BAYOU HEAT
COLLECTION TWO

Bayou Heat
Collection Two

Alexandra Ivy and Laura Wright

ISBN: 0989990761

ISBN 13: 9780989990769

Sebastian/Aristide: BAYOU HEAT 7-8

Copyright © 2013 by Alexandra Ivy and Laura Wright

Editor: Julia Ganis

Cover Art by Patricia Schmitt (Pickyme)

Lian/Roch: BAYOU HEAT 9-10

Copyright © 2014 by Alexandra Ivy and Laura Wright

Editor: Julia Ganis

Cover Art by Patricia Schmitt (Pickyme)

Hakan/Séverin: BAYOU HEAT 11-12

Copyright © 2014 by Alexandra Ivy and Laura Wright

Editor: Julia Ganis

Cover Art by Patricia Schmitt (Pickyme)

BAYOU HEAT

Book Seven

SEBASTIAN

New York Times and USA Today Bestselling Authors

ALEXANDRA IVY

Book Eight

ARISTIDE

LAURA WRIGHT

SEBASTIAN

By
ALEXANDRA IVY

PROLOGUE

THE small cabin with a thatched roof wasn't a traditional prison. There were no bars. No locks. No uniformed guards.

Instead, it was hidden on an isolated island in the Wildlands, surrounded by thick, untamed foliage and a treacherous bog that could kill the unwary. Just outside the door, several large Pantera in cat form stood on constant guard. But it was the magic of the elders which ensured that no one was going in or out of the small structure.

It was a place that only a handful of Pantera even realized existed. They didn't need to know, because it was where those Pantera who lost control of their cats and became feral were taken to be put to death.

Not precisely a tourist attraction.

Today, however, it housed a far more dangerous predator than a crazed panther.

The ultimate evil.

And the Wildlands would never be the same.

Inside the cabin, Shakpi sat on the narrow cot that was the only furnishing in the room.

She didn't care about the stifling heat, or the bugs that crawled over the dirt floor.

In fact, she rejoiced in them.

After what felt like an eternity of being trapped beneath the Wildlands, she had broken out of the prison her sister, Opela, had created by sacrificing her own life. Now she savored the sensation of freedom.

Oh, she hadn't entirely escaped. Opela's magic had effectively bound her to this land...the bitch. But over the past century, Shakpi had slowly and patiently weakened the edges of the prison. Once she could touch the world, she began calling her human slaves, using them to spread her infection that started the slow destruction of the Wildlands. As her power grew she could begin to manipulate the Pantera themselves, using them as pawns in their own annihilation.

Still, she remained stuck, her incorporeal form trapped by her sister's spell.

It wasn't until the Shaman had started to use his skills to contact his ancestors that she realized she could tap into his connection to the dead. Carefully she began infusing a small part of herself into the human male. The spell that had held her captive was meant to recognize the power of a goddess, not a human. She was slowly camouflaging herself in the guise of the Shaman.

It'd taken years. But Shakpi had learned to be patient. Even when the Shaman had seemingly disappeared just when she was prepared to complete her transformation. She knew he would return.

Her destiny was to rule the world.

It was written in the stars.

And her faith had been rewarded. Just a few hours ago the man had reappeared in the Wildlands, arrogantly opening himself to her possession. Fool.

Unfortunately, she hadn't quite anticipated the downside of being sheathed in a human form.

Not until she'd been so rudely attacked by the Pantera.

It was only then that she realized that while she was immortal, her new body was vulnerable to damage. Which was the only reason she was currently trapped in the cabin instead of destroying the bastards who'd dared to try and kill her.

Thankfully she was able to use her powers to hold off the initial rush of Pantera, managing to kill at least a half dozen before they'd driven her into this tiny cell and retreated.

No doubt they were even now debating how to kill a goddess without losing more of their warriors, but Shakpi wasn't particularly worried. At least not about escaping from the cabin. She had telepathically linked with one of her disciples who was swiftly approaching to release her.

Her only concern was how she was going to complete her destruction of the Wildlands.

The human form she was forced to use was too fragile to allow her to use the full might of her powers. And worse, it was susceptible to injury.

She glanced down at her male body that was covered by bloody clothing.

The deep gashes that had nearly sliced off the arms and one leg were healing, thanks to her magic, but it would take days before the pathetically weak body would be fully recovered.

Clearly she would have to find another way to complete her revenge.

Starting with an army.

And speaking of an army...

Shakpi rose to her feet as she heard the soft sound of voices outside the door. It seemed her rescue had arrived.

There was a brief delay as if the approaching Pantera was being questioned about his right to enter the cabin. Then at last, Shakpi could detect the fading scent of her guards.

A smile curled her lips, or rather the lips of Chayton, as the door was pushed open and the male Hunter entered the cramped room.

"Hello, Hiss." The words echoed through the air, filled with a power that proved she was no human. "Be the first to welcome your goddess into the world."

CHAPTER ONE

THE Suits' private headquarters near the center of the Wildlands looked more like a mansion from "Gone With The Wind" than an office building. A sweeping Colonial-style structure, it was painted white with black shutters, and had six fluted columns that held up the second-story balcony.

Inside, however, it was a buzzing hub of activity, filled with the sort of high-tech equipment usually reserved for the military. Pantera Diplomats often used the Geeks to hack and spy and infiltrate the human world. It was the easiest way to keep track of their enemies.

Then there were the Suits who preferred to do their job the old-fashioned way.

By getting their hands dirty.

And no one was better at getting his hands dirty than Sebastian Duval.

A tall male with bronze skin, he had a chiseled body that was currently covered by a pair of black chinos and a white silk shirt left open at the neck. He had pale green eyes swirled with yellow that most women called hazel, and tawny hair threaded with gold that brushed his broad shoulders.

He had a sophisticated gloss that allowed him to move among humans without them sensing that a lethal animal prowled just below his skin.

It was a skill that had served him well over the past century as fewer and fewer people remembered the presence of the strange puma shifters that lived in the deepest part of the bayous. Now they were mere myths to all but the highest human government officials who had agreed to keep their presence wrapped in secrecy.

Or at least their presence had been a secret until two weeks ago.

Prowling from one end of the long room that held a half dozen desks and a line of monitors on the paneled wall, Sebastian had a phone pressed to his ear, rapidly reassuring the governor of Arkansas that there wasn't a feral pack of Pantera ravaging their way across the country.

Christ...it was a pain in his ass.

He didn't know who or what was behind the strange attacks that had started in New Orleans and were rapidly spreading across the South. And he was pissed as hell that he was being forced to waste time dealing with hysterical politicians who'd somehow gotten a bug up their asses that there were wild pumas hunting innocent humans.

Idiots.

He needed to be concentrating his attention on the hunt for Shakpi, or even helping the warriors to prepare for the coming war.

And there would be a war...there was no doubt about that.

Now that the goddess had been released from her prison it was only a matter of time before she tried to destroy the Pantera.

Offering his solemn promise that he would give his full coopera-tion to the governor, Sebastian ended his call just as Raphael stepped through the open door.

Instantly a silence filled the room.

The head of the Suits was that kind of man. It wasn't his golden good looks or his large body, or even the arrogance etched onto his lean face that captured and held attention of the dozen Pantera. He was, quite simply, a natural born leader who commanded respect.

Today his expression was grim as he glanced around the gath-ered Pantera. "Clear the room," he barked.

Sebastian felt a stab of concern as the men and women swiftly exited by a side door, leaving him alone with the older man.

Two good things had come out of Shakpi's escape. The first was that the rot that had been destroying the Wildlands had suddenly stopped spreading. And the second was the fact that Raphael's mate, Ashe, was no longer fighting for her life, or the life of their unborn cub.

Or at least, she hadn't been the last time he'd checked in with his leader.

Now his heart slammed against his ribs as he studied his companion's stark expression.

"Ashe?" he rasped, barely daring to breathe until Raphael flashed a reassuring smile.

"Is well."

"Thank god," Sebastian breathed. Ashe was not only Raphael's mate, but she was currently carrying the first Pantera child in over fifty years.

A priceless treasure they would all protect with their lives.

"No, thank Isi," Raphael muttered.

Sebastian arched a brow. Isi was Ashe's long-lost sister, and since her arrival the infection or poison or whatever it was that had been slowly killing the fragile young woman had nearly disappeared.

"You believe she's responsible for your mate's recovery?"

Raphael folded his arms over his chest. "No doubt in my mind."

"So why does she remain in isolation?"

"Because the elders refuse to admit they could be wrong." Disgust laced his words. "They are convinced that she is destined to destroy the Wildlands. And they have enough influence to sway a large number of our people."

"The rumor is that Isi's blood did scorch the earth," Sebastian said, repeating the gossip that was swirling among the Pantera.

"Isi isn't the danger," Raphael snapped, clearly not there to discuss the mystery of his sister-in-law. "We have to be united if we are to defeat Shakpi."

Sebastian shivered. No one asked the question of how exactly they were going to achieve that little miracle.

Not when no one had the answer.

3

"True." Sebastian had been a witness to the moment Chayton, the human Shaman, had tried to close his connection to the trapped goddess. In fact, Sebastian had more than one scar from the fierce battle when they'd realized that Chayton had been possessed by Shakpi. "Have you located the Shaman?"

"No, but Parish has his Hunters on the trail."

Sebastian nodded, a familiar ball of frustration lodged in the pit of his stomach. "I'd give my left nut to know how the bastard escaped."

"No shit." Raphael rammed his fingers through his hair, a low growl rumbling in his chest. "I'm still trying to sort through that little clusterfuck."

Sebastian grimaced, not envying his friend's job. There were at least ten different stories of who was supposed to be where when it was discovered their prisoner had escaped.

"If this isn't about Ashe or Chayton, then what has you in such a twit?"

Raphael narrowed his golden gaze. "Twit?"

"Twit. Snit." Sebastian shrugged. "A mood."

"I'm a Pantera." Raphael peeled back his lips to reveal his elongated fangs. "I don't have moods."

Sebastian snorted. "And I'm about to sprout wings and flap around the room."

Raphael pulled out his phone, searching for a webpage before shoving it into Sebastian's hand.

"Read."

Sebastian glanced down, scanning the front page of a prominent New Orleans newspaper. His brows snapped together at the lurid headline:

LOCAL WOMAN MAULED, AUTHORITIES ON HIGH ALERT

"Shit." Sebastian gave an annoyed shake of his head. "Another wild animal attack?"

"It gets worse. Keep reading."

With a growing sense of dread, Sebastian skimmed through the short article.

"Pantera," he snarled, rereading the last paragraph to make sure he hadn't misread the shocking claim. Nope. There it was: the female was convinced that she was attacked by a Pantera. "How? Only top human officials are aware the Pantera truly exist. Which is bad enough." He made a sound of disgust. "I've spent all morning on the phone with the governor of Arkansas."

Raphael grimaced. "It could be that the humans are remembering the stories of their grandparents. When they're frightened, they often turn to myth and legend."

Sebastian didn't need to be a Diplomat to know that Raphael didn't believe this was a random accusation made out of fear.

"Or?" he prompted.

"Or traitors have been whispering our name among the masses."

"Damn." Sebastian understood better than anyone this new, unexpected danger. It was bad enough to be outed just when they were threatened with extinction. But to be revealed and then blamed for the violent attacks was a guaranteed way to make enemies of the humans. "What do you want from me?"

Raphael reached for his phone, stabbing a finger at the screen. "I want this stopped."

Sebastian blinked in surprise, anticipation heating his blood. Damn. It'd been far too long since he'd been on the hunt.

"Not that I'm not ready and willing to kill the bastards, but you don't usually give me the opportunity to release my inner cat."

"And you're going to have to keep it leashed." Raphael squashed his brief hope for a taste of blood. "At least for now. The FBI are demanding answers."

Sebastian grudgingly bridled his eager cat, forcing himself to return to his role as Diplomat. As much as his animal side longed for a good fight, he preferred to avoid violence whenever possible. Besides, they had Hunters who were trained to kick ass.

"I bet they are," he said dryly, already considering his various contacts in New Orleans. "I have someone in the mayor's office who can smooth things over."

Raphael shook his head. "Not this time."

Sebastian stiffened. He didn't have to be a psychic to know he wasn't going to like what Raphael had to say.

"What do you mean?"

"The human officials have demanded that we work together to discover who's instigating the trouble."

Nope. He didn't like it.

Not even a little.

"They can demand whatever they want," he growled.

Raphael held up a warning hand. "We need to cooperate."

"Since when?"

"Since our presence has gone from being fiction to fact."

Sebastian clenched his teeth in frustration. He understood that it made sense to work with the human authorities. Until they knew who was behind this, the Pantera had to foster all the goodwill possible.

But that didn't make it any less annoying.

"It would be easier to track down the villains responsible for the attacks without the interference of the FBI."

Raphael's eyes glowed with the power of his cat, revealing he wasn't any happier than Sebastian.

"I agree, but the public are swiftly becoming convinced that we're a threat to their safety and we both know what happens when fear rules among humans."

"Mob mentality," Sebastian muttered.

"Exactly."

Sebastian paced toward the large window that overlooked the communal meadow where the Pantera often gathered for meals. Surrounded by trees draped with Spanish moss and bathed in the early autumn sunlight, the Wildlands was a place of peace.

Home.

Instinctively his gaze moved toward the clinic that was barely visible through the trees. His parents were both Healers. Gentle souls who were so deeply committed to their vocation they wouldn't harm another creature, even if they were being attacked.

It was his duty to protect them.

Whether he wanted to work with the humans or not.

"Shit." He turned back to meet Raphael's bleak expression. "Is there more?"

The older man reached into his back pocket to pull out a folded piece of paper, handing it to Sebastian.

"This is your contact."

Sebastian read the name scribbled on the paper. "Reny Smith?" He scowled in confusion. "Never heard of her. They're sticking me with some damned rookie?"

"She's coming in from New York."

The knowledge didn't appease his irritation. There were a handful of agents who had high enough clearance to be aware of the Pantera. It didn't make sense to bring in a stranger.

"Why?"

"She's supposedly an expert in interrogations."

Sebastian made a sound of disgust. He knew the seedy underbelly of human politics.

"As if I need a human to help me with interrogations."

"Be nice."

"Is that an order?"

Raphael allowed his cat to prowl close to the surface, the air heating with his power. "Yes."

"Shit."

———

Reny Smith ignored the glances of the local agents who strolled past the small conference room that she'd claimed as her office.

She'd known she would be the subject of curiosity and even resentment when she'd asked for an opportunity to work on this case.

She had all the ingredients to piss off the local boys club.

She was an outsider. She was a woman. And she was barely out of Quantico.

Still, she'd been oddly convinced that she could help to sort through the mangled stories and hysterical accusations before the situation escalated into public panic. Even after her boss had granted her the top secret clearance and grudgingly confessed that the ancient stories were true. That there were real life puma shifters who lived in the bayous, and that she would have to work with one of them.

Well, she would work with him if he ever bothered to make an appearance.

Clicking her tongue with impatience, Reny rose to her feet, smoothing her hands down the black jacket that matched her slacks, and paced toward the window overlooking the majestic Lake Pontchartrain.

It was a mesmerizing sight with the sunset painting the water in vivid shades of pink and lilac. Of course, everything about New Orleans was mesmerizing.

No doubt it was because it was a city of such intense contradictions.

The decadent mixture of old world charm and modern high-rises. The sound of sweet jazz that filled the air, lacing its way among the dark, grinding poverty that lurked just out of sight. The aroma of chicory coffee overlaid with the earthy scent of the bayous.

It all combined to create a feast for the senses.

Reny told herself that was the cause for the restlessness that had plagued her since her plane had landed two days ago.

It didn't entirely make sense. But it was the best explanation she had for the weird feeling that something inside her was struggling to get out.

Besides, over the past years she'd become adept at telling herself small lies.

Her superior speed was just a matter of training. She was stronger than she should be because of genetics. Her unnerving ability to tell when people were lying to her was a god-given talent.

And that feeling that she was somehow more aware of the world around her? Well, she'd built a shield in her mind that allowed her to lock out her acute awareness so she could pretend to be just like everyone else.

What else could she do?

Ever since she'd awakened in a New York hospital eight years ago with complete amnesia, she'd felt like a freak. If she actually accepted she was different on a fundamental level, then...

Then she wouldn't just feel like a freak, she'd become one.

She abruptly shivered, rubbing her arms as electric tingles raced over her skin.

There was something approaching. No, not something... someone.

Feeling a ridiculous sense of premonition, Reny slowly turned, her breath wrenched from her lungs.

Holy...shit.

The man filling the doorway was drop-dead, heart-stopping, get-him-naked-now gorgeous.

Her gaze did a lingering inventory, starting with the thick, tawny hair that was pulled into a tail at his nape, moving over the bronzed male features and down the hard, perfectly sculpted body shown to advantage in black chino slacks and white shirt.

Her dazzled gaze returned to his gorgeous face, her heart slamming against her ribs.

Those eyes...she'd never seen anything like them. A green as pale as spring grass with yellow swirls that seemed to glow in the fading light.

Pantera, a voice whispered through her mind.

It didn't take the memory of her boss explaining that the age-old stories were true to warn her that this male was one of the elusive puma shifters.

Or even his inhuman beauty.

She could physically *feel* the cat that crawled beneath the surface.

"You're Reny Smith?" he murmured, his voice whiskey smooth with a hint of a southern drawl.

9

The sound of it wrapped around her like heated honey, warming places that shouldn't be warmed in public.

Damn.

Something stirred deep inside her. Not just the strange restlessness that had been plaguing her, but an aching need that was suddenly ignited in the pit of her stomach.

She determinedly squared her shoulders. What was wrong with her?

This was her big opportunity.

She wasn't going to blow it because this man was making her squirm with unfamiliar sensations.

"I am. I assume you're Mr.—"

"Sebastian," he interrupted, prowling across the institutional gray carpet to stand directly in front of her.

Heat licked over her skin.

"You're late."

The yellow in his eyes deepened to gold as his gaze skimmed down to where her white blouse was opened just enough to give a hint of her breasts.

"Actually, I would say I'm just in time," he murmured.

Reny should have rolled her eyes. She'd learned to ignore the typical male response to her looks since entering the academy.

Now, however, she was instantly on the defensive.

"Look, I'm here to work. If you…" She stiffened as he leaned forward, his nose flaring as if he were dragging in her scent. "What?"

"They told me you were human," he growled softly.

"Human?" She blinked in confusion. "What the hell are you talking about?"

"I can smell your cat."

A cold chill inched down her spine as she met his unnerving gaze. "Is that supposed to be some kind of joke?"

A tawny brow flicked upward. "Why would it be a joke?"

"I don't know what you think you smell, but I can assure you I don't even own a cat." The words had barely left her mouth when he'd closed the small space between them and pressed his nose to the curve of her neck. She sucked in a terrified breath. Not because she was frightened of the overtly beautiful man. But because his touch was sending jolts of savage arousal through her trembling body. "Please don't," she husked.

"I'm not going to hurt you, sugar," he drawled, allowing his lips to trail down her throat, lingering over the frantic beat of her pulse before he slowly straightened, his searching gaze sweeping over her face. "I assume you have a reason for your charade."

Attempting to squash her panic, Reny stepped around his large body and headed toward the door. She'd prepared herself for a rough, ill-mannered lout. Someone more animal than man. Not this gorgeous, sophisticated stranger who was making her skin feel as if it was too tight for her body.

"I don't think this is going to work."

"Stop."

The command in his voice had something inside her instantly halting her retreat, slowly turning to face him.

The fact that she'd obeyed pissed her off. "Don't give me orders, Mr.—"

"Sebastian," he smoothly reminded her, his beautiful face unreadable. "I thought you requested to be the FBI liaison?"

She scowled. "I asked to be given the opportunity to use my training."

"And at the first hurdle you're willing to walk away?"

The prickles continued the race through her body, her heart beating way too fast. "You're a massively large hurdle," she retorted.

His smile was filled with sin. "Oh, sugar, you have no idea."

"That's it."

She turned back toward the door, but before she could take a step he was standing directly in front of her.

Holy shit. Just how fast could he move?

"Let's start again," he murmured, holding up his hands as if to convince her he was harmless. Yeah. The very air sizzled with danger. "Please, tell me what you've managed to discover."

Reny wavered. Common sense told her to walk away. She didn't precisely understand why being in the same room with this man was making her so edgy, and she suspected that it was better not to know.

But the part that had allowed her to survive waking in a sterile hospital with no name, no family, and no past refused to allow her to quit.

He was right. If she allowed the first obstacle to send her scuttling back to New York then she might as well give up her career, because she'd never get another opportunity to prove herself.

Stiffening her spine, Reny crossed toward the long table at the side of the room where she'd spread out her files.

She'd never been a coward. She wasn't going to start now.

"I've interviewed the female who claims to have been attacked by the…" She fumbled over the word. "Pantera."

Moving in near silence, Sebastian was abruptly standing at her side, his heat wrapping around her with seductive force.

"Claims?" he demanded.

Reny clenched her teeth. Dammit. She would not shiver. Or whimper. Or melt into a puddle at his Italian leather shoes.

"She was lying."

"How do you know?"

Good question.

She had no intention of sharing the truth.

"I'm very skilled in reading body language," she said.

"I bet," he drawled, almost as if he knew her little secret. "No wonder you're an expert in interrogations."

"Yes." She deliberately stepped away from his intoxicating heat.

Not that it helped.

Sebastian's presence consumed every inch of the room.

"If it wasn't a Pantera that caused her wounds, then what did?" he asked. "And more importantly, why did she lie?"

"She was paid."

CHAPTER TWO

SEBASTIAN'S cat prowled anxiously beneath his skin.

What the hell was going on?

Was Reny Smith pretending to be a human to infiltrate the FBI? Was she one of the traitors?

Or did she truly not realize she was Pantera?

The vital questions should have consumed him, but instead he couldn't think beyond the intense awareness that had punched into him the moment he'd walked through the door.

God. Damn.

He didn't know what was setting him on fire.

Was it the dark hair streaked with fiery highlights that begged to be freed from her tight ponytail? The pale oval face that was dominated by a pair of moss green eyes? The slender, athletic body she tried to hide beneath the black suit? The rich, exotic scent of her cat?

All he knew was that he was barely leashing the urge to toss her onto the long table and strip away those starchy clothes and lick her from head to toe.

His cat purred at the thought of spreading her legs and lapping up her spicy arousal that was already perfuming the air. Her human mind might be wary of the desire that was setting off sparks between them, but her cat was ready and eager.

The only thing halting him was the knowledge that he couldn't be sure this female wasn't a trap.

"Do you have proof?" he demanded, forcing himself to concentrate on his reason for traveling to New Orleans.

Eventually he would figure out the puzzle that was Reny Smith.

And when he did, he'd have his aching cock buried so deeply inside her she'd be screaming in pleasure.

Perhaps sensing his brutal hunger, Reny inched away to grab a file from the neat stack on the table. Then, sucking in a steadying breath, she flipped it open to reveal a stack of photos.

"No, but look."

Sebastian allowed her the small space. For now.

"What am I seeing?" He reached to spread out the photos.

"This is Koni Handler's apartment." Reny pointed to the shabby brick building that was squeezed between a laundromat and an abandoned bookstore. She moved her finger to a photo of a cramped living room. "She shared it with three other girls. Her portion of the rent was three-fifty a month."

"It's not the best neighborhood," he said. "It could have been a local thug who attacked her. That would explain why she tried to make up a wild story. She couldn't risk the truth."

Reny shook her head, shuffling through the photos to reveal one of a pretty, dark-haired woman. She looked to be in her early twenties, although there was a hardness in her dark eyes and a petulant curve to her lips that hinted that she'd seen more than most females her age.

"Now, this is her at the police station."

Sebastian was confused. Reny had shown him the apartment, but not the actual crime scene, and the pictures of the victim didn't reveal the wounds from her supposed attack.

"I think it will save us time if you just tell me what I should be looking for."

Reny tapped the photo. "This is a Coach bag. Retail it costs five hundred dollars," she said. "Her jacket is Gucci." Her finger moved to point at the woman's diamond earrings. "And those earrings are at least a carat."

"They could be knockoffs."

"Are you kidding?" She sent him a disbelieving glance. "I'm from New York."

"And?"

"I could spot a fake at a hundred paces."

He hid a smile. Sassy. He liked it.

"I also recognize an original when I see it," he murmured, allowing his gaze to sweep over her exquisite face before returning his attention to the photo. "Maybe she has a sugar daddy."

She cleared her throat, her face flushed with an excitement she was desperately trying to hide.

"If she does, he has to be new," she said. "She pawned her laptop last week to pay her share of the rent."

Sassy and smart.

His cat preened with pleasure.

"Good catch." He brushed the back of his fingers over her cheek. "I think I should speak with this Koni."

She shivered before she was abruptly yanking from his touch, her chin tilting to a militant angle.

"We."

"We." His cat purred. "I like the sound of that."

She rolled her eyes, reaching for her purse on the table. "My car's in the lot."

He followed a step behind her as she headed for the door, enjoying the view of her tight little ass.

Soon he intended to be cupping that fine booty in his hands as she rode him to paradise.

Fully erect, he ignored the curious glances as they headed toward the back of the building. So far as he knew, only Reny and the top brass realized that he was a Pantera, but humans instinctively reacted to his power.

Men hurried to step out of his path, while females did their best to capture his attention.

His gaze never strayed from Reny's delectable backside. "What if I want to drive?"

Reny stepped into the elevator, waiting for the doors to close before shooting him a smoldering glare.

"I don't let any man take me for a ride."

With a fluid speed, he had her backed against the paneled wall of the elevator, his hands bracketing her shoulders as he leaned down to stroke his lips down the vulnerable curve of her throat.

"Oh, sugar, don't ever challenge a Pantera," he husked, drowning in her spicy scent. "We bite."

She shivered, but it wasn't fear sending tremors through her body.

Still, she held herself rigid, refusing to acknowledge the heat that simmered in her moss green eyes.

"Are you trying to frighten me?" she rasped.

He nipped the skin above her racing pulse. It was nothing more than the smallest taste, but the essence of her exploded on his tongue.

A growl rumbled in his chest.

"Just giving you fair warning."

He could sense the storm of emotions that battled inside her.

Fear. Confusion. And a hunger so fierce it dampened her skin in a fine layer of sweat.

But with a willpower he could only admire, she kept her brittle composure intact.

"Then let me return the favor. I always carry a Taser in my purse," she warned, lifting her hands to press them against his chest. "Move back."

Sebastian instantly dropped his arms and stepped away. He would push, but he would never force.

It was only a matter of time before Reny gave herself freely.

"Aggressive." He flashed his most charming smile. "I like it."

She muttered a curse beneath her breath. "Do you ever stop?"

"No." Not when it came to this female.

Sebastian pulled his cellphone from his pocket as they left the building and slid into the standard midsize cop car. He not only wanted to update Raphael on Reny's suspicions, but he intended to discover just what sort of game the female FBI agent was playing.

With his various texts at last sent, he slid the phone back into his pocket and studied the pure line of Reny's profile, his cat restlessly stirring beneath his skin. His animal didn't understand being so close to this delectable female and not being allowed to touch. It was the increasingly dismal homes that lined the narrow street that at last jerked him out of his brooding thoughts. They weren't far from their destination.

"Can you park a few blocks from the apartment building?"

She sent him a startled glance. "Why?"

"I want to see if I can catch any scent of Pantera in the area."

Without hesitation, Reny slowed the car, pulling into a loading zone next to the curb. Sebastian hid a satisfied smile. She instinctively trusted him.

Even when she wanted to kick him in the nuts.

He had a premonition that very soon he was going to need that faith.

"I'll drop you off here and park around the corner." She nodded toward the north. "The apartment building is at the end of the next block. I'll wait in the lobby."

He stepped out of the car, sending her a teasing grin. "There won't be any waiting."

"Arrogant ass," she muttered as he jogged away.

"I can hear you, sugar," he called.

"I know, dumpling," she called back.

He chuckled, anticipation sizzling through his body.

Oh, Special Agent Reny Smith, you are playing with fire...

———

Shakpi had to admit there were unexpected benefits to possessing a human form.

She'd discovered a passion for the spicy gumbo that she ordered from a local restaurant, as well as an addiction to the sugar-coated beignets that she demanded every morning.

There was also the unexpected pleasure that could be found between the talented lips of her devoted disciple.

Seated in the library of the large mansion that was built along the bluffs of the Mississippi River, she gave a low groan as she climaxed into the female's mouth. Who knew a cock could be the source of such pleasure?

There was the sound of the door being pushed open, then a small gasp as a woman with silver hair pulled into a bun and wearing a loose cotton dress stepped into the room.

"Oh." The face leathered by years in the hot Louisiana sun twisted into an expression of disgust. "Forgive me."

"Enter," Shakpi snapped, motioning away the disciple kneeling between her legs so she could rise to her feet and pull up her pants. She felt no embarrassment, only irritation that she'd been kept waiting. "You're late."

With the clanking from the dozens of bracelets that lined the voodoo priestess's scrawny arms, she moved across the wooden floor.

"I was forced to walk from the highway."

Shakpi narrowed her gaze. It had been an easy task to find a suitable lair and kill the humans who were currently occupying it, but she'd discovered that while there were a handful of benefits to her physical body, there were far more disadvantages.

She was weak, vulnerable to injury and she had an acute reaction to the stench of human technology.

The sooner she could find the means to release her spirit from the bonds of the mortal form, the sooner she could rule the world.

"I dislike the smell of fumes," she snapped, her gaze flicking dismissively over Lady Cerise. The woman possessed an arrogance that Shakpi was eager to shatter. "I also dislike being kept waiting. Don't allow it to happen again."

"I told you—"

The chandelier above them swayed, a crack forming in the cove ceiling. "You have been a dedicated disciple, Cerise." Shakpi's male voice held a quiet, deadly warning that couldn't be mistaken. "It would be a shame to have to destroy you now."

Cerise fell to her knees, her head bowed. "I am your servant."

"Hmm." Shakpi strolled forward, savoring the spiky fear that filled the air. "So you say."

"I have proven my loyalty," the priestess insisted, her head still lowered. "I have gathered disciples to spread your infection through the Wildlands. I have devoted years to searching for the Shaman to help open your pathway—"

"And yet, I still wait for the war you promised."

"The opening battle has begun."

Shakpi made a sound of disgust. She'd read the reports of the escalating violent attacks spreading across the South, and the rumors that had started to spread about the rabid puma shifters who were crawling out of the swamps to hunt humans. But she wanted instant results.

"Do you know how long I've waited to see the Pantera destroyed?"

"Which is why we must not risk your ultimate success by pressing too hard, too fast," Cerise urged, her body tense. "The humans are becoming increasingly fearful. Once they believe their local officials can't protect them it will be a simple matter to push them into violence."

"Don't fail me, Cerise." Shakpi reached down to grab the female by the neck, lifting her off her feet and squeezing hard enough to make her moan with pain. "You won't like what I do to disciples who prove themselves to be unworthy."

———

Reny took her time strolling along the street, despite the fact that dusk was cloaking the buildings in shadows.

She was a well-trained agent with a gun tucked in a holster beneath her jacket. Besides, she'd never had the trouble of many women. Men might leer and whistle and harass her from a distance, but none of them tried to get into her private space.

It was almost as if they were...intimidated by her.

Until Sebastian Duval.

She absently wiped her damp hands down her slacks, trying to concentrate on her surroundings. She could sometimes get a vibe from a crime scene and the neighborhood around it.

Tonight, however, she couldn't concentrate on anything but the nagging ache in the pit of her stomach.

Dammit.

She'd hoped that a little space would allow her to shake off the disturbing arousal that scorched through her. But ridiculously, it only seemed to grow worse.

It didn't make sense.

She never noticed guys. Not because she was some man-hater. It was just that she'd been so focused on her career that she'd never had time to play the games other women seemed to enjoy.

But from the second that Sebastian had strolled into the room her entire body had been on fire. As if he'd tossed a match on her long-dormant libido.

Okay, he was gorgeous.

No, wait. He was way beyond gorgeous. Reny wasn't certain there was a word that could capture his tawny beauty. Or the incandescent animal magnetism that the designer clothes and polished charm did nothing to mute.

But he was annoying, and arrogant, and clearly demented if he thought for a second he could make her believe she had some sort of cat smell.

Oh yeah, and there was the little fact that he wasn't even human.

If he weren't her current partner and vital to her future success, she would...

The image of what she wanted to do to him seared through her mind.

That long, chiseled body stretched across her hotel bed. His bronzed skin glistening with a light sheen of perspiration. His hair tousled and his hazel eyes darkened with pleasure as she kissed a path down his stomach to the hard cock...

She gave a strangled sound, a heat staining her cheeks.

Where the hell did that come from?

The answer hit her as she rounded the corner to discover Tall, Tawny and Tantalizing leaning against the apartment building.

Her nerve endings tingled as if they'd been scrubbed raw, as she studied the predatory male. Even wrapped in dusk he commanded full attention, creating chaos among the group of women walking down the sidewalk as they tripped over their feet at the sight of him.

Oddly annoyed by the lingering female glances, Reny moved to stand at his side, her brows pulled together.

"How did you…" She cut off her words as a smug smile curved his lips. "Never mind."

With a shake of her head she turned to pull open the door to the apartment building, stepping into the lobby.

Sebastian was directly on her heels, moving around her to investigate the bleak space. Across the peeling linoleum floor was the elevator, as well as the narrow door to the stairs. Opposite were a dozen mailboxes built into the wall. And closer to the door was an orange couch that she'd bet had been there since The Brady Bunch was on the air.

Reny shuddered. Had anyone actually sat on those lumpy cushions in the past decade?

"The attack supposedly happened here?" Sebastian demanded.

"Yes," she said, watching him pace from one end of the lobby to the other with a lethal grace that was mesmerizing.

"Cameras?"

She pointed toward the hole cut in the ceiling near the flickering florescent lights. "The owner of the building said they were temporarily out of service, but I suspect they've never functioned."

Sebastian nodded, crouching next to the mailboxes. "There's blood, but no scent of Pantera."

"It happened three days ago," she pointed out.

He straightened, turning to meet her guarded gaze. "After such a violent encounter there should be some trace of the attacker."

"Unless he could mask his scent."

"Impossible." Irritation emphasized the yellow-gold in his amazing eyes. "Just as the wounds on the female are impossible."

21

"Why?"

"A Pantera can't shift into his animal form unless he's in the Wildlands."

Reny hesitated. Her briefing had been lacking any details about the Pantera. No doubt because there wasn't much information to share.

The puma shifters had been elusive for so long that even the rumors of their abilities had died away.

"Are you telling me the truth?"

He shrugged. "It would serve no purpose for me to lie."

She held his fierce gaze, even when instinct told her to look away. "Of course it would. The Pantera have gone to a lot of trouble to remain hidden. If you have a rogue psycho attacking women it's going to reveal your presence to the entire world."

Without warning he was standing directly in front of her, his hand cupping her chin as he glared down at her.

"Whoever did this—" With a hiss, Sebastian abruptly jerked his hand from her face, shaking it as if he'd felt the blaze of ruthless need that jolted through her body. Then he went still, something dark and dangerous glowing in his eyes.

Puma.

It wasn't threatening. It was…watchful. Intent. Hungry.

She shivered, and lifted her hand to touch her chin. The skin felt like it'd been scorched.

"What did you do to me?" she husked.

He gave a slow shake of his head. "It wasn't me."

"It had to be you. It was your touch that started this."

"Reny—"

"No."

With a jerky motion she was headed across the foyer and up the stairs, unwilling to acknowledge the brutal arousal that was spreading through her body with every beat of her heart.

God. What the hell was wrong with her?

"Where are you going?"

"The victim's apartment is on the first floor."

Reny walked up the narrow steps, pretending to ignore the image of a stalking panther just inches behind her. He remained silent, but she could sense his tension. The very air sizzled with the heat of his edgy unease.

It was a relief to step out of the stairwell and into the dark hallway, despite the unmistakable stench of urine. Wrinkling her nose, she hurried to knock on the nearest door, forced to wait for a tense minute before it was pulled open to reveal a young woman who clearly was preparing for a night out.

Dressed in nothing more than her bra and panties, the woman pushed her dark hair still damp from the shower out of her eyes and glared at Reny.

"Christ, not you again," she muttered in disgust. "What now?"

"I need to speak with Ms. Handler."

The roommate leaned against the doorjamb, her pretty face already showing signs of her party lifestyle.

"She's not here."

"Do you know when she'll be back?"

"Never."

Reny frowned. "What do you mean, never?"

The woman shrugged. "She packed her bags after the attack and said she had a new place to stay."

Damn. Reny shook her head at her stupidity. She'd already suspected the female victim had received money to lie about her story. She should have known the first thing Koni Handler would do was flee this shithole of an apartment.

"She didn't give you an address?"

"The bitch didn't even leave enough money to cover the utilities. When you find her, tell her I'm going to kick her—" The roommate forgot how to speak as Sebastian suddenly stepped into view. Abruptly straightening from the doorjamb, the woman gave a toss of her hair, arching her back to make sure Sebastian hadn't missed the large tits that were spilling from the tiny lace bra. "Hello there."

Sebastian flashed his killer smile, and Reny had to clench her hands to resist the urge to shove the young woman away and slam the door.

"Did she leave any clothing behind?" he asked.

The woman continued to wave her tits like flags of invitation. "Just a bunch of worthless shit."

"Show me."

Turning, the roommate offered Sebastian a full view of her rounded ass. "I'll show you anything you want, big boy."

Sebastian shot Reny a covert glance, almost as if he sensed the violence that was boiling just below her brittle composure.

"I'll wait here," he murmured. "If you could just get me a shirt?"

The woman didn't bother to hide her irritation at Sebastian's lack of appreciation for her near-naked body, flouncing to snatch a thin top from a sofa that looked remarkably similar to the one in the lobby.

Eww.

"You're not a freak, are you?" she demanded, shoving the shirt in Sebastian's hand.

Sebastian kept his gaze locked on Reny's flushed face. "That's a matter of opinion."

Reny made a choked sound, the arousal pulsing through her reaching a near painful level.

Oh...hell. She had to get away from this man.

Now.

"If you hear from your roommate please give me a call," she muttered, shoving her business card into the woman's hand. She was already headed down the stairs by the time she heard the door slam.

CHAPTER THREE

SEBASTIAN gave a low growl at Reny's hasty retreat.

The sensible part of him urged him to bring a halt to the dangerous game.

It was one thing to play along until he could discover if she was an innocent who'd truly been unaware she was Pantera. Or if she was a traitor who was leading him into a trap.

It was another to become lost in the siren song of her mating heat.

A shudder shook his body as his cat savored the spicy arousal drenching the air.

Christ.

It'd been so long since any female had actually been fertile, let alone had broadcast her need with such potency, that it was like a kick in his gut.

Which was all the more reason he should get her to the Healers.

They needed to discover who she was, if her cat had been damaged, and how the hell she was able to project a mating heat when other females had tried and failed for years.

Yeah. That's exactly what he should do.

But as he headed in pursuit of the female, he wasn't reaching for his phone to make the call. His cat had been snared by the intoxicating scent of Reny Smith, and it was on the hunt.

Moving with lethal silence, he jogged down the stairs and out of the building.

Reny drew him on a level that was impossible to resist.

Stalking her through the darkness, he waited until she'd turned the corner before he was moving to stand directly in her path.

"Where are you going?"

"I assume you want the shirt so you can track Ms. Handler." Her words were cool, controlled. But her eyes glowed with a raw need that made his gut twist. "It only makes sense for me to return to the office and start a trace on her finances."

"That can wait." He brushed the back of his fingers over her cheek, groaning at the dewy heat that dampened her skin. His cat roared, not understanding why he was waiting. It didn't care they were on a city street where anyone could see them. It wanted what it wanted and it wanted Reny Smith. "We have something to take care of first."

"What?"

He stepped closer, watching the pulse at the base of her throat flutter out of control. A low growl rumbled in his throat. He wanted to bite that soft flesh. Preferably while he was climaxing, deep inside her, filling her with his seed.

"Come with me."

She licked her dry lips, no doubt seeing the cat glowing in his eyes. "Actually, I don't feel well."

He lowered his head, nuzzling a line of kisses down her stubborn jaw. "Trust me, I have the only cure."

"How would you know?" she breathed, her body trembling beneath his light caress. "Did you infect me with something?"

He nipped the side of her throat, reveling in her soft gasp of pleasure. "Not exactly."

Her hands landed against his chest, but she didn't push him away. Instead, she gripped his shirt as if her knees were threatening to collapse.

"What is it?" she husked. "What have you done to me?"

His tongue traced the delicate vein that ran the length of her neck. "Not here."

"I'm not going anywhere until you—" She hissed in outrage as he brought an end to the argument by the simple process of grasping her by the waist and tossing her over his shoulder. "Dammit." She pounded her fists against his back, at the same time trying to kick him in his balls. Wildcat. "Put me down."

A feral smile curved Sebastian's lips as he headed toward a far more prosperous neighborhood north of town. He was a Diplomat who'd always preferred to use charm when it came to seducing his women, but he had to admit that the caveman approach did have its appeal.

"You're going to thank me," he assured her, his voice laced with a possession he didn't bother to hide.

"Like hell."

"Trust me," he murmured, moving with a blinding speed humans could never hope to match.

"Never," she snapped, aiming a kick that would have brought him to his knees if he hadn't turned just enough for her blow to catch his upper thigh.

"Careful, sugar," he purred, his tone oddly pleased. "I intend to use that before the night's over."

She tried to twist her upper body, hoping to reach the gun that was pressing painfully into her side. Not to shoot the aggravating beast. Well, at least not a killing shot. But a slug in his ass would teach him a little respect.

But as if reading her thoughts, he managed to kick up the pace another notch, making her bang and jerk against his back until she feared she was going to be knocked out. She hissed in frustration, her arms wrapping around his waist as the passing buildings became a mere blur.

He continued at the mind-numbing pace as he kept his attention locked on their surroundings, making sure there were no hidden enemies as the streets widened and the houses became mansions hidden behind the veil of Spanish moss.

The quicker he had answers, the better.

For both of them.

At last reaching a white, plantation-style home set well away from the street, Sebastian circled to the back entrance, forced to halt at the steps to place his hand on a scanner. The lock would only open to a Pantera.

With a small swoosh, the heavy metal door swung inward, and Sebastian stepped into the cramped entry, waiting to be electronically scanned by the security system.

A full minute passed before a hidden panel silently slid open, allowing Sebastian to enter the house.

A part of him wished he could lower Reny to her feet and escort her through the large rooms with the molded ceilings and sweeping staircases that captured the airy, graceful beauty of the old South. She deserved to be treated as a treasured guest, not a prisoner. But until he could convince her that he was only trying to help her, he didn't have the luxury.

Regaining her breath, Reny loosened her grip on his waist and gave him another thump on the back.

"What the hell is this place?"

"A safe house for Pantera," he said, using the servants' stairs to reach the second floor.

"Why would you bring me here?"

Sebastian entered the first bedroom. With two long strides he had her dumped on the wide, ivory-canopied bed and had turned to head back out the door.

"Wait here."

"No…don't—"

He shut the door on her furious protest, touching the small lever that would trigger the lock.

The knowledge that he was damaging her trust in him was like a knife through his heart, but he grimly hurried down the stairs and toward the front of the house where he could sense one of his brothers.

Opening the door to what had once been the library, Sebastian stepped into a room that had been stripped of its original furnishings

28

and fitted with the sort of high-tech equipment that could rival the Pentagon.

Pantera might be creatures who'd been born of mist and magic, but they lived in the modern world.

A dark-haired Hunter with whiskey-gold eyes turned away from the line of computer screens he'd been monitoring and rose to his feet.

Lian looked his typical badass self in a pair of faded black jeans and Metallica T-shirt, his long hair pulled into a braid that hung down to his waist.

"Troubles?"

"Here." Sebastian moved forward to shove a long strand of hair into the startled Pantera's hand. "Have this sent to the closest lab and tested."

Lian frowned. "For what?"

"DNA. I want to know what family this comes from."

The Hunter lifted his brows in surprise. "Okay. Anything else?"

"A full background check on Agent Reny Smith, FBI," Sebastian said.

Lian turned to open a desk drawer, pulling out a small baggie to store the hair in. There were several Pantera who worked undercover in the local labs and could expedite the necessary tests.

"It will take at least twenty-four hours for the DNA. I can start the background check now."

Sebastian nodded. "Contact me as soon as you have something."

"You got it."

Confident that he could trust Lian to take care of the search into Reny's past, Sebastian retraced his steps, his body tensing as he reached to push open the door.

God. Damn.

He could physically feel the pulse of Reny's arousal. It was like a fire in his gut.

But slipping into the room, concern was his overriding emotion.

29

Closing the door, he leaned against it as Reny launched herself at him, her face flushed and tendrils of dark curls that escaped her ponytail pasted to her damp skin.

"You rat bastard," she snarled, slamming her fists against his chest.

Thankful she hadn't shot him the minute he'd opened the door, Sebastian wrapped his arms around her trembling form, pulling her tight against him.

"Shh." He lowered his head, brushing his lips over her temple. The mating heat shouldn't be this intense. It was like a violent force that was pummeling the two of them, instead of the gentle temptation that used to be common among Pantera. "I have you."

"God." She collapsed against his chest, her breath a loud gasp. "What's happening?"

His lips skimmed down her cheek, nuzzling the edge of her mouth. "It's the mating heat."

She pulled back her head to study him in confusion. "You're in heat?"

"Not me." His hand ran a soothing path up and down her back. "You."

"Dammit." Her brows snapped together. "I don't have to listen to this."

"You don't." His fingers cupped the back of her nape, his thumb stroking the pulse that beat at the base of her throat. "But denying the truth isn't going to help either of us. You can feel it, sugar." He peered deep into her gaze, glimpsing the frustrated cat who prowled just below the surface. "Burning deep inside you."

She gave a choked sound. "This has to be a trick."

"No trick." He fiercely held her gaze. The time for games was over. "Your cat has decided to take command."

"I'm not..." She halted to lick her lips, a fear that she could no longer hide tightening her face. "I can't be."

He ignored her ridiculous protests. "You can have your identity crisis later," he assured her. "For now, we need to deal with your discomfort."

"And how do you intend to do that?"

"I can ease you."

She gave a humorless laugh. "Yeah, I bet you can."

His thumb stroked the line of her jaw. "Or I can take you to the Wildlands."

"Why?" she snapped. "So some other puma can ease me?"

A blinding fury raced through him at the mere thought of another man touching this female.

Hell, he'd rip apart anyone stupid enough to get near her.

"Never," he snarled, grimacing as she winced at his feral expression. Sucking in a deep breath, he attempted to calm the beast inside. "Damn. The need shouldn't be this overwhelming," he confessed.

She glared at him, as if it was his fault. "Then why is it?"

"It could be a result of your cat being shackled for too long," he said, his voice a rough growl as he pressed her lower body against his swelling cock. "Or it could be the result of our returning magic. It's been a very long time since we've had a female in heat."

She shook her head, unconsciously curling her fingers into his chest as if she had claws. "Stop saying that."

He bent down until he was pressing his forehead against hers, his nose flaring to capture her deepening musk.

"Tell me what you want, sugar."

"Sanity," she muttered.

No shit. Sebastian could use a hefty dose of that himself.

But it wasn't happening.

Not until the heat was eased.

"Answer me, Reny, before I take the decision out of your hands," he commanded, the edge in his voice warning he was at the point of snapping. "Do we stay, or go to the Wildlands where the Healers might be able discover some pharmaceutical way to lessen your need?"

She trembled, her human mind no doubt urging her to demand to be medically cured of her ache. But it was the cat who was currently in charge, and the too-long suppressed feline wasn't at all confused about what it wanted.

"Stay," she whispered, her eyes glowing. "We stay."

Arousal slammed into him with the force of a cement truck, making it difficult to think as her hand boldly stroked over his chest.

He grasped her wrist, hissing as pleasure poured through him. "You're sure?"

She answered the strained question by lifting her free hand to continue his torture with bold, searching fingers.

"I don't know what's happening to me, but right now all I want is to wrap myself around you."

Sebastian cursed, his body swiftly threatening to explode. "Be careful what you say to me, sugar. I prefer to be a tender lover, but my cat is ready to devour you."

She didn't look nearly as frightened as she should. "You speak of your cat as a separate being."

"We are one in spirit, but he's far more...primitive. Life is simpler when I'm in my cat form. Life. Death. Hunger." He tangled his fingers into the thick satin of her hair, loosening it from the ponytail so it could spill over her shoulders. His heart skipped a beat as the overhead light shimmered in the fire hidden in the dark satin of her hair. "The thrill of the hunt."

His acute hearing picked up the sudden leap of her heart.

Ah. She liked the idea of being on the prowl.

"Don't think you can hunt me." Leaning forward, she trailed her lips along the curve of his throat. An instinctive provocation that was more Pantera than human. "I'll never be your prey."

Sebastian's fingers loosened on her wrist, his thumb brushing the rapid beat of her pulse. Foolish female. Challenging a Pantera male was a certain way to provoke his most primal instincts.

Strong females were as potent as the finest aphrodisiac to the animal inside him.

Sliding his hand to the front of her neck, his fingers circled her throat, holding her in a gesture of pure possession.

"If I decide you're mine," he murmured softly. "I will hunt you to the end of the earth."

"Is that a threat?" she demanded, her tone distracted as her fingers began to unbutton his shirt.

He gave a low growl, tugging her tight against his hard body.

"It's a promise, sugar," he rasped, his senses inflamed to the point of pain.

"This is madness." She pulled open his shirt, trailing her tongue down the bronzed skin she'd just revealed. "Complete lunacy."

His soft groan rumbled in his chest as he moved to cup her ass, compulsively pressing her to his rock hard cock.

"You won't get an argument from me," he muttered, for the first time fully appreciating the power of the mating heat.

Her hunger was a savage ache that clenched his body, the temptation of her spicy scent drowning him in need.

His cock throbbed in concert with every beat of her heart.

"Have you ever done this?"

He gave a startled laugh. "Had sex?"

She arched back to meet his searching gaze, an unexpected hint of vulnerability in her eyes.

"Have you been with many females in my...condition?"

Unable to resist the sight of that slender neck arched in open invitation, Sebastian lowered his head.

"No," he murmured, his voice a husky growl. "Never."

She gave a low groan as his tongue ran a searing path along the line of her throat.

"Then how do you know this will put an end to it?" Her fingers dug into his upper arms, as if her knees had suddenly become too weak to support her.

He nipped her earlobe, wryly acknowledging that the mating heat was only an excuse to give in to his desire.

He would have done everything in his power to get her in the nearest bed without the heat driving him.

"There's only one way to find out."

Before she could even guess his intention, Sebastian was easing her out of her jacket and unbuckling her holster to set aside her gun before swiftly dealing with the white cotton shirt. Then, reaching the end of his patience, he rid her of the lacy white bra with one sharp tug.

Sebastian made a sound of appreciation, his hands moving to cup her breasts with a reverent care.

Damn. He'd suspected she'd be beautiful beneath all that starch, but she was…perfect.

His thumbs teased the pink tips of her nipples, rumbling in pleasure as they hardened with excitement.

"Do you like that?" he demanded.

"Yes," she whispered.

His head lowered, his lips closing over the sensitive nipple. "And this?"

Her head dropped back, a low purr vibrating in her chest.

"Oh…hell, yes."

Softly chuckling at her eager response, Sebastian leashed his urge to pounce. Falling on her like a rabid puma probably wasn't the best idea. Not for their first time.

Continuing to tease her nipple with his tongue, Sebastian deftly slid down the zipper of her slacks, eager to feel her naked body pressed against his. When there was no protest from Reny, he slowly began to peel them downward, lowering himself to his knees as he efficiently tugged off her sensible shoes before he finished stripping her.

Then, still kneeling, he allowed himself to drink in her beauty.

She was long and slender, but had the firm muscles of a Pantera rippling beneath her smooth skin.

Excitement scorched through him as his attention lingered on the tiny triangle of silk that was all that covered her. Well…it didn't actually *cover* much.

Who would have suspected that beneath all that starch Reny Smith, FBI agent, was a woman who wore a bright red thong?

His cat snarled, urging him to rethink that whole 'no pouncing' decision.

Once again, however, he restrained his primitive impulse.

Instead, he skimmed his lips up the flat plane of her stomach, the valley between her breasts, at last halting at the pulse that beat wildly at the base of her neck.

She made a sound of impatience, her lips parting willingly as he at last claimed her mouth in a kiss of sheer possession.

"Sebastian," she moaned.

"If you have any intention of changing your mind, it'd better be quick, sugar," he warned. "My control is about to snap."

"Let it snap," she whispered against his lips.

"Last chance," he offered, his hands clenching the gentle swell of her hips.

He knew once he had a taste of her it would not be enough.

Because this is way more than the mating heat.

This woman belongs in my arms.

The unnerving words seared through his mind before he could halt them.

"My last chance ended when I arrived in New Orleans," she retorted, shivering as his tongue swiped between her lips in a very feline gesture. "I should never have left New York."

"I would have found you, Reny Smith," he said, grasping her hand to gently place it against his pulsing arousal. "This moment was fated from the day we were born."

She held his gaze as her fingers traced his hard cock that strained against his zipper, her eyes glowing with the power of her cat.

Hunger clawed deep within him. Okay, maybe no pouncing, but a raw, pagan night of sex was becoming far more likely.

As if deliberately attempting to drive Sebastian out of his mind, Reny tugged down the zipper of his slacks, releasing the heavy thrust of his erection.

"And I've never been so damned happy with destiny in my entire life," Sebastian managed to croak, shuddering at the hot surge of pleasure.

Heat spiked the air as she lightly skimmed her fingers down his thick length.

"I don't believe in that mumbo-jumbo," she muttered.

"You should. Fate brought you to me," he growled, his hands tightening on her hips as he sought to leash his eager cat.

"No, I control my own life," she stubbornly insisted, her hand moving steadily lower.

"Reny..." He muttered a curse, his eyes clenching shut. How the hell was he supposed to argue when he was one stroke away from a climax? "Are you deliberately trying to torture me?"

She discovered his tender sack and lightly squeezed. "Would I do that?"

"Yes," he choked, grasping her wrist to halt the exquisite torment. "No more."

"Why not?"

Forcing his eyes open, he met the glowing moss green eyes. "Because just your touch is about to make me explode."

The spicy scent of her arousal spiked at his blunt words. "And that's a bad thing?"

"Not bad," he husked. "But I want to be buried deep inside you when I come."

She shivered, responding to the stark need in his voice. "Then what are you waiting for?"

Good question.

Granted, he wasn't like many of his people. He was calm, calculated. Capable of considering a situation from multiple viewpoints.

That's what made him such a successful Diplomat. He didn't allow his instincts to rule him.

But now...

Now he wanted to plunge into the incandescent pleasure that was heating his blood to a fever pitch. He wanted to forget the danger that continued to threaten the Wildlands. And the knowledge that Raphael was depending on him to bring an end to the humans' mounting fear.

He just wanted to become lost in his hunger for a woman who was stirring emotions that should have terrified the hell out of him.

With a slow, sensuous gesture, Sebastian loosened his grip on her wrist at the same moment he captured her lips with a blazing kiss. She opened her mouth to invite the invasion of his tongue, her hand moving down his cock with a stroke that made his back arch in pure bliss.

Gliding his lips over the flushed skin of her cheeks, he discovered the sensitive spot just below her ear. She shivered in response, her heart pounding so loudly that Sebastian didn't need to be Pantera to hear it.

He used her soft sighs to guide his growingly insistent caresses, focused on her pleasure even as his hips began to pump in rhythm with her forceful strokes.

Oh…hell.

This wasn't how he expected this to play out, but it felt so fucking good.

Reaching that surprising thong, Sebastian ripped it away with one firm tug. Screw subtle.

He had one goal in mind, and nothing was allowed to stand in his way.

Skimming his hand over the curve of her thigh, Sebastian gently urged her legs to part, giving his fingers access to her most tender flesh.

A low growl rumbled in his throat as he parted her folds to discover that she was already damp and eager for his touch.

"Christ," she muttered, her hand unwittingly clenching on his cock as he pressed a finger into her body.

Not that he protested. Hell, no. He was all about muttering soft words of encouragement as he caressed her with a growing urgency.

His cat growled in frustration, wanting to possess the female in a far more intimate way, but Sebastian ignored the burning need to press her against the wall and fuck her until she screamed in pleasure.

Reny wasn't used to having sex with a Pantera male.

He needed to blunt the savage edge of his need.

Besides, the blissful pressure clenching his lower body was swiftly reaching the point of no return. He was fiercely determined to ensure her pleasure before claiming his own.

Lowering his head, Sebastian sucked the tip of her nipple in his mouth, using his teeth to tease her as his finger slid in and out of her slick channel. She whimpered softly, her hand stroking him with greater urgency.

He could sense that she was close.

Her spicy heat filled the room, intoxicating his senses.

Her breath locked in her throat, her back arching. Then, with a soft cry, she shuddered in completion, her last, insistent tug of his erection causing him to cry out as his climax slammed through him and the world shattered in pleasure.

Wrapping her in his arms, Sebastian had to smile.

Reny was wrong.

This had to be fate.

Nothing less than divine intervention could have brought this exquisite, mysterious female into his arms.

CHAPTER FOUR

PLEASURE scalded through Reny, making her knees weak as she clung to the man who'd just given her the most shattering climax of her life.

Good. God.

That was…

Her fuzzy mind struggled to form the words that would capture the spasms of pleasure that continued to clench her body.

It didn't make sense.

Sebastian was barely more than a stranger. Hell, they hadn't even had full intercourse.

She wanted to blame the blinding enjoyment on the weird-ass mating heat.

Any man would do while she was being forced into sex by a chemical-induced frenzy.

Problem was…she knew that wasn't true.

Yes, she'd been driven by a hunger she'd never felt before. At least, not that she could remember. And her logical mind would never have allowed her to get up close and personal with a man she'd just met if it wasn't for the lust that had thundered through her body.

But, there was no way that she'd have given in to her desire if she hadn't been attracted to Sebastian on a deep, primal level. And she certainly wouldn't still be aching to push him onto the nearby bed and impale herself on the hard length of his cock.

Almost as if able to read her thoughts, Sebastian lowered his head to nuzzle his face against her cheek in a very feline gesture.

She shivered. How could such a simple caress be so amazingly erotic?

"Better?" he murmured against her ear.

She gave a small nod, still trying to catch her breath. "It's not as..." She hesitated, allowing herself to consider the faint buzz of arousal that continued to race through her. It was there...waiting...but it was no longer a clawing, almost painful desire. As if Sebastian's touch had reassured the strange hunger that her needs were going to be met. How crazy was that? "Persistent," she at last muttered.

His lips touched her temple before following her hairline to trace the shell of her ear. "Good."

She sucked in a deep breath, discovering the exotic musk of his skin was as enticing as his hard, chiseled body and the soft caress of his fingers as they trailed up and down her back.

"Good?"

"When I take you, we'll both know that it's because you want to."

She pulled back to meet his eyes that still glowed with blatant lust. "You're so certain I want you?"

"Yes."

"Arrogant."

He flashed a smile filled with sinful promise as he released her to shrug out of his shirt. Reny nearly choked as she caught her first full glimpse of Sebastian's bare chest.

He was delectable.

Her fingers itched to explore the broad expanse of bronzed skin, lingering on the six-pack before lowering to the cock that was rising and thickening at her appreciative glance.

Or maybe she'd use her tongue, she abruptly decided, giving up any pretense that she wasn't eager to finish what they'd started.

It wasn't like he didn't sense her reaction to his striptease.

Just as she could feel the pulse of his mounting desire beating against her.

Heat prickled over her skin, her mouth going dry as he kicked off the Italian leather shoes and shoved down the black slacks.

Oh, man. He looked like he'd been sculpted by an artist.

The urge to touch him was too much to resist. Reaching out, she was caught off guard when Sebastian shackled her wrist in a strong grip.

"No," he growled, the cat so close to the surface that Reny would swear she could *sense* it.

She lifted her brows in surprise. "You don't like my touch?"

"Too much," he confessed with blunt honesty, tugging her against his naked body. Reny swallowed a startled gasp at the skin to skin contact. It felt like she was being branded. Claimed in a way she didn't fully grasp. Sebastian gave a low growl of approval, his smile smug. "The last time I let you to take control, allowing you to take what you needed from me. It's my turn."

His dominance was like a physical push against her. It should have annoyed the hell out of her.

Reny was far too independent to put up with a man who treated her as anything less than an equal.

So why was the feel of his raw, predatory strength sending tiny tremors of anticipation through her body?

Annoyed by her traitorous response, she narrowed her gaze.

"I like to be in control."

His hands skimmed up her back to tangle his fingers in her hair, tilting her head back so he could have full access to the vulnerable length of her neck.

"Yeah, I noticed." His lips traced a path of havoc along her jaw, before nibbling down the curve of her throat. "But you're going to like my way better."

Like?

She was freaking *loving* it.

"Oh, really?" she forced herself to mutter, even though she wasn't fooling anyone.

He chuckled, swiping a rough tongue over the sensitive spot between her neck and shoulder.

"Sugar, I'm going to make you scream."

"You can try."

"Ah, a challenge," he whispered, as his hands slid over her shoulders and toward her aching breasts. "I can be very persuasive when I'm motivated."

She made a choked sound as his thumbs brushed over her straining nipples. Why had she never noticed how sensitive they were? Probably because she'd never been touched by Sebastian.

Just having him near was enough to make her entire body sizzle with eagerness.

The reluctant acknowledgement had barely formed when it was buried beneath an avalanche of pleasure as his mouth skated over the curve of her breast. Reaching his destination, his lips closed over the tip so his tongue could tease her with merciless skill.

"Not fair," she muttered, her fingers shoving into the tawny silk of his hair.

He turned his head to torment her other breast.

"I never play fair," he warned her, lifting his head to meet her heated gaze. "I play to win."

With a motion too swift for Reny to anticipate, Sebastian swept her off her feet and tossed her into the center of the bed, her arms and legs splayed wide.

"Hey."

"We're doing things my way this time, remember?" he demanded, covering her with the welcome weight of his body.

She lifted her hands, intending to hold him off so she could tell him exactly what she thought of his arrogance. Only her hands were no longer connected to her brain. Rather than pushing against the hard planes of his chest, her fingers were lingering on a small tattoo of a crouching puma that was barely noticeable against the bronzed skin of his chest.

"I never agreed," she said, her voice a husky rasp.

Lowering his head, Sebastian nibbled at the corner of her mouth. "Do you need me to convince you?"

A harsh shudder shook her body. Oh, yeah. She was ready and willing to be convinced.

Somewhere in the back of her mind she knew that this was a brief moment of madness, first brought on by the strange sexual compulsion and now by her purely feminine desire.

And perhaps the need to forget the world for just a little while.

Beyond the closed door was her duty to finish the job that had brought her to New Orleans. And impressing her bosses to ensure her promotion.

And, oh yeah, somehow processing the suspicion that she wasn't entirely human.

Sometimes a woman needed a few hours of fantasy to make her reality more bearable.

And Sebastian was the perfect fantasy.

As if sensing her capitulation, Sebastian growled low in his throat, his hands moving with a possessive confidence over her naked body.

"Spice and musk," he muttered, his tongue outlining her lips. "I need a taste."

Reny gave a small squeak as one roaming hand slid between her thighs to stroke through her wet pussy.

"Do you bite?" she asked, breathless.

"Absolutely." He held her gaze as he dipped his finger into her thickening cream. "But only if you beg nicely."

Reny dug her heels into the black silk sheets as she arched her hips upward.

"As if..." She forgot how to speak as his finger began sliding in and out of her. "Oh."

His lips brushed over her cheek, then down the line of her jaw. "Let yourself go, Agent Reny Smith." He pressed a kiss to the pulse racing at the base of her throat. "Just." His mouth trailed down her collarbone. "Let." He covered the aching tip of her breast. "Go."

Oh, hell. Maybe he was going to make her scream. Her entire body was going up in flames.

43

Fisting her fingers in his thick hair, she instinctively wrapped her legs around his hips.

"Stop giving me orders and do this thing."

Pulling back, he regarded her with a lift of his brows. "Do this thing?"

"You heard me."

"Hmm." His smile was mysterious. "I wonder if your cat is as demanding as you are."

She deliberately rubbed herself against the granite-hard length of his erection, not ready to consider what sort of animal lurked inside her. "Does it matter?"

The yellow in his eyes glowed until they appeared incandescent in the dim light.

Bracing himself on his elbow, he altered his position until the tip of his cock pressed against her entrance. "You are going to be all kinds of trouble, sugar."

She sucked in a breath of anticipation, her pussy parting in welcome as he surged deep inside her with a slow, relentless thrust.

Moving her hands, Reny clutched at Sebastian's shoulders, her nails digging into his skin. Holy crap. He was huge. Deliciously, heart-stoppingly huge. She groaned. There wasn't pain. Despite Sebastian's considerable size, her body eagerly accommodated his entry. But there was a sensual sense of fullness, and a startling intimacy that she hadn't been expecting.

In this moment she felt utterly bonded to Sebastian. Bonded in a way that seemed far more poignant than two bodies simply having sex.

It was...

No. She slammed a mental door on the dangerous thoughts. She couldn't afford for this to be more than a meaningless, transitory coupling.

"Reny," he whispered close to her ear. "Are you okay?"

"Yes," she muttered, burying her face in the curve of his neck. "Don't stop."

"Christ, I couldn't stop if you put a gun to my head," he muttered, withdrawing from her body before pushing back in with a growing urgency. "I've never felt anything more perfect."

He was right.

It was perfect.

The heat and weight of his body as he pressed her deep into the mattress. The intoxicating musk that filled her senses. The beauty of his bronzed face, tight with the strain of tempering his hunger.

But before she could agree, he was once again pulling out and thrusting forward with a rhythm that stole her breath. Yes. Oh, yes. This was what her body had longed for in the depths of the night. This was what she needed.

Savoring the savage pleasure of his possession, Reny raked her nails down his back, delighted by the growl that reverberated in his chest. She dug her nails deeper, rewarded as he angled her head so he could sink his teeth into the vulnerable flesh of her neck.

He did bite.

His hips rocked faster, his hands tilting her upward to meet his deep, steady thrusts.

"Sebastian…please," she implored, her body coiled so tightly she felt as if she might shatter.

"I told you to let go." Dipping his head downward, he teased her aching nipple with his lips, pumping with a brutal pace as she wrapped her legs around his waist.

Reny's breath rasped in the silent air, her focus locked onto the point where Sebastian's body slammed in and out of her.

She was so close. So divinely close.

And then…pow.

It happened.

With one last surge he tumbled her over the edge, galvanizing her into an orgasm that exploded with blissful force. Her scream of pleasure reverberated through the room, her body shuddering with bliss as he continued to pump into her until he stiffened with his own release, his back arching beneath the force of his climax.

Wrenching open her eyes, she regarded him in horror.

Dammit. He'd made her scream.

Meeting her gaze, he allowed a smug smile to curve his lips. "Gotcha."

Chapter Five

SEBASTIAN purred, basking in the heat of Reny's body entwined with his own.

Mmm. He was satisfied on a level that went way beyond a good orgasm.

Sated lust was a good thing.

Hell, it was a great thing.

But this sense of...bone-deep rightness...it made him feel as if he'd just won the fucking lottery.

He was in trouble.

The kind of trouble that led a male Pantera into mating for life.

But he didn't care.

Fate had given him this female and there was no way in hell he was letting her go.

Nuzzling his lips against her temple, Sebastian trailed his fingers over her toned abs, relishing the spicy scent that fully captured this complicated woman.

Sassy, strong, unpredictable.

"That was—" His words were cut short when Reny pressed her fingers to his lips.

"No."

He arched a brow. "No?"

"I don't want to dissect what happened between us."

Propping himself on his elbow, he carefully studied her wary expression.

Her dark hair was spread across the pillows, hidden streaks of red shimmering like fire in the muted overhead light. Her face was still flushed from their combustible passion. And her slender body was perfectly formed to curve against him.

Her beauty was like an incandescent flame that drew him like a moth.

But it was the stubborn set of her jaw that captured his attention.

Reny Smith might have given her body with a generosity that had stolen his heart, but it was obvious her mind refused to accept the inevitable bond that was forming between them.

He smiled wryly. He didn't know whether to be annoyed with her stubborn resistance, or excited by the thought of continuing the chase.

It would make her eventual surrender all the sweeter.

Leaning down, he nipped the tip of her nose. "Are you always so romantic with your lovers?"

"I'm practical," she said in defensive tones. "I've had to be."

"Why?"

"When you have your past stolen from you by amnesia you swiftly discover the world isn't a place for fairy tales."

Amnesia…hell, that would explain so much.

"You were in an accident?"

"There was some sort of trauma." Old sorrow darkened her moss green eyes. "I was found hidden in the back of a semi-truck. I had wounds on my wrists and ankles that proved I'd been bound for several days, if not weeks. Maybe even longer. The doctors speculated that I'd been held by a psychopath and my mind had blocked out the memories of my torture."

Sebastian barely dared to breathe as fury exploded through him. This sweet, fragile woman had been abused by a madman?

It was no wonder she'd been forced to build walls in her mind. Not only to deal with the horror of her captivity, but to contain the cat inside her that had never been allowed to fully bond with her.

Christ, she had to be one of the strongest people he'd ever met to not only survive, but to have built a new life for herself.

His fingers gently stroked her cheek, the need to ease her pain a physical necessity.

"How did you join the FBI?"

She turned in to his light caress, unconsciously seeking the comfort of his touch. "The cops who found me took me under their wing when it became obvious I wasn't going to be able to find my family." A tremor raced through her body. No doubt she'd tormented herself over the years with the image of how her parents must have been frantic in their search for their missing daughter. "They encouraged me to apply to Quantico."

Sebastian frowned. How was it possible that he hadn't heard of a missing Pantera female?

Her parents would have come to the Wildlands for assistance in searching for her

Unless they were dead.

Which meant the bastard holding her might not have been a random psycho.

"Did they find the man responsible for holding you?" he murmured.

She shook her head. "They searched, but they couldn't even be entirely certain that's what happened to me."

"Perhaps they were looking in the wrong place."

"What do you mean?"

He absently smoothed a strand of hair behind her ear. "The Pantera have enemies."

Her lips parted, but before she could interrogate him, there was a series of beeps from across the room.

"That's the office," she muttered, wriggling out of his arms to hop out of bed.

Sebastian gave a low growl of protest, but he couldn't deny an appreciation of watching her naked ass as she moved to pick up her jacket and pull out the ringing phone.

It was a very fine ass, he acknowledged, wishing he'd done more exploring of the lush temptation.

Next time…

His indulgent fantasies of the various ways he intended to savor Reny were interrupted as he watched her expression become grim as she listened to the caller.

Instantly, he was off the bed and pulling on his clothes. Their all-too-brief moment of privacy was over.

It was time to rejoin the world.

"What happened?" he demanded as soon as she ended the call.

She dressed with a brisk efficiency. "There was another mauling."

"Damn." Sebastian tucked his shirt in his pants and smoothed back his hair. "I need to talk to the victim."

"You can't."

"Why not?" His brows snapped together as he watched her slip on her sensible leather shoes and tug her hair into a tight ponytail.

Once again she was the starchy Agent Smith.

His cat growled in disapproval.

She lifted her head to meet his annoyed glare. "She's at the morgue."

Oh…hell.

Sebastian's gut twisted with regret. He'd known it was only a matter of time before their enemies took their attacks to the next level, but he'd hoped he would be able to expose them before they actually killed someone.

"Do you know where they found the body?"

Reny grimaced. "It was propped next to the dumpster at the police station."

"Bold bastards." Sebastian pulled out his phone and texted the info to Raphael. The Wildlands needed to be prepared in case the humans decided to retaliate. "They wanted to make sure it was found."

"Yes."

Sebastian slid the phone back into his pocket. "We need to find the first victim."

"I agree."

With an obvious refusal to glance toward the bed that was a visual display of their recent passion, she headed to pull open the door.

Before she could step out of the room, however, he captured her from behind. Wrapping his arm around her waist, he whispered directly in her ear.

"You know this isn't finished."

She held herself stiffly, but there was no missing the rapid beat of her heart.

"Don't push your luck, cat," she warned.

He traced the curve of her ear with his tongue. "Sugar, I'm going to push until I hear you scream again." He planted a kiss in the hollow beneath her jaw. "And again." He gently sank his teeth into the tender flesh between her neck and shoulder, chuckling as she groaned in startled pleasure. "And—"

Giving a small hiss, Reny broke out of his hold, turning to meet his smoldering gaze.

"Are all Pantera so cocky?"

An unexpected, shockingly violent tidal wave of territorial possession surged through him. "I'm the only Pantera you need to worry about." There was a hint of warning in his voice. "Period."

Her eyes widened, but perhaps sensing the danger of poking his cat when it was anxious to pounce, she deliberately stepped into the hall.

"Where do we start?" she asked.

Sebastian squashed the urge to scoop her in his arms and carry her back to bed. His growingly urgent need to bond with Reny Smith would have to wait until they'd brought a halt to the bastards who were attacking defenseless women.

"Back at the apartment," he said, hoping Koni Handler had the information he needed to start his hunt. "I need to pick up the female's scent."

"Makes sense," she agreed, briskly heading down the stairs.

Sebastian prowled at her side. "You should return to your office and start running her financials."

She pulled out her phone and began typing in a message. "I can have one of the techs take care of it."

They moved down the stairs and toward the back of the house. "Then you can go have dinner."

"I already ate." She sent him a suspicious glare. "Why are you trying to get rid of me?"

"We don't know what's out there hunting women," he said.

A dangerous heat sparked in her eyes. "Exactly. It's my job to find out."

He was a Diplomat. He knew that tone.

It meant, 'You've just pissed on my last nerve. Now back off.'

But he was also a Pantera male who possessed an instinctive need to protect his female.

"You don't understand the danger."

Heat sizzled through the air, the power of her cat glowing in her eyes.

"Don't you dare treat me like a helpless little woman." She stepped forward, poking her finger into the middle of his chest. "This is my case." Another poke, this one hard enough to hurt. "If you don't want to be my partner then return to the Wildlands and send someone else."

Oh, hell. She was a born Hunter. He could read it in her fierce need to be out tracking down their enemies. It was no wonder that she'd chosen to go into law enforcement.

Sebastian smothered a wry smile.

She was going to make his life…interesting.

"Come on," he said.

———

Reny was prepared to remain on her personal soapbox. There was nothing she hated more than being treated as if she couldn't be good at her job because she had a uterus instead of a penis.

But the moment they'd returned to the desolate neighborhood where Koni Handler had lived, Sebastian wisely resisted any urge to try and prevent her from remaining at his side as he focused on following the scent.

A scent that teased at Reny's nose even while she slammed the door on acknowledging her abilities.

It was a trick she'd developed when she was in the hospital and realized how different she was from the other patients.

How else could she stay sane?

They'd traveled three blocks when Sebastian came to a sudden halt, his expression grim as he glanced around the corner that was bathed in the gaudy lights from a nearby bar.

"Why are you stopping?" she demanded.

"She must have gotten into a vehicle." He gave a frustrated growl. "Dammit."

"Then we do it the human way," Reny murmured, her trained gaze instantly searching near the doorway of the bar. She was rewarded by the sight of a small red light. "There." She pointed toward the surveillance camera.

He arched a brow, looking impossibly gorgeous despite his ruffled hair and the hint of tawny whiskers that shadowed his jaw.

"Good call. Can you get us access?"

Something eased in her chest at his ready willingness to accept her help.

Maybe he wasn't a complete jackass.

With a smug smile she pulled her badge from the inner pocket of her jacket and headed across the street.

Entering the narrow bar with a dozen worn tables scattered over a wood floor, Reny took a direct path toward the back of the room where a large, grizzled man was tending bar. A few of the drunken patrons gave her a lingering look before paling in fear as they caught sight of the predatory male who walked a half step behind her.

Less than ten minutes later they were in a cramped office that smelled of scotch and cheap cologne, skimming through fuzzy images that flashed across the computer screen.

"There she is," Reny said, halting the video as she recognized Koni Handler stepping into a white van with an emblem painted on its side of a spread-winged raven flying across a full moon.

"Shit." Sebastian leaned over her shoulder, his expression grim. "Can you enlarge it?"

She zoomed in on the blurred image of the driver. "Do you recognize him?"

The heat from his body pumped through the room. "Unfortunately."

Her breath caught in her throat as she glanced up to meet his bloodthirsty gaze. "Is he Pantera?"

"No," he instantly denied. "But I think I know how to find him."

She rose to her feet, heading out of the office. "We'll take my car."

"Yes, ma'am," he teased, allowing her to lead them out of the bar and down the street.

She waited until they were in her car and Sebastian had punched in the GPS coordinates that had them heading east before she asked the obvious question.

"How do you know the driver?"

There was another blast of heat, revealing that beneath Sebastian's façade of calm focus was a smoldering fury.

"We discovered that he's a disciple for our enemy."

"Disciple?" She sent him a puzzled glance. "That's a strange term."

"They worship the goddess who's determined to destroy us."

She searched his tense profile, looking for some indication he was screwing with her.

"A goddess?"

"Yes." His fingers tapped on his knee, clearly impatient to get to where they were going. "Which means this might be even worse than we originally anticipated."

Shit. He was serious.

"What goddess?" she demanded, wondering if the night could get any more bizarre. "And why does she want to destroy you?"

"I promise to explain it as soon as we find our missing victim," he said, his tone distracted.

Reny grimaced, not in the mood to insist on answers.

She was still trying to accept the thought that she might be a Pantera.

She didn't want to add in a mysterious goddess who might or might not want to destroy her.

They traveled in silence as Reny followed the GPS directions to the edge of town. At last, she turned into what looked like an abandoned industrial complex.

"Pull over there." Sebastian pointed toward a stack of pylons. She parked the car and shut off the engine, already prepared when he turned to send her a worried glance. "Reny."

"Don't." She pointed a warning finger into his face. "Start."

With a roll of his eyes, he shoved open the door and climbed out of the car. Reny pulled her gun from the holster before following him through the thick shadows toward a three-story brick building at the edge of the complex.

Expecting him to head directly for the loading doors that stood open, Reny was caught off guard when he took a wide path around the far edge of the building.

"Where are we going?" she demanded, keeping her voice pitched low so it wouldn't carry.

"There could be Pantera," he explained. "We need to stay downwind."

She jumped over a pile of coiled steel cable that was nearly hidden by the patches of weeds.

Damn. She was going to end up with a broken neck if she wasn't careful.

"I thought you said a Pantera couldn't be involved," she said.

His pace never slowed. "I said a Pantera couldn't shift away from the Wildlands, not that we haven't discovered traitors among our people."

"Great," she muttered. "Any other surprises you want to spring on me?"

He glanced over his shoulder with a grin that made her blood heat. "Not while you're clothed."

She cursed at the instant lust that raced through her body. "Arrogant cat."

CHAPTER SIX

SEBASTIAN reluctantly led Reny toward the narrow door at the end of the abandoned warehouse, knowing it would be a waste of breath to try and convince her to wait in the car.

Besides, he couldn't change her nature.

Reny Smith was a born warrior. To try and make her less would break something deep inside her.

Not that it wasn't going to make him crazy to have her charging into danger.

With one sharp tug, Sebastian had the padlock broken and was pushing open the door. Then, with a silence that no human could hope to achieve, he was sliding through the vast room that had once been filled with crates of animal pelts. The lingering odor might have masked the presence of the four humans if they hadn't been bonded to Shakpi. The sour stench that clung to her disciples couldn't be missed.

Halting in the shadows, Sebastian studied the humans who remained oblivious to his presence.

There was a young woman he assumed was Koni Handler. She was tied to a chair, her head bent down so her hair fell forward to hide her face, although he could hear her soft sobs from across the room.

Several feet away was an older woman with several bracelets on her scrawny arms, dressed in a brightly patterned dress. Her silver hair was pulled into a knot at the back of her head and she was currently giving two human males the evil eye.

Sebastian growled deep in his throat. There was a redheaded male with a scar that twisted one side of his face, but it was the man with lanky black hair and a rat face that Sebastian had recognized from the video surveillance.

Derek.

The bastard who'd been pretending to be an ally to the Pantera when all along he was working for their enemies.

On the plus side, it was Derek's stupidity that had allowed the Geeks to track his movements from the voodoo shop where he'd been spying on Isi to this warehouse. Which was how Sebastian knew exactly where to locate him.

Clearly not any more impressed with the thug's intelligence than Sebastian was, the older woman pointed her finger toward the bound woman, the heavy bracelets that circled her arms giving a loud rattle.

"You were told to kill her and dump the body."

"We did with the ugly one," the redhead muttered, hunching his shoulders. "This one we want to play with first."

"Idiots." The woman that he suspected was Lady Cerise stepped forward to slap the man on the side of his head. "My informant just called to warn me that a Pantera is in town working with the FBI. Do you want to lead them to us?"

Sebastian silently cursed, making a mental note to track down the informant. He wouldn't tolerate traitors.

"They have no way of finding this place," Derek boasted.

"You know nothing," Lady Cerise snapped. "It's easy to be a bully when you're dealing with the dregs of humanity. The Pantera will eat you alive." She allowed a dramatic pause. "Literally."

"I'm not scared," Derek muttered, ruining his cocky boast when he sent a nervous glance toward the shadows that shrouded the warehouse.

Did he sense they were near? Sebastian hoped so.

He wanted him afraid. To feel hunted.

"Because you're stupid." Lady Cerise pointed out the obvious. "Now get rid of her."

The redhead folded his arms over his chest. "You ain't in charge."

There was a shocked silence.

"What did you say?" the older woman at last rasped.

"Our goddess, Shakpi, has returned," the man said. "She's in charge now."

Sebastian covered Reny's mouth with lightning speed, easily sensing her shock at the revelation that the goddess he'd mentioned earlier was actually walking the earth. He'd hoped to avoid sharing that little tidbit of info. At least until she'd managed to process the other shocks she'd had to endure over the past few hours.

Across the cavernous room, Derek gave a nervous laugh. "Even if she does look like a middle-aged Indian dude."

"No shit," the redhead agreed with a chuckle.

Not amused, Lady Cerise deliberately grasped a small satin bag she had tied around her neck.

"You will do as I say or I will place a curse on you that will cause a body part to fall off each and every day. Starting with your very small dicks." The woman offered an evil smile. "Do you understand?"

The two men shuddered at the threat. "Fine."

Sebastian was distracted as Reny pressed against him to whisper directly in his ear. "I have to do something."

He wisely bit back his instinctive refusal, reminding himself that Reny would never forgive him if he tried to cage her.

Besides, he was going to need her if they were to get the female out alive.

Assuring himself that he'd soon have her back in the Wildlands where she would be safe, he turned to meet her steady gaze.

"I'll distract them," he murmured softly. "You circle around and get the girl." Something that might have been relief darkened her eyes, as if she'd been dreading his refusal to accept her help. Of course, he couldn't completely resist giving out at least one warning. "Don't take any unnecessary risks."

Narrowing her gaze, she abruptly framed his face in her hands and glared at his startled expression.

"You."

"Yes?"

"Be careful."

He blinked in surprise, having expected a lecture, not a warning. Warmth spread through his heart as she brushed her lips across his with a kiss that promised far more wicked pleasures to come.

"Careful is my middle name."

She gave a shake of her head. "I'm fairly certain your middle name is Aggravating Bastard."

He stole another kiss before straightening and nodding his head toward the west wall. "Take the female out the side door and call for backup."

With a smooth efficiency, Reny was moving along the edge of the room, her gun held in a professional grip.

Good girl, he silently approved, waiting until she was approaching the bound female before he stalked forward, using the sheer power of his presence to capture the villains' attention.

Even humans could sense when there was a predator in their midst.

Halting a few feet away, he folded his arms over his chest.

"You should listen to..." He glanced toward the older woman. "Lady Cerise, I presume?"

The redhead clenched his hands, deliberately flexing his muscles. As if Sebastian would be impressed. Twit.

"Who the hell are you?" he blustered.

"I could say I'm your worst nightmare but that would be so cliché." His smile was mocking. "Oh, the hell with it. I'm your worst nightmare."

Out of the corner of his eye, Sebastian watched as Reny silently crept forward and began working on the ropes that held the nearly unconscious female.

Confident she could complete her mission, Sebastian briefly watched Lady Cerise scuttle away, accepting he'd have to track her down later before he returned his attention to the redhead who was taking a step forward.

"Careful, Van," Derek warned. "He's one of those fucking animals."

Van turned his head to spit on the ground, revealing the image of a raven that had been branded on his neck. The Mark of Shakpi.

"I've had my rabies shots," he assured his friend, acting all badass with the knowledge they had Sebastian outnumbered.

Sebastian arched a brow. "Wanna play, tough guy?"

"Play with this." Pulling a gun from a holster at his lower back, Van squeezed the trigger.

Sebastian easily dodged the bullet and stalked forward.

"Shit, do something," the man rasped, emptying his magazine in an attempt to halt Sebastian's relentless approach.

"Like it's doing you any good?" Derek muttered, abruptly retreating toward a nearby storage room.

"Where are you going?" Van demanded as his companion fled, finally realizing that Lady Cerise had disappeared at the first sight of Sebastian. "Goddamn cowards."

Sebastian allowed his smile to widen, breathing deeply of the man's rising terror. These bastards had not only attacked helpless females, but they were deliberately trying to create trouble between Pantera and humans.

They deserved to be punished.

Still he forced himself to wait before he attacked the fool. Reny was still urging the stumbling female across the floor. Once he was sure she was safely out of the building, he would—

Concentrating on Reny, Sebastian failed to notice Derek stepping back out of the storage room with a small gun in his hand. Not that he would be worried even if he had.

A bullet would hurt like a bitch, but it couldn't kill a Pantera.

But it wasn't a bullet that he felt stab into his neck.

Instead, it was a tiny dart.

Baffled by the ridiculous weapon, Sebastian reached up to pluck the dart from his neck, instantly recognizing the toxic potion that the Pantera had recently discovered being used by Shakpi's disciples.

A numbing sensation spread through his body with terrifying swiftness, cutting off his connection to his cat.

Shit. He couldn't shift when he was away from the Wildlands, but his strength and superior senses were directly connected to the power of his animal.

Turning to charge the bastard, he felt his knees threaten to give away as the toxin pumped through his bloodstream.

"Damn."

His last thought was relief that Reny was headed away from the warehouse, before Derek slammed a two-by-four against the side of his head.

———

"Do you have to be so rough?" Koni Handler whined, trying to pull away from the arm that Reny had wrapped around her waist to keep her upright. "My side hurts.

Reny resisted the urge to remove her arm and allow Koni to drop to the crumbling cement that had once been a parking lot.

"You want to get caught?" she muttered, continuing to half-drag the woman toward the pile of pylons as she texted her commander for backup.

All she wanted was to get the woman into the safety of her car so she could return to the warehouse.

Her last glimpse of Sebastian had been him confronting the two men with an arrogant confidence, but she was anxious to return to make sure he didn't do something stupid.

She didn't know much about the stubborn Pantera, but she suspected that he could very well underestimate the danger of humans when they were scared. The sooner she could get back to help him, the better.

"God, no. Why would they be so horrible?" Koni muttered, her tone petulant. "I did everything they asked."

"Like lying to the police about who attacked you?"

"Are you a cop?"

Reny sent her an impatient glare. "I'm the person saving your ass."

The woman hesitated, as if considering the possibility of pretending innocence, before she gave a reluctant nod.

"Yes, I lied."

"Why?"

"One of my regulars at the bar where I work asked if I wanted to make some extra money," she explained.

Reny's gaze scanned the shadows for enemies, her weapon held in her hand. Her senses might tell her that they were alone in the darkness, but she'd devoted the past eight years to ignoring her instincts, preferring to depend on her training.

"What did you have to do?" she asked.

"Let them mark me up like I'd been attacked by an animal and then go to the police."

Reny grimaced. "And you agreed?"

"They gave me five thousand dollars," Koni said. "Of course I agreed."

"How did you end up in the warehouse?"

"I—"

"The truth," Reny interrupted as her companion hesitated. "Trust me, I'll know if you lie."

"When I first agreed, I didn't know they were going to leave scars," Koni complained, holding out her arm that was marred by what looked like four long claw marks. The wounds were certainly deep enough to leave lasting proof of her stupidity. "I can't make tips looking like a freak-show."

"You tried to blackmail them for more money?"

Her lower lip stuck out in a pout that had obviously been practiced in front of a mirror. "They owed me."

"Yeah, and scumbags you meet in bars always pay their debts."

"Okay, at first they said no," she admitted, stumbling over a chunk of concrete. "Then last night they called and said they changed their minds. I didn't know they were going to try to kill me."

The woman burst into tears, but Reny ignored them.

It wasn't just her lack of empathy for a woman who'd been ready to lie to the police and start an interspecies war just for money. But she'd caught a renewed whiff of that strange sour smell that had been in the warehouse, warning her that they were no longer alone.

Dragging her companion around the pylons, she opened the back door and shoved her inside.

"Stay here," she ordered.

"No." With unexpected speed, Koni reached up to grasp her arm. "Don't leave me."

Reny cursed, unable to struggle. Not when she was holding a loaded gun. "An ambulance is on its way."

The woman gave a loud wail that made Reny wish she carried duct tape. "Please, they're going to kill me."

"Not if I kill you first. Let go," Reny muttered, grabbing the woman's fingers and peeling them away.

Then, slamming shut the door, she carefully eased her way around the pylons, not surprised to find the older woman standing just a few feet away.

"I'm FBI. Don't move." Reny pointed her gun at the woman's head. "Who are you?"

"Lady Cerise," she said, her tense expression visible despite the darkness. "You're too late."

Reny frowned. "What do you mean?"

"They've taken the Pantera away."

Sebastian? Fear thundered through her even as she desperately tried to hold on to her training.

She couldn't afford to be rattled.

"Why would I believe you?"

Lady Cerise arched a brow. "You're a Pantera as well, aren't you? Can't you sense he's gone?"

Reny stiffened. She didn't want to think about the whole Pantera thing, but the woman was right.

The faint awareness of Sebastian's presence that unconsciously hummed through her entire body was absent.

Shit. Her fingers tightened on the gun. "Where did they take him?"

"I can show you."

"Yeah, right," Reny scoffed.

The woman held up her hand, the bracelets rattling around her wrist. "I swear."

Reny narrowed her gaze, studying the thin face lined with age. "Why would you help me?"

"Because I am beginning to realize that I've made a terrible mistake. I thought—" She broke off her words with a shake of her head.

"What?" Reny prompted.

"It doesn't matter." The woman squared her shoulders. "Shakpi must be stopped."

Shakpi. The goddess they were discussing in the warehouse?

"What does she have to do with Sebastian?"

"That's where they'll take him," Lady Cerise muttered. "And I know where to find her."

"Tell me."

"No. You'll need me to get you past the guards."

Reny studied the woman's stubborn expression, easily sensing the woman was telling the truth.

"Fine. As soon as the backup arrives—"

"No, the minute they sense the authorities are near they will kill your man and scatter," Lady Cerise insisted. "We will have to slip in unnoticed."

Reny grimaced, but she didn't hesitate. She didn't have a damned clue how to fight a goddess. The FBI academy didn't have classes on defeating crazed deities that walked the earth, but there was nothing that was going to keep her from getting to Sebastian.

Why she was willing to risk everything for a man she'd met only hours ago was a question she didn't intend to waste time pondering.

"Let's go."

CHAPTER SEVEN

SEBASTIAN hadn't actually expected to wake up. Pantera who were stupid enough to let themselves be outmaneuvered by mere humans usually ended up dead. And besides, he'd never received the same tactical training as the Hunters. He was supposed to flay his opponents with his tongue, not his fists.

Which meant that when he finally forced his eyes open, he was actually relieved to discover he was lying on the floor of a small room that had been stripped of furniture, with the windows boarded over.

And he didn't even mind the aching muscles and tender bruises that revealed he'd been violently beaten while he was unconscious.

In fact, he was counting his blessings until the door was shoved open and a male with a lean face and glossy dark hair worn in a braid stepped into the room.

Chayton, the former Shaman, looked familiar in his traditional leather pants and a beaded vest. But it only took a glance into the eyes that glowed with a sickening power to prove that it wasn't Chayton who was in command of this body.

"Shakpi," he rasped in horror.

"Good. I thought you would never wake." A humorless smile twisted Chayton's lips. "What's your name?"

Sebastian forced himself to a seated position, relieved to discover the toxin that had shut off his connection to his cat was beginning to wear off. He wasn't at full strength, but he at least wasn't completely helpless.

"Fuck you," he muttered.

Chayton squatted down in front of him, drowning him in a sour stench that made Sebastian gag.

"That could be arranged, if you want."

Sebastian shuddered, barely able to concentrate as the malevolent power pulsed through the room.

"Where am I?" he managed to rasp.

"At my temporary lair." The Shaman cast a dismissive glance around the room. "It's pathetic, but thankfully the Wildlands will soon be destroyed and I can create a setting worthy of a goddess."

Sebastian shook his head, hiding his stab of fear. "Never."

"Oh, it's going to happen," Chayton drawled, reaching out to run his finger down Sebastian's cheek. "Soon."

Sebastian jerked away from the cold finger, feeling as if he'd been tainted. "You don't have the power to defeat us."

Chayton chuckled. "I don't need to."

"What does that mean?"

"The humans might not have the strength or intelligence I would desire for my disciples, but they do have the numbers."

Sebastian made a sound of disgust. They'd suspected that the cowardly attacks were being caused by the human disciples, while Shakpi plotted a more direct battle. Now it was obvious that Shakpi was personally responsible.

Obviously the goddess preferred to hide in the shadows and allow her followers to take the risks.

"You're behind the supposed Pantera attacks," he muttered.

"It's so divinely simple." Chayton shrugged. "A few dead bodies littered around the world and they're foaming at the mouth to destroy something. The Pantera will be obliterated in a month."

The cat inside him stirred, gaining strength with every passing second.

Not that he was stupid enough to think he could challenge a goddess.

For now, it was more important he gain any information possible and try to pass it on to Raphael.

"Why am I here?"

Chayton slowly straightened, folding his arms over his chest as he studied Sebastian with that unnervingly evil gaze.

"When my disciples called to say that they had an unconscious Pantera I told them I wanted to speak with you."

"Why?"

"I intend to savor the death of my sister's creations, but I will need a few loyal servants." Chayton's face remained impassive, but Sebastian could sense the goddess's smug arrogance. "I'm offering you the opportunity to serve me."

Serve the goddess responsible for the death of Pantera? With an effort, Sebastian pushed himself to his feet, the air heating with the force of his fury.

"You can take your offer and—"

"Careful," the Shaman snapped. "You get one chance before I allow my disciples to play with you." Chayton glanced toward the door, watching as Derek and Van stepped into the room. "They can be a little...rough."

Sebastian curled his lips in a disdainful smile. "I'll walk through the fires of hell before I'd bow to you."

"Fine." The power surged through the room, but even as Sebastian prepared for a killing blow, Chayton was heading out the door. "Have fun, boys."

Momentarily baffled, it took Sebastian a few seconds to understand Shakpi's abrupt retreat. She might be a goddess, but she was in a mortal body.

She was afraid of a physical confrontation.

That's why she was hiding behind her disciples.

The realization had barely formed when Van pulled his hand from behind his back to reveal a baseball bat.

"Ready to play, kitty cat?" the thug demanded, strolling forward.

Sebastian shrugged, well aware the idiots didn't realize his body was swiftly ridding itself of the toxin.

"Do I have a choice?" He made his voice sound as if it was an effort to even speak.

The goons smiled as they rushed forward.

With a fluid speed that no human could hope to match, Sebastian had the baseball bat yanked from Van's hands and whirling to his left in time to bust Derek's skull open with one negligent swing. The traitor fell to the floor, his blood pooling on the wooden planks.

Van squeaked in terror, turning to flee.

He managed two steps before Sebastian grabbed him by the neck, dangling him off the ground as he whispered in his ear.

"Where are you going?" he snarled. "We've just started to have fun."

———

Reny kept her head lowered as Lady Cerise led them past the two armed men who stood at high, wrought iron gates and up the seemingly endless driveway. The older woman hadn't been lying when she said that Reny would never have gotten through the tight security without her.

Still, Reny kept her hand on the trigger of her pistol hidden in the pocket of her jacket as they climbed up the stairs to the columned terrace where even more men were standing guard. She was well aware that she was quite likely walking into a trap.

The only thing that kept her moving forward was the unmistakable awareness that sparked to life deep inside her.

Sebastian was near.

And he was alive.

The knowledge compelled her to remain just steps behind Lady Cerise as they entered the mansion and moved through the foyer into a formal drawing room. And gave her the courage not to flee in panic when she was hit by a pungent, sour stench that assaulted her senses.

With a muttered curse, she stepped around the edge of a large bookcase, hoping to avoid the notice of the slender man with a long, black braid and distinctly Native American features who stepped into the room.

She didn't have to be told that this wasn't just a man.

That there was some massive…spirit…contained within the body that she very much feared was the goddess, Shakpi.

She grimaced as a fierce power beat against her, barely resisting the urge to pull out her gun and start firing.

Thankfully the unnerving creature's attention was locked on Reny's companion, the narrow face clenched with disapproval.

"Cerise." The name was said as a curse. "Did I invite you?"

Astonishingly, the older woman managed a dignified bow. Reny was fairly certain she would have peed her pants.

"I wanted to make sure the Pantera arrived."

"He did." A cruel smile touched the man's lips. "My pets are playing with him."

Reny bit her lip, fear piercing her heart. She didn't know what they were doing to Sebastian, but she knew it couldn't be good.

She had to get to him.

"He's alive?" Lady Cerise asked.

"For now." The dark eyes that burned with a strange light narrowed. "What do you care? Your attention should be on causing panic among the humans."

"We have dumped the first body near the police station. It's already stirring outrage in the media."

"It's not fast enough. I…" Reny watched in confusion as the male abruptly dropped to his knees, his hands clutched to his chest. "No."

Lady Cerise stepped back, her eyes wide with alarm. Obviously this wasn't a usual occurrence.

"What's happening?" the voodoo priestess demanded.

Chayton grabbed his head, ignoring Lady Cerise as he tumbled onto his back, the odd power seeming to ebb and flow as he gave a cry of sheer frustration.

"This isn't possible. I escaped," he wailed. Then his back arched and he gave another earsplitting cry. "No."

Sebastian was stepping over Van's motionless body when he caught an unmistakable scent.

Reny.

Oh god, had she been captured?

Still holding the baseball bat, Sebastian raced through the maze of rooms, avoiding the guards who were focused on protecting the house from an outside attack.

Entering the formal drawing room, he easily spotted her standing next to Lady Cerise.

The tightness in his chest eased as his frantic gaze confirmed that she was uninjured. Dropping the bat he rushed forward, wrapping her in his arms as he sucked in a deep breath of her spicy scent.

"Sebastian," she sighed, pressing her lips to his throat before she pulled back to study his face with a frown. "You're hurt."

"It's nothing." He dismissed her concern.

She reached up to touch the swelling beneath his eyes. "Nothing?"

"Trust me, I'll heal." He studied her pale face. "How did you get here?"

"Not now." She pulled out of his arms, pointing toward the body in the center of the room. "We have bigger things to worry about."

Sebastian made a choked sound of shock as he realized that it was Chayton who was lying on the carpet.

"What the hell is going on?" he rasped, sending a suspicious glance toward Lady Cerise. "Did you do this?"

The voodoo priestess shook her head. "I don't have the power to hurt a goddess."

Sebastian ignored Reny's muttered curse as he stepped forward, leaning over the male body that continued to twitch.

"Then what did?"

Chayton's eyes snapped open, his hand reaching toward Sebastian. "Baby."

"Did he say baby?" Reny muttered.

Sebastian barely heard her as a red-hot fury blasted through him. He knew beyond a shadow of a doubt that the bastard was talking about Ashe's baby.

He fell to his knees, wrapping his hands around the man's neck. "God damn you, Shakpi."

The dark eyes were oddly pleading as they met Sebastian's lethal glare. "Chayton," he rasped. "I'm Chayton."

"This is a trick," Lady Cerise warned, but Sebastian suddenly realized that the savage power that had pounded against him earlier was now nothing more than a dull throb.

And even the sour stench had faded.

His hands eased their grip on the man's throat. "What's happening?"

Chayton grimaced, as if he were fighting some inner battle. "Shakpi is being weakened by Ashe's baby."

Sebastian sucked in a shocked breath. "She gave birth?"

"Not yet, but it's near." The man's voice was thick with pain. "The baby's magic is spreading."

A fragile hope began to bloom in the center of Sebastian's heart. From the second they'd discovered that Ashe was pregnant, they'd prayed that it would mean the return of fertility among the Pantera.

Now it appeared their entire future might depend on the child.

"Can it destroy Shakpi?"

Chayton gave a slow nod. "Yes."

"Thank the goddess," Sebastian breathed.

The Shaman reached up to grab Sebastian's arm, his expression rigid with fear. "No, listen."

"What?"

"Assassins," he hissed.

Sebastian frowned, wondering if he'd heard right. "Assassins?"

"They're coming."

"For who?"

"The baby."

Sebastian leaned forward, his hope being replaced by a crushing fear. "Where are they? How do I recognize them?"

Chayton's hand dropped as his eyes slid shut. With a growl, Sebastian grabbed the man's shoulders and gave his limp body a shake and then another.

At the same time there was a series of loud pops as the guards came rushing into the room, firing their weapons.

Lady Cerise swiftly turned to flee, while Reny calmly pulled her weapon and began picking off the henchmen one by one.

"Shit." Rising to his feet, Sebastian moved to shelter Reny with his larger body, steering her toward the French doors as she continued to thin out the herd of charging bad guys. "We have to get out of here."

"What about Shakpi?" she demanded.

Pushing her out of the house, Sebastian pulled his phone from his pocket and hit speed dial. "I'll have Lian gather the local hunters to secure the house," he growled. "They'll have the place surrounded and the guards disabled before the bastards know what hit them."

Reny hissed as a bullet flew past her ear. "What about us?"

"We're going to the Wildlands."

CHAPTER EIGHT

REACHING the edge of Shakpi's lair, Reny and Sebastian waited long enough to ensure the property was encircled by Pantera and that neither Shakpi or Lady Cerese had escaped before they were running through the streets of New Orleans.

Sebastian set a punishing pace, forcing Reny to release her natural speed that she'd kept hidden for years. Then, confident she could keep up, he accelerated his stride as they hit the edge of the city and headed toward the bayous.

Not that she was going to complain.

She didn't fully understand what was going on, but she knew if there was a baby in danger she would run until she dropped in exhaustion to try and save the child.

Concentrating on putting one foot in front of the other, Reny barely noticed the thickening vegetation until she felt a strange tingling rush through her and she came to an abrupt halt.

Oh...god.

She shivered, joy rushing through her as she felt the soggy ground beneath her feet and the early morning sunlight that began to peep through the Spanish moss draped over the surrounding trees.

Breathing deeply, she allowed the scent of rich, black earth and brackish water to fill her with...contentment.

There was no other word.

A delicious warmth pressed against her back as Sebastian wrapped his arms around her waist and pulled her against his chest. Leaning down, he spoke directly in her ear.

"What do you think of the Wildlands?"

"Home," she said, the word unfamiliar. She'd spent the past eight years in places where she never fit in, never felt as if she could ever reveal who she truly was.

"Home," he growled in approval, his arms tightening around her. "Tell me what you're thinking."

"It...smells right."

He chuckled, burying his nose into the curve of her neck. "Yes, it does."

She shivered, leaning against the welcomed strength of his body as she slowly, painfully lowered the shields that she'd kept in place for so long.

At first, she was overwhelmed. Christ. Her senses felt as if they were under assault as she truly experienced the world without a human filter.

Suddenly she could hear the thump of Sebastian's steady heart and the flap of a heron's wing overhead. She could catch a thousand scents that could be traced by single strands to the world around her.

The tang of a frog hidden beneath a rotting log. The sweetness from a floating lily. The intoxicating musk from the man behind her.

And then there was the acute sense of the animal that lived deep inside her.

An animal that was suddenly desperate to be free.

"Now that I'm here, I think I can shift," she abruptly said.

He skimmed his lips up the side of her neck. "When you're ready."

"I want to try."

Sebastian went rigid. "Now?"

She turned in his arms, meeting his worried gaze. "I know you're in a hurry—"

He cut off her words with a kiss. "We've already warned Raphael about the assassins," he murmured against her lips. "He'll already have the search going for the hidden enemy, as well as organizing a constant guard to keep Ashe and her baby safe. We have time."

"Okay." She stepped back, taking a deep breath as she concentrated on the sense of...well, the only way she could explain it was *awareness* that prowled just below the surface.

"Just relax and let it happen," he urged softly.

She did as he commanded, loosening her tense muscles and allowing her thoughts to float.

At first she felt nothing more than a gentle warmth that flowed through her, making her wonder if she was supposed to mutter magic words or do some sort of weird-ass dance. Then, without warning, an explosion of sensations blasted through her body, making her feel as if she was being ripped from the inside out.

Oh, god. It was...glorious.

Astonishing.

Shifting into cat form, Reny surged into motion, bounding over the boggy ground with a sense of freedom that made her soul soar.

There was a roar from behind her and suddenly there was a tawny puma with yellow eyes running at her side.

She didn't know how far they ran, she only knew that when she entered a meadow that was dappled with morning sunlight, it seemed perfectly natural to turn and leap onto Sebastian, tumbling him to the side.

His eyes shimmered with pleasure as they rolled across the soft ground, nipping and growling and even swiping his claws over her shoulder as they played with a glorious joy.

Reny might have stayed in her cat form for the rest of the day if she hadn't known that despite his seemingly carefree enjoyment, Sebastian was desperately worried about the lurking assassins.

They would have plenty of time in the future to indulge her long overdue exploration of what it was to be Pantera.

Closing her eyes, she once again relaxed her muscles, allowing the magic to race through her blood as she shifted back into human form.

A painful rapture that could easily become addictive.

Stretched out on the mossy ground, she was only partially aware that her clothing and even cellphone survived the transformation. Her focus was centered on the blazing awareness of Sebastian that was buried deep inside her.

It wasn't just sexual, although there was plenty of lust burning with an incandescent heat in the pit of her stomach.

It was more the sensation of being connected to him on a primitive level.

Lying directly in front of her, Sebastian gently framed her face in his hands, his eyes dark with concern.

"What is it?" he demanded. "What's wrong?"

She gazed at his exquisitely beautiful face in wonder. "I feel as if we're connected."

A slow, unexpected color crept beneath Sebastian's bronzed skin. "Because we are," he said, reaching down to pull her jacket and blouse to the side, revealing four silvery slashes that marred the skin just above her collarbone.

She blinked in surprise. "What's that?"

"I marked you."

"Marked me?"

He grimaced. "My cat was a little…overenthusiastic."

Reny felt a small flare of amusement. Was he embarrassed? It seemed impossible that the suave, perfectly composed diplomat could actually be flustered. "What does that mean?"

His fingers gently traced the silver slashes. "I've chosen you as my mate." His voice was low, reverent. "And I'm very much hoping you'll choose me as yours."

"Mates?"

"For eternity."

She should feel overwhelmed by the soft words. Just a day ago she was a career woman who cherished her independence.

Now...

Now she felt nothing but a wild exhilaration that fizzed through her body like champagne bubbles.

Her fingers stroked through the tawny satin of his hair, recalling the beauty of his pelt when he'd been a puma.

"There's no doubt?" she demanded, her vulnerable heart not ready for any unpleasant surprises.

She needed to be absolutely certain that this gorgeous, insanely sexy cat wasn't going to disappear from her life.

A wry smile twisted his lips. "My cat knew from the moment I entered the office to see you standing there..." His fingers moved toward the buttons of her shirt, slowly tugging them open. "Your passionate nature buried beneath the starch."

Heat curled through the pit of her stomach, a hungry ache pulsing through her body.

"Is that why I wanted to rip off your clothes and lick my way from your very sexy lips to the tips of your toes when I first saw you?" she asked, her voice husky with need.

There suddenly seemed to be something incredibly erotic in the thought of making slow, delicious love surrounded by the bayou.

"The mating heat is only a signal that our cats are sexually compatible and that you're fertile," he explained, his finger tracking the lacy line of her bra. "The actual mating is a melding of our souls."

"Melding." She sighed in pleasure as his lips nuzzled a path of kisses just beneath her jaw. "Yes. That's exactly what it feels like."

"Reny." With a groan he found her lips, claiming them in a kiss that spoke of blatant ownership.

Which was just fine with Reny.

She belonged to Sebastian. Just as he belonged to her.

The thought had barely formed when instinct took over, and scarcely aware of what she was doing, Reny's claws emerged and she was swiping them across his chest.

"Jesus," he rasped in shock, yanking back to glance down at the four perfect rips in his shirt.

"Did I do it right?" she demanded in concern, catching sight of blood on his beautiful bronzed skin before the shallow wounds were healing before her very eyes.

Raw, primal satisfaction smoldered in his eyes as a slow smile curved his lips. "Oh, sugar, it couldn't be more right."

Reny watched in sizzling anticipation as he started to lower his head. The mating heat was flaring back to life with a vengeance. Then with a low curse he was pulling back, and with swift efficiency had her shirt buttoned and her jacket smoothed back into place.

"What's wrong?" she demanded as he rose to his feet and pulled her upright.

"Someone's coming." He kept hold of her hand as a male appeared between two cypress trees. "Hiss," he murmured.

The Pantera male, with dark hair pulled into a tail at his nape and gray eyes, moved forward, his expression impatient.

"Finally," Hiss muttered.

Reny felt Sebastian tense. "What is it? Have the assassins been found?"

Hiss gave a shake of his head, something about the action oddly familiar to Reny.

"No," he said, "But Ashe has gone into labor."

Sebastian gave a short, strained laugh. "I suppose Raphael is a fucking basket case."

The other Pantera snorted. "Worse. He needs you..." With a shocking speed, Hiss was abruptly focusing his attention on Reny, his hand lifting toward her face. "What the hell?"

"Hey." Sebastian slapped the man's hand away, his voice filled with aggression. "That's my mate."

"Mate? I'm..."

"What?" Sebastian snapped.

Hiss gave a shake of his head. "Never mind. Are you coming or not?"

Sebastian wrapped his arm around Reny's waist, gazing at her with blatant devotion. "Ready for this, sugar?" he asked softly.

She leaned her head against his shoulder, giving a firm nod. "With you at my side, I'm ready for anything."

ARISTIDE

BY
LAURA WRIGHT

CHAPTER ONE

HOT.

Smoking hot.

And by the smell of her, human.

Aristide tracked the waitress with his dark gaze even as he sent the solid green ball into the far right pocket of the one decent pool table at The Cougar's Den. Around him, a couple of his Pantera brothers hissed and cursed at the clean shot as they finished off their beers. But Aristide barely heard them. His eyes and his nose were trained on the wickedly hot human female working the room. The human female he shouldn't even be acknowledging, much less lusting over. Dressed in The Cougar's uniform of black miniskirt and white tank top, she took orders, stopped traffic and made tongues loll. Small, maybe five foot two, she had the body of a pin-up: round and lush up top and around back, where it counted. The perfect amount of succulent flesh for a horny male to fondle and kiss and grip and lick.

Aristide growled low in his throat and sank another ball with only a quick glance in the side pocket's direction. He was utterly captivated. As in, his eyes just refused to remain on anything but her for longer than a second. With her shoulder length, night-black hair and pale skin, she was truly stunning. But it was her large blue eyes that really drew him in. They seemed both highly intelligent, and unmistakably vigilant. An unlikely pairing for a Saturday night in The Cougar's Den.

Though a Nurturer, Aristide didn't work in the emotional or mental sciences, but he could always sense panic, confusion, anxiety and fear within others. Sometimes it was so close to a being's skin, it seeped out into the air around them. And this human woman, who he couldn't seem to turn away from, had all four infusing her delicious scent. He wondered why.

She started walking in his direction then, her gaze jumping from a table of older guys, to her cellphone, to some bikers, then to the small Pantera crowd around the pool table. If he wasn't mistaken, Aristide saw her jaw tremble slightly when she eyed the latter. When she eyed him. He purposely missed his next shot so that when she reached them, he could speak to her first. Human women were always a curiosity to Pantera males, but the Suits he was with tonight were notorious in their preference. Normally Aristide wouldn't give a shit. Normally, he'd back the hell off and let Roch and Damien make their not-so-subtle moves—moves human women seemed to enjoy and seek out whenever a Pantera male was in The Cougar's Den. But tonight wasn't a normal night, and for some reason Aristide couldn't understand or quell, this human female wasn't getting near his friends, much less landing on their to-be-fucked list. Hell, if Roch or Damien even tried to touch—

Aristide's feral thoughts came to an abrupt halt as those fever-inducing hips he'd noticed a second ago swayed tantalizingly toward him as she rounded the table of bikers. Thank Opela by the time she reached him, his basic ability to communicate had returned.

"How are you tonight?" she asked in a smooth, feminine voice as her gaze flickered nervously from his eyes to his chin to his mouth.

"Thirsty," he said stupidly, his tone lower, harsher, hungrier than he'd intended. *What the hell is wrong with me?*

"Sounds about right," she said with a small smile and a bite to her lower lip.

Aristide's groin tightened with the action.

"What can I get you?" she asked.

84

He was about to tell her nothing, to go away and don't come back. And definitely don't ask his friends the same question or he might have an aneurism right on top of the goddamn pool table. But then her eyes slid upward, over his collarbone, chin, mouth. And those baby blues met his black stare, and he felt a pull on his guts and his heart and his dick unlike anything he had ever experienced before.

Attraction? Hell, yes. But this was unlike any swipe of attraction he'd ever felt. This was attraction times ten. No. Times a thousand. And without thought, the fingers on his right hand closed around the hem of his jacket as his gut, heart and dick instructed him to order the woman to drop her tray and slip inside his shelter of leather. Inside, against his chest, where it was warm. Where Aristide could keep her close and scent her. Where he could protect her—from the males in the bar, both human and Pantera.

But who's going to protect her from you, asshole, a voice inside of him whispered viciously. From what you want to do to her this very second? This stranger. This HUMAN.

"We have a few beers on tap," she began, her words a little breathless as she dropped her gaze and quickly checked her cellphone. "Or maybe you'd like something stronger?"

Something stronger...yes, and maybe hotter, too...something that involved her, naked, laid out on the top of the bar, him poised over her with a bottle of tequila in his hand and a lime wedge in his mouth.

Once again, Aristide made a growling sound deep in his throat, but he didn't turn away as he should. Didn't tell her to leave him be, as he should. He couldn't. Like it or not, comprehend it or not, this woman held him, and the puma residing inside of him, captive. His gaze traveled over her. Her exquisite face and her smooth, night-black hair...oh, and that mouth. He'd never seen her before, but she reminded him of someone. Who was it? Her dark hair, those shockingly blue eyes and that unpainted mouth that seemed as though it had been stained a deep, berry red.

His lips twitched as an image popped into his mind. Ah, yes... Snow White. A movie he'd seen as a child. She was Snow White in a tight black miniskirt and three-inch heels. Heels he would make her keep on after he stripped her bare and placed her gently on the bar.

A hum moved through his body, down below his waist where the evidence of his attraction was straining against the zipper of his jeans. Clearly, he'd been stuck in quarantine with Ashe's sister, Isi, for far too long. There was no other excuse for this impossible reaction. He'd been desperate for a female before, but nothing like this. And never for a human woman. He needed to get his shit together or get the fuck out of here before he did or said something unforgivably stupid.

"I'll take a beer," he said, forcing his gaze away and back to the pool table. "Any beer. But cold."

"Coming right up," she said.

Aristide knew that humans had a place in the lives of some of his Pantera brothers and sisters, but that would never be his reality. No matter how hot they were. Or how their skin or their voice or their scent called to him.

Teeth grinding against each other at the back of his mouth, Aristide grabbed the chalk from the edge of the table and worked the end of his cue. He was one of the males in his species who seriously wanted a mate, and—Opela be blessed—a family to go with it. And his mate *would* be a Pantera female. Looking, panting or drooling over a human woman was a waste of his goddamn time.

As he stretched over the table, he heard her taking drink orders from Roch and Damien. Doing her job. Her human job that had nothing to do with him. As his hand tightened around the stick, he tried to block the conversation out and focus on his shot. But it was impossible. His friends were being irritating pricks.

"I'll have a beer, beautiful," Damien said, his tone oozing sexual charm. "And your phone number."

"Smooth," Roch said, chuckling. "Forgive my friend here, darlin'. He's under the unfortunate impression that women find him attractive."

"And my friend here is under the impression that he's going to have a beating heart after tonight," Damien said on a playful growl.

Aristide lined his cue up with the ball. *Don't look over there. Because if one of those idiots is touching her...*

"Forget the phone number, gorgeous," Damien continued. "Let me take you out tonight. Somewhere real nice. What time do you get off work?"

"Sorry," she began tightly. "I'm busy."

"Busy for him, right?" Roch said with a smile in his voice. "But not for me."

"Not interested, but thanks," she said. "I'll get those drinks."

"Ah. You have a male," Damien said quickly.

"Something like that."

Crack.

The sound echoed throughout the bar, and Aristide instantly felt all eyes swing his way. *Ah, shit.* He was hoping everyone would think it was the satisfying sound of his last solid ball dropping into the right corner pocket. But he wasn't that lucky.

"What the fuck, Ari?" Roch said, all sexual heat gone from his voice. "You broke the cue."

Yes, the cue, and your attempt to hit on the woman.

My woman.

Fuck.

Aristide groaned at the asinine thoughts inside his head. What was wrong with him? Why was he having such predatory, possessive feelings about a complete stranger? One who didn't have an ounce of shifter blood? And one who had basically said she was taken? He needed to get out of here. Forget the beer, forget the game.

His eyes came up, narrowed on the Suits. Both Roch and Damien were staring at him like he was crazy. The woman, however, was a few feet away, her gaze completely focused on the screen of her cellphone. She looked pale as shit, and that foursome of emotions was coming off of her in waves now. Panic, confusion, anxiety and fear—all drifting into Aristide's nostrils.

Aristide dug into his pocket for some cash. After weeks of being locked up with Ashe's sister, testing blood sample after blood sample, hypothesizing until his brain felt close to exploding, all he'd wanted to do was have a night off, a few drinks and a game of pool with some knuckleheads. Not cause a scene, driven by his overwhelming desire for a woman who shouldn't even be on his radar.

"I'm out of here," he mumbled, placing the broken cue down on the table and tossing a few more bills than necessary to cover the damage. "Sorry about that."

Aristide heard both males call after him as he headed for the door, but he didn't so much as slow his pace. Heat and desire and confusion and ire were barreling through him at top speed, and he needed some cold air on his skin. Then maybe he needed to get laid. Bury himself inside a willing and warm Pantera female for a few hours and get his sanity back again. Shit, he had a few doors he could knock on. And an empty house he could use.

He busted out of the front door and into the cool autumn air. The moon was full overhead, lighting the landscape of half-full parking lot in a pale, yellow glow. Sex had always been easy, hot and fun. But it seemed like lately, ever since his sister had mated his best friend and moved out of their family house, Aristide had wanted something else to go along with that heat, that fun. Something lasting and real. Something that filled his empty house, and shit, his empty heart. A true Pantera mating. It was something he wasn't about to find in The Cougar's Den. He needed to return to the Wildlands where he belonged.

As he headed down the steps and into the parking lot, something caught his peripheral vision and he turned. A woman, he thought. No. It was *the* woman. His waitress. Snow White. He paused near a black pick-up truck and watched as she rounded the corner of the bar and walked swiftly toward a rusted green hatchback. Was she done with her work already? And where was she going in such a rush? Home? *To her male?* he ground out inside his mind. Damn, he despised how much his body screamed at him to go after her, question her, convince her to look for comfort and pleasure elsewhere. With him.

She was talking animatedly on her cellphone, while searching her purse for something. A moment later, she fished out a set of keys, her hand shaking terribly as she tried to slip one into the lock of her car door. Something rippled through Aristide as he remembered her face in the bar, the worry in her eyes, the fear in her scent, the constant checking of her cellphone. Was she in trouble?

His puma scratched at his insides, but Aristide shoved the cat away. He shouldn't be concerned about her. No matter what his mind said or his dick begged for, she wasn't for him. She belonged to someone else. A human male, no doubt.

Yet Aristide remained where he was, watching as she slipped inside her vehicle, hurriedly backed out of the space and hauled ass out of the parking lot. Yes, something was wrong.

Aristide's gaze flickered toward the bayou in the distance, the Wildlands where he should be headed, first on foot, then on paws. Then a sound yanked his attention back. Another car had pulled out directly after the woman, and was following her way too closely to be anything but a problem.

"Shit," he uttered as he abandoned all reason and sense and left the shelter of the truck.

He sprinted across the lot, his puma hovering close to the edge of his skin. Keeping up with a vehicle for any length of time wasn't going to be possible, but they were in town and things moved slower with stop signs and traffic lights. Eyes narrowed and vigilant in the moonlight, Aristide ran, faster than he'd ever run before. Over potholes and uneven pavement, the taillights of the car following her blinking scarlet, beckoning him forward. As they hit a red light and a few stopped cars, the woman veered into the empty turn lane. Tires squealed as both cars took the turn at too high a speed.

His puma driving him, Aristide rounded the corner. He was nearly to the hotel when the sudden and fierce slam of metal against tree trunk erupted in the air. His heart dropped into his shoes, and without forethought he raced forward, uncaring, not stopping until he had the woman's car door open and her unconsciousness body in his arms.

"Come on," he whispered way too goddamn frantically for the total stranger in his grasp. "Wake up. Look at me. Please."

On his knees near the door, Aristide stared down at her. She had a gash on her forehead and she looked far too pale for his liking, but her breathing wasn't labored.

"Shit," he cursed when she remained still. "Come on, Female. Open your eyes and look at me."

Behind Aristide, car doors opened and slammed shut, and in an instant, it all rushed back to him. And to his puma, as well. Someone was after this woman.

A fierce and feral growl vibrated in his throat and he eased her closer to his chest as he prepared himself for a battle. It was illogical and strange, but he knew he'd fight to the death for this female. And that would take awhile. A Pantera male didn't die easily.

"Ari?" came a voice Aristide recognized instantly. "What the hell are you doing here?"

Ice froze the blood in Aristide's veins. Coming to a stop beside him, towering over him, was the leader of the Hunters. Parish. *What the hell?* And beside him was his sister, Keira, and another massive, dark-haired Hunter called Lian. They were all staring down at him nonplussed, the moon overhead illuminating their stern body language and expressions. All three were in pure Hunter mode.

Suspicious and massively protective of the woman in his arms, Aristide bared his teeth at them and hissed, "You answer first. What are you doing here?"

Parish knocked his chin in the direction of the woman in Aristide's arms. "We've come for her."

Aristide's wariness deepened. "Why? She's a human."

"Yes," Lian said with a fierce glare. "And our enemy."

Enemy? The word slid through Aristide's gut, hot and painful. Yet his arms only tightened around the woman. He had no idea what she'd done—or what the Pantera believed she'd done—but in that moment it didn't matter. He and his puma would protect her, no matter what.

"Release her, Aristide," Keira said in calm but authoritative voice. "Release her and walk away. Let us take care of this."

Aristide leapt to his feet. The sound that rumbled in his chest, then erupted from his throat and echoed down the deserted street, was so low and so terrible, both male Hunters stepped back.

"That's right," he snarled at them, his puma screaming to emerge. "Keep backing up, shifters. All the way to your vehicle. Then get inside, start the engine and return to the Wildlands. Because this woman will not be touched by anyone but me."

Chapter Two

THE first thought Katherine Burke had when she awoke was: *Am I dead?* Followed closely by: *No, I can't be. I can't leave Noah.*

Panic struck her and she tried to move, to sit up, but strong, gentle hands held her down.

"Easy," came a voice she recognized. "You're all right."

Forcing her eyes open, she groaned at the intense light that instantly shrank her pupils and caused her head to ache. "Too bright. Please."

The hands left her, and in seconds she heard a click and felt the shocking burst of light recede. Blinking to gain back her vision, Kat took in her surroundings. It was still night, the intense light obviously coming from a bright lamp. She was in a hospital room. Everything was white and sterile, and as her heart kicked against her ribs, her mind bent back to remember what had gotten her here. It didn't take long for the chase and the accident to come back. Oh, god. Someone was after her. One of those cat shifters she'd written about. No. That she'd lied about.

"How are you feeling?"

On a gasp, her head came around and her eyes made contact with the man from The Cougar's Den. One of the pool players. Mr. Cold Beer. He was in the same clothes, minus the leather jacket. Her gaze rolled over him. Tall, broad, shockingly handsome with short, thick sandy brown hair and black eyes. Her heart kicked. *Cat's eyes*. Yes, she remembered. He was one of them. The Pantera. Which meant what exactly? She glanced around again. On second look, the hospital room seemed different than the rooms she'd seen before. Her breath stalled in her lungs. Was she in the Wildlands?

"Do you remember what happened to you?" he asked, his voice so husky, so male, Kat felt its vibration all through her body.

Her heart beating furiously inside her chest now, Kat nodded.

Light brown eyebrows raised over deep, dark and curious eyes. "Do you remember me?"

The vibration in her body dropped low in her stomach. Good lord, how did one forget a face like that, a body like that? A voice like that? She eyed the white lab coat he was wearing. "Are you doctor?"

"Of sorts," he said. He glanced over his shoulder at the door, then returned his gaze to her. "Why were you running from the Pantera? Did someone threaten you?"

He seemed genuinely concerned, but Kat knew how men were. How they acted when they wanted something from you, and how they acted afterwards when they got it.

"This is all a mistake," she said, trying to sit up. "I don't know where you've put me or why, but I need to go home."

"And where is that?"

She hesitated for a moment, then spat out the truth, "New Orleans."

As the man came to sit on the bed near her waist, Kat drew back against the pillows. She felt breathless and warm, but not from her fear and anxiety. Up close, he was even better looking. He seemed to ooze strength and raw maleness, and she felt her curiosity flare. This was the real deal, and the Pantera males she'd written about—the fiction she'd invented—seemed positively puny in comparison.

"Listen," he began, his voice soft but threaded with warning. "Very soon we're going to have people in here asking you a lot of questions. Before they do, do you want to tell me anything? Who you are? Why you were running last night from—"

"The Pantera?" Kat said quickly and without thinking.

93

The man's eyes shuttered, and he growled softly. "You know about us?"

Pressed back against the pillows, Kat stared at him, her breathing shallow. This was bad. How could she be so stupid as to show her hand when she might've gotten out of here? This man—it was him—he unnerved her, made her drop her guard. Even back at The Cougar's Den she'd felt that from him.

"Shit…" The man sighed. "So what they said is true. You wrote a story about us for an online magazine?"

She didn't answer. "You can't hold me here."

"Can't we? After all you said about us in that article? Calling us monsters who eat children?" He chuckled darkly. "Saying that we are not magical beings at all, but a cult of sociopaths?"

Panic flooded Kat's body, and she glanced around the room. There had to be a way out of here. A way to escape.

"What do you say to this, Katherine Burke?"

Her eyes darted back to him. One brow lifted, his gorgeous face tight with tension.

"Yes. I know your name." He leaned toward her. "How are you going to fix this? These lies you told? These families you've put in danger?"

Kat's eyes widened and her heart stalled. "Danger? What are you talking about?"

"Ah," came a female voice from the doorway. "The guards told us she was awake."

Both Kat and the male turned to see three people walk into the room. They were tall and fierce, even the one female, and dressed very causally in faded jeans and tank tops. The lean muscles on each made Kat's breath catch.

"What do you want from me?" Kat said slowly, fearfully.

The female spoke first. "Besides telling the entire world you lied about us? Immediately and on camera?"

Kat shook her head. "I can't do that."

"Why the hell not?" the woman growled, moving toward her.

But the man who sat on Kat's bed was already on his feet and standing in the woman's way. "Calm down, Keira."

"Fuck you, Aristide," she said. "We need answers."

"Why did you spread those lies, Miss Burke?" asked one of the men behind Keira. He had gold eyes, long black hair and scars near his right ear and mouth.

Keira shook her head. "It was just a satire piece. Like The Onion."

No matter how scared she was, or how much she hated herself for the article she was forced to write, she couldn't tell them the truth. Not if she wanted to see Noah again.

"And yet you won't tell the world that," Keira spat back.

Kat remained tight-lipped. She had to find a way out of here. But if she truly was in the Wildlands, how would escape even be possible? She had no idea where she was, or how far it was to the outside world.

"Who are you working for, Miss Burke?" the golden-eyed man asked, his calm demeanor unnerving her. "Because even though you have no tattoo, no Mark of Shakpi on your body, we know you must be working for our enemies. The ones who are desperate to tell the human world to be afraid of us, to attack us."

Oh, god. Was that true? Was that why Marco had forced her to do this? Was the man called Aristide right? Would she truly be hurting families? And what was the Mark of Shakpi?

"I work for the Jefferson Post," she said, shaking her head against the desire to tell the whole truth, and the fear of what would happen if she did. "I'm one of their staff writers, and I wrote a satire piece. That's all. That's it."

"Bullshit," Keira said, flipping her off.

"Hey," the man called Aristide growled beside her. "Rein in your sister, Parish. She's about to get her ass kicked out of here."

Parish sniffed. "Good luck with that, brother."

"Fuck you, Aristide," the woman returned, her own set of gold eyes flashing. "You can't do that."

"You're in my jurisdiction now, Keira."

Her eyes narrowed and she cocked her head, studying him. "You obviously have a hard-on for this human, but it isn't going to get in the way of our investigation."

Kat's eyes lifted to Aristide. He stood beside her bed, his expression hard, resolute, his body language screaming defensiveness. What was Keira talking about? A hard-on for her? Was this man interested in her? And why did that idea make her entire body hum?

"Okay, let's take a breath everyone," Parish said, though his face and expression were tight with tension as he turned his gaze on Kat. "Will you or will you not recant your story publically, Miss Burke?"

"I will not," she said softly. *I can't.*

"Then you will stay in the Wildlands until we have answers to our questions."

Ice raced into her veins and her breath caught in her throat. "You have your answers."

He shook his head. "We want the truth. Names. Locations. The plan."

"There is no plan!" Kat burst out, sitting up completely now, ignoring the slight pain in her head. "I don't know about any plan!"

"Okay," Aristide growled, placing his hand on her shoulder. "That's enough."

"You know something," Keira hissed, coming to the edge of the bed.

Aristide growled at her. "She needs to rest, Hunter."

Hunter? Confusion mingled with the fear, and the shame inside Kat.

"You said she was fine, Ari," Parish said tightly, his golden eyes narrowed.

"Nothing serious, nothing's broken. But she's had a shock. Give her some time."

"We don't have much of that, and you know it," Parish said darkly.

The room seemed to grow cold as everyone in it fell silent. Kat looked from face to face. Worry and hope etched each taut expression. What was happening? What had that bastard Marco gotten her into?

Checking his phone, the man behind Parish, who had been quiet up until that point, spoke in a harsh whisper. "We have a possible breach at the south border."

Parish cursed. "How many?"

"Seems to be a single." He shrugged. "Could be another lost traveler."

"Or it could be because of her." Keira glared at Kat, pushing away from the end of the bed.

"Out," Aristide growled.

"Fine," Keira muttered. "But we'll be back."

As all three of them filed out of the room, Kat released the breath she'd been holding since they walked in, and dropped back against the pillows. She was so lost. Deeply in trouble. How in the world was she going to get out of this unscathed?

She turned to Aristide, to the one person who had championed her, and offered a very sincere, "Thank you."

"Don't thank me," he answered, his eyes still pinned to the door. "Thank my puma. I believe he's the one who can't resist protecting you."

"Your puma?" she repeated, confused.

He didn't elaborate further. "Rest, female. You're going to need it." He headed for the door, adding, "And don't try to escape. There are guards at every exit."

Kat opened her mouth to respond, but no words came out. Only a puff of air. In the doorway, the man called Aristide had completely disappeared, and in his place stood the most beautiful and terrifying cat Katherine had ever seen. It was large and had sandy brown just like...

Oh, god. She'd known...she'd known this. Maybe not exactly believed it, but she'd known that the Pantera were shape shifters. But to see it...actually witness the transformation...have it confirmed.

She covered her mouth and watched as he stalked out the door, his massive head held high and proud, his thick tail twitching.

———

Hiss cased the perimeter of the small house on Geradon Street, wishing he was about five miles west, inside the borders of the Wildlands, and able to access his puma. He never felt as powerful without it. But this was where he needed to be, and this was how Parish, Raphael and the elders wanted it. Shakpi and her accomplice locked up nice and tight where her disciples couldn't find her. And even though the goddess was unconscious, the Pantera didn't trust that her devastating magic couldn't unfold at any second.

"You two stay here," Hiss commanded the two Pantera guards who were stationed at the back of the house. "Rage and Elise, you take the front. One at the door, one patrolling. And try to be inconspicuous."

"And inside the house?" Elise asked him.

Hiss raised one eyebrow at the pale blond Hunter. "I'll be guarding the prisoners myself."

The female nodded and took off with her partner. With Hiss, there was no questioning, no suspicion. He was trusted and respected by all.

So foolish. So goddamn foolish. To trust him or any Pantera. Because, truly, they were all capable of treachery.

Hiss entered the small, one bedroom home and headed for the door to the basement. The Pantera had made a practice of this, buying land, houses, all over the United States to use for their particular purposes. Hiding, escape, holding prisoners. This property was a brand new acquisition. To keep the Pantera's enemies close—but not too close.

Hiss descended the short flight of stairs, lit only by a single bulb hanging from the ceiling. The cold space was sparse, dank, and housed two side-by-side cages. Both of which were occupied.

Hiss's gaze moved over the human male, Chayton, who had been taken over by Shakpi several weeks ago. The male was still unconscious after his recent attempts to flush the goddess from his body, but Hiss knew that the powerful spirit still dwelled within him, hovering just beneath the surface of the male's aging skin, waiting for its chance. It would be Hiss's job to assist in her awakening. Just as soon as they had the blood of the child.

"Do your kind know you're a traitor yet?"

Hiss turned sharply at the interruption to his thoughts, his eyes narrowing on the woman in the other cell. "The only traitor here is you, Cerise." He clucked his tongue. "Leading that female to where Shakpi was holding her mate captive? You are as good as dead when she wakes."

The silver-haired woman with the sharp eyes shrugged. "Perhaps. But at least I won't die a fool. Like you."

Hiss laughed. He was no fool. Ruthless and without mercy, yes, But not a fool.

"I realized too late that Shakpi was only using me," Lady Cerise muttered, her fingers closing around the bars of her cage. "She was never going to grant me the power she dangled in front of me daily."

"See, that's the difference between us," Hiss stated evenly. "I'm not looking for power. Only justice."

Her stoic gaze connected with his. "And this is justice? Allowing a Pantera infant to be killed before it even takes its first breath?"

A painful heat snaked through Hiss's body. The death of Ashe's child would cause him no amount of grieving. He knew that. He knew he was about to become a monster. But it was justice. The deep and abiding pain the Pantera had caused him when they'd sacrificed his entire family to keep themselves hidden still bloomed within him. He was without anyone because of the Pantera. His Diplomat parents and his sister had been exposed to the human world, and instead of bringing them home, sheltering them, the Pantera leaders had allowed the three to be taken out, to be killed.

For the good of the Pantera.

He growled low and hateful in his throat. Just as they hadn't stopped his family's death, Hiss wouldn't stop the death of their young 'savior.'

"You look tired, Cerise," he said before turning back toward the staircase. "But remember to sleep with one eye open. Shakpi will awaken."

CHAPTER THREE

"I hate this," Raphael uttered, pacing back and forth in front of the door to the room that housed his beloved mate.

Ashe was still in labor, Isi by her side. The sisters seemed totally connected, supporting and giving power and healing to each other, and Aristide had seen Raphael leave the room several times to give them space.

Aristide eyed the guards who were lined up on either side of the door. With the threat of harm to Ashe and her child, no one was taking any chances.

"She's doing very well," Aristide assured him.

"It's taking so long."

"It's her first cub, Raphael. And a Pantera. And we all know better than to rush a Pantera, don't we?"

The Suit's eyes lifted. They were tired, but Aristide's words had granted them a flicker of humor. "I'm just..."

"An anxious father," Aristide finished.

"Yes. And seeing her in pain..."

"But it's a beautiful pain. One that gives hope to us all."

"Nurturer," Raphael growled half-heartedly.

"Damn right. And better than having to wear one of those silk cat collars." He grinned. "Or as you Suits call it, a tie."

Raphael laughed for a moment, then his eyes narrowed a fraction. "Do I hear correctly that we have a human woman in custody? Somewhere in this very medical facility?"

Aristide's body tensed. "We do."

"And is she working for our enemies?"

"Parish and the Hunters believe so."

The Suit's eyes darkened. "What do you believe, Ari? It was you who found her, wasn't it? And your judgment has always been top notch."

Yes, it had. But that was before his puma had set its dark eyes on a secretive Snow White in heels. "She is definitely hiding something, but I don't think she wishes us ill. She seemed genuinely shocked when she realized the trouble she caused."

"Then why did she do it? I saw the article online." Raphael glanced at the guards, then looked back, his voice lowered. "And it's not one of those bullshit tabloids no one takes seriously. It's reputable. My spies have told me that the humans are taking it as a call to action."

"She claims it was satire," Aristide said.

Raphael sniffed his disbelief and his annoyance. "Well, whatever it was, it's already made the humans who live in our vicinity, the ones who've always wondered about us, start organizing. Search parties, investigations. We can't have humans raining down on us right now with our enemies closing in, our magic waning, and Ashe in labor."

Aristide's nostrils flared as he inhaled sharply. "I know, and I'll find out the truth."

"How?"

"I'm not sure yet."

Raphael took a deep breath and let it out. "Well if you don't, the Hunters will. Any way they can. And they'd better." His gaze flickered toward the door. "I won't have a traitor here, Ari."

Aristide's puma scratched beneath his skin. It didn't like this conversation. It didn't like what the Suit was insinuating. All it wanted was to get to the woman again and be close to her, protect her. Shit, maybe even rub up against her.

Fool cat.

"I'm going back to my Ashe now," Raphael said with a nervousness that completely contradicted his normally hard-ass demeanor. "Maybe she'll let me do something. I offered to let her hold my hand when she was having contractions, break the goddamn thing if she wanted to. But she needs her sister…"

"Everything's going to be fine, brother," Aristide said with a quick touch to the male's shoulder. "And soon you'll be holding your cub."

The look Raphael gave him before he disappeared inside the room made Aristide's chest tight. Nothing was going to harm this little family. This new Pantera life. This chance and hope for them all to have a future. Damn, maybe cubs of their own someday. He had to find out what the woman knew, what was coming for them and when.

He moved down the hall with long, purposeful strides. He had a meeting in the labs in ten minutes with two of his pathologist colleagues, but he was going to check on the woman first. Try and get her to talk to him, tell him why she would write such lies about people she didn't know, or a world she'd only guessed at while working at The Cougar's Den. But when he opened the door to her room, he didn't find her alone. The guards who were supposed to be outside her door and window were instead standing over her bed, trying to pin her down.

Aristide's puma burst to the surface of his skin, causing him to shift in and out of his cat state. Adrenaline rushed through him. He started to pant and his vision went crystal clear.

He launched himself at the bed, growled at the guards. "What the hell is going on here?" he demanded.

Never in his life had he experienced something like this. He was in pure attack mode, and it took everything inside of him to rein in his fitful cat.

One of guards glanced up, his eyes going wide at whatever he saw on Aristide's face. "She tried to escape."

"That's not true!" Katherine cried out, fighting the female who was trying to hold her down. "I just wanted to get up, walk around, go to the goddamn bathroom!"

The male shook his head at Aristide. "She can't be on the floor, sir, not today. We can't risk it. We need to strap her down."

"No." This time it was Aristide and not his puma who answered.

The female guard turned to look at him with a shocked expression. "Sir?"

"I agree she can't be loose on the floor," Aristide said through gritted teeth, keeping his tone as even as possible. "But I won't have her strapped down like a mad creature."

Katherine stopped struggling, but her breathing remained erratic and her eyes were filled with tears.

"Then, how—" the male began.

"She's well enough to leave Medical," Aristide said quickly.

The female guard's eyes widened. "Parish will not allow her to leave the Wildlands, sir."

"And neither will I." Aristide's eyes locked onto Katherine Burke. "She's going home with me."

———

Her mouth agape, Kat moved underneath the rose-trellised archway and up the path toward the one-story house. A charming, freshly painted home with several mature trees bracketing it, and a sweet two-person swing on one side of the porch. It wasn't the only dwelling like it in the lush Wildlands. In fact, Kat had seen several of the darling cottages dotted here and there as she walked with Aristide.

"Not exactly the rat traps tossed together by savages who don't care about the sewage they live in or the hordes of unfed children running around," Aristide said, heading up the porch steps in front of her. "The near-animals who could break free from their land at any moment and go hunting in the human world."

Kat flinched at his words. No. At *her* words. God, she hated that article, hated that she'd had to say 'screw you' to her love of writing in exchange for such damaging fiction. But she couldn't help it. In fact, she'd do it again if it would keep her Noah safe.

As she moved up the steps to the porch, she took in the man who held the front door open. All six feet two inches of lean muscle and captivating presence. She knew now that his name was Aristide, knew that he was something in the medical community here, knew that he was an actual puma shifter—and god, she definitely knew that he was about the most gorgeous thing she'd ever seen in her life. But what she didn't know was why he'd brought her here—why he'd saved her from being restrained, from being an immobile prisoner in a hospital bed.

"Come inside, Katherine," he said in a calm voice.

Damn, she liked his voice. Liked it way too much. It made her feel safe somehow, no matter how insane that sounded in the situation she was in. Because no matter what, no matter where she was, she had to remember that she was still a prisoner. A prisoner who had to find a way to escape.

She walked past him into the house and saw that the interior of the place was just as comfortable and well appointed as the outside. Warm rugs and leather couches...desks and artwork, and a fireplace. Her heart sank a touch inside her chest. She'd always dreamed of having a place like this for herself and Noah. She wondered if, after all of this, after it was over, she could really have a normal life.

"Come. Let me show you your room," Aristide said, leading her down the short hallway that was lit by skylights. "Bathroom is there," he said, gesturing to the end of the corridor. "And this is where you'll stay."

This is the most perfect room in the world, she thought the very second she stepped into the large, warm and incredibly inviting space.

"My sister fixed it up as a guestroom before she moved out," Aristide explained behind her. "It's a little too white and has way more flowers than I'm comfortable with, but if I don't have to sleep in it then I suppose it doesn't matter."

"It's beautiful," she said in a whisper, taking in the rosebud wallpaper and blush-colored pillows.

"Good. Glad it suits." He was a quiet for a moment, then cleared his throat. "Well, I'll let you settle in, rest. You really should rest. Doctors orders."

"Wait," Kat blurted out, her back to him. "Why, Aristide?"

"What?"

She turned around and stared at him. At this man who, because of his size and muscles and intensely black stare, should be feared. But to Kat, his presence gave her peace and warmth, and—dare she think it—hope?

"Why are you doing this?" she asked. "Why did you bring me here? Why wouldn't you just leave me in the hospital, let them keep me hostage?"

His eyes remained a dark, calm sea. "Would you like to return, Katherine?"

She shivered. "No."

"Then it doesn't matter what my reasons are, does it?"

"Yes, it matters," she said with a touch of heat. God, she was so confused, so scared. She hated being scared. She needed Noah, needed to know he was all right and that Marco was keeping his word. Maybe she could find a phone, or borrow Aristide's cell. She'd lost hers in the wreck. But would he let her contact anyone?

"People don't do nice things for no reason," she said.

"I have no doubt of that," he agreed, leaning against the door-jamb. A sudden glimmer of amusement lit his eyes. "But I'm not *people*, Katherine. I'm Pantera."

His words—no, that one word—entered her body and melted like sweet chocolate. Oh, if only she could believe in the goodness of others again. That a man could be honorable, faithful...

"What does that mean, exactly?" she asked. "You must want something from me."

His eyes shuttered and he nodded. "I want the truth. And I want to protect you."

"But why? I'm nothing to you."

He started for the door. "Rest now. We'll speak about this later."

"You're not going to chain me down or lock me in?"

"There's nowhere you can escape to that my puma can't find," he called over his shoulder before closing the door to her room.

His words pulsing in her brain, Kat plopped down on the bed, on the snowy white comforter. Oh, lord, she wanted to believe him. What he'd said about protecting her, and how he'd said it. He'd looked so sincere, like he truly meant it—like he might have some burgeoning feelings for her.

Idiot. Have you learned nothing from your relationship with Marco? Your mistakes? You cannot risk Noah's life, his future, by risking your heart again.

Katherine knew Marco wouldn't hurt Noah, not if there was another story possibility in the works. But she needed to get to him to tell him so.

Lying back on the bed, she gazed out the window at the lush green Wildlands, every leaf, every blade of grass glistening in the warm light of the sun. Night would be the best time for her escape. When Aristide was asleep. And when the beautiful Wildlands she'd trashed so successfully grew still and silent and cool.

CHAPTER FOUR

ARISTIDE was a shit cook. Normally he grabbed midday meal with the Pantera outside near the bayou, but today was different. Ashe was in labor and everyone was on edge. No one wanted to sit still long enough to eat anything. And then there was the fact that he had a guest in his home.

A guest.

His nostrils flared. What was he doing, calling her that? Having her here under the guise of finding out information about the Pantera's enemies when, even now, his puma purred beneath his skin? The annoying animal was finally content for the first time since he'd scented Katherine Burke at The Cougar's Den. Aristide wished he knew what it meant, and how this would all turn out in the end.

Stepping back, he assessed the meal he'd prepared for them. Fried chicken, one of the Geeks had made for Xavier and Amalie. But, as usual, his best friend and his sister had brought some over for the poor, hungry bachelor. And there was fruit, and of course, bread pudding. It was the one thing Aristide could actually make with success, and without a kitchen fire. His mom had taught him how before she'd passed. Thought it was important for a male to know how to cook a desert. "Sweets to catch a sweetie someday," she would say. Just the thought of those special times made Aristide's guts twist painfully. He missed them. His parents. Even Amalie now. Shit, he missed having a family.

The scream that rent the air tore Aristide from his thoughts and made the blood in his veins turn cold. *The woman.* Was she hurt? Had someone gotten into his home?

Abandoning the food, he tore out of the kitchen and ran down the hall. When he reached her room, he wasted no time knocking. He wrenched the door open and burst inside. He found her fully clothes and writhing on the bed, moaning, twisted in the sheets. Midday sunlight washed over her face, illuminating the sheen of sweat as she continued to dream.

Relief snaked through Aristide's body. No one harmed her. He rushed the bed until he stood over her. She was still asleep, her mind conjuring fearful images or scenarios. His puma wanted out. It wanted to crawl on top of the mattress and lie beside her, lick her face until she awoke from whatever hell she was finding herself in.

Goddamn cat!

"Noah!" she screamed, lying flat on her back, her face and neck muscles tense. "Please, Noah. No! Don't take him!"

Aristide didn't know who this Noah was—if he was Katherine Burke's male—but he didn't care, and neither did his puma. He only wanted to soothe her.

He knelt on the bed, gently gripped her shoulders and lifted her into a sitting position. "It's all right, Katherine," he said softly. "You're dreaming."

Instantly, her arms went around his neck, and she burst into tears. But her eyes remained closed. She was crying. In her sleep! Christ.

"Noah, I'm coming," she whimpered. "I swear I'm coming."

"Hush, now. Everything's all right." Aristide started rocking her like he remembered his own parents rocking him when he was a small, scared cub.

"I need him," Katherine cried into Aristide's chest. "I love him."

A quick flash of unmistakable jealously moved through Aristide as he felt her body relax, as he felt her come awake. And he was glad for it because having her in his arms, soothing her, scenting her, was doing something to him. And not just behind his zipper. He was connecting with her on a level that was inappropriate for the situation they found themselves in. She was not here for his pleasure, or to bond with him. She was a possible link to the Pantera's enemies, and he needed to release her, get up and walk away before he did something stupid. Before he pulled her even closer and forced her eyes to his. Before he told her that right now, raging inside of him, was an animal that wouldn't allow another male to get close to her ever again—touch her ever again.

"You're all right now, Katherine," he said almost formally, easing her back, placing her against the pillows.

"Aristide," she began, her voice still thick with tears. "I...I'm sorry. I was dreaming about—"

But Aristide was already on his feet and headed for the door. He didn't want to know. "It's nothing, Katherine. Nothing at all."

———

Fifteen minutes later, her face washed and her head clear, Kat ventured out into the hallway. She was mortified by what had happened, how she'd reacted, and she felt she needed to give this man—this man who had been so kind to her—some semblance of an explanation.

She found him in the kitchen, setting a small table with knives and forks and plates with delicious looking food piled on them. For two. Him and her, presumably. A sweet warmth coated Kat's insides at the strange, yet very sexy sight. This six-foot-two beast of man, with all his muscles and tightly caged ferocity, fixing lunch. She'd never seen anything like it. Experienced anything like it—like *him*. Total maleness on the outside and compassionate, nurturing soul on the inside.

"Can we talk?" she asked.

His dark eyes lifted to meet hers and he nodded. "Are you hungry?"

That question had so many different meanings to her in that moment, it was crazy, but all she said to him was, "Yes."

After placing a pan of something that looked absolutely delicious, and smelled even better, on the table, Aristide came around and eased back one of the wood dining chairs. "Please. Sit."

Really? Kat mused with a touch of sad humor. Manners, too? Seriously, this man had to have a rotten side. He had to be hiding something. He had to have an ulterior motive for the way he was treating her.

He does, Kat. He wants information about Marco.

Aristide sat down in the chair opposite her and picked up a chicken leg. "Dig in, Katherine. You need to regain your strength."

Yes, to escape, her mind tossed out quickly. But she pushed that truth back for the moment.

"You made this?" she asked, fork in hand.

"Only the bread pudding," he said, his eyes warm as he studied her. "The rest was donated to the cause."

"What cause is that?" she asked, curious.

His mouth twitched with amusement. "The lonely workaholic bachelor fund."

She laughed. "Ah, that. So, no woman?"

His eyes darkened. "Not officially."

The way he was looking at her, it was almost as if he knew what she looked like without her clothes on. Heat surged into her and pooled low in her belly. Eyes down, she stabbed a piece of the bread pudding with her fork and popped it into her mouth. The moment it hit her tongue, she sighed. It was delicious. It was *him*. This man. Warm and comforting, yet with every bite, more and more addictive. She mentally rolled her eyes—at herself and at such foolishly sensual thoughts.

"Do you have any family?" she asked him, abandoning the pudding for the chicken.

"A sister," he told her. "But she's mated. To my best friend. She's the donator of the chicken."

"You miss her." It wasn't a question, and Kat wondered if she'd crossed a line with the observation.

But Aristide didn't seem put out at all. "Family's a tricky thing," he said, popping orange slices into his mouth. "You appreciate them more when they're not around," he added.

His words had Kat's shoulders falling, and her appetite receding. Something that didn't go unnoticed by Aristide. For the first time that day, his eyes grew cool.

"You miss your male?" he asked tightly.

She placed her chicken down and sighed. "Yes. I suppose he's my male. And I miss him very much."

Aristide also stopped eating. His jaw looked very tense now. "Where is he? This male of yours? Home waiting for you?"

Why was he getting so irritated? Kat chewed her lip. He had no idea what was going on with her little male. No idea how scared she was, how she counted the seconds until she could see him again.

"Is he one of our enemies, Katherine?"

The question brought Kat's head up. "What? Who?"

Aristide's eyes narrowed, the plate of food on the table before him now completely forgotten. "This Noah."

Enemy? Was he serious?

"Tell me, Katherine," he said forcefully, his glittering, black eyes narrowing. "Is he the one who wishes Ashe's child harm?"

"Oh my god!" She pushed away from the table and stood up. "Hurt a child? No! God, no! Look, I had no idea why Marco wanted me to write the article. I had the connection to the online magazine and he used me for it. I hate that I did it." Tears pricked her eyes and her voice grew shaky. She couldn't stand him looking at her with that dark, probing stare. Couldn't stand how weak and foolish she was.

"Excuse me. I need some air." She turned from him and went to the door leading to the backyard. Yes, she needed air, but more than anything she needed his probing gaze off of her. He had a way about him that sucked her in, and made her feel like unleashing everything that was on her heart. And shit, she'd said too much. She prayed she hadn't risked Noah with her outburst. She blinked back

111

tears. She was lost. So lost. She had to get out of here and see her baby.

Strong yet gentle hands cupped her shoulders and turned her around. And a voice, so soothing, so masculine, hummed in her ears.

"Look at me," Aristide said. "Please."

She didn't want to. She was afraid of what she'd see there. Pity? Attraction? Disappointment? Or worst of all, a mask of honor she'd want desperately to believe in. Her gaze lifted. But on that tan, sharply angled, devastatingly handsome face was only an expression of curiosity.

"Who is Noah, Katherine?" he asked, his warm breath moving over her face.

She couldn't stop the words, the truth. Not from him, and she didn't know why. "My son," she said, tears streaming down her cheeks. "My five-year-old son."

Aristide's mouth formed a thin line. "And this Marco?"

"Noah's biological father, and a mistake I made when I was young and stupid. I thought I was in love with him." She shrugged, feeling the weight of the secret she'd held onto lift. "I only knew him for a month."

"And the boy is with him now?" Aristide asked, his voice near to a growl.

"Yes."

"Does this Marco hold your child hostage, Katherine?"

The look on Aristide's face made Kat draw back. It was so fearsome, so unlike the man who had made her lunch just a few minutes ago. This was as close to a pissed off animal as he could look without shifting.

"Marco has no rights to him," she said. "He doesn't want him. Never has. And I thanked god for that every day."

"But…" Aristide ground out.

This was it. Telling him the truth—what would it cost her? And yet she couldn't lie to him. Something was there, between them now. He'd pulled her out of that wrecked car, and he'd held her close and soothed her during her nightmare. Maybe it was a foolish and inconvenient attraction, but neither one of them could deny it's amazing strength.

"Marco took him." Kat's voice trembled and tears rolled down her cheeks. "He said he wouldn't give him back to me unless I wrote the article."

"The article that makes us look like a threat," Aristide finished. Then his brows knit together. "The police? Have you gone to them?"

Kat laughed, but it was dull, sad sound. "He warned me against doing that."

A soft growl exited Aristide's throat. "But you've written it. Why do you still not have your boy?"

Kat's heart lurched and she shook her head. "He wants one more," she said. "It's why I've been working at The Cougar's Den." Her eyes implored him as the tears continued to fall. "I need you to believe me. I didn't know why I was writing that horrible article, just that if I didn't I'd never see my son again."

Aristide released a heavy breath and brought his hand around to cup her face. He gently brushed away her tears with the pad of his thumb. "I believe you, Katherine. I believe you."

CHAPTER FIVE

"SHE'S no enemy," Aristide declared.

With twilight descending, he stood at the darkening shore of the bayou just outside Medical, the leader of the Hunters on his left, his sister, Amalie, on the other. As a Hunter herself, Mal was fully aware of what was going on both with the threat to the Pantera and with Aristide's houseguest.

"How can you say that after what she's done?" Parish asked him. "Everything she's written? Knowing none of it was true."

"Because I know her motivations," Aristide said. "Her belief that if she didn't write whatever this Marco wanted her to write, her child would be harmed."

"Maybe she just wants you to feel sorry for her," Amalie suggested. "Maybe she just wanted to get into the Wildlands, get another story."

"Well, then this one would actually be true, wouldn't it?" he countered.

Parish sneered, his gold eyes darkening to amber in the dying light of day. "I should never have allowed you to take her home."

The puma inside of Aristide snarled. "You could never have stopped it."

"Goddammit, Aristide, you're not taking this seriously!"

A deadly calm moved over Aristide. "You're very wrong about that. I will get you this Marco's location."

Parish's eyebrows lifted.

"How?" Amalie asked.

"I'm certain he's connected to the assassins," Aristide said, looking out over the moonlit bayou. His home, the one he would always protect. "Maybe we can stop him before their plan can be carried out."

"We?" Amalie repeated slowly.

He turned to face her. "I'm going with you."

Mal blanched. "Ari, you're no Hunter."

Aristide shook his head. "No negotiations. You take out the assassins before they can get to Ashe and the cub, and I'll get Katherine's boy."

"And do what with him?" Parish demanded. "Bring him here?"

Aristide nodded.

"We can't house a human, Ari," Amalie said. "Not for any length of time, anyway."

"Not unless she's mated to a Pantera," Parish put in.

"This I know," Aristide said in a clipped voice. "I'm going back to her now."

"Be careful," Amalie said as he turned to go.

"Always, sister," he returned.

But Parish wasn't done with him yet. "Why are you doing this for the woman?" he called after him.

Aristide stopped and turned around. Both his sister and Parish were backlit by the yellow moon. "It's for the Pantera."

"Why are you doing this for the woman?" Parish repeated.

Aristide sighed. Looked away. Then back at the pair. "I believe my cat wants her."

Amalie gave him a worried look. "Just your cat?"

"It must be," he said with a little too much passion.

"Why, brother?"

He cursed. "I am Pantera, Mal. You know me. You know what my plans for the future have always been. I must mate a Pantera. It's what I want." *No. It's what I used to want.*

A smile tugged at Parish's lips. "My mate's human, and she's helping another human give birth to a Pantera cub as we speak. Things aren't what they used to be here, Ari. Our past is not our future, it seems." His chest puffed up a little. "My Julia would give her life for me, and for any Pantera, I believe. She's my everything; my happiness, my soul. I'm so proud to call her my mate." He lifted one dark eyebrow. "With all that's gone down, there are many reasons to reject your attraction, your need for this woman, Katherine Burke. But being human shouldn't be one of them."

Aristide didn't answer. He couldn't. His past wants and desires were engrained in him. In the idea of a true Pantera mating. Like what his parents had. What his own sister had. Right now, he needed to get back and talk with the human woman. The woman who he cared for, certainly, and who he would help. But not a female he would ever call his mate.

He gave them both a quick nod before turning away, leaving the ever-darkening bank of the bayou.

———

The moonlight clung to the tops of the trees, refusing to filter through and offer her safe passage. Kat followed the bayou, hoping, praying it led her out of the Wildlands and into La Pierre. Once there, she could find a way back to New Orleans. And to where she knew Marco was staying.

Hearing something, she stopped near the shore and glanced around. She'd never been in the bayou at night, but it was definitely not the still and silent place she'd believed it to be. Noises came from everywhere: the water and the land, and the sky. Kat hissed as a small nutria ran past her feet, the semiaquatic rodent heading straight for the bayou. Once it was safely underwater, Kat started moving again, waiting for that familiar sense of relief to wash over her, the relief that stated, 'You're fine. That was just a little animal who probably has very small teeth.' But what she felt instead as she jogged along the shoreline in a stolen pair of what she'd assumed were Aristide's sister's shoes, was a strange shock of guilt.

Aristide. He'd trusted her. Enough to leave the house without locking a door—or locking her up. What would he think when he returned? That she'd lied to him? About everything, about Noah? Her heart lurched. She hated the idea that Aristide would ever think she'd betrayed him. And yet, that was exactly what she was doing, wasn't it?

Betraying him to save her son.

The snap of a twig on the shoreline made her jump, and she picked up her pace. What was she going to say to Marco when she got there? Would he understand that being taken by the Pantera had not her fault? Was there any possibility that she could end this now? That her one awful writing mistake about the Pantera could be her last? That she could take Noah and just…disappear? She didn't even want to contemplate what might be coming her way. What her future, and Noah's, might look like if Marco was as 'above the law' as he'd claimed.

Up ahead, she saw an open area, almost a field, with high grass, and stopped for a moment to catch her breath. Was this the border? she wondered, looking around. Was she close to town?

But her questions went completely unanswered as a rush of heat hit the back of her neck, and a very male voice whispered near her ear.

"Big mistake, Katherine," Aristide said.

Panic flooded Kat's body. Large hands encircled her waist and he spun her to face him. Dressed in jeans and a thin black long-sleeve shirt that accentuated every hill and valley of muscle he possessed, Aristide stared down at her under the wash of moonlight. Lips pressed together in a frown, and eyes darker than the sky, he looked ominous. His nostrils were flared, and he was breathing heavily. She wondered if he'd just shifted, if it had been his puma who had found her, scented her, chased her down. Or the man himself had tracked her.

"I'm sorry," she said, struggling to free herself from his grasp. "But I have to get to Noah."

Aristide bared his teeth and his black eyes glittered like polished stones. "You think when you show up on that bastard's doorstep he's just going to hand the boy over to you?"

"I don't know, but I have to try."

"That he's going to be suddenly caring and honorable?" Aristide continued. "That he's going to be the boy's father now?"

Kat felt the blood drain from her face and she stopped struggling. "Don't call him that." She shook her head. "Never call him that. Marco was a sperm donor, nothing more. As far as I'm concerned, Noah has no father."

Aristide's face tightened. "Don't you understand? Going to that man could endanger Noah even more. What do you have to give him? A new story? Or the tale of your failure and capture?"

"Maybe he'd give me Noah if I tell that story, too," she cried out, hating herself with every word she uttered.

But Aristide didn't admonish her for her ugly threat. Instead, he loosened his grip on her and released a breath.

"You won't do that, Katherine," he said. "You don't want to do that."

"I will do anything for that boy. He and I...we're the only family we got." Her voice broke. "Don't you get that?"

"I do." His eyes moved over her face. "My life has always been about family. Cherishing the one I had and lost, and waiting for the one I hope to have in the future."

His words cut into Kat, so deep she sagged in his grasp. Why didn't a man like this exist outside the magical world of the Wildlands?

"Why are you doing this?" she asked him wearily as a breeze off the bayou ruffled her hair.

His brows drew together. "What do you mean?"

"Acting like you care."

"I'm not acting, woman," he growled.

"Then...why? What do you want from me?"

His answer came swiftly, and in the form of the most breath-stealing kiss Kat had ever experienced. One moment he was holding her arms, and the next, he'd taken her face in his hands and captured her lips with his own. Heat radiated off his body, yet his soft, full mouth felt cool. Kat groaned into his kiss and wrapped her arms around his neck, reveling in the feel of him so close. He tasted like fresh air and stars, and she never wanted him to stop.

His hands plunged into her hair, held the back of her skull while he nipped at her lower lip, than lapped at it with his tongue. Kat's legs felt like water, and her belly ached. Not with pain, but with a need, a desire, she hadn't felt in years. A desire she hadn't thought existed inside of her anymore. Something long dead, surely. Something she had refused to even contemplate trying to revive.

Something this man—Aristide, with his kindness and his fierceness–had resurrected with just one kiss.

Knowing it was probably her one and only shot, Kat gave herself over completely to the amazing feeling running up and down and in and out. She gave herself over to all the hot, wet sensations driving through her body. And when Aristide groaned and changed the angle of his head, deepened his kiss and let his hands travel down her back and over her hips to cup her backside, Kat pressed against his palms. She thought of the bread pudding. How every bite had made her want more. Kissing him, being touched by him, was like that—but times a thousand.

God, she wanted everything. She wanted to be on her back with this man naked above her. She wanted him looking at her, those amazing eyes of his, the ones that made her hope, gazing down at her as he pushed inside her willing and very wet body. She wanted him to say her name, over and over, as he came. And then she wanted him to hold her, whisper in her ear that everything would be okay before he kissed her asleep.

Aristide eased her forward, pressed her against his chest as he kissed her, hard and excited now, his tongue ruthlessly invading her mouth. Kat's breasts tingled and tightened, and her sex grew slick with arousal. She wanted him. She wanted him like she'd never wanted anyone. And when his fingers wrapped around the hem of her skirt and he lifted the fabric up to her waist, she nearly broke from his kiss and shouted, "Thank God!"

As cool air played over her ass, Kat gripped Aristide's scalp tightly and suckled his tongue into her mouth. Aristide responded with a growl and a quick, heady squeeze to her backside. *Oh, yes. Oh, god, yes.* The growl continued, moving down his throat, vibrating in his chest, causing Kat's breasts to ache terribly. It was only when one of his hands slipped inside the waistband of her panties and headed south, down over her buttocks to where she truly ached, that Kat believed she might know pleasure for the first time in years.

Panting against his mouth, she arched her back, giving him easier access to her sex, silently begging him to touch her. And when he did, when he found her drenched and ready, he slipped two fingers inside of her and cursed.

Electric heat flowed through Kat's body at the delicious invasion, radiating in all the right spots. Feeling full, feeling desperate, she clung to him, moaning and crying out and suckling his heavy lower lip as he slowly worked his fingers in and out of her. It had been ages since she'd been touched like this. And truly, her own hand didn't count—was a joke in comparison to this, to him. But she did know the burgeoning sensation of impending climax, and all of it was coming upon her now. Rocking her hips, rubbing herself against him, she wanted to scream at the rising tide of orgasm—tell it to go away, give her more time. Just a little bit more time. She even thought of begging Aristide to stop, but she knew if she was given a voice, she'd only beg him to continue—and god, continue hard and deep...and rough.

As if he could read her thoughts, Aristide quickened his pace, then drove up inside of her so deep, Kat gasped. *Yes. This was perfection. This was heaven.* Holding her close, Aristide worked that soft, G-spot close to her womb. That spot that would send her flying and crashing at any moment. But it was when he pulled his mouth from hers and commanded that she look at him, that Kat knew she was done for.

"Come for me, Katherine," he whispered on a growl. "Damn, if it's possible you're even more beautiful when you're aroused."

Kat stared up at him, her lips parted, panting. "How do you make me feel this way?"

"What way is that?"

"Sexy, and so safe."

"Because I want you, Katherine. I want you more than you can imagine." His eyes pinned to hers, the moonlight shimmering overhead, the bayou breeze rushing over their skin, Aristide thrust into her over and over as his thumb expertly massaged her clit. "And if you'll let me, I'll make sure you feel all of that and so much more."

Waves of heat crashed over Kat and her body stiffened. She didn't want it...didn't want it to end...

But she was powerless against the pleasure that radiated out from her sex. Her cries echoed throughout the Wildlands as she gave in, gave up, to the most intense and wondrous feeling in the world.

As her body bucked, and cream coated his fingers and her inner thighs, Aristide just held her steady, and continued to gaze upon her as if she was something amazing. As if she was precious to him.

Was she? She knew he wanted her. But was she precious to him?

The question undid her, exhausted her, and she dropped her head against his chest, sated. Breathing heavily, she whimpered, and Aristide kissed her hair and slid his fingers from her body. With gentle hands, he eased her skirt back down where it belonged, then gathered her into his arms. For several, wonderful minutes, Kat allowed him to hold her. But after awhile, as her skin cooled, the feeling of vulnerability and closeness was almost too much to bear, and she forced herself to move away from him.

With some distance between them, Kat found his gaze and held it, wishing this—whatever was going on between them—could last. No...could *grow*. But it wasn't possible. They were from two completely different worlds and life paths.

"What now?" she asked him.

He gave her a soft smile. "Come back with me."

Kat closed her eyes on a sigh. "Please tell me you didn't come after me because I'm your prisoner and you want information."

"I can't tell you that, Katherine," he said, his eyes studying her.

The pain that ripped through Kat at his words, his admission, nearly stole her breath. But she could still manage a terse, "Bastard." Tears tightened her throat and she backed up another foot. She knew it. God, she knew it. They were all the same. They all lied and used—

"But that's not the only reason I came after you," he said, his expression rigid. "Or, Opela help me, the most important reason."

"What?" Her anger still humming at the surface of her skin, she just stared at him. "What are you talking about?"

"I want to protect you, Katherine," he continued, moving toward her. "I want to find your cub. And I want to save the one who is about to be born here in the Wildlands."

Her mind raced over what he'd just said. Find her cub? What? Was he saying he wanted to help her? Help her get Noah? And if so, how could she believe him?

"Oh, Katherine," he whispered, reaching for her hand, lacing his fingers with hers. "My puma knew it before I did."

"Knew what?"

His eyes glowed black fire. "Please. Just trust me."

Her belly clenched. "I don't know you, Aristide."

He squeezed her hand. "And yet, you kind of do. Right? I know I feel that way. Shit, I felt it at The Cougar's Den the first time I saw you."

She shook her head, her fingers curling around his even as she warned herself to stop touching him. "But how is that even possible?"

He sighed. "Oh, the magic of the Wildlands is a curious thing. It exists inside every Pantera, and when a male or female recognizes their other half, the one they are connected to on a level that surpasses reason, that magic's released. It finds the match, the mate, and grabs on tight until both parties realize it."

He smiled at her. He was so gorgeous, so sexy, so convinced of what he was saying. But how could that be? He cared for her, wanted to protect her, help Noah...

"Keep that in mind for your next article, by the way," he added, then brought her hand to his lips and kissed the palm.

Kat shivered. Not with fear or pleasure. But with all that he'd just said to her.

"Let's work together," he said. "To bring Noah back to you, and to make sure that his sperm donor never gets near him again."

Kat didn't know if she believed in magic, or god—if she even deserved it. But in that moment, her heart believed. In Aristide and all that he promised. She felt somewhere deep inside of her soul, somewhere she had always refused to access for fear of being hurt further, disappointed further, that he would do everything possible to help her and her cub. She smiled at that. Her *boy*.

Aristide broke away, releasing her hand. "Now, let's go home."

Home. No, she wouldn't think on that right now. Right now was all about getting Noah away from that monster.

"Climb on my back and hold on."

Kat's eyes widened at his words. "Your back?"

He flashed her another killer smile before dissolving completely into the spotlight of moon glow and reemerging as the gorgeous, growling, and fiercely protective puma she'd seen only once before. She wasn't used to his shift yet and her breath caught in her throat at his size and fierceness.

With a quick snarl, he made an impatient gesture for her to get on his back. Still trembling slightly from both the residual effects of her climax and from the anxiety of all she knew, feared, wanted and prayed for, Kat climbed onto Aristide's muscular, golden back and wrapped her arms around his neck.

The satisfied purr that broke from his cat's throat echoed throughout the forest as he took off into the trees.

CHAPTER SIX

"MOVE and you're dead," Hiss uttered in his most deadly voice.

"Easy, friend," came the reply. "I come in peace."

Just outside the back door of Shakpi's and Lady Cerise's makeshift prison, Hiss had discovered someone camped up under the small deck. It had been pure luck that the Hunter had even spotted the male, as the bastard had been hiding incredibly well. All the way to the back under the stairs. And even more worrisome, he had masked his human scent.

Hiss pressed the butt of his gun a quarter inch farther into the man's soft temple. "How did you get past my guards?"

The male—the human—seemed completely unfazed by the weapon, or by the puma shifter who wielded it. "Shakpi chose well," he said, his starkly pale face splitting into an ugly smile. "You are ruthless."

Shakpi? Hiss's lip curled. "Show me."

The man's near-manic eyes widened. "Show you what, Kitty Cat?"

Hiss didn't even bristle at the man's attempt to ruffle his fur. "If you have true knowledge of Shakpi, then you know exactly what I'm asking for."

The man laughed softly, the movement causing his long, pale red hair to fall about his face. "Are you going to shoot me if I move?"

Hiss pulled the gun from the man's temple, but kept it aimed at his chest. "You can move. Just don't fuck with me. How 'bout that?"

"Sounds like a very solid plan," he said, reaching down and grabbing the hem of his shirt.

Hiss watched as the man yanked the black fabric up to his right nipple. Below it, inked into the ribcage, was the raven and the moon he sought. But something else caught Hiss's eye, something he didn't expect. Two slashes of red, of blood, across each raven's wing.

His eyes jacked up, and his gut went tight. "Who the fuck are you?"

The man's eyes glistened. "My name doesn't matter. All that matters is Shakpi. Has she awakened?"

Hiss hesitated, his mind rolling backwards. If there was one thing he remembered about his training long ago, it was the description of the very tattoo he'd just witnessed. Shakpi's disciples had warned him that if he was to come across a male with such a marking, he must do whatever was asked of him. Not to help Shakpi, per se, but because that male would be nearly as powerful as Shakpi herself.

"She remains unconscious," Hiss told the man, holstering his weapon and getting in fight position. He had a feeling if this male had wanted to, that gun at his hip—that gun he'd held to the man's temple—could've easily been turned back on him.

"That is no matter," the man said tersely. "We will take her there ourselves."

"Take her? Where?" Hiss had heard no part of this plan.

"Into the Wildlands." With his red hair and the strange moonlight filtering through the slats in the stairs, the man looked like a circus clown. A very powerful, very deadly, circus clown.

"Shakpi must be awakened," he continued. "And we will need the blood of that brat to both revive her and sustain her."

For the second time in two days, a wave of foreboding moved through Hiss. It was true that he hated the Pantera for what they had done to him and to his family. But in that moment everything inside of him—his puma—wanted to scream YOU WILL NEVER DESTROY US.

"Are you sure?" Hiss asked. "That the cub's blood has this power?"

"It is foreseen, traitor," he snarled. "Take me to Shakpi. Then go and get rid of your guards. Send them back to the Wildlands. My own disciples are here, waiting."

"If you cross the borders into the Wildlands, expect a fight," Hiss said tightly.

"But of course, puma shifter." He grinned evilly. "It's a fight we've been waiting a long time to engage in. One we expect—if my little writer monkey did her job correctly—to be followed by a human infiltration." His nostrils flared. "Now. Take me to her."

Hiss hesitated, a moment of second thoughts. But it was too late for him now. He'd crossed over his own traitorous borders long ago. It was time to see the job finished, and his vengeance taken.

He slipped out from under the stairs and motioned for the man to follow him. "This way."

"I can see the fear in your eyes, Katherine," Aristide said, watching her pace the wood floors of the kitchen. "And I swear to you, I will do whatever it takes to find the boy."

She stopped and gave him a pensive look. "I want to go with you."

"I know, but it wouldn't be safe or smart. If what you say is true about this human, Marco—and what I believe about his involvement with our enemies—he won't give a shit who he hurts as long as he gets what he wants. I need to focus on Noah. Without distractions."

"What if I promise not to be a distraction?"

Aristide laughed softly and went over to her. "You, beautiful Katherine, are destined to be my endless distraction." He reached for her, and this time she nearly flew into his arms. The action made Ari's heart muscle squeeze.

She nuzzled her face into his chest. "If this doesn't work—"

"Shhhh," he whispered smoothly. "Please don't do that."

"I'm scared. For him, and god...for you."

Aristide placed a finger under her chin and lifted her eyes to his. "Tell me you trust me."

She bit her lip. "I wish you could understand where I've come from. *What* I've come from. I haven't trusted anyone in five years."

"Oh, *ma chère*, that's no way to live."

Her eyes pricked with tears, but she nodded. "I still don't understand why you're doing this for me."

He dropped his head and kissed her. "Yes, you do," he whispered close to her perfect mouth. A mouth he had to claim. Just as he wished to claim her heart. He kissed her again. But this time with all the heat and desire and faith that was crashing through him.

When he eased back, he smiled. "If all goes well, I'll be back by dawn."

"Make it go well," she said on a stilted laugh.

"I like you in my house, Katherine Burke." Grinning, he pulled away. "Wait up for me?"

She nodded. "Be careful."

"Always," Aristide called back as he headed out the door and down the porch steps.

He was meeting Parish, Keira and several other Hunters at Medical to do a quick rundown of the plan they'd created. Outside the gate of his house, Aristide shifted into his puma. He was halfway down the road when he heard Katherine calling to him on the wind. He stopped and glanced over one massive shoulder, watching her run, his cat's eyes narrowed and his nose picking up her heady, yet anxious scent.

When she stopped before him, out of breath and face flushed, Aristide contemplated shifting back into his male form. But before that thought had time to truly take root inside his cat, Katherine broke out with the most perfect, most amazing, most needed verbal eruption in the world.

"I do understand," she said, her gaze pinned to his cat's. "I understand why you're doing this. I'm just so afraid to want it. To want you. Because I couldn't bear to lose you, or to have you turn me away." Her eyes grew liquid and supple. "I trust you, Ari."

For so long, Aristide had wanted a mate, a family. A true partner. And the last place he'd ever thought he'd find her would be the human world. But he remembered something his mother had told him once: *love knows no boundaries.* It would seem she was right.

His puma purred at Katherine, then rubbed its large head across her belly before turning away. With a howl of pleasure, of purpose, he broke into a run, knowing all the while that she was there, watching him until his tail disappeared from view.

CHAPTER SEVEN

KAT had read, walked around the backyard and the front yard, eaten some leftover bread pudding, even showered in Aristide's amazing outdoor shower. Anything and everything she could think of to keep her mind from racing. But it was impossible. Her mind raced like a crazy person, and her pulse jumped every time she thought she heard something near the house. It had been three hours since Aristide had left, and she was losing herself in worries and fears about what was happening. Had the directions she'd given him worked out? Was Marco still there? Noah?

Pulling a blanket around her shoulders, she padded out to the porch and sat on the swing, looked out at the quiet, dark lane in front of the house. She should've gone. She should be there if something happened. She could go now, couldn't she?

Stop, Kat. God, stop right now.

She inhaled and exhaled a couple of times to get her bearings back, to push out the panic. Aristide was right. Having her there would be a distraction and possibly even a match to Marco's unstable flame.

Pushing off the swing, she was just about to head back inside, maybe try that book again, when she heard a sound behind her. She turned to see an enormous black puma kicking up dirt as it raced down the lane. Her heart jumped into her throat as it stopped in front of the gate and shifted into a tall, broad shouldered, caramel-skinned man with shockingly blue eyes and short black hair. His tense gaze traveled the pathway and eased slightly when he spotted Kat.

"Katherine?" he asked, raising one black eyebrow.

She nodded. "Who are you?"

"My name's Xavier." He opened the gate and walked in. "I'm Ari's best friend, and mate to his sister, Amalie."

Recognition dawned within her. Aristide had spoken many times of this man, and of his sister. "Is he all right? Have you heard from him? Anything about my son?"

He smiled gently, cautiously. "He hasn't returned, but Mal has sent me to stay with you."

Kat felt instantly cold, even inside the blanket. "Why?"

"We've been infiltrated by our enemies."

"Oh my god. Where are they?"

"They've breached the borders of the Wildlands and are moving toward town. Our Hunters will stop them before they get here."

"Humans?" she asked, feeling sick. She'd done this. She was responsible for this. She'd never forgive herself if the Pantera were harmed. Or the baby. She vowed she would do whatever it took to help them, to undo her lies.

"They're disciples of Shakpi," Xavier continued. "The evil spirit who has one goal: to destroy the Wildlands." His jaw tightened. "Her followers are out for blood. They believe it's the only way to revive Shakpi and return her to power."

It was almost too much to take in, but there was one thing Kat understood. The blood they wanted wasn't from battling the Pantera. "The baby?"

Xavier nodded gravely, though his eyes shimmered with happiness and hope. "Ashe's cub has just been born. A beautiful little female."

———

A battle of distraction raged behind Hiss as he ran toward Medical, Chayton's body, near lifeless, in his arms. He tried not to think about what he was doing, what he was allowing to happen, and all the Pantera lives that were at stake back near the border. He just kept moving. The human male weighed practically nothing, making it an easy feat, but it wasn't the man's weight that was Hiss's biggest concern. If Shakpi couldn't be revived by the blood of Ashe's cub, she would certainly perish along with this man—the host who sheltered her. Hiss couldn't let that happen. If he survived this monumental act of treason, if he was going to out the Elders and the leaders of the Pantera for all they had done to his family, he needed the evil one's power to keep him alive and safe outside of the Wildlands.

All around him, dawn threatened to break, and Hiss quickened his pace. He'd created the camouflaged shelter he was headed for. Had scoped out the spot himself. It was perfect. Near enough to Medical so the blood could be delivered while it was still warm, but far enough to be hidden from sight.

His eyes vigilant, his nostrils widened for the scent of any Pantera who might be headed his way, headed into battle with the magic-laced humans, Hiss spotted the heavily wooded area up ahead. It was untouched, and he blew out a breath of relief.

Kneeling down, he placed the male inside the small shelter made up of leaves and bracken, wishing he'd brought something to cover him with. Chayton's breathing was worrisome. It seemed overly shallow and his skin looked ashen.

Hiss glanced up at the sky. The human male should've been there by now. What the hell was keeping him? Hiss would be discovered if he remained longer than a quarter hour. But the wave of concern that moved through him was overtaken by the sudden and strong scent of a Pantera he knew well. She was smart and cunning, and she was upon him in an instant.

"Hiss?"

Heart thundering in his chest, Hiss rose. He kept his body in front of the shelter. He didn't want to have to hurt her, his closest friend within the Hunter community, but the human male was on his way. And that bastard would show no mercy to anyone who stood in his way.

"What are you doing here?" she asked, coming toward him. "You're needed—" She stopped a few feet away, caught sight of the shelter and blanched. Her gaze slid to his, then back to the shelter.

Thinking fast, Hiss blurted out, "Shakpi awakened. I followed her here. I'm guarding her—"

"No," Mal said tightly.

Hiss could practically feel her mind working.

"Oh, Hiss," she whispered, dropping into a crouch.

"Don't do that, Mal. You have no idea…"

His words were ripped from him a rush as Amalie simultaneously shifted to her puma, and knocked him backwards. She was on top of his chest in an instant. Hiss had never seen her so feral. With a curse, he shifted too, and bit into her puma's neck with his fangs. Mal cried out, but drew back and battered his face with her paws, drawing blood. Rolling on the ground, fur flying everywhere, the two cats clawed and bit at each other, vying for dominance. Finally, Hiss got his legs underneath him enough to push her off. Twin snarls rent the air as both of them scrambled to their feet, then shifted back to their human forms.

Breathing heavily, Hiss growled at her. "I don't want to hurt you, Mal! Goddammit!"

A few feet away, Mal glared at him and spat on the ground. "You already have."

"Get out of here now," Hiss returned.

But she didn't move. "I trusted you with my life."

"We all trusted you."

Hiss whirled around at the male voice. Moving through the trees toward them were two Hunters: Lian and Rosalie. They looked ready to kill.

Panic swirled through Hiss. Could he run? Make it to the border? Fuck, no. Lian was one of the fastest males he knew.

"Don't even think about it," came another male voice behind him.

Again, Hiss whirled. This time it was Mercier who blocked his way.

The massive Hunter shook his head, his sable eyes flashing pure hatred. "You deserve death for this, Hiss."

"And you won't get that blood," Lian called.

Hiss turned back, utterly fucked now. Lian was standing beside the shelter that housed Shakpi.

"The cub is born," Lian said. "Healthy and beautiful. Your plan has gone to hell. And the one you're waiting for? He's dead." The male sniffed. "The asshole's name was Marco something. A real piece of shit. Like the bottom of your shoe."

Rosalie shook her head. "Nice company you've been keeping, Hiss."

Exhaustion barreled down on Hiss. Some of it from all the shifting, but most of it from the burden he'd been carrying for too damn long.

"The battle?" he ground out.

"Over," Rosalie said told him. "Two casualties."

Hiss's head came up, nausea snaking through him at the thought of a dead Pantera. "Who?"

"Human. The disciples." She stared at him. "But you can bet your ass someone will find out about it—that human blood was spilled inside the Wildlands. They're going to be coming for us now. Maybe not today, but soon."

"None of ours were hurt?" Hiss said without thinking.

Mercier laughed bitterly. "There's no *ours* anymore, Traitor."

But Rosalie nodded. "A Pantera Hunter was hurt. An apprentice."

"Which one?"

"Why should it matter?" Lian uttered blackly. "You don't give a shit about us. You betrayed us."

"I was betrayed too, Lian!" Hiss spat. "So go fuck yourself!"

"What?" Rosalie asked. "What are you talking about?"

He knew it was pointless, knew they wouldn't care or believe him. But he told them anyway. "The leaders of our kind, Rosalie. They allowed my family to be killed all those years ago, for the good of the clan." He growled. "Where is my justice? I'm not the only traitor here."

All three Hunters were silent for a moment, then Mercier spoke. "Mal, you and Rosalie take Hiss into custody. Lian and I will follow with Shakpi."

"Oh, yeah, that's right," Hiss said, wanting to run as Rosalie came toward him, but knowing he wouldn't make it out alive. And goddammit, he had to stay alive. "Ask them! Any of you. Ask the elders. Shit, ask Raphael."

But they weren't listening now. They had a job to do. Hiss knew how their minds worked, because once upon a time he was a loyal Hunter, too.

Chapter Eight

KAT was going crazy. Dawn had broken a good thirty minutes ago and there was no sign of Aristide. She and Xavier were both feeling the stress of not knowing what was going on. Inside the house one moment, pacing the gardens the next. No one had come by to tell them anything. No one seemed to be around. Kat was ready to beg Xavier to go and find out some news and come back. But she knew he wouldn't go. There was a sort of silent code between the males here, especially best friends like Xavier and Aristide. They looked out for each other, and Kat couldn't help but be moved by it.

"Coffee?"

Shivering in the gray morning light, she glanced over her shoulder to see Xavier walking down the porch steps, two cups in his hand. "No, thanks."

"Come on now," he said, holding one steaming mug out to her. "It gives you something to do. Something to sip and hold while you're slowly going mad."

He grinned at her on that last bit, and she laughed softly and took the cup. "Thank you, Xavier. For the coffee, and for the company."

"Anytime," he said. He came to stand beside her at the gate. "He'll succeed, Katherine. I know him like no one else. His word is everything to him."

Her heart squeezed inside her chest. Yes, she believed that. "How long have you two been best friends?"

"Seems like forever," Xavier said with a sniff. "Since we were cubs. I did think we might be headed for a breakup a short time ago when I fell in love with his sister."

Kat turned to look at him. "Really? I'd think he'd find that comforting. His best friend, who he trusts, and his sister."

"Well, it turns out he did end up feeling that way." His dark brows lifted over his extraordinary eyes. "But I was worried. That male is family to me, and I did not want to lose him. Nothing's more important than family." He smiled a very wicked smile. "You'll see."

Heat surged into her cheeks and she nearly choked out, "What?"

Xavier laughed, but the sound died away nearly as quickly as it came. He glanced past her, craned his neck and narrowed his eyes. "Katherine, come."

"What?" Kat followed him out the gate and onto the dirt road. For a second, she couldn't see anything. Dawn had broken, but there were some low hanging clouds about. But after a moment, she caught sight of something in the distance. Her heart lurched, then started slamming against her ribs. *No...it can't be.* Without another thought, she started toward it. Walking slowly at first. She thought she heard Xavier call to her, but she didn't look back. She swore she saw the cat she wished to see. But what of the boy?

She slowed, stared, not believing what she was seeing. Because truly, how could it be possible? Then she gave a muffled cry and took off. Running toward the puma, and its small, blond, five-year-old rider.

"Noah!" she cried, and barely gave Aristide's puma time to stop before snatching the boy up in her arms and squeezing him tight. "Oh, my baby. Oh, my boy. I missed you so much."

She pulled back and inspected him, every inch she could see, and when she found him perfect, unharmed, she squeezed him again.

Aristide was shifting, returning to his tall, strong, capable, honorable, wonderful self. And when he caught Kat's eye, he winked at her and gave her a grin.

"Someone's happy," he said.

"You have no idea," Kat cried, touching her boy's hair and his face. *Was he real? Was she truly this lucky?*

"Mommy can we stay here?" Noah asked near her ear. "For a little while at least? I don't like it out there. I'm scared. But here..." He giggled. "I've got my own puma protector." He lifted his head. "Right, Ari?"

"You know it, Cub," Aristide said with a playful growl, reaching over to tousle the boy's hair.

"We'll talk about that later, honey," Kat said, feeling slightly embarrassed. Aristide had been so kind, so amazing to her, the last thing in the world she wanted to do was put him on the spot. "Right now, I want you to come inside and get some sleep."

"But it's morning," Noah whined. "I'm not tired."

"Who's hungry?" Xavier called, loping up to meet them. He enveloped Aristide in a hug, and slapped his back a few times. "Damn. It's good to see you, brother."

"You, too," Aristide said.

"I'm hungry," Noah called out. "I'm pretty sure I could eat a whale."

"A whale?" Xavier repeated, his blue eyes going wide. "That's some serious fish food, little cub."

"Whales aren't fish, they're mammals."

Both Aristide and Xavier laughed, and the former ruffled Noah's hair again. Kat wished the moment could go on for hours, days... The jokes, the love, the family. How could she have ever written such things about such a wonderful place? She would fix it. Even if she had to deal with Marco. She owed everyone here, Aristide most of all, a good story. A true love letter to the Wildlands.

"Come on, ya'll," Xavier said, dropping an arm over Aristide's shoulders. "Let's go to my place and see if Mal's back. Find out what's happened and where we stand while we stuff our faces."

"Yippee!" Noah screamed, making everyone laugh again.

Aristide turned to Kat and gave her look so intense, so hot, it sent shivers of desire through her. But his voice remained as cool as the air around them. "No one's going to be able to sleep anytime soon. There's much to talk about, and much to celebrate." His eyes burned into her. "Right?"

She nodded. "Right." She wasn't sure what he meant. If he was just talking about their small party. Or her. And him. Either way, she had to find out.

"Did I say how much I missed you?" Kat said in between kisses as she and Noah walked down the street next to the two grown Pantera males.

Noah giggled. "Yes. But I already knew."

"You did?"

"Ari told me."

Kat glanced over at the man, the male—the guy she was so desperately falling for. He was walking side by side with Xavier, but his eyes were pinned on her.

"When he came and found me in that mean man's house," Noah continued. "He told me how much you love me and that you missed me and that if I just trusted him, he'd bring me to you."

Tears pricked Kat's eyes. "I'm so glad we both trusted him, baby."

As she hugged her boy closer, she felt Aristide's hand at her back, guiding her, protecting her, treating her with such care as they all walked together through town.

———

A few hours later, Aristide led Kat into the house. His house. His family's house. A house that craved, and deserved, to have happiness again. For so long, it had been just him and Amalie. But now, Aristide was hoping for a fresh start with two humans he knew in his guts he didn't want to live without.

He closed the door and eased Katherine into his arms. She melted into him at once. Noah had been having so much fun at Mal and Xavier's place, he'd refused to leave. After eating more than a boy twice his size—maybe he had a touch of the Pantera in him?— Xavier had pulled him into a game he was creating on the computer.

Noah had begged to stay for another hour. Which was a perfect amount of time for what Aristide had planned for his mother.

"Ashe's cub is well and safe," he said, gazing down at her, his puma purring inside his chest. The feel of her against him was making his body roar to life. "And your boy is well and safe, and will never have to fear that monster again." He raised a brow. "But what about you, Katherine? Do you feel safe? Here, with me?"

Her eyes sparkled with undeniable happiness as she gazed up at him. "I feel so much more than that, Ari."

A low, hungry growl escaped his throat. "Oh, I love when you call me that."

She grinned. "Then I'll always call you that."

Always. Yes, he liked that.

"Do you think the Pantera would allow Noah and I to stay for a little while?" she asked, a touch of her contentment, her happiness, stolen by a momentary thread of concern.

Aristide lifted one eyebrow. "Only mated humans can live in the Wildlands, darlin'."

It was as if her entire world came tumbling down in that moment, in that stupid comment, and Aristide felt like a giant asshole for chiding her. "Katherine, I'm sorry."

"No. No." She shook her head and tried to ease herself away from him. "That's okay. I understand. We can go this afternoon."

Oh, shit. He was not doing this well. Holding her close, he allowed his puma a moment of possessiveness with a soft snarl. Then he held her gaze. "Listen to me, Katherine Burke. And listen well. Right now I ache for you so badly I can barely contain it. I need to touch you. I need to kiss you. Christ, I need to feel what it's like to be inside of you. So deep, we both lose our minds and our breath."

She stared up at him confused. "I don't understand."

"But first you need to know how I feel," he continued, his strong jaw tight and his eyes flashing black fire. "I want you. Here. With me. Forever. I want to mate you. I want to wake up every morning to your face, and have you fall asleep in my arms every night."

Her mouth dropped open and she stilled. "I want that, too. Oh, Ari, I want that more than anything. But are you sure? I'm not a Pantera female."

"You are my female," he said roughly, bending down and scooping her up in his arms. "And I'm taking you to our room and to our bed to make sure you understand that fact."

"Our room," she repeated. "Our bed?"

"Fuck, yes, Katherine Burke. Our everything."

He felt her shiver in his arms, knew that right then her nipples were getting hard. He licked his lips. "Noah can have the room you've been staying in," he decreed, moving swiftly down the hall. "Unless he hates the flowers. I'm not too into the flowers myself. So maybe we could fix it up together, him and me."

"Aristide?"

He stopped just inside the bedroom and turned to look at her. She was so beautiful. Her cheeks flushed with desire. Her eyes wide with desire, and a need for reassurance from him.

"You do want this?" he asked savagely. "Say you want this, that you want me. Because I want you and Noah more than anything. I know what you said about him not having a father, but it's not right. He needs that. And...I need him."

Tears welled in her eyes, and she nodded. "Yes, Ari. All of it. A million times, yes."

It was all he needed to hear. He stretched her out on the bed, then started undressing her. First her shoes, then her skirt and top, his eyes never leaving hers. But when she was completely naked before him, he drew back and allowed his gaze move over her, explore, covet. Oh, she took his breath away. Pale, long limbs, narrow waist, lightly muscled arms, full breasts with edible nipples that seemed to call to him.

"Mine," he growled, feeling his male self collide with his puma.

"Then take me, Ari," she said passionately, her arms outstretched. "I need you. I need you inside me. I've never wanted anything more."

Aristide wanted hours to explore every inch of her, kiss every peak and valley, lick every drop of sweet cream from her nearly shaved pussy. But when she spread her legs wide and showed him just how slick and pink she was, he couldn't be contained any longer. After all, they had tonight and tomorrow, and forever, to explore.

Aristide quickly stripped, then growled softly at her as her eyes dropped to his heavy shaft. "See something you like?"

She smiled wickedly. "Oh, Ari, so many things. But right now, I need you over me, inside me, against me."

He was on the bed in seconds, had her thighs spread a few inches wider and his cock sliding home before she said another word. Liquid heat enveloped him, and when she wrapped her legs around his waist and arched her back, he thrust into her so deep, she gasped. He dropped his head and captured her mouth, taking her gasps and her groans into his lungs. It was perfect, like fine wine.

"My Katherine," he whispered against her lips, moving inside of her, claiming her, taking her all the way to the brink of climax. "My life, my family, my love."

And when she cried out and exploded around him, Aristide went with her. Followed her over the edge and into a new and wonderful life for them both.

Epilogue

THE small cabin on the isolated island in the Wildlands was surrounded by heavy flora, and a perilous swamp that had claimed a few unwary Pantera over the years. It was used to imprison those who had done the Pantera wrong, and those who couldn't control their cats any longer. Hiss belonged to the former group. The wrongdoers and the traitors.

Standing over the cot that only days ago had hosted the evil Shakpi, Hiss wondered at his future. Should he give up? Give in, break with this life and move on to the next? Or should he fight to free himself? Was it important that the ones who imprisoned him now knew why he had turned against them? That it was their own treachery, their callous disregard for his family—and shit, for three of their own—that had brought this about?

The door was pushed open and one of his fellow Hunters, Rosalie, appeared. She was in her human form and she could barely look him in the eye as she announced that a visitor had come to see him.

"I don't want to see anyone," he growled. Every second he breathed, his shame grew like a cancer.

"What you want doesn't matter anymore," Rosalie said, before motioning to whoever was behind her to come inside.

Only days ago, Hiss had stood sentry outside that door. In his quest for revenge, he'd fallen so far down it would be impossible to crawl back up. He knew that, knew he was done for, and he didn't want anyone else in his face telling him so.

A female with green eyes and dark hair pulled back into a pony-tail stepped into the room. She wasn't remotely tall, but there was a toughness about her, a sharpness that didn't suffer fools well.

Hiss turned to the Hunter near the door. "You can go, Rosalie. I'm not about to paw my visitor."

"Not a chance, Hiss." This time her eyes met his, and they were filled with hot, raw disappointment.

It was a look that scratched at Hiss's insides, that snaked into the very core of his own Hunter nature and bit at shards of his remaining moral compass. He pulled his gaze from her and settled it on the female in front of him. "Who are you and what do you want?"

Her green eyes narrowed. Not with malice, but with keen inter-est. "Do you remember me?"

"I believe we've met before," Hiss answered caustically. "Sebastian's mate, right?"

The female nodded. "But that's not all I am, it seems."

"Why do I care?" He couldn't imagine why the female was here, what she wanted from him.

She took a deep breath and let it out. "Before coming here I really didn't know what I was. I knew I wasn't like the other humans I worked with, was friends with, but I didn't really try and go digging for answers." Her eyes softened. "Until Sebastian."

Hiss cursed and dropped down on the cot. "Have you come here to tell me about your perfect little love story, Female? Because that would be a true form of torture for me."

"Sebastian wanted to know who I was, where I'd come from, how a Pantera female could grow up among the humans without anyone ever looking for me," she continued, unfazed by his vicious attitude. "He took a hair sample from me." She grimaced. "Without me know-ing about it—"

Hiss growled. "Get on with it, Female. I have all day and night, true, but not for this pointless bullshit."

Her face fell. "The sample was tested, and DNA—my DNA—matched another shifter here in the Wildlands."

Something hot and aching rolled through Hiss at her words. Why the hell was she here? What kind of game were the Pantera playing? Or maybe this was the elders—

"I'm your sister, Hiss."

The words popped out of her mouth like bullets from a gun. At first, Hiss wasn't sure he'd heard it correctly. Then he replayed it. Again. And again in his mind.

"You're lying," he uttered tersely, coming to his feet.

"No." She shook her head.

"That's impossible. My sister is dead. My parents are dead. I have no family."

Tears pricked in her green eyes and she shrugged. "I don't know how this happened, how we got separated. If our parents are truly gone, or what. But DNA tests don't lie. I'm your blood, Hiss." She lifted her chin. "I'm your sister."

Bayou Heat

Book Nine

Lian

New York Times and *USA Today* Bestselling Authors

ALEXANDRA IVY

Book Ten

Roch

LAURA WRIGHT

LIAN

BY
ALEXANDRA IVY

CHAPTER ONE

THE streets of the small town of La Pierre, Louisiana were empty and the handful of houses locked up tight.

It could be because it was well past midnight with the faintest hint of an autumn chill in the air.

Or maybe it was the fact that the town was perched on the edge of the bayous where anything might crawl out and attack the unwary. Including a race of puma shifters known as Pantera who the humans had just learned weren't creatures of myth and legend.

Yeah, that might make the locals a little twitchy.

There was, however, one business in town that was still open to customers no matter how late or dangerous it might be.

The Cougar's Den was the local bar that doubled as a meeting place for the Pantera.

The two-story wooden building was built on tall stilts with a tin roof that was faded to a miserable shade of mustard. There were also shutters painted a dull green that could offer protection during hurricane season, and a rickety staircase that had nearly been the death of more than one human trying to make their way home after a long night of drinking.

Inside there was the mandatory bar with tall stools, a cramped dance floor and a couple of shabby pool tables at the back of the long, darkly paneled barroom.

There was even an old-fashioned jukebox that was currently blaring out Lynyrd Skynyrd to the dozen Pantera males lined up at the bar or playing pool.

Perched on one of the stools, Lian sipped his chilled water, looking every inch a badass Hunter.

It wasn't just the fact he was well over six foot, with broad shoulders and muscles that looked like they'd been carved from granite. Or the dark hair that had been pulled into a long braid that hung to his waist. Or even the jeans and faded Iron Maiden shirt.

It was the restless hunger in the whiskey-gold eyes and the barely leashed violence that buzzed in the air around him.

Of course, the Suit seated next to him didn't look much more civilized.

Michel might be a Diplomat, but there was no mistaking the fact that a lethal predator prowled behind those cunning green eyes. Oh, and if that wasn't scary enough, there was also the skull-shaved head, and broad body that was currently covered by a casual cotton shirt that was tucked into his black slacks.

At the moment, he was tossing back his favorite shot of whiskey as Lian filled him in on the latest happenings in the Wildlands.

Raphael, the leader of the Suits, had been careful not to share too much information when he sent out word to call his Diplomatic staff home. They'd discovered the hard way that not everyone could be trusted. Not even among the Pantera.

"Hiss is a traitor?" the Suit breathed in horror. "Fuck me."

Lian nodded. There were a lot of 'fuck mes' going around the Wildlands over the past few days.

Not only because Hiss had been actively working with their enemies, but because the Pantera had been attacked by the disciples of Shakpi who'd been determined to sacrifice Ashe's baby.

Oh, and the fact that they had the evil goddess—who was currently unconscious and trapped in a human body—locked in a secluded cabin in the middle of the Wildlands.

"Yeah, that's the general consensus."

Michel gave a shake of his head. "Why would he betray us?"

"He claims the elders were responsible for the death of his family. Only—"

Lian halted, glancing around the room to make sure there weren't any humans lurking in the dark corners.

"Only what?" Michel prompted.

He pitched his voice low enough that it wouldn't carry. Even if there weren't any humans close enough to overhear his words, and the jukebox continued to blare out Sweet Home Alabama, he simply assumed that the place had been bugged.

At least in the public rooms.

Paranoid? Maybe. But the past few weeks had taught him that they had enemies hiding everywhere.

Hiss was proof of that.

Damn him to hell.

"Only Sebastian's new mate, Reny, is his sister."

Shock widened Michel's eyes. "Hiss's sister?"

"Yep."

"I thought his entire family was dead."

"That's what we all thought."

"Shit. I need another round."

Michel motioned to the tall, golden-haired male who was lazily washing glasses. The Pantera spy who was currently acting as a bartender tossed the bottle in Michel's direction, obviously sensing the Suit needed more than one shot.

Lian reached for his water, lifting it toward his friend. "At least we have some good news."

"We do." Michel abruptly smiled. "The babe."

Despite the fact they were ass-deep in trouble, the birth of Raphael and Ashe's baby was something they could all celebrate. The first child born to the Pantera in over fifty years.

"She takes after her mother," Lian murmured. "A true beauty."

"To Soyala," the Suit announced, his voice deep in tribute as he touched his glass to Lian's. "Our future."

"To Soyala."

They both took a drink before Michel was setting aside his glass and studying Lian with a somber expression.

"Did Raphael tell you why he was calling the Suits back to the Wildlands?"

"He wasn't comfortable sharing the fact that Shakpi is still alive over the phone," Lian pointed out in wry tones. "Plus, he wants to hear firsthand what's going on in the world. He's worried about the humans and their reactions to learning the Pantera aren't just a figment of their imagination."

"Yeah, he should be." Michel rubbed the back of his neck, his expression troubled. "The stories of rabid man-beasts who sneak out of the swamps to eat babies and rape women are all over the streets of New Orleans. Half the population wants to drop a nuke on the Wildlands to get rid of the dangerous mutants, and the other half wants to gather us up and put us in protective custody." Michel gave a dramatic shudder. "I don't know which one scares me the most."

"No shit," Lian agreed with an answering shudder. "It's going to get even worse when they discover two of them were killed when they tried to get ahold of Ashe's baby."

Michel scowled. "They attacked us."

"You're the supposed expert on humans, dude," Lian reminded his friend. "You know they won't care that we were only protecting ourselves."

"True." His hand curled into a fist on top of the bar, a sudden heat blasting from his body. "For now, we're terrifying monsters who've stepped straight out of their horror stories."

"Exactly. They don't need a reason to want us dead."

There was a brief silence as they considered the potential clusterfuck that waited for them, then Michel gave a shake of his head.

"Okay, I get that things are tense, but Raphael can't expect us to cower in the Wildlands forever?"

Lian shrugged. "I'm guessing it's temporary, but right now our leader is a little—"

"Ape-shit crazy?" Michel helpfully supplied.

Lian gave a sharp bark of laughter. Raphael was always aggressive. Now he was downright…well, ape-shit crazy was the perfect description.

"Yeah, that about sums it up," he wryly admitted. "I don't blame him. Not only is he a new father to a baby who carries the fate of the Pantera on her tiny shoulders, but we have a half-dozen Pantera traitors we have to deal with, and a powerful deity who might awaken any second and continue her evil plot to destroy us."

"Fair enough." Michel poured himself another shot of whiskey. "Has anyone come up with any bright ideas of how to kill the bitch?"

Lian swallowed a sigh.

No one wanted the bitch goddess dead more than he did, but he wasn't happy with his current assignment.

He was supposed to be a Hunter, not a damned babysitter.

"The Geeks are studying the ancient scrolls," he muttered.

Michel arched a brow. "Isn't that a little old-school for them?"

"Desperate times, *mon ami*."

"You can say that shit again. Did they find anything that can help?"

"Not really, but they did locate a few scrolls that'd been stashed at the bottom of the original receptacle," he said. The receptacle was an ornately carved chest that had been discovered in the back of the caverns. It was believed that it had belonged to Opela. Most of the writings contained a history of the Pantera, along with the laws that still governed their people. "They hope the hidden texts will reveal how Opela stopped her insane sister the first time."

"Why do they only hope?" Michel demanded. "Can't they tell?"

Lian folded his arms on the bar, his muscles bulging beneath the T-shirt.

"They're written in an ancient script," he explained. "The Geeks haven't been able to translate them yet."

Michel rolled his eyes. Lian didn't blame his friend. Like their current streak of bad luck wasn't enough. Now the scrolls they needed had to be written in some weird chicken scratches?

"So we're fucked?"

"Maybe not." Lian once again lowered his voice. "Xavier asked me to fetch some scholar who specializes in obscure languages and bring him to the Wildlands."

Michel blinked, looking exactly like Lian had felt when Xavier had approached him.

Baffled. And dubious.

Extremely dubious.

"How would a human be able to translate the words of a Pantera goddess?"

"He was trying to explain the tedious methods of philogy—"

"Of what?"

"Some fancy way of saying someone who studies languages."

Michel grimaced. "Christ."

Lian nodded in agreement. There was nothing like a Geek to make you feel like an idiot.

"Exactly. It all sounded like blah, blah, blah after a while. Still, if this scholar can help then I'll track him down and bring him back."

Michel remained confused. "Why do you have to track him down? Can't Xavier just invite him to come to the Wildlands? It's not like we're flying under the radar anymore."

Wasn't that the truth? Lian suppressed the tiny frisson of unease. He was trying to ignore the looming human confrontation. Right now he had more pressing troubles to deal with. One disaster at a time, thank you very fucking much.

"Supposedly this researcher is some sort of hermit who never leaves his home," he told his companion. "Xavier didn't even have a name beyond GoliardRetro."

"What kind of name is that?" Michel demanded.

"Some nerdy screen name thing," Lian said. In all honesty he wasn't interested in the language professor. His job was getting the man to the Wildlands as quickly as possible. The Geeks would take it from there. "Xavier managed to trace the computer to a general location in the northwest corner of the state. I'm going in to find him and convince him to join us here."

"And if he doesn't want to come?"

A smile of anticipation curled Lian's lips, the song on the juke-box appropriately changing to Eye of the Tiger.

Or in this case...puma.

"I can be very persuasive."

Michel narrowed his gaze, studying Lian with an oddly curious expression.

"Why you?" he abruptly asked.

Lian blinked. "Excuse me?"

Michel leaned an elbow on the bar, his steady gaze never wavering from Lian.

"Why did Raphael choose you to go get this scholar?" he pressed. Michel might look like a Hunter, but he was a perfect Suit. He had the insatiable curiosity of a trained spy. Every stone had to be turned over before he was satisfied. "There are Hunters in Bossier City."

Lian glanced toward the window, half expecting to see a member of his extended family standing at the edge of the bayou, waiting to walk him home.

"Because I told him if I had to spend another day in my house I was going to shove my head in a wood chipper," he admitted in rueful tones.

Michel gave a sudden laugh. "That bad?"

Bad? Lian rolled his eyes. He could barely breathe when he was forced to spend more than a few hours in his childhood home.

"I have an entire family of Nurturers who are constantly looking for someone to smother," he said, his expression one of disgust. No one loved their family more than he did, but yeesh. A full-grown male didn't like to feel as if he was still in the nursery. "I swear to the goddess, I can't step out of my private rooms without one of them trying to brush my hair or slap a band-aid on one of my boo-boos, or shove a cookie down my throat." He shook his head. "Yesterday I twisted my ankle during a training session with Parish and my mother threatened to tie me to my bed if I didn't spend the after-noon resting."

"Awww." Michel smiled with mocking amusement. "It's sweet."

"It's...humiliating," Lian muttered. "If I don't get away I'm going to lose my fucking mind." Rolling his shoulders, Lian slid off the stool. "Speaking of which, I need to get on the road."

Michel stood, his expression somber as he placed a hand on Lian's shoulder.

"Take care, *mon ami*. These are dangerous times for a Pantera to be on his own."

Lian nodded. "Always."

———

The pretty cottage situated several miles south of Shreveport was built well away from the dirt path and hidden behind a tall hedge. And if that wasn't enough to discourage unwanted visitors, there were a number of nasty traps hidden around the property.

After all, a young woman living on her own couldn't be too careful, Dr. Sage Parker had always assured herself. And if that made her seem antisocial, well...so be it.

She had her work.

Not only as a researcher, but she taught online classes for a local college.

It was all she needed.

At least, that's all she would admit to needing.

If she spent her nights lying awake, a restless need that she didn't entirely understand plaguing her body, she wasn't going to admit it.

Not even to herself.

Finishing her breakfast, Sage left the sun-filled kitchen to enter the main room of the cottage that her father had transformed into a library.

The walls were hidden behind floor-to-ceiling shelves that held her rare collection of leather-bound books. In the center of the room was a long, glass case that held fragile texts that needed constant temperature control. And in the far corner was a small desk nearly hidden beneath the crates of books that had arrived during the past week.

Sage halted to pull her pale, silvery blonde hair into a lopsided ponytail. As usual, she'd forgotten to comb it when she'd climbed out of the shower. Not that it mattered. There was no one to notice if her hair was tangled, or her delicate features that were dominated by large grey eyes were bare of makeup, or her tall, slender body was covered in a pair of yoga pants and faded Harvard University sweatshirt.

Her mother had complained that she had too much of her father in her.

He'd been a history professor who'd been little more than a shadowy figure to Sage. More often than not he was off on some archeological dig. And when he was home, he spent his days locked in the library instead of devoting any quality bonding time to his only child.

Her mother, on the other hand, had been a local midwife who'd dabbled in voodoo. She'd been determined to have her daughter follow in her footsteps, but Sage had adamantly refused.

Okay, maybe she had some weird...abilities.

But she'd rather be labeled an eccentric scholar, than a witch.

Especially now that both her parents were dead.

With her hair out of her face, Sage reached for the box of protective gloves she always used when handling her books only to drop them on the worn carpeting when the sound of a startled male cry echoed through the air.

An intruder.

Holy...crap.

Instinctively moving to grab the silver letter opener off her desk, Sage headed out of the library and into her parents' bedroom that she'd converted into a storage area for her overflow of books.

It didn't occur to her to call 911. It would take the cops a half hour to get to her place. If they even bothered to come. Her mother had placed a curse on the local chief of police when he'd cheated on his wife. He'd laughed at first, then he'd broken out in painful boils. He still held a grudge.

The putz.

Pushing open the door, she tentatively stepped into the room.

At first she could see nothing through the gloom.

She kept the curtains closed to guard her books against the sun. Now she had to strain to catch sight of the intruder who was struggling against the net that had fallen over him the minute he'd forced open the French doors and stepped into the room.

Her first thought was that she was glad the net had been magically enhanced by her mother to keep any intruder trapped until Sage released them.

Clearly the man was furious and ready to do some damage.

But as she snapped on the light to get a good look at her unwelcomed visitor she forgot how to breathe.

Oh...my.

His male beauty hit her like a punch to the gut.

The dark, perfectly chiseled features. The long black hair pulled into a tight braid. And the eyes that smoldered with golden fire in the shadows.

There was a raw sensuality that shimmered around him, calling to her most feminine needs.

Without warning the gnawing hunger that had only bothered her at night was suddenly flooding through her body, the strange sensations making her heart race and her palms sweat.

Good lord. She swallowed, feeling as if her skin was too tight for her body.

She'd been aroused before. She'd even had sex, although it'd been a colossal disappointment.

But nothing had prepared her for the blistering awareness that sizzled through her as a rich, intoxicating male musk seeped deep inside her.

"What the hell?" the man snarled, glaring at her in fury. "Get me out of here."

She felt a ridiculous stab of disappointment.

Why?

Did she think he was going to be struck with the same tingling, breathless fascination?

Yeah. Fat chance.

Holding the letter opener in front of her, she took a hesitant step forward.

"It's very rude to trespass," she informed him.

His hands gripped the net, his large body tense with outrage.

"Maybe if you answered your damned door I wouldn't have had to trespass," he said between clenched teeth.

Sage frowned, belatedly recalling the pounding she'd heard when she was in the shower. She'd assumed that it was the wind banging one of her loose shutters.

Now she shrugged, not about to admit that she didn't recognize the knock because no one ever came to see her.

That was just…pathetic.

"I didn't answer because I don't want visitors."

"Fine." The golden eyes narrowed. "I'm not looking for you, anyway."

Oh. Another stab of disappointment.

"Then why are you here?"

"I'm looking for Dr. Parker."

She frowned in confusion. Did he mean her father? Surely not. He'd passed away ten years ago.

"Why?"

He gave the net a frustrated shake. "Get me the hell out of here."

She clutched the letter opener, trying to ignore her uncontrollable reaction to the stranger.

Not easy. He really was a magnificent specimen of manhood.

Tall, muscular, starkly beautiful…

She shivered, heat licking over her skin.

Why was it suddenly so hot?

"Not until you tell me what you want with Dr. Parker," she forced herself to demand.

A low growl rumbled in his throat. "Xavier sent me"

Sage made a sound of shock. "XavierTopGeek?"

The stranger's eyes widened, something that might have been amusement shimmering in the golden depths.

"Top Geek?" He gave a sharp laugh. "Oh hell, I'm going to have to share that sweet nugget with my fellow Hunters."

"I don't understand."

All humor was wiped from the intensely male face. "You don't need to," he snapped. "Let me out or you're not going to like the consequences."

Sage frowned, turning to study a nearby pile of books. Her mind didn't work properly when she was looking directly at the intruder.

"Hush, I'm thinking..." Her inner debate of whether or not to try and contact the man she'd been chatting with online for the past few years was brought to a sharp and painful end as arms wrapped around her and she was tossed onto the nearby bed. "Eek."

She slashed the letter opener toward her attacker only to have it knocked out of her hand as the man leaped on top of her, pressing her into the mattress.

"Not so fun being trapped, is it?" he rasped, his eyes darkening as she struggled beneath him. Heat abruptly sizzled between them as his body hardened. "Although I'm beginning to realize there are a few unexpected benefits."

A combination of fear, and anger, and potent arousal exploded through Sage.

"Get off me." She slammed her hands against his chest, panic thundering through her.

Regret softened his harsh expression as he gazed down at her, but he refused to budge.

"Where is Dr. Parker?" he demanded.

"Why?"

"I need to speak with him."

"About what?"

He hissed in frustration. "Do you always answer a question with another question?"

"No." Sage grimaced. Even being held hostage by a stranger she found it impossible to lie. "Okay, maybe I do. It's a habit."

"Look, I have no intention of hurting you, but this is important," he said, an unmistakable sincerity in his voice. "Can you just tell me how to find the scholar?"

Sage cleared her throat. If Xavier had sent the man, then he couldn't be looking for her father. And it was obvious she wasn't going to get rid of him until he'd spoken to 'Dr. Parker.'

"You already have."

CHAPTER TWO

SAGE watched shock tighten the man's expression, something in the back of his eyes making her stiffen in alarm.

What the hell?

She could have sworn…

The thought wasn't allowed to fully form as the stranger pushed himself off the bed, glaring at her in disbelief.

"Is that supposed to be a joke?"

Sage pushed herself to a seated position, her body still carrying the heat and scent of him.

"Why would I joke?"

He scowled, folding his arms over his chest. "You're the expert in ancient languages?"

"Yes."

"You're—" He halted, giving a shake of his head.

"I'm what?"

"Young."

"Not really. I'm thirty-two." She tilted her chin. This was a familiar argument. "And not to boast, but I had my doctorate by the age of twenty so I've had more time than most to concentrate on my own research. Plus, I've been an adjunct professor for the past ten years."

He glanced around the room that was nearly overrun with books.

"You live here alone?"

She absently rubbed her hands over her bare arms. His presence seemed to fill the entire room.

"I think it's your turn to answer some questions."

He pressed his lips together, impatience crackling around him. Then, with an obvious effort, he leashed his temper.

"Ask."

Her hands gripped the handmade quilt that covered the bed. "Who are you?"

"Lian."

"Just Lian?"

He shrugged. "Just Lian."

She narrowed her eyes. He might be gorgeous, but he was clearly a jackass.

"You're a friend of Xavier?"

"More of a relation."

Hmm. There was something in the way he said relation that made her think he wasn't talking traditional brother or cousin.

"What do you want from me?"

"Xavier has several scrolls he wants you to translate."

Okay. That didn't seem so...creepy. She was contacted several times a week by people who wanted her expertise in decoding ancient texts.

She was, without false modesty, the best in the business.

Still, most of her potential clients didn't send someone to break into her house.

"Why didn't he just ask me? I would have had him mail them to me."

"The scrolls are too fragile," he said. "They can't be moved."

Sage was prepared for the complication. Her work often dealt with fragile parchment.

"He could scan them or even take a picture and send me the images in an email."

Lian took a step forward, studying her with an alarming intensity.

"I thought scholars salivated over the opportunity to get their hands on rare artifacts?"

She lowered her gaze, well aware that her face revealed her every emotion.

One of many reasons she didn't play poker.

"I don't travel."

He heaved a harsh sigh. "Why not?"

"That's none of your business."

"Do you have a medical condition?"

She swallowed a humorless laugh, shoving herself off the bed. A medical condition would almost be preferable.

"You've wasted enough of my day," she informed her aggravating guest. "You can leave the same way you came."

She started to edge past his large body only to be forced to a halt when he deliberately moved to block her path.

"What's your name?"

"You know my name," she snapped.

"Your first name."

Her gaze moved to the forgotten letter opener on the ground. Not as protection. If this man wanted to hurt her there was nothing she could do to stop him.

No. But she wouldn't mind stabbing the annoying creature in the leg.

His persistence was pissing her off.

"Sage," she at last admitted.

"Sage." Her name rolled off his tongue with a hint of a Cajun accent. A tiny shiver raced through her.

Nope, she wasn't ready for that level of intimacy.

"You can call me Dr. Parker."

His lips twitched. "Fine…Dr. Parker." His brief amusement faded. "This is important."

Excitement fluttered in the pit of her stomach.

He was close enough she could feel his heat wrap around her, the spicy musk clouding her mind with thoughts of smooth, bronzed skin beneath her tongue.

Good lord. She needed to get this man out of her house before her brain turned to complete mush.

"So is my research, plus I have papers to grade and—"

"This is life or death," he interrupted sharply.

"If you say so."

A strange growl rumbled in the air. Was that coming from Lian?

"Did you hear me?"

"We all believe our work is vital."

"No." He grabbed her chin, tilting back her head so she was forced to meet his fierce gaze. "This is a matter of life and death."

Heat blasted through her at his touch.

"Would you please…" Her words faltered as she once again caught sight of that shadow moving in the back of his eyes. There was something in there. Something that was focused on her with the smoldering hunger of a predator. "Oh…you're not human."

———

Lian cursed at his odd reaction to the female.

It wasn't just his astonishment at discovering that she was a she, not a he. Or even that she wasn't the old, slightly batty professor he'd been expecting.

It was the intense, blistering awareness that had slammed into him the second she'd stepped into the room.

Man. He could think of nothing but the overwhelming need to somehow get her beneath him so he could be buried deep inside her.

It was only because he'd been pissed as hell at being caught sneaking into the cottage—like he was nothing more than an unskilled cub—that had allowed him to leash the animal inside him that was roaring for a taste.

There would be no ravaging until he had her in the Wildlands, he'd warned himself.

Now he realized that his intense awareness had allowed him to overlook the obvious.

There was no way in hell he should have been trapped in that net unless there'd been a magical spell attached to it.

"I see your cat," she murmured, looking more curious than frightened.

Lian gave in to the impulse to run his fingers down her cheek, savoring the warm satin of her skin. This female obviously had magic running through her veins.

But it was the fact she could detect the animal inside him that made his heart leap.

Could she be a Shaman?

The mere potential was a cause for celebration.

There was an elder Shaman at the Wildlands who had long ago retired, and of course, Chayton, who was now lying unconscious with an evil goddess trapped inside him. Neither had been capable of serving his people for the past thirty years.

To have a young, clearly healthy Shaman just when the Pantera could once again breed would be nothing less than a miracle.

Suddenly the need to get her to the Wildlands became even more vital.

"How do you see my cat?" he asked.

"I just...do." She licked her lips, sending a jolt of white-hot excitement searing through Lian. Oh, hell. The things those lips could do to his body. "Is Xavier a cat as well?" she demanded.

He nodded. "Yes."

She wrinkled her brow. "I'm surprised I didn't suspect."

Lian scowled. He didn't know where the completely irrational stab of jealousy came from, but he sure as hell didn't like the implication she knew Xavier well enough to suspect he wasn't human.

Just how often had the two communicated?

"What do you know about my people?" he asked in abrupt tones.

"A great deal, actually." She glanced toward the stacks of books, offering Lian the opportunity to appreciate the delicate perfection of her profile. "I've read a number of books that describe the Wildlands and the puma shifters who live there."

"Do you know the legend of our creation?"

"There were two goddesses, Shakpi and Opela." She turned back to meet his watchful gaze. "I believe there was some sort of rift between the two."

His lips twisted.

Rift was a mild way of saying that Opela had sacrificed herself to lock her sister, Shakpi, in a prison so the crazy-ass bitch wouldn't destroy the Pantera.

"You could say that."

She tilted her head to the side, the end of her ponytail sliding over her shoulder.

Lian instinctively moved his hand to touch the silvery strands. Oh...man. It felt just like silk.

She stilled, but made no effort to pull away. "Are you a religious scholar?"

He gave a choked laugh. He fully admired the Geeks, but the thought of being stuck in a library or seated in front of a computer for endless hours gave him a brain cramp.

Give him open space, fresh air, and cunning prey to pursue and he was a happy cat.

Or give him a beautiful woman in his bed. Preferably one with silver-blonde hair and fascinating gray eyes rimmed with black.

"Hell to the no," he assured her, his fingers sliding around her neck to cup her nape. The crisp scent of lemon teased at his senses, the smell oddly erotic to the cat that stroked against the inside of his skin. It wanted a taste of this female. "I'm a Hunter."

"A Hunter?" She cleared her throat, pretending she wasn't burning up with an arousal that matched his own. A wasted effort. Her need was obvious in the flush that stained her cheeks and darkened her eyes. Even if he wasn't able to detect the sweet honey that was making her pussy slick and ready for his cock. "What does that mean?"

Maintaining his hold on her nape, he stroked his free hand down the curve of her spine.

"The obvious." He tugged her tight against his stirring arousal, his head lowering to press his face into the curve of her neck. "I track my prey until I have them cornered." He licked a rough path to the pulse that thundered at the base of her throat. "Then I pounce."

She made a strangled sound of shocked pleasure, her hands grabbing his arms as if her knees had suddenly threatened to collapse.

"You're in my personal space."

He chuckled, rubbing his cheek against her smooth skin with a gesture that was pure feline.

"I'm deciding whether or not I intend to play with you before I pounce."

He heard her breath catch, her body instinctively arching closer to the hard thrust of his cock.

"I'm not your prey," she breathlessly protested.

Lian allowed his teeth to press into the flesh of her neck, not breaking the skin, but offering a warning.

He might be able to convince his cat to take the seduction of Dr. Sage Parker at a slower speed, but it wasn't going to tolerate any denial of the desire that smoldered between them.

"Of course you are," he growled. "I was sent to retrieve you."

She shivered, her fingers tightening on his arms even as she gave a shake of her head.

"I told you," she rasped. "I don't travel."

Muttering a curse, Lian lifted his head. As much as he wanted to toss this female on the bed and ease his throbbing cock deep inside her, he had to concentrate on fulfilling his duty.

They had to find some way to translate the newly discovered scrolls.

And for now, this woman was their only hope.

"And I told you. The future of the Pantera is depending on you," he said.

She pulled from his lingering touch, her hand pressed to her chest as if trying to slow the pounding of her heart.

"What makes the scrolls so important?"

He hesitated before giving a small shrug. She'd have to know the truth eventually.

"We hope it can tell us how to kill Shakpi."

CHAPTER THREE

SAGE felt the breath being wrenched from her lungs at the blunt explanation.

God almighty.

This was all happening too fast.

Her life was supposed to be a series of predictable, well-planned days that never varied.

She worked hard to make sure that there were no surprises.

Now her house had been invaded by a Pantera male. Her body was burning with an unfamiliar passion. She was being told she had to leave the safety of her house to travel to his homelands.

Then, to put icing on the crazy cake, he was implying that they needed her to translate a scroll that they hoped would kill a goddess...

Yeah. That tripped over the edge of what her poor brain could process.

"This isn't funny—" she started to sputter.

"Trust me, I don't joke about a psychotic goddess who's determined to commit genocide," he interrupted, his beautiful features grim.

Genocide?

She widened her eyes. "You suspect Shakpi is trying to destroy your people?"

"I don't suspect it," he snarled, the temperature of the room amping up a few degrees. Was the heat coming from Lian? "I know it."

"How?"

"She told us."

"Okay." She took a step backward. Until this moment she'd been willing to play along. But when people started saying they'd spoken directly to a god or goddess, and claimed to have direct knowledge of their holy plans, she had to draw a line. "And people think I'm crazy."

"I'm not crazy." He stepped forward, grasping her chin in his hand. "Listen to me, Sage. I'm going to give you the condensed version of Pantera history and then we're going to the Wildlands."

"I told you—"

"Just listen," he commanded, then, before she could remind him this was her house and she didn't take orders from anyone, he was swiftly revealing the events of the past months.

She wanted to laugh at his absurd story.

To assure him that he was out of his mind and that he needed to return to his home. Without her.

But the words wouldn't come.

Quite simply because she believed him.

Not only because of the sincerity in his voice, but because she'd always possessed the ability to sense when someone was telling her the truth.

She wasn't a lie detector. Her gift wasn't that precise. It was more an overall 'feeling' of honesty.

At last she gave a slow shake of her head and studied him with a growing sense of horror.

"You have a goddess locked in a shed in the Wildlands?" she breathed.

Lian turned to pace the worn floorboards, his movements possessing a fluid grace that no human male could match.

"Basically."

171

She wrapped her arms around her waist. "And you want me to translate a scroll in the hopes that it will reveal how to kill her?"

He turned, his face hard with determination. "Or return her to her prison. If she awakens and escapes she'll eventually discover a way to destroy us." He held her gaze, as if daring her to deny the truth of his words. "It's that simple."

She chewed the inside of her lip. She believed him. She didn't want to, but she did.

"You'll have to bring the scrolls to me," she at last conceded, holding up her hand as his lips parted in protest. "There are ways to ensure they're transported without harm and I'll need my research books to help with the translation."

"No."

Her brows snapped together. Annoying, arrogant...ass.

"You claim to need my help, then you go out of your way to be difficult," she protested. "It isn't logical."

He moved back to stand directly in front of her, his potent male musk making it difficult to think about anything but ripping off his clothes and exploring every inch of his hard, bronzed body.

"We can't allow the scrolls to leave the Wildlands when we're surrounded by enemies," he informed her.

She clenched her teeth.

Concentrate, Sage, she silently chided her embarrassing thoughts. The man was here to stop a potential genocide.

Now wasn't the time to be distracted by her suddenly overactive libido.

"What enemies?"

Fury flared through the whiskey-gold eyes. "The disciples of Shakpi have gone into retreat, but they continue to watch from the shadows for the chance to strike." He glanced toward the French doors, almost as if expecting to discover one of the disciples standing in the overgrown bushes. "If they learn that there was a scroll that could destroy their goddess they would stop at nothing to get their hands on it." His gaze snapped back to her, his expression bleak. "Including killing you."

Her heart squeezed in fear. Oh...lord. She spent her life trying to avoid attracting attention. The last thing she wanted was to piss off a bunch of homicidal fanatics.

"I can give you the name of another translator," she said, inching toward the open door leading to the hallway.

If she was lucky, she could make a dash for her upstairs bedroom where there was a nice, sturdy lock on the door.

His eyes narrowed. "Are they as good as you?"

She shrugged, taking another step toward the door. "I know several who are very competent."

His lips twisted as he deliberately stepped into her path, his arms folded over his chest.

Busted.

"Who is the best?" he prodded.

She heaved a resigned sigh. "I...I can't come."

"Why not?" He reached to cup her cheek in his palm as she tried to turn her face from his unwavering scrutiny. "Dr. Parker?"

She forced herself to pull away, latching onto the first excuse that came to mind.

"I should think it was obvious," she said. "I am a genius, after all."

"What's that supposed to mean?"

"I'm smart enough not to take off with a stranger who broke into my home and claims he needs me to help kill a goddess."

"Good point." The cat lurked in his eyes...lethal, prepared to pounce. "Now tell me the real reason."

"I did." Her mouth was dry. Not from fear. No. This was pure, unadulterated excitement. "I think you should go."

He reached to trail his fingers down her throat, hooking one finger into the neckline of her sweatshirt to pull her toward his hard body.

"You know I'm not leaving without you."

"Lian, don't."

He ignored her breathless protest, his gaze lowering to the full curve of her lips.

"Tell me, sweetheart. Why do you use these books to hide from the world?"

Trapped beneath the ruthless golden gaze, she found it impossible to lie.

"I'm different."

"Because you're smart?"

"That, and I…" She faltered. She didn't talk about her strange abilities. Not even with her mother, who'd always suspected her daughter wasn't normal. "I see things other people don't."

Most people would have laughed.

Or immediately assume she was a lunatic.

Lian didn't even flinch.

"What do you see?" He asked. "Images? People? His free hand reached to lazily play with the end of her ponytail. "Pink elephants?"

She glared at him. "It's not funny."

"I'm sorry." He went motionless, belatedly seeming to sense she was more than a little sensitive when it came to her 'gift.' "Please tell me," he urged in a soft voice.

A part of her wanted to walk away. This man already disturbed her on a level she didn't entirely understand. Did she really want to make herself more vulnerable by revealing her deepest secrets?

But another part sensed that this stranger was one of the few in the entire world who could understand.

"When I truly looked at you I could see your cat. Not with my eyes, but…" She gave a shake of her head. "It's hard to explain."

His fingers cupped her chin, his attention focused on her with an unnerving intensity.

"What else?"

She blinked. His interest wasn't just a polite pretense. Or a fascination with the local weirdo.

It was a genuine, intense desire to know.

God. Could he actually reveal what was wrong with her?

"There are some people who have outlines of shapes that dance around them," she said, unable to actually describe the peculiar forms that she could see.

Some were so vague they were nothing more than wisps of white. Others were solid human outlines that were filled with vibrant colors. Yellow, scarlet, plum and a dozen other hues. Each color seemed to represent a characteristic of the form. Loyalty, honor, courage, anger, lust...

She wrinkled her nose. "I assume they're ghosts."

"Not ghosts," he corrected, his voice...reverent. "Ancestors."

Her heart gave a leap of hope. Yes. Ancestors who stood as protectors for their family.

That seemed right.

"How do you know?"

He gripped her hands, his eyes blazing with the force of his cat.

"Come with me, Dr. Parker," he commanded. "I have the answers you've been searching for."

———

The mansion in the Garden District of New Orleans was set behind high hedges and surrounded by a well-manicured lawn. The white two-story home was framed by a large pool on one side and a sunken rose garden on the other.

At the back was a large grotto that was surrounded by several marble statues that were rumored to have been stolen from Versailles.

The ten million dollar estate had once belonged to a prominent Louisiana family who were now buried beneath the recently remodeled garage.

Stepping onto the balcony that ran the full length of the second floor, Stanton Locke leaned against the ornate wrought iron balustrade and pressed his cellphone to his ear.

A tall man with dark hair he kept pulled into a short tail at his nape, he had a lean, dignified face, blue eyes and a slender form that was currently attired in an Armani suit.

The sort of man who looked as if he should be living in a posh mansion.

175

Few people would recognize him as the brutally poor orphan who'd grown up in the East End of London.

Stanton, however, never forgot his cruel beginning. Or who had snatched him from the inevitable life of drugs and early death that had been his certain destiny.

"You managed to locate him?" He spoke into the phone, his British accent honed until it sounded as if he'd attended a posh boarding school.

"Yes," Hank answered him, his voice rough. Unlike Stanton, the local thug had no desire to try and better himself. Which was fine. There was always a need for expendable soldiers. "But it doesn't make any sense," Hank added.

"Explain."

"The house he's visiting belongs to some hermit researcher."

"Researcher of what?"

"Languages."

Stanton tapped an impatient finger on the railing, his mind racing.

Could this be the opportunity he'd been waiting for?

It was risky.

"A human?" he demanded.

"Yep."

"Intriguing." He paused, weighing the danger of tipping his hand against the knowledge they were running out of time. "We need that Pantera," he abruptly announced.

He heard his soldier suck in a shocked breath. "Are you fucking kidding me?"

Stanton understood the man's reaction. Trying to capture a Pantera, even when they were away from their homeland, was like trying to trap a wild animal.

Thankfully they'd stumbled across the information that malachite could weaken the beast inside them, making it possible to bind them in the heavy-duty chains that Stanton had personally designed.

It wasn't always successful, as they'd discovered on more than one painful occasion.

But it was all they had.

For now.

"Ah, Hank, I did question whether you were suitable to take on a position of authority and clearly my fears were well-founded," he drawled.

Despite his lack of intelligence, Hank did possess a finely honed instinct for self-preservation.

"No…" he rasped, his fear throbbing in his voice. "I mean, of course I'll get him."

"Good." Stanton smiled, his gaze sliding toward the tree-lined street just visible over the high hedge. "You know what happens to people who disappoint me."

"Yes, sir. I'll contact you as soon as I have him."

"You do that."

Stanton returned the cellphone to his pocket, lingering on the balcony to enjoy the morning sunlight. The autumn air was crisp, but still warm enough to encourage him to delay his return to the house.

It was the unmistakable ping of his computer that at last forced him to turn and enter the long, ivory and gold room he'd chosen as his office.

The lofted ceiling with gilt cornices matched perfectly with the Louis XIV furniture and Persian carpets, creating a Versailles vibe. The ornate elegance might offend some men, but Stanton had spent his early days dreaming of the day he would be surrounded by luxury.

This suited him just fine.

Crossing to the cherrywood desk, Stanton settled himself in his chair before he touched the button on his computer to connect with the caller.

"Yes, master?"

The screen flickered, but it remained too dark to reveal more than a vague outline.

"Have you managed to retrieve my prize?" a dark voice demanded.

Stanton felt a chill inch down his spine. He'd only seen his master in the flesh on one memorable occasion. He still had nightmares.

But the man had turned Stanton's life from one of grim survival to endless possibility.

For that he was willing to give him unwavering, unconditional loyalty.

"We are still searching," he was forced to admit.

The man made a sound of annoyance. "My patience grows thin."

"I understand," Stanton soothed. "I have several warriors poised to infiltrate the Wildlands, but the Pantera remain on heightened alert." He resisted the urge to clench his hands in frustration. Emotions were the enemy. Success came from a clear head and a precisely formulated plan. And if events outside his control interfered in his scheme, then it was his duty to find a way to use that interference to his advantage. That was how he'd earned his current position on top of the Organization. And how he intended to stay there. "It is impossible to enter their territory unnoticed."

There was a husky rattle as the Master struggled to breathe. "What we need is a distraction."

"My thoughts precisely," Stanton promptly agreed. "I hope I might have one."

"The sooner the better, Stanton." The warning was unmistakable. "For all our sakes."

CHAPTER FOUR

SAGE felt hope spike at Lian's soft promise to reveal the truth of her strange powers, only to be swiftly replaced by a wary disbelief.

"How could you know what's wrong with me?" she demanded, pulling her fingers out of his hands.

He scowled, but he allowed her to step away. "To start with, there's nothing wrong with you," he growled.

"I'm not normal."

"Thank god," he assured her. "Normal is boring. You're blessed."

Blessed? She shuddered when she remembered the neighborhood children who ran away when she started to talk to the misty figures that no one else could see. Or worse, when she had a vision of a disaster before it happened.

Ah yes, and then there was the time she'd accidentally set the classroom on fire.

After that little incident her mother had decided it was safer for her to be homeschooled and she'd retreated into her father's library.

Even then she'd been harassed by her mother, who'd been convinced her 'gifts' could somehow be used to increase the family income.

"That's easy to say when you're not…"

"Different?" he helpfully offered when she hesitated. "Trust me, sweetheart, I know all about being different."

Okay. That was true enough. Still, it wasn't the same.

"But at least you know what you are, and you were raised with people who are just like you."

A wicked smile touched his lips. "Oh, sweetheart, no one is like me."

She rolled her eyes, even as her heart gave a leap of excitement.

He was just so…gorgeous. And charming. And sexy.

Sexy enough to melt a reclusive spinster into a warm puddle of aching need.

"You know what I mean," she forced herself to accuse. "You didn't have to worry that someone was going to think you were weird or—"

Her words were cut off as Lian unexpectedly pressed a finger to her lips.

"Shh."

She watched in confusion as he moved with a blurring speed to press himself against the far wall, tilting his head to peer out the French doors.

Sage froze, speaking in a whisper. "Did you hear something?"

"An intruder outside the house." He gestured toward Sage, waiting until she hesitantly moved to join him. "Do you recognize him?"

She glanced out the glass door, a sharp fear clenching her stomach at the sight of the large man with a shaved head and multiple piercings. Wearing a black motorcycle jacket and heavy leather boots, he looked so much like the typical 'bad guy' she couldn't believe he was real.

"No." She gave a shake of her head. "I've never seen him before."

They watched as the stranger pulled a gun from beneath his coat, unaware he'd been spotted as he began to wrestle his way through the tangled overgrowth of her yard.

For once Sage was happy she didn't have interest in keeping a neatly tended lawn. It would take him at least a few minutes to reach the house.

"I'm sorry, sweetheart, but time just ran out," Lian said on a low growl.

Her brows lifted as he turned back to reveal his obstinate expression.

"What do you mean?"

"We have to go."

She bit her bottom lip. "Go where?"

She knew the answer before he ever said the words.

"The Wildlands."

"No." She gave a violent shake of her head. "No way."

He reached to grab her shoulders, his grip firm enough to warn he was barely resisting the urge to toss her over his shoulder and force her to leave with him.

"Do you want to stay and see if he's in the mood to shoot you?"

Panic skittered down her spine at the mere thought.

"You could get rid of him."

He held her gaze, allowing her to glimpse the predatory cat that lurked just below the surface.

"Yes, but I don't think you'd like my methods."

She glanced back toward the man creeping ever closer.

Shit. He was right. She didn't want to force Lian to kill the intruder.

But the mere thought of leaving the security of her home and traveling across the state with a man who stirred her most primitive needs sent a flutter of nerves through the pit of her stomach.

"I can't," she breathed.

His hands lifted to cup her face, thumbs brushing her cheeks with a tender caress.

"I promise I'll take care of you, sweetheart." The heat of his hands scalded her skin, his musk wrapping around her to offer a drugging sense of comfort. "Nothing's going to hurt you."

Did she really have a choice?

There was no way in hell she was going to stand around and wait for the scary man dressed in leather to break into her home.

But that didn't mean she had to like it.

"You've already put me in danger," she accused, assuming the man had to have followed Lian to her house.

She hadn't had a problem with gun-toting strangers before.

"Trust me." He reached to grab her hand, tugging her until she was pressed against the solid strength of his chest. "Can you do that?"

"I don't know," she admitted with a stark honesty.

Without warning he swooped down to capture her lips in a kiss that jolted through her with blistering pleasure. Sage gasped, her mouth instinctively parting beneath the enticing demand of his tongue.

Good lord.

Who knew a mere kiss could feel like she was being struck by lightning?

She shivered, her fingers clutching his T-shirt as he spoke against her tingling lips.

"Come with me, sweetheart," he urged.

"Fine," she grudgingly agreed, allowing him to tug her out of the room and toward the side door in the kitchen. "But I don't like this."

Keeping her hand tightly clenched in his, Lian steered her toward a small opening he'd obviously cut into the hedge surrounding her house. Then, keeping in the shadows, he moved along the dirt path at a swift pace.

Sage remained silent, periodically glancing over her shoulder to make sure they weren't being followed.

There was something distinctly unnerving in the thought that there was a very real possibility of being shot in the back.

But after running for over a mile, her thoughts altered their focus from flying bullets to the growing ache in her side.

She was a researcher, not a marathon runner.

About to inform her companion she couldn't jog all the way to the Wildlands, Sage was caught off guard when Lian tugged her around a thicket of trees where a car had been parked.

No. Not just a car.

This was a sleek work of art.

"What is it?" she breathed in awe.

Lian ran a hand over the streamlined roof, a strange smile curving his lips.

"A Lamborghini Gallardo."

Sage didn't know much about cars, but she sensed the white automobile with black accents was worth a rather large fortune.

"It's yours?"

The sinful smile widened as Lian opened the passenger door so she could slide onto the butter-soft leather seat.

"Actually it belongs to Jean-Baptiste," he explained as he took his place behind the steering wheel, revving the powerful motor to life. "He's going to shit when he finds out that I borrowed it."

Despite the fear that continued to pound through her, she couldn't help but laugh.

The man was impossible, but he was so boyishly charismatic that she couldn't be mad.

"Borrowing implies that there was mutual consent," she informed him.

He stomped on the gas. "It was an emergency," he countered, taking obvious pleasure in flying down the road at a speed that made her hair stand on end. "And it was just sitting in the garage, begging to be taken. How could I resist?"

She shook her head. She'd bet her rare Kish tablet that this man had never heard the word 'no' before.

"Are you an only child?" she abruptly demanded.

"Nope. I have three older sisters."

"That explains it."

He sent her a quick glance. "Explains what?"

"Your assumption you should always get your own way."

He chuckled, his attention thankfully returning to the road. "What about you? Are you an only child?"

She turned her head to study the scenery that passed them in a dizzying blur.

"Yes, but I wasn't spoiled."

"Why not?"

She hunched a shoulder, her stomach cramping at the unpleasant memories of her childhood.

"My father was rarely home and my mother washed her hands of me when I refused to embrace my gifts," she confessed.

"What about your extended family?" He was forced to slow as they hit the interstate. The morning traffic wasn't heavy, but she was certain the last thing Lian wanted was to be stopped by a cop. "Your grandparents and aunts and uncles?"

"I never met them."

She sensed his astonishment. Not surprising. From what she'd learned of the Pantera, they were a tightly knit community that put an emphasis on the pack.

"Never?"

"My father emigrated from England and my mother's family disapproved of her choice to practice voodoo." Her hand reached to unconsciously grab his hard thigh as they darted off the interstate and hit a side road with a sudden burst of speed.

She understood he was trying to determine if they were being followed, but…yikes.

"You must have been lonely," he said, taking several more turns before they were back on the interstate.

It took a minute for her to catch her breath. "Yes."

"I can't even imagine," he mused. "I was smothered to the point of near insanity. I love my family, but a male needs his space."

Her lips twisted, hiding the envy that sliced through her heart.

How many nights had she dreamed that she was surrounded by a loud, loving family that actually cared whether she did her homework or ate her vegetables?

"Spoiled," she said beneath her breath.

Naturally he heard her. It seemed they actually did possess the acute senses of a puma.

"Don't worry, they'll be anxious to smother you as well."

Her head jerked around to meet his teasing glance. "Me?"

"Of course."

"Why would they care about me?"

"Because they're Nurturers and they're morally compelled to fuss over people."

She scowled, telling herself that he was being ridiculous.

And even if he wasn't, she didn't want complete strangers fussing over her.

Did she?

"I won't be there long enough for anyone to notice me," she protested.

A mysterious smile touched his lips. "We'll see."

Knowing it was pointless to argue with the stubborn man, Sage settled back in her seat and concentrated on the world that whizzed past her. Anything to keep herself from thinking of how far away she was from the safety of her tiny cottage.

She lost track of time as Lian concentrated on weaving through the increasing traffic, one eye on the rear view mirror to make sure they weren't being followed.

Then, just as they reached the outskirts of Baton Rouge, she was jerked out of her inner thoughts as a black truck zoomed from a side ramp and slammed directly into their rear bumper.

"Lian," Sage cried in fear, certain they were about to die in a fiery crash.

Lian, however, expertly turned into the spin, somehow managing to avoid the other cars as he whipped them around and then headed for the nearest exit.

"Hang on, sweetheart."

———

Lian didn't have the same skills as Jean-Baptiste behind the wheel, but he did have a car with a finely tuned engine that could hit two hundred miles an hour, and the lightning quick reflexes of a cat.

Within a few miles he'd managed to shake the black truck and disappear among the suburbs of Baton Rouge.

Still, he remained on full alert.

There was no way in hell the intruder could have followed them from his researcher's house.

Which meant that the bad guy had enough cohorts to watch the roads for the very distinctive Lamborghini. Or he'd managed to tag the car with a tracking device.

Either way, Lian had to get off the streets.

Winding his way toward the older district that lined the banks of the Mississippi River, he at last turned onto a dead-end street that had seen better days.

Beside him Sage sucked in a deep breath, clearly suffering from shock.

"Why are you slowing?" she demanded in husky tones.

"We need to lie low for a few hours."

She furrowed her brow, studying the dilapidated homes and air of aging decay that shrouded the entire neighborhood.

"Here?"

"Trust me."

She brushed back a silvery curl that had come loose from her ponytail, her hand unsteady.

"As if I have a choice."

Lian pulled into a narrow alleyway, regret stabbing through his heart.

When he'd gone to collect the mysterious Dr. Parker for Xavier, he hadn't considered that he might put the man in danger. And even when he'd discovered that the researcher was a fragile young woman who was terrified to be forced from her home, he'd still insisted that she leave.

He'd been confident that he could protect her. That nothing could get past him to hurt her.

Now he realized that his arrogance had very nearly gotten both of them killed.

Shit. If something happened to this female he would never forgive himself.

Not only was she vital to the future of his people, but his cat was insisting that she belonged with him.

There was nothing more important in the world than keeping her safe.

Halting in front of a chain link fence that blocked the path, he reached beneath the seat to retrieve his gun. Then, rolling down the window, he used his acute sense of smell to ensure there was no one lurking in the shadows.

Once confident they were alone, he swiftly left the car to press his hand to the sensor hidden in a box on the brick wall that lined the alley.

Instantly the gate slid open.

The locks were rigged to sense the touch of a Pantera, which meant as soon as the gate closed behind them, nothing but another Pantera could open it again.

Returning to the car, he drove past the fence and through a garage door that lifted as they approached.

As the door slid down behind them, the lights flickered on to reveal a large, surprisingly well-maintained space that was attached to the two-story Colonial-style home next door.

Climbing out of the car, Sage glanced toward the steel storage cabinets that held the expected tools and auto parts expected in a garage, as well as several emergency firearms and ammo.

"What is this place?" she asked.

Joining her, Lian placed a hand on Sage's lower back and urged her toward the door connecting the garage to the main house.

"A safe house."

They walked down a short hall, then together they stepped into a large, airy kitchen that had been recently remodeled to include white cabinets, granite countertops, stainless steel appliances and a white and black tiled floor.

Sage blinked, seemingly astonished to discover the inside didn't match the dilapidated outside, but her attention was clearly more focused on what might be hidden just around the corner.

"Are we alone?"

"Yes." He pulled his cellphone from his pocket, needing to pass along word of their attack, as well as getting help as quickly as possible. "Raphael has called most of the Pantera back to the Wildlands."

She nodded, wrapping her arms around her waist as she glanced toward the windows.

"What if they find us?"

He moved forward, brushing the back of his fingers down her cheek. "They can't get through the locks."

"How do you know?"

His heart twisted. Man. He hated the fear that edged her voice.

And the knowledge that he was entirely responsible.

"They're specifically designed to react only to a Pantera's touch. There's no way in hell any human could get past them," he said, not bothering to share the fact that there were traitors among the Pantera. She was freaked out enough. "Besides, I made sure we weren't followed." Leaning down, he brushed his lips over her forehead. "If you need the bathroom there's one just through the dining room, next to the office."

She gave a jerky nod, wiping her hands on her sweatshirt before she forced herself to head out of the kitchen.

Lian resisted the urge to yank her in his arms and offer her comfort.

She was still trembling from their nerve-shredding trip to the safe house. She needed time to gather her composure before she would be ready to accept anything from the male she no doubt held to blame for her current situation.

Completing his phone call to Raphael, he searched through the kitchen for something to make for lunch.

It would be a few hours before the nearest completely trustworthy Pantera could reach them. Until then, he intended to do his best to prove to his companion that he wasn't going to let her down again.

He'd demanded her trust.

It was time he earned it.

Opening a can of soup, he poured it into a pan and set it on the stove, then he pulled out a loaf of bread from the freezer along with sliced cheese.

He'd just laid the buttered bread in the hot skillet when Sage returned to the kitchen, her face pale but her expression calm.

"Are you hungry?" he asked, keeping himself busy as she settled on a stool that was pulled up to the breakfast bar.

The urge to touch and hold her was nearly overwhelming, but he compelled himself to be patient.

Not his finest talent.

Hell, it didn't even make the top hundred.

"Yes," she admitted. Not that she had much choice when her stomach gave a loud growl.

"How about a grilled cheese, and tomato soup?"

"You cook?"

He sent her a startled glance, the agonizing pressure in his chest faintly easing. Her teasing might be forced, but it proved she hadn't completely decided to hate him.

"Only the basics," he warned, spooning the soup into bowls as he finished browning the sandwiches and slid them onto paper plates. They were far from perfect. One side was too dark and the other barely toasted. But he couldn't deny a strange surge of pure joy as he watched her sip the soup and take a large bite of the grilled cheese. Ignoring his own food, he leaned his elbows on the counter and studied her with blatant pleasure. "To be honest, I rarely get the chance. Now I'm starting to understand why it makes my mother so happy."

She glanced up in confusion. "You are?"

"I like taking care of you," he told her in soft tones.

Her gaze dropped, a blush touching her cheeks. "I'm not a child."

His lips twisted as the violent awareness he was desperately trying to keep leashed blasted through him.

"Believe me, Dr. Parker, I'm painfully aware you're all woman."

Her blush deepened, the pulse at the base of her neck fluttering. Not fear.

Arousal.

She cleared her throat. "How long are we going to stay here?"

Unable to resist temptation, Lian reached out to touch his fingertips to that pulse, his cat purring at the blatant assurance she was far from indifferent to him.

"Until Raphael can send someone to escort us to the Wildlands." His fingers drifted down to the loose neckline of her sweatshirt. Her warm, citrus smell filled the kitchen, making him instantly hard. "I'm not going to risk trying to move you without backup."

She polished off her sandwich, trying to pretend her heart wasn't racing as his finger slipped beneath her sweatshirt to trace the line of her collarbone.

"Why do you think they followed us?"

That was the question, wasn't it? Their enemies had one purpose, and that was to return Shakpi fully to this world. So far they'd infiltrated the Wildlands, lured a handful of Pantera into becoming traitors, and tried to turn the humans against them. So attempting to predict their next move was enough to give any poor Hunter a headache.

He gave a frustrated shake of his head. "Maybe they hope to kidnap me to use as leverage in getting ahold of Shakpi. Or—"

"Or?" she prompted.

He hesitated before finishing his sentence. Sage was too intelligent not to reason out what was bothering him.

"It could be they've learned you hold the potential to translate the scrolls."

"What if I can't?" She bit her lip, the stunning gray eyes shadowed with fear.

Not for herself. But at the thought of failing his people.

With a smooth leap he was over the breakfast bar and pressing a finger to her lips.

"You will."

"You can't be sure," she protested. "My skill with languages isn't magic."

His thoughts fragmented as his finger traced the full temptation of her lips.

There were a thousand reasons his thundering need to claim this female was a bad idea.

A demented goddess who might wake at any moment. Enemies who were even now searching for them. Sage's potential position as Shaman.

Not to mention the fact that the female was still feeling vulnerable.

But nothing could convince his cat that she didn't belong in his arms...oh hell, who was he kidding?

It wasn't just his cat.

The man very much needed her stripped naked and spread beneath him.

"You're magic," he assured her, lowering his head to bury his face in the curve of her throat.

She lifted her hands to rest against his chest, but they didn't try to push him away.

"What are you doing?" she demanded.

He shuddered. The raw ferocity of his need was enough to scare him, let alone a poor female who couldn't possibly understand how quickly a Pantera could become addicted to one special partner.

"I'm sorry." He nipped at her tender flesh, his arms sliding around her to tug her off the chair and against his chest. "I know I keep pushing you, but my cat doesn't understand why it can't have a taste."

She trembled, her head tilting back to give him greater access.

"A taste of me?"

A roar of approval rumbled in his chest at the open invitation, his tongue tracing the delicate line of her throat before he indulged in another nip.

The delicious, lemony taste of her exploded on his tongue. His hunger spiked. Oh, man. He was going to *devour* her.

"Maybe more than just a taste," he warned, the image of her spread across the breakfast bar searing through his mind.

She grabbed his T-shirt, as if her knees were threatening to collapse.

"Lian," she breathed.

He nuzzled the sensitive spot just below her ear. "Tell me no and I'll stop."

"And if I don't say no?"

Chapter Five

SAGE felt Lian stiffen, clearly shocked by her low words.

Hell, *she* was shocked.

She was the typical scholar.

Introverted, socially awkward, and embarrassingly timid when it came to flirting.

But somehow this man managed to bring out a side of her she didn't even know existed.

When she was with Lian she wanted to be the sort of bold, daring, sexually exciting woman who could drive a man crazy. It didn't make sense. Certainly not when they were virtually strangers.

But in this moment, she didn't care.

She'd been alone for so long.

Too long.

Now her entire body hummed with a desire that she refused to deny.

Lifting his head, Lian searched her upturned face with a wary expression. She sensed that he expected her to have a sudden panic attack.

Not surprising.

She'd never been particularly courageous. Nothing at all like the Pantera females who he no doubt usually chose as his lovers.

The thought only stiffened her spine.

He gently cupped her cheek in his palm, his thumb stroking her lower lip.

"You're stressed."

His senses were too acute for her to lie.

"True."

Regret scorched through his golden eyes. "And I'm taking advantage."

She frowned, rebelling at the realization he thought she was too weak to say 'no' to his seduction.

Dammit.

She might not be Xena warrior woman, but she wasn't spineless.

Fisting his shirt in her hands, she went on tiptoe to kiss him with a blatant need.

"I might not be a Pantera Hunter, but I'm not completely helpless," she warned, biting his lower lip hard enough to make him hiss with pleasure. "If I wanted to stop you, I would."

A sudden heat blasted from his body, his hesitation forgotten as his eyes glowed with a golden fire.

"Ah yes, I'd nearly forgotten your little trick of trapping me in that net." A slow, sinful smile touched his mouth as his arms tightened around her. "Someday you're going to pay for that."

The tension that had gripped her since being forced from her home was seared away as she arched into the hard warmth of his body.

"It isn't my only trick," she whispered, rewarded for her bashful flirtation when he gave a soft purr of appreciation and abruptly swept her off her feet.

"I have a few of my own," he promised, rubbing his cheek against the top of her head.

Sometimes he was such a cat.

"Where are we going?"

"I need to have you someplace more comfortable."

She wrapped her arms around his neck, vaguely aware of the glossy paneling and tiled floors as he headed toward the stairs at the back of the home. She'd already discovered when she went in search of the bathroom that the house was beautifully maintained, despite the appearance from the outside, with all the modern conveniences a person could want. Now she had far more important things to occupy her mind.

They entered the nearest bedroom that was decorated in a pale ivory and lilac. Without hesitation Lian was crossing the floor and lowering her onto the massive four-poster bed.

Sage's heart thundered in her chest, the spicy scent of his musk stirring her arousal until she could feel a damp heat bloom between her legs.

Straightening, Lian stared down at her, his entire body Hunter-still as he studied her with a predatory gaze.

She shivered, her mouth dry. Everything about this man screamed danger, but she'd never been more excited in her life.

"You have me more comfortable," she husked, the anticipation flowing through her like the finest aphrodisiac. "Now what are you going to do to me?"

"First I'm going to strip off these highly unnecessary clothes."

Moving to plant one knee on the side of the mattress, Lian leaned down to grasp the hem of her sweatshirt, tugging it over her head with a smooth motion. He offered her a boyish grin of satisfaction as he easily performed the same service for the rest of her clothes, revealing that this was far from the first time he'd stripped a woman.

But once she was stretched naked on the lilac comforter his amusement faded, to be replaced with an expression of savage ferocity.

"Oh shit," he muttered.

She licked her lips, struggling to breathe. God. She needed to feel his hands on her skin.

It was becoming a near painful force.

"Is something wrong?"

"Hell no," he growled, his heated gaze inspecting her with unnerving intensity. "You're perfect."

"Aren't you going to take off your clothes?" she urged in husky tones.

As if sensing she wasn't as bold as she wanted him to believe, Lian swiftly stripped off his clothing, standing in front of her like a bronzed, exquisitely sculpted work of art.

Her eyes widened. God almighty. She'd never seen anything more beautiful. He was all male. A feral animal with his broad chest that tapered to a narrow waist and the long, muscular legs.

On his upper right shoulder she could glimpse a stylized tattoo of a crouching puma that looked ready to pounce.

And then there was the proud thrust of his arousal...

Her stomach clenched, her breath hissing between her teeth.

Okay. She needed this man.

Now.

"Better?" he murmured, watching as she stirred with restless frustration.

Daringly she patted the mattress. "You should be here."

"Soon," he assured her, placing a hand next to her head as he leaned over her. "First I intend to lick you from head to toe."

"That sounds—"

Her words were forgotten as his lips captured the hard point of her nipple.

She gasped as his tongue flicked over the tender tip, teasing her until she was arching in need. Good lord. She'd never felt anything so amazing.

It was as if she'd waited her entire life for his touch.

Licking and biting his way to her other breast, he reached up to tug her hair out of the rubber band to allow it to tumble over her shoulders.

Instantly his fingers smoothed through the silvery strands.

"Such glorious hair," he sighed. "Like liquid moonlight."

"Can I feel yours?"

The gold of his eyes darkened, his cat lurking just beneath the surface.

"God, yes," he pleaded.

He held perfectly still as she slowly undid the long braid, delighting in the midnight texture.

"It's soft," she said in a wondering tone. "And it smells like musk."

She combed her fingers through the long strands, allowing it to brush over her naked skin. The sensation triggered a low groan of approval from her parted lips.

"You smell like summer. Warm days and lemonade," he breathed, his hands tracing a scorching path over her body even as his teeth sank into the base of her throat.

The feel of his bite should have shocked her.

Instead she squeezed her eyes shut as her back arched with excitement.

"Lian," she cried out.

"I told you I was going to taste you." He returned his attention to her breast, tormenting the tip with his tongue as his hand eased between her legs. "Slowly." One finger slid between her slick folds. "Thoroughly."

"Does it have to be slow?" she rasped as he pressed his thumb against her clit.

"Oh sweetheart, we can go any speed you want later." He used the edge of his teeth to bite her nipple before he soothed the small pain with nuzzling kisses. "But this first time I want to savor."

Her hips instinctively lifted off the mattress as his finger slid into her aching body, his thumb rubbing her sensitive bundle of nerves at a steady pace.

"Savoring is good," she decided, her voice thick with need.

He gave a soft chuckle. "Just good?"

She tentatively slid her hand down his back, fascinated by the heated silk of his skin. She hadn't expected fur. Not in his human form. But who knew that he would be so smooth? And hard. And delectable.

"Maybe excellent," she conceded.

"Maybe?" Nuzzling a path up her neck, he teased the corner of her mouth before he kissed her, a stark demand. Sage melted, allowing her tongue to tangle with his as his finger thrust deep inside her. "I see you're one of those tough professors," he at last whispered against her lips. "What does it take to get an A from you?"

Sage scraped her nails over the rippling muscles of his back, delighted when he shuddered in pleasure.

She could have told him that the few classes that she taught online had earned her the nickname 'Hard-Ass Parker.' Right now, however, she was fully prepared to be generous.

Especially as he kissed a path down to her aching breasts, giving each nipple a lingering caress before heading ever lower.

"Sometimes I grade on the curve," she assured him.

He glanced up, his eyes smoldering with a hunger that sent a thrill of anticipation inching down her spine.

"A challenge," he said, his expression one of wicked promise.

Sage tried to swallow, her body vibrating with an acute tension.

"Not really—" Her words broke off in a strangled cry as his lips skimmed down the flat plane of her stomach. Her fingers clenched in his hair, her muscles trembling with delicious anticipation. "Oh."

He traced the curve of her hip, the abrasive sensation of his five o'clock shadow against her skin oddly erotic.

"I thought some extra credit would help."

"It's—" She hissed as settled between her legs and licked the liquid heat that pooled in her pussy.

Raw lust blasted through her, making her toes curl and her thoughts fracture.

"Yes?" he teased, tugging her legs farther apart.

"Stop talking," she commanded, sliding her foot down his bare back.

His eyes sparkled with mischievous humor. "Yes, Dr. Parker. I was always better with my hands." Another mind-destroying lick. "And tongue."

Oh, yeah. He was really, really good with his tongue, she silently applauded.

Running her foot up and down his back, she groaned in pleasure as he fucked her with his finger at the same time he licked her clit with skillful expertise.

She writhed beneath him, desire spiraling toward a critical peak.

"Lian," she hissed in warning.

Easily sensing she was close, Lian kissed his way back up her body, balancing on his elbows as he peered down at her.

"I see your cat," she murmured, hypnotized by the feral wildness that lurked deep in his eyes.

"And he sees you." His voice was rough as his animal prowled near the surface. "He wants you in the worst way. Are you ready?"

She groaned, her hands cupping his face as she allowed him to see the depth of her need.

"So ready," she rasped, not about to confess that after years of celibacy she'd been ready for him the instant he'd snuck into her cottage.

That was just…pathetic.

"Thank god. I don't think I can wait another second," he confessed, his musk teasing at her senses. "You've gutted me, Dr. Parker."

Her fingers explored the chiseled line of his jaw before moving down to chart the broad width of his shoulders.

"Is that bad?"

He pressed a kiss to her forehead. "We're both about to find out."

Even prepared, Sage cried out as he angled his hips and pierced her with one smooth thrust. Good lord. She felt invaded. Stretched to the limit, until she slowly became accustomed to his large cock.

She grasped his shoulders, shivering as his hair slid around them like a curtain of satin as he rocked in and out of her, each time thrusting deeper.

It was slow and tender and shockingly intimate.

She was being overwhelmed by Lian, lost in the heat and beauty of the moment.

The thought should have terrified her. She was a reclusive spinster who never allowed anyone close. But at this moment she wanted—no, she *needed*—to share herself on a primitive level.

Muttering low words of encouragement as she lifted her hips to meet his growingly urgent thrusts, Lian cupped her breasts, using his thumbs to tease at her nipples.

Sage groaned, digging her nails into his shoulders as he hit a magical spot that made her gasp as shocking pleasure jolted through her.

"Lian."

"I've got you, sweetheart," he muttered against her mouth, his body pressing even deeper.

She struggled to breathe.

She was close.

So deliciously close.

His hands lowered to grasp her legs, urging them around his hips as he pounded into her. At the same time, he buried his face in the curve of her neck, sinking his teeth into the tender flesh.

She screamed as her orgasm slammed into her with shattering force at the same time Lian groaned and released his seed deep inside her.

Bliss splintered through her before she was slowly floating back to earth, wrapping her arms around Lian.

She held him close, wishing this moment never had to end.

For the first time in forever, she wasn't alone.

———

Lian reluctantly pulled out of Sage's body, pressing his lips to the mark he'd made on her neck before he was gently gathering her boneless body into his arms.

Gutted indeed, he wryly conceded.

It wasn't just the savage ferocity of their lovemaking.

That had been...spectacularly fantastic. And he fully intended to indulge his sexual hunger as frequently as Sage was willing.

But it was the soul-deep realization that destiny had just crashed down on him that made him smile in wonderment.

His mate.

His cat had known from the minute he'd caught her citrusy scent, although his human nature had taken just a little longer.

It was, after all, a life-changing event.

Now both sides were in perfect agreement.

This woman belonged to him.

And he was never going to let her go.

Silently running his fingers through the silken strands of her hair, he contemplated how long he had to wait before informing her that she was fated to spend the rest of her life with him, when the chime of his phone made him groan in frustration.

Reluctantly releasing his hold on Sage, Lian rolled off the mattress and dug his phone out of the pocket of his jeans.

"Damn," he muttered, reading the text message.

Sitting up, Sage modestly tugged the sheet up to her chin. As if he hadn't kissed every satin inch of her pale skin.

"What's wrong?" she asked.

"Our escorts are almost here."

A satisfying hint of disappointment darkened her eyes to charcoal.

"So soon?"

"They were coming from Bossier City," he said, not sharing the information that they'd been traveling through the south to gather families of the Pantera and return them to the Wildlands.

He'd already terrified her enough, thank you very fucking much.

"Oh."

Lian watched in amusement as she scrambled off the bed and hastily began to jerk on her clothes.

Clearly she was embarrassed by the thought of getting caught in bed during the middle of the day.

He dressed at a much more leisurely pace, anticipating the pleasure of challenging that modesty on a regular basis.

Not that he would ever change her.

His shy, scholarly beauty was perfect.

But Pantera were openly affectionate creatures who craved touch from their mates. And of course, his family was extremely high maintenance when it came to demanding attention.

It was going to be interesting to watch her adapt.

Crossing the short space, he smoothed her hair behind her ears and dropped a kiss on her forehead.

"It's okay. They're going to wait for us in the garage," he assured her, a stab of fear twisting his heart as he felt her stiffen beneath his touch. Lifting his head, he studied her with a growing concern. "Hey, are you okay?"

Her lashes lowered to hide her expressive eyes. "Why wouldn't I be?"

Blatant deflection.

His thumbs brushed the inside of her wrists, monitoring the unsteady pulse.

"Because we both know things just changed between us," he said, unwilling to try to pretend their time together was anything less than life-altering.

She kept her head lowered. "I don't know what you're talking about."

He clicked his tongue, releasing her hands so he could gently tip her face up to meet his wry smile.

"For the record, you're a piss-poor liar."

She heaved a small sigh. "I need time to…process."

He wrinkled his nose, sliding a finger down the length of her jaw. "I'm pushing again."

"Yes."

"Sorry."

She arched a brow, her lips twitching with a burst of humor. "No, you aren't."

Relief jolted through him. She might be stunned by the force of their attraction, but she wasn't frightened.

At least not yet.

"Busted," he admitted with a chuckle, rubbing their noses together. "It's my nature to go for the kill, but anytime you need me to back down just tell me, sweetheart." He stole a soft, lingering kiss. "I don't ever want you to feel overwhelmed."

"Hmm." She gave a tug on his hair. "I suspect you overwhelm most people."

True. He didn't have the brooding intensity of a Raphael or Parish, but his feral power tended to make most people avoid pissing him off.

"Not you," he swore, holding her gaze. "Never you."

Unexpectedly she reached up to thread her fingers through his hair that he hadn't bothered to braid.

Hell, he might never braid it again if Sage liked it loose.

And if that made him pussy-whipped...good.

"Only in the best way," she assured him in husky tones.

On cue his entire body went up in flames, his erection pressing painfully against his zipper.

"Oh hell, Dr. Parker, you might be a genius, but your timing sucks," he growled, wrapping his arms around her so he could press her tight against his aching cock. Then, knowing it was going to leave his balls blue, he kissed her with an urgency that had both of them panting before he reluctantly released his tight hold and headed toward the door. "Wait here," he muttered.

Promising himself an entire month alone with Sage once the scrolls were translated and the threat from Shakpi ended, Lian made his way through the safe house into the attached garage.

He caught the scent of the waiting Hunters before he ever pushed open the door. Which meant he was prepared to discover Mercier standing in the center of the cement floor. The dark, sable-eyed male had a broad, heavily muscular body that was currently covered by a white tee and camo pants. It took a second, however, to locate the other Hunter who was hidden beneath Jean-Baptiste's Lamborghini.

"Any problems?" he asked Mercier, ignoring the older male's narrow-eyed gaze.

There was no disguising the scent of sex that clung to his body, but he wasn't prepared to discuss his bonding with Sage. Not until she'd accepted that she belonged to him.

With a shrug, Mercier conceded to the unspoken warning.

"Nothing obvious, but..." The male scowled, giving a shake of his head. "Something's out there."

Lian knew exactly what he was talking about. It wasn't a precise smell, or a tangible sound. Just a vague sense they were being watched.

"Yeah, I'm getting the same vibe," he muttered.

Dammit. He wasn't afraid of his enemies. But how the hell did you fight them when they lurked in the shadows?

There was a muffled growl before Rosalie was sliding from beneath the car, holding her hand up.

"I found it," the tall, golden-haired beauty proclaimed, her pure green eyes smoldering with grim satisfaction.

The two males moved to inspect the tiny tracking device that'd been hidden on the undercarriage.

"Shit," Lian muttered, wondering if it'd been attached to the car while he was at The Cougar's Den or if it had happened while he was in Sage's cottage. Either way, he now knew how they'd followed him. "That didn't come from Radio Shack."

"No." Mercier's expression was hard as he plucked the device from Rosalie's fingers to inspect it with an expert eye. He was one of the Hunters who worked closely with the Geeks to develop weapons to protect themselves in the event the magic surrounding the Wildlands ever failed. "Military grade."

"Our enemies seem to have stepped up their game," Rosalie said, her puzzled expression reflecting her companion's growing confusion.

The disciples of Shakpi had always shown a preference for low tech, using the mystic power of their evil goddess to destroy the Pantera.

When had they gained access to this sort of equipment?

Lian made a sound of annoyance. "What the hell are they up to?"

"I don't intend to find out," Mercier snapped, taking charge. "Rosalie and I will drive your car along with the tracker and head west. Wait an hour, then go south with your cargo," he commanded. "We'll meet you back at the Wildlands."

Lian resisted the urge to argue. As much as he hated putting anyone else in danger, he had to concentrate on making sure that Sage was safe.

Besides, there were few things the two Hunters couldn't handle.

"Don't take any unnecessary risks," he ordered.

"*Moi?*" Mercier widened his eyes with a faux innocence. "Would I do that?"

"Don't worry," Rosalie said before Lian could remind his fellow Hunter of the day he'd leaped in front of a human poacher who'd been about to shoot a red fox who was nursing her young. Mercier had taken the shot to his chest, but had never halted as he grabbed the gun from the human and broke it in two. "He does anything stupid and I'll put his balls in a vise."

Mercier sent his a companion a heated glance. "I have a better place for my balls."

Rosalie leaned forward to nip the male's chin with an astonishingly intimate gesture.

"Keep it up and you won't have any," she warned in a throaty voice.

"Ouch," Mercier breathed, looking as shell-shocked as Lian felt.

Holy hell.

He hadn't seen that coming.

"Just be careful," he said, not surprised that neither noticed when he walked out of the garage and headed back to his waiting mate.

CHAPTER SIX

THE morning sunlight streamed through the open windows as Sage made her way down the narrow staircase of the large three-story house.

It'd only been two days since she'd arrived at the Wildlands, but she'd already been overwhelmingly welcomed into Lian's family, even as he'd been condemned to reside at the communal home of unmated Hunters.

She smiled at the sound of half a dozen voices all speaking at once that greeted her before she ever stepped into the large kitchen.

She'd lived alone for so long the noise and constant chaos that filled the Pantera home should have been overwhelming. And, at times, she couldn't deny it did make her head spin. But overall, she savored the warmth and companionship that surrounded her.

Sensing her arrival, the crowd of people that included Lian's grandparents, his parents, his eldest sister and her mate, all turned to regard her with blatant interest.

"Here she is," the silver-haired grandmother said, wiping her hands on a flower-patterned apron.

Lian's father moved forward to press a cup into her hand, his lean face that reminded her strongly of his son wreathed with a kind smile.

"Your coffee, just as you like it."

She wrapped her hands around the cup, a dangerous stab of pleasure warming her heart.

No one had ever known how she took her coffee.

Not ever.

"Thank you." She sipped the hot liquid. "It's perfect."

Lian's mother wasn't about to be outdone as she handed Sage a large bagel that was fresh from the oven.

"And a warm bagel to tide you over until breakfast," she said.

Lian's sister had the same dark hair and eyes as her brother although her face was far more rounded, with pretty features. Currently she was standing at the stove, frying bacon.

"Yes, we had to hold back the meal until Lian could get here," she informed Sage.

Sage's brief sense of cozy comfort was shattered.

Being surrounded by his family had offered her an unexpected comfort, but spending time with Lian was just the opposite.

The minute he walked into one of the shabbily comfortable rooms her entire body prickled with a fierce awareness that was downright embarrassing. For god's sake, everyone in the house could catch the scent of her arousal.

It was humiliating.

And worse, she was beginning to feel as if something vital was missing when he wasn't nearby.

How could he have become such an important part of her life in just a few days?

It was obvious she needed to limit the time they spent in each other's company.

"Oh, he's coming for breakfast?" she asked in what she hoped was a casual tone.

Lian's mother sent her a teasing grin. "After being on duty during dinner last night you didn't think he would miss the opportunity to see you first thing this morning?"

"That boy can't keep himself away," Lian's father agreed.

"Like you could?" The silver-haired grandmother gave a roll of her eyes. "I remember having to lock the windows at night to keep you out of the house."

With an unrepentant grin the male moved to wrap his arm around his mate's shoulders.

"How could I resist?" He pressed a kiss to her dark hair. "She's still the prettiest girl in the Wildlands."

Lian's mother tilted her head back, regarding her mate with an open devotion that made Sage's heart ache.

"Flattery will get you whatever you want, my love."

Sage backed toward the door. "You know, I think I should be working on those scrolls."

"But what about breakfast?" Lian's sister demanded.

She took another step back. And another. "This bagel is really enough, thank you."

"Lian is going to be disappointed," his mother sighed.

"Nonsense. He's a cat. He likes the chase," his father announced, sending a Sage a nod of approval. "Smart girl."

Sage gave a choked cough, her entire body sizzling at the thought of being chased by the dangerous puma.

"Yes…well, I'll see you later."

Turning on her heel, Sage bolted from the house, swiftly making her way to the communal center.

The first day she'd been amazed by just how civilized the Wildlands truly was.

The few books that had mentioned the Pantera implied that they were savages who lived like animals in the bayous.

Nothing could be further from the truth.

There might be a large part of the secluded lands that remained gloriously untamed, but the Pantera lived in beautiful homes that were cleverly built to incorporate the thick cypress trees, and were draped with Spanish moss. There was also a communal area where the land had been cleared to create a manicured park where they shared meals or enjoyed lazy games.

Perhaps most shockingly, there was a modern medical facility, a guest house, and a mansion straight out of "Gone With the Wind" that served as the headquarters for the Diplomats as well as the computer whizzes known as Geeks.

She'd been amazed when she'd entered the large plantation-style structure with fluted columns to discover it was filled with high-tech computers and monitoring equipment.

Thankfully, she'd been shown to the top floor that held the Pantera's most fragile books and scrolls. She wasn't a complete idiot when it came to technology, but she preferred to feel the weight and texture of a book. To smell the leather and dust and crumbling paper.

It was like holding history in her hands.

As she entered this morning, however, she was careful to spread the five ancient scrolls across the long table that Xavier had shoved to the middle of the wooden floor.

Not only was the fraying linen too fragile to be handled more than necessary, but she'd at last realized that the scrolls weren't individual texts, but instead, they were each a part of a whole.

Now a sense of…rightness…flowed through her as she studied the lines of glyphs.

It wasn't just her years of research, or even a natural intelligence that allowed her to decipher complex symbols.

She possessed an instinctive gift that went way beyond most scholars.

Yet another secret she kept hidden.

Losing track of time, she was bent over the scrolls when a low, male voice whispered directly in her ear, shattering her concentration.

"Any luck?"

Straightening, she turned to discover Lian standing mere inches away. Instantly her heart lodged in her throat and a vicious hunger twisted her gut.

Even after three days in the company of the large, outrageously gorgeous man, the sight of him was still a punch to her gut.

It wasn't just the perfect, bronzed features, or the whiskey-gold eyes that smoldered with wicked charm, or even the chiseled body she seriously wanted to lick from head to toe.

It was the sheer…maleness that stirred her on a primitive level.

She wanted to crawl into his arms and never leave.

And the knowledge scared the hell out of her.

Not because she thought he would ever hurt her. She understood the dark possessiveness that he felt for her would ensure he'd always protect her, even from himself.

But her past had taught her that she was asking for pain to open herself to another.

People left. They always left.

And then she was alone.

Far better to keep her heart well-guarded.

And of course, there was that embarrassing problem of wanting to climb on top of him the minute she caught sight of him.

It took only a glance, however, to realize that Lian had reached the end of his patience.

"You startled me," she muttered, absently pulling off the gloves she always used when dealing with fragile texts.

"Sorry." He crowded her against the edge of the table, his finger reaching to smooth a stray curl behind her ear. "I did knock."

She sucked in a deep breath, savoring the spicy musk that sent heat jolting through her body.

Good lord. If he could bottle that scent and sell it as an aphrodisiac he could make a bazillion dollars.

She cleared her throat. "I tend to become lost in my research."

His lips twitched, his fingers stroking a decadent line of fire down her throat.

"Lost or hidden?"

She stiffened. Did he know she was deliberately trying to keep a distance between them?

"I don't know what you're talking about," she tried to hedge.

His fingers circled her neck, blatant ownership in his light grasp.

"I warned you that you're a terrible liar, Dr. Parker." He brushed his lips over her forehead. "Not that I blame you. My family can be—"

"Terrifying?" She cowardly latched onto his unintentional excuse for her elusive behavior.

"That's one way of putting it," he said wryly.

She felt an instant pang of guilt. "They're very kind," she forced herself to admit. It was the truth, after all. "And they've made me feel very welcome."

His lips skimmed down the narrow length of her nose. "Yes, they adore you, but they tend to overwhelm the unwary."

She shivered, her hands clenching against the temptation to run her fingers through the long, glossy strands of his dark hair.

Why did he leave it free to flow down his back? It was a constant temptation.

"Is there something you needed?"

"Just to be near you," he said with his usual blunt honesty. Then he held up a hand that held a wicker basket. "And to bring you this."

Suddenly Sage's stomach growled as she was hit by the most delicious aromas.

Spice, and shrimp, and vegetables combined with a heady scent of freshly baked bread.

"It smells divine."

"My mother's gumbo and corn pone, still warm from the oven," he revealed. "She was concerned that you didn't eat enough breakfast."

"I wanted to get back to work," she said, turning to point at the scrolls she'd unrolled and aligned side by side. "During the night I realized that I'd been looking at the hieroglyphs all wrong. You see, it doesn't read from top to bottom, but across each scroll."

"Fascinating," he murmured.

She glanced up to discover him studying her with an unwavering focus.

"You're not even looking."

"Of course I am." Hunger shimmered in his eyes as they lowered to her lips. The air prickled with a heated arousal as he grabbed her hand and led her across the floor and through the French doors. "I just happen to be interested in something other than musty scrolls."

"Lian, I'm supposed to be translating," she protested even as she crossed the balcony and allowed herself to be seated at the small wrought iron table.

He efficiently emptied the wicker basket, taking the lids off the bowls of steaming gumbo and divvying up the corn pone. Then, pouring them each a glass of wine, he settled in the chair next to her.

"I admire your dedication, Dr. Parker," he said, taking a sip of the wine, the gentle breeze tugging at his hair. Even in the afternoon sunlight he looked dark and dangerous and entirely edible. "And I swear I'll do my best to give you all the freedom you need to pursue your interests so long as you give me permission to distract you when I think you need a break."

Anticipation licked through her body. "What sort of distraction?"

A slow, sinful smile curved his lips as he easily caught the scent of her arousal.

"First, we eat."

Sage sucked in a deep breath, grabbing for her spoon.

Yeah. Eat.

No jumping on top of the yummy Pantera and having her wicked way with him...

Concentrating on the food, Sage cleared her plate, giving a small groan at the savory burst of flavors. After years of surviving on salads and frozen dinners she could pop in the microwave it was a delight to indulge her senses with homemade meals.

Watching her lick her fingers with obvious satisfaction, Lian lounged back in his chair.

A big, lazy cat with the eyes of a lethal predator.

"More wine?" he asked.

"No." With an abrupt motion she was on her feet. She wanted to rub her cheek over his unshaven jaw so badly it was a physical pain. "I'll fall asleep."

With a fluid motion he was standing next to her, threading their fingers together.

"I know how to wake you up."

Instead of heading back inside, he pulled her toward the edge of the house where a narrow staircase led from the balcony to the ground.

Sage frowned, but made no effort to pull away. "Where are we going?"

"I intend to take you on a tour of the Wildlands." He led her away from the communal area into the lush vegetation of the wetlands. "It's too beautiful a day to be locked inside."

"I'm really close to a breakthrough on the scrolls," she weakly protested.

He shrugged, following the narrow path that weaved between the cypress trees.

"An hour or so away from them will help you clear your mind."

"But I thought you brought me here to decipher the scrolls?"

"I did."

"And now you want me—"

"Yes." He came to an abrupt halt, bracing Sage as she slammed into his hard body. Framing her face in his hands, he regarded her with the raw hunger that made her toes curl. "I want you." His fingers traced down her cheeks and along the line of her jaw. "Your delectable body. Your daunting brain." He offered a rueful smile. "Your wary heart."

An aching need raced through her.

She wanted to believe.

She truly did.

But...

"Lian."

He leaned down to press a tender kiss to her lips before straightening and once again grabbing her hand so he could lead her forward.

"Today, however, all I ask is that you come and play with me."

Sage swallowed a sigh.

213

How could she resist?

Her logic might warn she was bound to regret giving into temptation, but her heart was demanding she savor every moment she could spend with this man.

"You are a very bad influence," she muttered.

He flashed her a grin that could make her bones melt.

"Sometimes very bad can be very good."

No. Shit.

She gave up any hope of being sensible, instead allowing herself to be led astray by her naughty cat.

"Where are we going?" she at last asked.

"Someplace my family won't find us." An edge of a growl was in his voice. "As much as I love them I'm tired of having a constant chaperone. I want to be alone with you."

With one last tug of her hand, he urged her through a swathe of Spanish moss and into a small meadow.

"Oh," she breathed, taking in the narrow channel of water that was spanned by a wooden bridge. "It's beautiful."

Lian stood at her side, his hand skimming up and down her back. "Can you feel it?"

She tilted her head to meet his watchful gaze. "Feel what?"

"The magic."

She frowned. "I'm not Pantera."

"Just feel," he urged softly.

She parted her lips to argue, only to snap them shut as she realized that she could feel...

Something.

The warmth of the sun. The breeze that brushed her skin. The spongy ground beneath her feet.

And an unmistakable tingle that filled her body.

Easily sensing the second she accepted the truth of his words, Lian moved toward the middle of the meadow.

"Now watch," he urged.

Sage's eyes widened as a shimmering mist suddenly surrounded Lian's large body, the air filled with a burst of heat that made her take an instinctive step backward.

Holding her breath, she pressed a hand to her heart as the mist slowly cleared to reveal a huge cat with fur as black as ebony and whiskey-gold eyes.

He was beautiful.

Proud. Powerful. Primitive.

For a breathless moment he held himself still, perhaps waiting to see if she would run away screaming in terror.

But Sage wasn't frightened.

She felt nothing but awe as she dropped to her knees and held her arms open in invitation. Slowly Lian prowled forward, nudging her with his wet nose.

Wrapping her arms around his neck, she stared directly into the eyes that held the essence of the man who'd stolen her heart.

"I see you," she whispered.

Parting his jaws, he released a roar that shook the earth.

———

An hour after luring Sage from her work, Lian grudgingly allowed her to leave the meadow.

As much as he was enjoying their rare time alone, he understood that his people were desperate for a way to halt Shakpi's determination to destroy them. If the scrolls had the slightest potential to offer them hope, then he couldn't allow his selfish desires to stand in the way.

And just as importantly, he understood his sweet, serious scholar.

He could momentarily distract her, but her clever mind wasn't going to be satisfied until she'd achieved the goal of translating the hieroglyphs.

It would take time to thoroughly corrupt her.

She was disappearing through the Spanish moss when a tall male with golden hair and gold eyes flecked with jade appeared from the opposite direction.

Raphael was the head of the Suits, and father to the first baby born to the Pantera in the past fifty years.

"I heard your female was a beauty, but I didn't realize she carried the gift of our ancestors."

Lian sent his friend a startled glance.

He'd been careful not to share his belief that Sage was a potential Shaman, although he was certain his family already suspected the truth.

But it was a shock that his companion had noticed from a mere glance across a meadow.

Either Raphael was a mind reader, or Sage's powers were growing now that she was in the Wildlands.

He was betting on Sage's magic becoming more pronounced.

"I suspected, but I couldn't be certain," he confessed.

The golden gaze narrowed. "Does she know?"

"She accepts that she has powers that she doesn't fully understand," he said, forcing himself not to follow as she disappeared from view.

Dammit. He'd promised he'd give her the space she needed to finish her work.

Raphael moved so he was standing directly in front of Lian, his smile wry as if he understood how difficult it was for the younger male to concentrate on anything but his mate.

"So why don't you explain it to her?"

Lian grimaced, reaching into the pocket of his jeans for the narrow leather string. He'd left his hair down because he knew that Sage enjoyed running her fingers through the long strands.

And he'd do anything to please her.

Now he wanted it out of his way.

"In the past few days I've stolen Sage from her home, placed the fate of our people on her shoulders and discovered that she's my mate. That doesn't even include being mauled by my family." He

216

gave a short, humorless laugh, tying off the braid. "I think we can wait a few days to dump more surprises on her."

Raphael nodded, one of the few who understood. His own mate, Ashe, had gone through her own shocking transformation.

"She's stronger than you think," he assured Lian.

"I don't want her to *have* to be strong."

"Anyone who has to deal with you and your family will need a spine of steel."

Lian's lips twitched. "I suppose that's true enough," he said. He suspected that Sage was already bonding with his family, but she would have to develop well-defined boundaries if she didn't want them running her life. "Tell me what's going on."

Raphael's face hardened to a grim mask. "Mercier and Rosalie are missing."

"Fuck," Lian snarled, his gut clenching with a combination of fear and fury. As Hunters they understood that their duty was to put themselves in danger when necessary. But that knowledge didn't stop Lian from feeling a savage stab of guilt at their disappearance. "When was the last time you heard from them?"

"Yesterday morning," Raphael said. "They checked in from Dallas."

"And?"

"They said they were at the safe house and intended to return to the Wildlands last night." Raphael's eyes glowed with the power of his cat. "They never showed."

"You think our enemy has them?" he asked, even knowing the question was ridiculous.

Mercier and Rosalie would have contacted Parish if they were going to be late.

No way in hell they would just have dropped out of contact.

"What other explanation—" Raphael's words broke off on a low growl, his claws piercing his skin as a foul odor filled the meadow. "Do you smell that?"

The stench was impossible to miss.

It warned their enemies were near.

"Intruders?" he muttered, his gaze searching the shadows between the trees.

"No. Shakpi." Raphael sent him a warning frown. Your Shaman just ran out of time."

God. Damn.

Could they just once get a break?

Lian shook his head, frustration a toxic knot in the pit of his stomach.

"The translations aren't done."

Raphael flexed his claws. "I'll try to slow her down, but we need a miracle to stop her from escaping."

There was a burst of mist and sparkling colors as Raphael shifted into a massive puma with caramel fur and golden eyes.

Lian didn't bother to watch Raphael bound across the meadow toward the cabin where they'd stashed Chayton's unconscious body.

He was already headed toward the Suits' headquarters. Once he'd checked in with Sage he would join Raphael in his battle to try and halt the goddess from escaping the Wildlands.

Reaching the large mansion he released his claws and climbed the post of the balcony. Then, vaulting over the edge of the balustrade he was bursting through the French doors.

Sage had clearly just entered the room, the white gloves dropping from her hands as she caught sight of his somber expression.

"Lian, what is it?" She crossed the floor to stand directly in front of him. "What's wrong?"

"Shakpi is awake."

She made a sound of shock, her head turning to glance toward the scrolls neatly laid out on the table.

"She can't be," she argued. "It's too soon."

"Look at me, sweetheart," he commanded, cupping her cheek with his hand and urging her back to meet his searching gaze. "Have you discovered anything that can help us?"

She bit her bottom lip. "I'm just now learning how to translate the symbols to sounds."

"What does that mean?"

"I can phonetically pronounce the glyphs, but I don't know what they mean." Distress darkened her eyes to slate. "I'm sorry. I failed you."

His brows snapped together as he wrapped her in his arms and rubbed his cheek on top of her head.

Dammit. It was bad enough he'd thrown her into the middle of their war with the evil goddess. He wouldn't have her blaming herself for something that wasn't her fault. Especially when he was the one who'd lured her away from her work.

"Don't say that," he chided. "Even if Shakpi escapes, these scrolls might help us prepare our defenses." Lifting his head, he peered down at her pale face. "We need you, Dr. Parker."

She gave a small nod, then abruptly wrinkled her nose as a blast of putrid air swept through the open French doors.

"Good lord, what is that?" she muttered.

Grabbing Sage's arm, he gave her a push toward the far door. "Run."

"What?" She dug in her heels, looking at him as if he'd lost his mind.

She wasn't wrong.

The mere thought that Shakpi was headed in this direction was enough to send him over the edge.

The evil bitch was supposed to be trying to escape.

It's what she'd done the first time they'd tried to hold her captive.

Snatching the phone from his pocket, he sent a quick message to his mother.

"Go to my family," he rasped. "They'll take you back to your home."

She was shaking her head before he ever finished speaking. "No, I'm not leaving you."

He glanced over his shoulder, a shudder of revulsion wracking his body as Shakpi reached the edge of the clearing.

"Don't be stubborn." He jerked his attention back to the female who was making his heart squeeze with terror. He could face a thousand crazy-ass goddesses before he could contemplate the thought of Sage in danger for even a second. "There's nothing you can do here."

Her chin tilted. "I'm not helpless."

He fisted his hands. Where the hell was this coming from?

He was impulsive and always ready to dive into danger headfirst. Sage was supposed to be the sensible, cautious, blessedly logical one.

"You can't stop a goddess," he pointed out in rough tones.

She remained stubbornly in place. "Can you?"

"Sage."

Without warning, she moved forward, going on her tiptoes to press a kiss to his lips.

It was a gentle caress laced with the promise of a future.

Oh...hell.

"You do what you do and let me do what I do," she commanded in soft tones.

In that second, she could have ordered him to stop the world from turning and he'd have done everything in his power to fulfill her wish.

Accepting he'd lost this particular battle, he turned to run out of room, shifting into his cat as he sailed over the railing of the balcony and prepared to battle a goddess.

CHAPTER SEVEN

SAGE ran her fingers over the glyphs, desperately trying to ignore the vicious roars and occasional snarls of pain that filled the air.

She didn't have claws or teeth. Or even a damned gun.

For now, the only way to help Lian was by concentrating on the scrolls.

She was so close, the symbols forming into words in her head as a tingle of power raced through her blood.

This wasn't a history of the Pantera as she'd first assumed. Or even a detailed explanation of how to destroy Shakpi as Lian had hoped.

This was...magic.

Lost in her thoughts, Sage didn't sense the approaching man until he lightly tapped on her shoulder.

She jerked her head around to discover a tall man with milky brown skin, blue eyes and dark hair that was closely buzzed to his scalp.

Xavier was the Geek she'd been in cyber contact with for the past four years. Of course, she'd assumed he was another researcher, not a mythical puma shifter.

"What are you doing?" the man snapped, his expression grim as he towered over her. "You need to evacuate."

"No." She turned back to the scrolls to point toward a hieroglyph shaped like a bluebird. "What does the word Hielar mean?"

With an effort, Xavier leashed his obvious desire to be in the clearing below with his pack mates.

"Hielar?" His brow furrowed as he searched his mind for the answer. "In the old language it meant 'come.'"

Sage felt a flicker of hope.

Was it possible she was on the right track?

"Come or summon?" she demanded.

"What are you suggesting?"

"I think this is a spell."

Xavier stiffened, suddenly offering her his full attention. "A spell to get rid of Shakpi?"

She gave a shake of her head. "No. To summon someone." She bit her bottom lip, touching her fingers to the glyphs. The strange prickles continued to race through her body, as if urging her to speak the words, but the symbols remained frustratingly out of focus. "Or something."

"Dammit." Xavier glared at the scrolls in frustration. "I was so certain these could help."

"I think they can," she insisted.

He shook his head. "Dr. Parker, I appreciate you traveling here and trying to decipher the scrolls, but the last thing we want is to risk summoning some unknown spirit."

She flinched as she heard a heavy body crash into a tree below.

She was a scientist at heart. The sort of person who depended on logic and fact. Which was why she'd tried to suppress the magic that bubbled deep inside her for so long.

Since arriving in the Wildlands, however, she'd allowed herself to lower her barriers and 'see' the scrolls with her emotions, not the eyes of a researcher.

At the beginning she'd thought she'd sensed the lingering echo of the goddess because she assumed Opela had written the scroll.

Now that she realized it was a spell...

Well, the only reasonable explanation was that it was meant to summon the elusive goddess.

"Even a spirit that has the same power as Shakpi?" she asked.

Xavier made a sound of impatience. "There isn't any."

"Her sister."

Not surprisingly, the large male glared at her as if she'd just committed sacrilege. Even though it'd been centuries since Opela had disappeared from the Wildlands, the Pantera deeply mourned her loss.

"Opela sacrificed herself to imprison Shakpi," he said in harsh tones.

Sage reached out to lightly touch his arm. She didn't mean to offend Xavier, but she didn't have time to do this in a more diplomatic way.

"You don't truly believe she's gone," she insisted.

He scowled, no doubt assuming she was arguing semantics. "Not completely gone, but—"

A loud yelp sounded from below. Lian. Sage pressed a hand to her heart. She could physically feel his pain.

"Oh hell," she breathed, sending Xavier a pleading glance. "We have to do something."

He hesitated for less than a heartbeat before giving a sharp nod of his head.

"Say the spell."

That wasn't what Sage had been expecting.

"Me?" She blinked in confusion. "I'm not Pantera."

"You have the magic," he told her, his gaze boring into her with a fierce determination. "You're the only one who does."

She stepped away, wrapping her arms around her waist.

It was one thing to be asked to translate the scrolls. She had full faith in her abilities to decipher even the most obscure languages.

But what did she know about magic?

A big fat nothing.

"What makes you think I can cast a spell?" she rasped.

His huge body vibrated with the need to join the battle, but easily sensing her rising panic, he reached to grasp her upper arms in a light grip.

"Do you remember the first time we met?"

She licked her dry lips. "In the chat room?"

"Yes, I sent a fellow Pantera a message in our private language. Imagine my shock when you managed to translate it."

The internet chat rooms she'd discovered after becoming an adjunct professor had proven to be a godsend.

She might be too introverted to mix easily with people in public, but she'd been astonishingly capable of joining in the numerous debates and scholarly exchanges in the various rooms.

"I thought it was a brainteaser," she confessed, easily recalling the strange conversation that had popped up on her screen. It'd taken her several hours, but she'd eventually worked out the basic construct of the unknown words and sent a message back to Xavier in the same language. "But a talent for translations doesn't equate to mystic abilities."

"No, but over the years I sent you more and more obscure texts, most of which were nothing but gibberish to me."

She arched her brows. "Were they Pantera texts?"

He shook his head. "They'd been written by a Shaman."

"Oh." Suddenly she realized that this man had been subtly testing her over the years. He'd suspected all along that there was more to her than just another scholar. "That's why you had me brought here."

"I'd hoped you could decipher the scrolls. I didn't know they were a spell," he readily confessed, his fingers tightening on her arms. "Will you help?"

What could she say? She didn't know how or when it'd happened, but she knew with absolute clarity that Lian was now the most important thing in her world. She would give her life to protect him.

"I'll try."

"That's all we can ask." His eyes glowed with a lethal lust for blood as his cat broke free of its leash. "I have to go," he growled, already shifting into a huge black puma before he was pouncing across the balcony and over the railing.

Savagely squashing the need to follow behind Xavier, Sage instead turned to place her hand flat on the scrolls.

This was how she could help.

She couldn't allow herself to be distracted.

"Okay, Sage, you can do this," she muttered. "Lian needs you."

Emptying her thoughts of everything except the hieroglyphs, she allowed the magic to flow through her blood and softly spoke the words that felt like fire on her lips.

It took several minutes to complete the entire spell that was spread over five scrolls, but reaching the last glyph, she straightened from the table and sucked in a deep breath.

She didn't know what she'd expected.

Lightning. Earthquakes.

The sky falling.

Instead, she smelled...fresh grass as a misty shape formed and floated out the French doors.

Was that the goddess?

With a shake of her head, Sage was headed toward the door. She'd done everything possible with the scrolls.

Now she intended to be with Lian.

They would face the danger together.

———

Lian snarled as he watched the tall man with a lean face and dark hair braided down his back raise his hand. Chayton, the one-time Shaman, was looking decidedly worse for wear with deep claw marks down one side of his face, and a bloody nose. But while his body was human, he was infected by the spirit of the goddess who had the sort of magic that was making it impossible for the gathering Pantera to completely halt his progress across the large clearing.

To prove his point, the man released a bolt of energy that slammed into the charging golden puma.

With a pained yip, Raphael was tossed into a nearby tree, the crunch of bones making Lian wince.

Shit.

Even in his puma form, he understood that things weren't going well. Unfortunately, they didn't have any choice but to try and keep the spirit contained in the Wildlands. If Shakpi managed to get past their borders she would disappear and they would once again be under constant threat of attack.

There was a blur of black as Xavier leapt through the air and hit Chayton from behind. The Shaman muttered a curse before he reached over his shoulder and blasted the clinging puma with enough force to knock Xavier unconscious.

Ignoring his shattered ribs and painful wounds that had been scorched into his flesh, Lian leaped forward, his jaws wide as he went directly for Chayton's throat.

He managed to get close enough to scrape his elongated canines across the bastard's shoulder, but before he could latch onto the flesh, he felt fingers close around his neck to bring him to an abrupt halt.

With an inhuman strength, Shakpi held him off the ground, studying him with glowing eyes.

"Why do you fight me?" the goddess demanded, an unmistakable frustration etched onto the lean, bloody face. "You can't possibly win."

Lian shifted to his human form, using the abrupt change to free himself from the brutal grip.

"Not alone," he snarled, backing toward the edge of the clearing. Maybe if he could piss her off enough, he could lure the evil bitch away from his people. "But we are pack. You can't defeat us all."

"I don't need to defeat all of you." A smug smile touched Chayton's lips. "Just one."

"One…" Realization smacked into Lian. Shakpi wasn't trying to escape the Wildlands, because she was convinced that the key to her ultimate destruction of the Pantera was the child. "Raphael," he shouted toward the golden puma slowly rising to his feet. "She's after Soyala."

Raphael's roar made the trees tremble as he raced across the grass to the house he shared with his mate.

At the same time, Lian was charging forward to halt Shakpi as she tried to follow the fleeing puma.

He wrapped his arms around Chayton's slender body, intending to knock him to the ground. But clearly tired of playing with him, the goddess pushed him away with a jolt of her power.

"No, nothing can stop me now."

Instantly Lian's entire body was filled with a shocking pain that forced his heart to a shuddering halt and wrenched the air from his lungs.

Fuck.

He was going to die.

There was no way to survive the massive injuries to his inner organs.

The thought had barely formed when the enticing scent of lemon teased its way past the fog in his mind.

No.

He wasn't going to give up.

Not when Sage needed him.

With a groan of agony, he opened his swollen eyes, discovering Shakpi standing over him.

"Why?" He forced the question past his numb lips. "Why do you hate us?"

The glowing eyes filled with envy. "You are an abomination."

The goddess truly was mad, Lian acknowledged in horror.

"We're the children of Opela," he ground out.

"She should never have created you. It was a mistake."

"She loves us."

"No. She loves me." With a burst of fury, Shakpi reached down to grab Lian by the throat, yanking him back to his feet. "She promised to love me."

"And I do," a soft, lyrical voice said.

The fingers on Lian's neck tightened as the goddess turned to study the small cloud of mist that hovered a few feet away.

"Opela?"

"It is I, sister." The soft voice came from the mist that shimmered in the late afternoon sunlight, the air suddenly filled with the scent of fresh grass. "What have you done?"

Lian blinked in confusion.

Could this truly be Opela?

It was certainly as good an explanation as any other.

Awe spread through Lian even as he struggled against the shattering pain.

"Release him, Shakpi," the female voice commanded.

Shakpi shook her head. "This is a trick."

"No trick." The scent of grass thickened even as the misty shape floated closer. "I've come for you."

The hand that was squeezing Lian's throat eased, as the goddess concentrated on the shadowed form standing directly in front of them.

"You tried to destroy me."

Lian could actually feel the sorrow that pulsed from Opela. "I would never wish to hurt you, my sister."

"You locked me away," Shakpi hissed, the earth quaking beneath her remembered sense of betrayal.

"I couldn't allow you to attack my children."

"You should never have created them." Shakpi glanced toward Lian, her eyes filled with hate. "They took you away from me."

"I have always been here for you." The mist swirled, expanding to touch Shakpi.

The evil goddess dropped her hand from Lian, but not before he felt the sheer love that was gently wrapping around her.

A love that was as vast as the universe.

"You left and I was alone," Shakpi whispered.

"Come with me, sister."

Shakpi shook her head. "I won't return to the prison."

"Let's go home," the female voice gently urged.

The lean face softened with a yearning that came from the very soul.

"Home? You swear?"

"Yes, Shakpi. It's time."

Chayton's body trembled and then collapsed as the dark shadow of Shakpi's spirit left The Shaman's body to join with her sister.

Barely capable of standing, Lian dropped to his knees, instinctively reaching to feel for Chayton's pulse before he glanced up at the mist that now shimmered with a dazzling display of color.

"You're leaving?"

He felt something like the brush of a finger over his swollen cheek, offering a warmth that seared away the most grievous of his injuries.

"It's for the best, my child."

"But you just returned."

His heart twisted with regret. To be surrounded by her gentle glory was going to be a memory he would never forget.

"I've been here, Lian, just as I always will be," she promised in musical tones. "The Wildlands are a part of me." There was another burst of color from the mist. "And a part of Shakpi. Life and death. Night and day."

He battled the darkness that was threatening. Even with Opela's healing he remained painfully weakened from his battle.

"What about the magic?" he demanded, unable to believe their struggles were over.

"It's in the land and in you, but the source now rests in the child." There was a hint of warning in her voice. "Guard her well."

"Yes," he murmured, a sense of pleasure filling his heart as the scent of lemons surrounded him.

A second later, Sage was kneeling beside him, her arm wrapping around his shoulders.

The mist began to fade, but before it completely disappeared, Opela's voice whispered on the breeze.

"Welcome home, Sage."

CHAPTER EIGHT

THE private room at the back of the clinic that was reserved for patients who were hurt, but capable of healing on their own, was big enough to hold a large, comfortable bed and two leather seats for visitors.

It wasn't, however, large enough to contain a dozen full-grown Pantera who were determined to fuss over the man who was lying on the mattress with his ribs bandaged and healing herbs rubbed onto the burns that marred his upper arm.

Sage hovered next to the heavy walnut headboard, needing to be near Lian, but understanding his family were anxious to assure themselves he was going to make a full recovery.

Enduring the avalanche of concern for nearly an hour, Lian at last reached his breaking point when his grandmother decided she would comb and braid his hair.

"That's it. Everyone out," he roared, pointing to the door. There was a shocked silence as the visitors stared at Lian with wide eyes, then with a sudden smile Lian's father was firmly ushering the crowd out of the room. Prepared to follow, Sage had barely moved when slender fingers wrapped around her wrist. "Not you," Lian growled. "You stay."

She arched her brows, hiding her flare of relief.

When she'd seen Lian kneeling on the ground with his face swollen and covered in blood she'd been terrified he was dying.

Even now she felt compelled to reach out and brush her fingers down his cheek to convince herself he was alive and well.

"Bossy," she murmured.

"Frustrated," he corrected. Pulling up the sheet that covered his naked body he sent her a smile of smoldering invitation. "Join me."

Her heart jolted with instant arousal. Just being near Lian was enough to make her pulse race and her stomach clench with excitement.

To have a full view of all that bronzed deliciousness…

It was enough to make any female tingle in anticipation.

But she hadn't forgotten that he'd just had the shit beat out of him by a crazed goddess.

The last thing she wanted was for him to interrupt his healing.

"You're hurt," she forced herself to say.

He shrugged. "I'll feel better once I have my mate next to me."

Her breath caught at his blunt words. "Mate?"

He studied her pale face, his body tensing as he searched for her reaction.

"Does that frighten you?"

Barely aware she was moving, Sage crawled onto the bed and allowed Lian to wrap her in his waiting arms.

It wasn't just that she sensed his need to feel her pressed against him, but his question had touched her most vulnerable nerve.

She *was* frightened.

Not at the thought of being this man's mate.

Every part of her desperately longed to believe that they were destined to be together.

But she'd been taught that she couldn't depend on love. Not when it could be so easily snatched away.

Trust wasn't easy for her to offer.

"How can you be sure?" she demanded, burrowing against his warm body as his intoxicating musk saturated her senses. "You barely know me."

His hand slid beneath her sweatshirt to stroke a soothing path up and down her back.

"My cat decided the moment he saw you," he told her, his lips brushing her temple. "The human side wasn't far behind."

Her fingers unconsciously stroked over the hard muscles of his chest, seeking reassurance in his solid strength.

"What if you grow tired of me?"

"Tired?" Lian gave an unexpected chuckle, tugging the sweatshirt over her head and tossing it onto the floor. "Impossible."

"Lian—"

Her words were forgotten as Lian methodically stripped away the rest of her clothes with heart-jolting impatience.

"No, it truly is impossible," he assured her, his tone absent as his gaze surveyed her naked body with a hungry urgency. "Pantera mate for life. There will never be another for me."

Sage felt her pussy clench in need, the damp heat filling the air with the scent of her arousal.

She struggled to concentrate on her point.

She did have a point, didn't she?

She groaned as his fingers skimmed down her stomach, heading for the aching void between her legs.

"I'm not Pantera." She managed to grasp the unraveling threads of her argument.

"You belong to us." His lips nuzzled over her cheek to the corner of her mouth. "To me."

He lifted his head to reveal eyes that glowed with the raw need of his cat.

The same need that was churning through her.

"Belong?" she tried to chide, only to have the word come out as a groan.

He nipped her lower lip. "Just as I belong to you." He kissed her with a slow, thorough brand of possession. "Forever." He nibbled a path of destruction down the curve of her neck. "Stay, Dr. Parker. Be my mate and our Shaman."

She braced herself for another surge of fear, but instead, a sense of...rightness settled in her heart.

Lian wasn't her parents.

He was loyal and supportive, and lethally charming.

Precisely the sort of male to teach an aging spinster how to enjoy her life.

Sage, however, wasn't yet entirely convinced she was a mystical Shaman.

"I don't even know what a Shaman is supposed to do," she protested.

His finger slid between her slick folds, a smile of satisfaction curving his lips as she instinctively lifted her hips in response to his intimate caress.

"Each has their own skills," he explained. "But most have been able to sense the faction of a newborn Pantera."

"Faction?" The question came out as a squeak as his finger slid into her tight channel, sending shockwaves of pleasure through her body.

His teeth toyed with the lobe of her ear, the hard length of his cock pressed against her hip.

"If they're destined to be a Hunter or a Diplomat or a Healer."

That sounded...

His thumb found her sensitive clit, circling it with teasing strokes.

"Oh."

"They can also decipher messages from the ancestors."

He kissed his way to the curve of her breast, latching onto the aching tip with an urgency that made her whimper.

"Lian." Sage threaded her fingers through the dark strands of his hair.

"Hmm?"

Her back arched, bliss shuddering through her as his finger thrust in and out of her body with a growing insistence.

"We're having a conversation."

He lifted his head, his bronzed features tight with the strain of leashing his desire.

"The only thing I want to discuss is our mating."

A rueful smile curved her lips.

For years she'd hidden away from the world, trying to hide her abilities as if they were something shameful.

It'd taken a puma shifter to teach her that her gifts were special. And so was she.

"You're pushing," she teased, lifting her head to steal a quick kiss.

His eyes were molten gold as he stared down at her with a somber expression.

"I know," he said, his voice husky with emotion. "I've claimed your body. Let me claim your heart, Dr. Parker."

She framed his beautiful face in her hands, smiling with sheer joy.

"You already have."

Heat licked over her skin as the power of his cat blasted through the air.

"Is that a yes?" he growled.

Sage didn't hesitate.

She'd felt alone her entire life.

Now she not only had a mate, but an entire family who were anxious to make her feel at home.

"That's a definite yes."

He didn't give her the opportunity for second thoughts.

With his cat shimmering in his eyes, he swiped his hand over her lower stomach, the claws slicing through her flesh.

Sage gasped, but shockingly, there was no pain, only pleasure as he swooped his head down to claim her lips in a kiss that made her toes curl in pleasure.

"Mine," he growled, rolling on top of her to settle between her spread legs.

Then, sliding his cock deep inside her body, he physically connected them even as their souls entwined to become one.

EPILOGUE

LIAN heaved a sated sigh as Sage ran a brush through his hair.

He'd protested when she'd pulled on her clothes and grabbed the brush his grandmother had left behind. He wanted another few hours of having her naked and sweaty beneath him, but he couldn't argue with her point that the clinic wasn't the most private place to indulge his endless lust for his mate.

In a few hours the Healers would be satisfied he was strong enough to leave and he intended to choose one of the empty cabins that was on the opposite side of the Wildlands from his family home.

Once he had Sage alone he was going to lock the door and throw away the key.

Until then he had to be satisfied with the feel of her hands running through his hair as she pulled it into a braid.

Savoring her soft touch and the lemony scent that clung to his skin, Lian scowled as a sharp knock intruded into their peaceful silence.

"Go away," he snapped.

The door was shoved open to reveal Raphael, who was dressed in jeans and a T-shirt despite the fact his wounds hadn't fully healed.

Lian tensed, a sudden anger racing through him as he caught sight of the male's bleak expression.

Dammit.

They'd just survived yet another attempt by Shakpi to commit genocide.

Hadn't they earned a few centuries of peace and quiet?

"I have news," the leader of the Suits announced.

"Do you want me to leave?" Sage asked, already moving off the bed.

"No, you're pack now." Lian wrapped an arm around her shoulder and pulled her tight against his side. "Our business is your business."

She stiffened, as if waiting for Raphael to deny her right to be at Lian's side.

Of course he didn't.

Sage was pack.

"He's right," Raphael said with a simple honesty. "You belong to us."

Feeling Sage relax against his side, Lian focused his attention on his friend.

"What's wrong?"

"We had word from Mercier and Rosalie's kidnappers."

A growl rumbled in Lian's chest.

So they had been taken by the enemy.

"Bastards," he ground out. "Did you inform them that their goddess has abandoned them?"

"Yes."

Lian narrowed his eyes. "And?"

A sudden heat filled the air as Raphael struggled to contain his fury.

"And their demands have nothing to do with Shakpi."

"Then what the hell do they want?" Lian asked. Without their evil goddess to give them a purpose, he'd expected them to slink into the shadows. "Money?"

"No." Raphael's expression was hard as stone. "An exchange for one of our prisoners."

An icy chill of premonition inched down Lian's spine.

"Who?"

Raphael clenched his hands, the name coming out like a curse.

"Hiss."

ROCH

BY
LAURA WRIGHT

Chapter One

AFTER a quick shift from puma to Pantera, Roch stood on the dirt path outside Medical and slid the knot of his wrinkled tie into place.

"Isn't that the same suit you had on last night, brother?" Damien asked, his black eyes heavy with amusement.

Roch regarded his friend and colleague. "Yes, it is." He didn't like it, but time demanded it be so. The position of Diplomat deserved the respect of a suit—even if that suit was rumpled and carried the faint scent of a night gone awry.

As a morning breeze off the bayou moved over them, the tall, black-haired male chuckled. "You're such a manwhore, you know that?"

"Don't insult me, Damien," Roch said, running his fingers through his thick, disheveled blond hair. He was never sleeping on a couch again. No matter what the circumstance.

"What? By calling you a whore?"

"No. By calling me a man." Roch turned his ice blue gaze on his fellow Suit. His brows lifted a fraction of an inch. "Besides, nothing happened with the female."

The male snorted. "Yeah, I believe that. Remember, I know you. Have seen how the females respond to you. It's unfair as hell." He paused to wave to a couple of female Hunters passing by. When they barely gave him a second glance, he turned his attention back to Roch, his expression hopeful. "Teach me."

Roch cracked a dry smile. Damien was a good male; funny, honest and loyal. Not to mention a brilliant Diplomat. But this understanding of his, this belief that Roch possessed some kind of sexual magic, or—pardon the phrase—catnip with the females he encountered was complete bullshit. All he had was an open and respectful desire. And maybe the belief that a female's pleasure came before his own.

"I saw you leave The Cougar's Den with her," Damien pointed out. "And you show up this morning in the same clothes, looking like you hardly slept." He grinned. "That's what I call a successful night."

Roch growled softly with impatience. The night before had been anything but successful. In fact, it had been pretty much hell. Owning to it wasn't high on his priority list, but he knew Damien wouldn't stop questioning him until he was tossed a little something to satisfy his curiosity.

"The female is getting married in a week," Roch said, wishing he'd had time to stop home for a shower. No matter how he tried to play this, Raphael and the other Suits were going to give him some serious shit about the wrinkled jacket and pants—not to mention the lingering odors of alcohol and a pissed-off stomach.

Damien looked genuinely confused. "So she's getting married. And?"

"I don't play with claimed females, Damien."

The confusion on the male's face deepened. "Then what did you do last night?"

Her roommate.

Roch grinned at that. At his foolish, yet highly decadent thoughts. It had been the plan. He'd even agreed to let the engaged human female watch—which she'd been damn keen on doing. But then hell had pulled him under, shaking and churning his guts until he'd become violently ill. First all over the white sheepskin rug on their living room floor, then in the bathroom for a good two hours. He'd passed out on their couch shortly after, like a hammered teenager.

Granted, Pantera had their share of medical issues to deal with, but stomach sickness was a rarity. He'd woken up late and apologized profusely to the women. And on his way back to the bayou, he had called to arrange for a new rug to be delivered and maid service to come to their apartment.

"Forget last night," Roch said, motioning for Damien to follow as he headed toward the doors of Medical. "Today is what matters. And the work ahead. But I will say that Hiss had better give us the answers we're looking for. My cat is just aching to attack something."

"Hiss?" Damien repeated, his brows slamming together in confusion. "Is that who we're meeting with this morning?"

"You didn't know?"

The male shook his head. "Didn't know who we're meeting, and sure as hell didn't know he'd been brought to Medical."

A flicker of unease moved through Roch. It wasn't like the leader of the Suits to keep information from his faction members. "I'm sure Raphael meant to inform you."

"Maybe he doesn't trust me."

The bitterness in Damien's voice wasn't hard to miss. It was difficult being the newest member of any faction, but with the Diplomats it was doubly so. There was so much information, so much protocol—so many secrets that needed to be kept to protect the Pantera.

"Why would you think that?" Roch asked him.

The male shrugged. "Hiss was a friend back when we were cubs."

With a sniff of amusement, Roch yanked the door wide. "Hiss had many friends. Raphael is no doubt suffering from intense stress due to Shakpi's dramatic departure, and that we've been outed to the humans—and then there's the lack of sleep due to the incessant squawk of one called Soyala."

That seemed to both smooth the male's raised hackles and cause him to grin. "The cub. I'm sure he doesn't mind her cries. A young is a great blessing to a male."

"To some males, that's true," Roch answered. "I, however, prefer work—and the cries of a male who's just come clean after a particularly rough interrogation."

Damien laughed. "So, why was Hiss brought here?"

"They're testing him," Roch said as they moved down the hall. "His blood, heart, mind—even his cat. While his tongue remains quiet, the Nurturers are hoping to glean some information as to why our new enemies would trade two Pantera for one. Why Hiss is so important to them."

"I still think loyalty to these humans could be a factor," Damien put in, giving a quick smile to a passing female who was in her puma state. "Maybe they have a long history. Maybe they consider Hiss one of their own. And the exchange for Rosalie and Mercier is their way of demonstrating that."

Medical was alive with activity, as it always was in the morning hours. Roch spotted Raphael up ahead. The leader of the Diplomatic Faction was dressed sharply in a tailored black suit and was speaking intently to one of the head Nurturers, Jean-Baptiste.

"Well, they can have him," Roch said with a growl. "As soon as he tells us everything he knows, and we have our loyal Pantera back again."

A few feet from his boss, Roch gritted his teeth as his stomach rolled hard and fast again. What the hell was going on with him? Bad alcohol? Bad food? What? And why was it still affecting him? As he neared the two Pantera, he shoved the feeling back. He didn't have time for ailments. He had a job to do. And, he mused with a forced grin, the cries of a traitor male to elicit.

———

Fired.

FIRED!?!

Lydia Page stared at the trees swaying in the breeze outside the picture window and wondered why she hadn't anticipated the reaction from the partners at her law firm. Maybe because they were both women, and had children of their own? Of course, they also had husbands and nannies to go along with those children. But surely they understood that she'd be committed to the firm even if she had a child?

Nope.

To be fair, they hadn't said they were firing her because of her pregnancy. Because, you know, that would be highly illegal. Instead, they'd claimed they were firing her for excessive absences. Which was such crap. With the illness and subsequent death of her mother six months ago, she'd taken some time off. Two days over her allotment, to be specific—two days both partners had verbally agreed to. But as a lawyer, she knew how well oral agreements stood up, and how quickly they were forgotten.

Behind her, the office door opened. "Ms. Page," came the doctor's voice. "Thank you for coming in today."

"Of course," she said.

It was this very lunchtime appointment at The Haymore Center that her assistant had both scheduled and shared with one of the partners' assistants a few days ago. Clearly, the partners didn't believe that a single mother could put in the kind of hours they wanted.

Well, screw them, Lydia thought, her eyes now set on the doctor seated across from her. She could get another job. Hell, maybe she'd even open her own practice.

"How are you today, Ms. Page?" the doctor inquired, his gaze trained on the paperwork before him on the desk.

"Fine," she said brightly. "No morning sickness yet. But I'm sure that will come. My mom was really sick with me from six weeks to four months. Barfing all the time." She smiled and touched her flat belly. "But what's a little barf when you get something so precious at the end of it, right?" She laughed softly.

The doctor took a deep breath and let it out slowly. "Ms. Page, I'd like to discuss your blood test and ultrasound results."

It was then that he looked up from his paperwork and met her gaze. His eyes were a cold brown and deep set. His mouth a thin, tense line. Lydia felt the blood drain from her face, and her heart start to pound. "What's wrong? The baby—"

"The baby looks fine," he said evenly. "Healthy."

"Oh my god." She put a hand to her chest. "Oh, thank goodness. I—"

"But there is something we need to talk about," he amended.

The relief from a moment ago evaporated and heat prickled through her. "What?"

"The embryo's development is further along than it should be." His tone was unsympathetic at best.

Lydia's hands started to tremble. "What does that mean? How far along is it?"

"The fetus should be measuring four weeks. But instead, it's twelve."

Lydia stared at him, her heart beating so fast now it actually hurt. She'd only met Dr. Ambrose twice. Once for a consult, and the second time when he performed the insemination. The man was purported to be a genius so she had overlooked his lack of warmth and bedside manner. With the job she'd hired him to do, skill was far more important than kindness. But right then, staring at him across his desk, feeling as though she might implode from fear and grief, she wouldn't have minded a little bit of gentleness.

"What does this mean?" she asked in a near whisper. "And why did it happen?" *My baby...*

Once again, the door opened behind her and a woman's voice called out, "Knock, knock."

"Come in, Erin," the doctor said in a grave tone, avoiding Lydia's gaze as much as possible now.

The woman strode past Lydia and came to stand beside the doctor. She was somewhere in her mid-thirties, with pale brown hair and dark, intelligent eyes. She looked from Lydia to the doctor, then back again. "I see you've been told."

Her words were meant to sound sympathetic, but they came out detached and clinical. Lydia clasped her hands together. Her palms were cold and wet. "Yes," she said.

"I am sorry, Ms. Page," she said, handing Lydia a document. "But I'm sure you understand why it's imperative that you terminate this pregnancy immediately."

CHAPTER TWO

"I'VE told Raphael and now I'll tell you," Hiss growled. "The only Pantera I will speak to are the elders."

The Hunter could be damn intimidating, even strapped down to a bed with needles sticking out of his arms. Though he felt like shit, Roch stood imposingly over the male, arms crossed over his chest. "You think you're in any position to make demands, traitor?"

"Yes, I believe I am."

"Arrogance won't get you anywhere but back in a cell," Roch threatened.

"The elders will never come here," Damien put in from his position at the foot of the bed. "So just do us all a favor and end this. Tell us why these humans want you."

"I don't know," he ground out, his dark grey eyes narrowing with hatred.

"Bullshit," Damien growled.

"Give us names, addresses and plans," Roch said calmly. "And we'll return you to your humans."

Hiss's lip curled. "They're not *my* humans, asshole. They're not my anything. I don't know them. My dealings were with the followers of Shakpi. And whatever I did, whoever I used, it was for myself and my family alone. Not for some human cause."

"Maybe we should bring Reny here," Roch suggested, watching to see if the male's cat flashed behind his eyes. It didn't. It hadn't in quite some time. "Let the long-lost sister have a visit with her traitor brother. Have a nice familial heart-to-heart."

"Fuck you," Hiss ground out.

Roch leaned in, bile forming in his throat. "No. Fuck you. No matter what your reasons for doing what you did, they weren't good enough. You screwed your kind, your blood. You have forced us out of hiding. You have created fear in the hearts of our females. Including your sister." Concerned that he could vomit on the male with all the seizing up going on inside his belly, he stood up again. "You know they have Rosalie, right?"

Hiss's expression turned pained. "Yes, I know."

"She's a good friend of yours, isn't she?"

This time Hiss didn't answer. He turned away.

"You know what, you don't even deserve to breathe, you—oh, fuck me—" Roch sucked in air, his legs threatening to buckle. A wave of dizziness was moving over and through him. If he remained, he was going to lose his shit. He pushed away from the bed and growled to his colleague. "Take over, Damien."

"Hey," the male called after him as he headed for the door. "You all right?"

"Just keep at it," Roch ground out. "I'll inform Raphael."

He stumbled out into the hallway. This was bullshit. Whatever was going on with him. He didn't do sickness. He didn't accept anything that pulled him away from his work. His cat scratched at his insides as he walked down the hall. The thing wanted out. No. It wanted to take over. It knew his male form was weak, and this scratching, pawing—it was a protective instinct.

"What the hell's wrong with you?"

Roch gave Raphael a quick nod as the male fell into step beside him. "Just something I ate." *Or drank. Or came into contact with. Or... who the hell knows.*

"You look like shit," the leader of the Suits remarked. "Come to think of it, you looked like shit when you got here. You should go get checked out."

"No," Roch said quickly and gruffly.

"Come on, brother. Jean-Baptiste can take a quick look. Or if you want a female, Doc Julia—"

"I said I'm fine." Roch picked up the pace. He needed to get outside. Air. Sun. His puma. A Pantera's digestive system was quick to flush out anything it didn't like, so whatever was going on with him should pass in a few hours. "I'm going home."

Raphael continued to follow him. "Are you sure you can make it on your own?"

The growl Roch tossed the male's way ended the question and answer session. But it also stole some of Roch's strength. "I left Damien with Hiss..." he managed to mutter before he hit the glass doors.

"Fine. Just go," Raphael called after him. "I got this."

Roch burst through the doors, and the second the sunshine hit his skin and the breeze of the bayou entered his nostrils, his cat took over. It was as though his male form melted into his puma, and he instantly felt strong and healthy.

With a quick snarl at the surrounding Pantera who were heading for the bayou and midday meal, Roch took off. For the forest, and for the border of the Wildlands—so sure about what he had to do next, he didn't question it.

After all, he was pure instinct.

———

"The baby will have defects, right?" Lydia said before the woman, Erin, could utter another word or thrust a pen her way. "That's what you're telling me? It may be born with a deformity." She tossed the papers on the doctor's desk. "Well, let me say I don't care. I don't care. This is my child."

Erin turned to the doctor and raised her eyebrows. Clearly, she wasn't expecting such a response. Well, she could just suck it. Her heart slamming against her ribs, Lydia inched forward on her chair and fought for a serious, businesslike expression. "I'm not going to sue anyone, if that's what you're worried about. I knew the risks when I had the procedure."

"Legal action isn't what we're concerned about, Ms. Page," the doctor put in.

Yes," Erin agreed. "As you said, you knew the risks, and you did sign a contract—"

"Then what else is there?" Lydia interrupted. "Look, there's got to be some chance. I'm sure you've seen situations like this before. Isn't it at all possible that the baby could turn out to be normal?"

"Normal?" Erin repeated, then sniffed as if she scented something vile. "No."

Tears pricked Lydia's eyes.

"We'd like to take care of this today, Ms. Page," the doctor stated.

"No," Lydia said. This was ridiculous. Why were they pushing her? Why weren't they at least letting her think? Have some time—

"We need you to trust us," Erin put in, her tone strangely calm.

"I told you, I'm not getting rid of the baby."

"It isn't safe," the doctor pressed.

"I'll take that risk."

The doctor sat back in his chair. "You'll be a pariah and your child will be a freak. Is that what you want?"

Lydia's heart stopped. Or that's what it felt like. Cold, alone, disgusted. Her hands shaking slightly, she stood up.

"What are you doing, Ms. Page?" Erin asked warily.

"Leaving," Lydia informed her. "And I won't be coming back."

The doctor cursed softly. Erin, however, wasn't giving up. "Wait. Please. The donor you chose—"

Lydia swung her purse over her shoulder. "What about him?"

The woman glanced at the doctor, then turned her attention back to Lydia. "He was a mistake, Ms. Page. He should never have been allowed in the program. I swear to god I'm going to find out who did this and—"

"What?" Lydia asked, her heart starting to pound hard once again. What was happening? What had she done by trusting these people? "What the hell is going on?"

"He isn't human, Ms. Page."

It was as if the lawyer switch suddenly flicked on and Lydia moved closer to the woman. "Really? That's how you're going to play this? Telling me I have an alien baby? Not only is that pathetic and ridiculous, but it makes you—"

"You have heard about the race of shape shifters discovered out in the bayous?" the doctor asked.

A thread of unease moved through her. "Yes, of course. I've seen them on TV and online. The Pantera, I think they're called. But what does that have to do with—" She whipped around to face Erin.

For the first time since Lydia had seen the woman, she genuinely looked distressed. "I don't know how this happened, Ms. Page. But I swear to you we will find out."

Flies were buzzing in her head. She couldn't hear very well. Her skin felt prickly too. And she was shaking her head. "No."

"I'm very sorry."

She started to back up. "That's impossible."

"Your blood tests confirm the match," Erin said.

Reeling, Lydia turned away and headed for the door. She had her fingers around the knob when Erin called out to her.

"Take the day. We'll schedule the termination tomorrow morning."

Tears pricked Lydia's eyes.

"You'll only need to wait a few weeks and we can try again—"

Her hand left the door and went to her belly. "No. Never." She whirled around. "This baby is mine."

Erin and the doctor both stared at her like she was insane. And maybe she was.

"Ms. Page," the doctor began. "Besides this being against our laws of nature, the Pantera will not look kindly on this mistake. Our government is working with theirs to foster a relationship. It's only at the beginning stages. We don't know how these...beasts...will react."

Beasts? It was as if the man had sent a knife through her heart. She didn't know what was coming. Didn't know how she was going to manage any of it. But she did know that she was going to protect this child from people like these.

"You could be in danger if anyone found out." Erin had her arms crossed over her chest. She looked pensive. "Not everyone has sympathy and understanding for these animals—this new species."

"Like you?" Lydia asked bitingly.

Erin's lips thinned. "I urge you to think very carefully about this, Ms. Page. And we hope to see you back here in the morning."

"I don't have to think about anything," Lydia told her fiercely, her hand finding the doorknob once again. "No one is taking this baby from me. Pantera, human—it belongs to me."

As she swung the door wide and walked out of the doctor's office, she felt both sets of eyes on her back.

CHAPTER THREE

HIS cat had taken him to the edge of the Wildlands, but after his shift into his male form, his mind and body, and something he couldn't explain—or resist—had led him into New Orleans. He'd been there a hundred times for both business and pleasure, but this was the first time he'd had no clear purpose.

As he roamed the sunlit streets, enjoying a respite from the many hours of sick stomach and fuzzy head, he wondered why he was drawn here—what his cat was after.

Who it was after.

It wasn't unusual for a Pantera to follow a feeling, an instinct—see where it led. But it was an unusual practice for Roch. He rarely used his instincts unless he was in his puma form. In his male form, as a Suit, he relied on information, deduction and logic.

Bracketed by a small crowd of people, Roch noticed a woman walking toward him. She was beautiful, with long red hair and green eyes—eyes that moved over him with interest.

"Hi there," she called out.

It was the strangest thing. Roch wasn't the kind of male who pursued a woman, hard and relentless, but he did show his interest with a few words and a smile. Today, however, he had neither. Nothing. No interest at all.

Well, not in the redhead, anyway.

Just as she passed him with an irritated eye roll, he felt a surge of heat so powerful and electric, he turned toward it, like a flower into the sun. Or a Pantera male into a storefront. He glanced up at the sign before him. *Break For Beignets*. What the hell was this, a diner? A donut shop? And why was he being drawn here?

With heat still blazing inside him, he opened the door and went in. He was immediately met with an overpoweringly sweet scent and a long line of customers. Clearly, everyone wanted a beignet this morning. Everyone but Roch. He wasn't hungry. In fact, despite the wondrous heat radiating from his chest, he was starting to feel sick again. *Goddamit. What the fuck is going on?*

He scanned the line, looking for something, anything that would stand out to him. When that turned up nothing, his eyes cut left, moved over the six tables and the people sitting at them. Lovers, businesspeople, family—

His gut screamed, then felt as if it had been split in half by a dull ax. He blinked to clear his vision, which was flickering black and white. Seated at the smallest table near the back was a woman he didn't know. Didn't recognize. And yet he did.

His breath seized inside his lungs and for a second, he just stared at her. Maybe twenty-seven or twenty-eight, and human, she was the most beautiful woman he'd ever seen in his life. She had delicate features that called to him to touch. But a strong presence that made him wary. The sunlight streaming in from the window at her right made her masses of tight blond curls glow like a halo, and when she glanced up from her coffee and caught his gaze, he saw that her eyes were an extraordinary shade of violet. Christ. Who was this woman? And why had he been drawn here to her? Because, hell, he knew she was the reason he'd come to New Orleans today.

He started her way, his gaze taking in her form-fitting gray suit. She was tall, with small, firm breasts, and long, lean legs that could wrap a male's waist and hold on tight while he—

He shut his thoughts down before they managed to take root. Take root and multiply.

He stopped when he reached her table, and found himself tongue-tied. Unheard of. What was going on? Why was he so attracted to her, by her? No. No…Attracted was too gentle a word for what he felt when he looked at this woman. Possessed was better. More accurate.

"You can take the chair."

She was speaking to him; a clear, sensual sound from lips so naturally full and pink they made his mouth water. *Shit.* And she was looking at him with those large, expressive, violet eyes rimmed with extraordinarily long lashes.

"Excuse me?" Roch said, trying to reason what he was doing, and why.

"You want that, right?" She pointed to the black iron chair across from her. "Feel free. I know it's crazy busy in here."

He glanced around, then came back to her. "The tables are all full." He sounded like a fool, an insane male. And yet he couldn't stop himself.

"I suppose you can sit here," she said, though her tone was cautious. "But I have to warn you, I'm not going to be great company. It's been a shitastic morning."

Tell me, his cat purred from inside his chest. *Tell me what's wrong and I'll fix it. Whatever it is.*

Ignoring the overzealous feline inside of him, Roch pulled out the chair and sat down. "I'm sorry about your morning. Nothing like a donut to make things right, though."

She smiled and the gesture seemed to light up her entire face. He stared at her. Hard. He couldn't help himself. Besides her beauty, she made him feel…right somehow. It was like walking in the front door of his house and sitting down on the couch. He felt comfortable and warm. And drawn. So fucking drawn.

"Have you ordered yet?" she asked, her eyes flickering with humor. "Maybe you need a donut too."

"Maybe." A smile tugged at his lips. "But alas, the line…"

She glanced past him and nodded. "Well, I'm not very hungry." She pushed her plate toward him. "You can have mine."

Roch's eyes settled on the pastry, then lifted to regard her. "Have we met?" he asked. "I feel as if I know you."

She laughed softly. "I want to say that's a pretty tired pick-up line. But," she stopped and shook her head, "I think we may have." Her brows drew together. "Are you an attorney? Or do you have a job in the legal profession?"

"No." Was she an attorney? He knew nothing about her. And yet he truly felt as though he knew everything.

"Maybe college?" she suggested. "Where did you go to school?"

"I didn't." His nostrils flared. She smelled like heaven. Flowers and some kind of spice. "Have you been to The Cougar's Den in La Pierre? Or out near the bayous?"

"No." She laughed. "You know what it probably is? I look like someone you know and vice versa."

No. No. "I don't think it's that simple," he said, his chest flickering with tension.

"I think it has to be. Or maybe online, Facebook or—"

He couldn't stand it any longer. He leaned in and whispered, "Are you connected with the Pantera somehow?"

Her eyes widened and her lips parted. "What did you just say?"

His jaw tight, he glanced around, then turned back to her. "Do you know of the Pantera?"

Her face went as white as the powdered sugar on top of her beignet. "Oh my god," she said on a gasp. "Oh my god. Those assholes." Her eyes narrowed on him. "Freaking Haymore works fast."

Haymore? Roch stared at her in confusion. Who the hell was Haymore? His gut rippled with tension. Was this her male?

"Listen up, dickhead," she ground out, trying to keep her voice low as she stared him down. "No matter what you've been sent here to do or to offer me, I will never end this pregnancy."

Roch's guts screamed with heat and sickness. Those violet eyes had turned fierce and protective. Pregnancy? She was pregnant? What the hell? Bile claimed his throat and he wished for his cat to take over so he didn't puke all over the untouched beignet.

"I'm leaving now," the woman said tightly. "Follow me and I'm going straight to the police." She leaned toward him then and whispered, "Leave me alone and you'll never hear from me again. No one will ever know this child is half Pantera."

Roch's body started to vibrate as the woman grabbed her purse and stood up. He reached for her, took her wrist, his eyes piercing into hers. "You are carrying a Pantera young?" he hissed, careful to keep his voice low. No doubt they were already attracting attention.

It wasn't possible. She couldn't be…With the curse…He froze. The curse had lifted only weeks ago. But, Christ, if it *was* true, who had planted their seed inside of her?

Feral anger rippled through him.

Which Pantera male had lain with this woman? Touched her? Ran their hands through those soft, blond curls while they—

She yanked her arm away, cutting off questions he had no right to be asking. "Fine. Play stupid." She seemed tough, hard, pissed off, but the fear was bright in her eyes. "Just don't bother me ever again."

Bother her? That's not what he wanted. "You're putting yourself in danger," he managed to grind out. "By being here. By being out—" He was about to say out of the bayou, but she stopped him with a hard stare.

"I don't care." She glanced around at the nearby tables, then turned back to him and whispered, "I will do anything to protect my child."

"Even if that child is part animal?" he asked, amazed.

"Fuck you," she ground out.

Stunned, every muscle in his body tense and ready to spring, his guts clenching with every breath he expelled, Roch watched as the woman left the table and hurried out of the shop.

———

A bag of Chinese take-out in one hand and a book on what to expect during pregnancy in the other, Lydia thanked her doorman and headed for the elevator. After the morning she'd had she just wanted to hide out in her condo this afternoon. Take a bath, and binge-watch Orange Is the New Black while stuffing her face with cream cheese wontons.

Once inside, she hit the button for the third floor and leaned back against the metal wall. She was trying to assure herself that the people at The Haymore Center would leave her alone now that she'd threatened going to the police, outing their mistake, but she couldn't help feeling afraid. Not for herself, oddly, but for the little life growing inside her. If this baby was truly half Pantera, how was she going to protect him or her? Especially if there were people out there who looked at her child and saw an animal?

The elevator door opened and she stepped out, headed down the hall. Was it possible to keep it a secret? Or would her half human child end up being able to shift into a cat one day in the middle of Show and Tell?

Okay, tomorrow, she mused, nearly dropping her book as she tried to free a hand to get her keys. She'd think about this tomorrow.

"Let me help you?" came a male voice a few feet away.

Lydia's head lifted and her heart nearly dropped onto the carpet under her feet. She froze, her keys instantly forgotten. Clutching the food and the book to her chest, she took in the man standing just outside her door. It was him. Of course it was him. The guy from the beignet place. Her insides pinched. From fear, and lord, from something else entirely. Something she refused to name. Something she should not be feeling at all.

Her gaze tracked over him. He was terrifyingly good-looking. Tall, lean, big hands, thick wrists, dark blond hair and icy blue eyes that warned of a highly intelligent mind. Just like earlier, he wore a black suit, white shirt, and dark purple tie, and as he walked toward her it was like witnessing the very essence of confidence, sexuality and ultra masculinity.

"This is disturbing," she said, trying like hell to remain cool and calm, and act like she could kick his ass if she had to. "You outside my door." Dammit. Her voice was shaking. Or maybe that was her insides. It was just…the way he was looking at her. Not like he wanted to do her harm, but like he wanted to know what her skin tasted like.

She blushed and walked past him to her door.

"I'm sorry," he said. "I'm not trying to scare you."

She could feel him behind her. His warmth. "Too late." She transferred the book and food bag to her left arm, then went searching—not for her keys this time, but her cellphone. If this gorgeous bastard from Haymore tried anything, she was calling the police.

"I just need to know," he said, coming around her and leaning all six feet, suit-clad, hard jawed gorgeousness against the doorframe. "Are you certain you're carrying a Pantera child?"

The need to drop everything and cover her belly with her hands, protect her tiny child, was intensely strong. But Lydia kept her composure. "That's an odd question for the man who's representing the very company whose samples I used."

"I'm not representing this Haymore you speak of."

She turned to look at him just as her hand closed around her cell.

His eyes darkened to a stormy sky blue. "And I'm not a man."

Heat and panic erupted within her. Her breathing shallow and uneven, she brought her cellphone out of her purse and quickly dialed 911. "You need to get the hell out of here. Maybe get yourself to a psych ward. The cops are coming."

But the cellphone never made it to her ear. The man slipped it from her so fast she hardly felt it leave her hand. He stabbed the off button, then turned to look at her.

"You need to come with me, Ms. Page."

Her heart was beating so fast, she worried she might pass out. "And you need to run before I scream my head off."

"I am not going to hurt you," he insisted tightly. In fact, he looked put out, insulted by her suggestion. "I am Pantera, and I want to help you."

The book she was carrying slipped from her arms and dropped onto the floor. Her mind whirred. And she tried to keep up with her thoughts—with what he'd just said to her. *Pantera*. This tall, imposing, stunning, gorgeous nut case was Pantera?

No.

She stared into his eyes. She didn't believe him. Couldn't. But then she saw something flash within those ice blue orbs. Something she couldn't explain, but something her body, skin, and blood recognized.

She gasped, covered her mouth. "It's not possible."

"What samples are you talking about?" he asked. "What did you get from this Haymore Center?"

Oh god. Was this really happening? "I was artificially inseminated." She couldn't believe she was saying this, telling him this.

Something flickered in his blue eyes. Gratification? Or relief? "So you have not lain with one of our males, then? No Pantera has a claim on you?"

Lydia stared at him. "No." The way he spoke. The words he used. Could this be real? Could he actually be a Pantera shifter?

"If the child is Pantera," the man continued as if what they were discussing was not completely insane-sounding, "wouldn't you want to know its origins, community, history and medical issues?"

"I don't want to do this," she said, digging into her purse, grabbing her keys. "Just go. Please. I don't know how you found me or who you really are, but—"

He sniffed with irritation. "Unless you're thinking of hiding the child? Is that it? Hiding it away so the humans don't have to see it." The sudden ferocity in his eyes was a living, breathing thing. "Perhaps you're ashamed of its—"

"Hey!" His words, and his accusation, were like boiling water on a hot day. Forgetting her fear, she whirled on him and air-stabbed him with her key. "Never," she said through gritted teeth. "Okay? I would never be ashamed of my child."

She turned back and jammed her key into the lock. This was madness. All of this. She needed time. She needed to think. Maybe he would go away. Maybe he'd leave a number where she could reach him. Dammit! She was so confused. She pushed the door open.

"Come with me, Lydia," he said.

Just as she stepped inside her hallway, her head came around. "You know my name."

He nodded, as if that was answer enough.

Apprehension tugged at her insides. "If I say no, you'll try and take me anyway, won't you?"

Sharp eyebrows lifted over intense blue eyes. "Are you saying no?"

Her breathing uneven, she slipped farther inside. She was just about to shut the door in his face and on those words, when she heard a noise coming from her living room. Her heart slammed against her ribs as true fear coursed through her.

The man's lip curled and his nostrils flared. "Don't move."

Without another word, he rushed past her—so fast she barely saw him. Lydia stood there frozen, trying to decide what to do. Suddenly, the sounds of fists hitting bone, and glass breaking against hardwood rent the air. Fuck! Where was her cell? Did he have it? Could she get into the kitchen and use the house phone?

But before she could make any kind of move, the man emerged from the shadows of her living room. Calm, cool, looking as though he hadn't been touched.

"Leave the food," he said tightly, his eyes moving over her, examining every inch of her. "I'll feed you once we get to the Wildlands."

Lydia noticed she'd dropped the bag of Chinese on the floor. The book, however, was still clutched to her chest.

"What was that?" she demanded in a thin whisper.

He took her hand in his. It was cool and large and callused. "Come on. It's not safe here. That bastard had a gun."

CHAPTER FOUR

"ROCH," he told her as she hesitated in the backseat of the cab they'd taken from New Orleans to La Pierre.

It wasn't his usual method of travel. He liked to run, or, when he was traveling for business, use one of the vehicles from the Pantera's car club. But he was in a hurry today, and he wouldn't have Lydia walking any farther than necessary.

She glanced up at him, her expression wary, yet intrigued. A look Roch was getting used to with her.

"That's your name?" she asked. "Roch?"

He nodded as the cab pulled to a stop in front of The Cougar's Den. He quickly paid the driver, then opened the door and stepped out. He offered Lydia a hand. "Come. We need to walk a little now."

She took it, and Roch tried not to purr at the feeling of her soft skin against his palm. If it was possible, she looked even more beautiful in the rich, afternoon light of the bayou. Her curls were pulled back off her flawless face in a loose ponytail, and the warmth of the day was making her cheeks flush pink.

He led her out of The Cougar's Den parking lot and toward the bayou and the Wildlands, making sure their route through the terrain was relatively uncomplicated. It had been nearly impossible to keep his eyes off of her on their drive. His hands, too. He'd felt her anxiety and had wanted to comfort her. But he needed to remember that she didn't belong to him. He was merely discovery, protection and delivery. If she truly was carrying a Pantera cub within her, priority number one was going to be to find out how that had happened. How a clinic in New Orleans had managed to get their hands on Pantera sperm samples.

Then they were going to have to find the father.

As they walked, heat and irritation slashed through him at the thought. Not to mention the words, and the warning: *I found her and I get to keep her.*

Foolish male, he chided himself.

"Just for the record," she said as they trudged through thick grasses and around massive cypresses. "I'm coming with you because I decided to."

"Of course."

"Not because someone forced me," she continued, her tone no doubt similar to the one she used in a court of law. "I don't do anything I don't want to do."

"I believe that," he said with a hint of amusement. He would like to see her in court, badgering witnesses, fighting for justice for her client. He imagined she'd be magnificent.

"Are you making fun of me?" she asked with just a touch of humor.

"Not at all," he said. "There is no denying that you're a strong-willed female. Much like our Pantera females."

"Really?"

"Yes. You'll fit in well."

"I'm not planning on fitting in, Roch."

Christ, his name on her lips was like a stroke to his skin with a goddamn feather. As they walked through the lush flora and the sun grazed his skin, he couldn't help but imagine her saying it again...in his ear...on his neck.

Against his mouth.

He growled softly and forced those thoughts and images back. Hell, he should kick them the hell out. Never to return again. He had no right to them. Dangerous. Impossible.

261

When the border of the Wildlands finally came into view he heaved a sigh of relief. She would be someone else's responsibility soon. He'd get her to Medical and under Dr. Julia's care. Parish's mate was human too, and she would serve this purpose well. Then he'd find out who the father of Lydia's cub was—and how this Haymore Center had gotten a hold of Pantera samples.

His stomach rolled suddenly and he groaned. *Shit.* What was going on with him? He stopped and took a breath, wondering if he was going to actually get sick in front of his new guest. That would be great. Really fucking fantastic.

Lydia moved closer and put her hand on his shoulder. "You okay?"

He sucked in air. Not because of his wrecked stomach, but because of her touch. It made his skin and chest tighten, and, Goddess help him, his cock twitch.

"What's wrong?" she asked, sounding surprisingly concerned. "Can I do something?"

"No. It's nothing. Just haven't been feeling well lately." When she eased her hand back and stepped away from him, he laughed. "Don't worry, Lydia. It's not catching. Something I ate or drank." Or who the hell knew?

"Sorry," she said with a soft laugh.

"No problem."

"I just want to protect the baby."

"As do I."

She stilled, her eyes finding his. They were the color of a Dyesse lily, and the warmth they gave off made him ache with a hunger he'd never known before. Shit, what was he going to do about this? This attraction. No, this...*crush* he seemed to have on a human female—a human female who was carrying a Pantera male's cub?

Maybe the male wouldn't want it.

Maybe the male wouldn't want her.

It was his cat. The puma's thoughts, not his own.

A deep growl erupted from his throat.

"Roch?" she said, sounding worried.

"It's okay," he said quickly, diffusing her concern. "We're just on the border of the Wildlands."

As they entered a thick cluster of trees, and the scent of the bayou wafted over them, Lydia stopped and looked around. The sun filtering through the treetops, changing the colors of the leaves from sunny yellow and green to pale orange. "Wow. It's beautiful here."

Roch felt a swell of pride at her words. It was good she could see what he saw. Good for her cub, if it was indeed Pantera. "You haven't seen anything yet," he said.

Her eyes met his and they were warm and excited, and Roch had to stop himself from reaching out and brushing her cheek with his fingertips.

"Well, let's go then," she said, starting off toward another massive cypress.

"Not on foot," Roch called out to her.

She turned, her brows knit together. "Then how?"

"Don't be afraid, all right?"

"Afraid of what?" she asked.

He took a deep breath, trying to calm his cat. He could feel it pacing inside of him, wanting to get out. Wanting to meet her. In a flash of movement, he shifted into his puma. The cat snarled and stretched, and instantly, Roch felt healthy and strong.

He turned and growled softly at Lydia. She was standing there staring at him, her eyes wide, her mouth open. But surprisingly, she didn't look scared. Just awestruck.

"Oh my god." She shook her head. "I know this is real, but it just feels...it looks...you are so beautiful..."

Roch's cat purred with pleasure, then gestured to its back with its enormous head.

She looked from his face to his back. "You want me to ride on you?" she asked, her voice reed-thin.

He stalked toward her, growling at her again. When he pressed his massive body against her side, she nearly toppled over.

"I guess that's a yes," she said with a reluctant laugh. She climbed onto his back, her sweet weight pressing into his muscles, then leaned over so her lips were near his cat's ear.

The puma nearly lost its mind. It lifted its head and howled into the fragrant bayou.

"I hope I'm not too heavy," she whispered, wrapping her arms around its neck.

A sound almost like laughter erupted from Roch's cat before it took off into the trees.

———

Lydia studied the pretty young woman with the pale skin and long black hair who had come into her room at the Medical facility just moments ago. Her name was Ashe, and she seemed nice. Hell, everyone Lydia had encountered so far seemed nice. She wasn't sure what she'd expected. After reading an article about them in one of the more reputable newspapers, maybe she'd imagined a more domineering species. But she hadn't encountered that yet. Unless she counted Roch. He definitely had a bit of the domineering side. But everyone else had been very welcoming, almost gentle. No doubt they wanted her to feel comfortable as they all figured this out together.

She felt so unsure about being here, yet so curious too. Riding on Roch's back, her arms around his warm, powerful neck, had been one of the most incredible experiences of her life. And seeing the Wildlands up close, its obvious beauty and quiet magic made her ache to see more, see everything. If her child was really a part of all this, a Pantera, then she wanted to explore, find out as much as she could about them and their way of life.

"I know you must have a million questions," Ashe said, coming over to the bed and sitting down. "And I'm sure Doctor Julia answered some of them when she took blood samples and your medical history earlier. But I can offer you something that no one else can." The woman's brown eyes flashed with companionable mystery.

"What's that?" Lydia asked, curious.

"I'm human," she said. "And my mate is Pantera. We have a new baby."

Lydia didn't say anything for a moment. She was kind of shocked. None of that was mentioned in the article she'd read. She had no idea that Pantera and humans were interacting. And mating? Was that like marrying?

"You're human?" she repeated.

Ashe nodded. "And let me just tell you, when I first came here and saw all of this, I was shocked and scared, and I didn't know what to do. I'd met my mate outside of the Wildlands without knowing he was Pantera."

"Oh wow," Lydia said. How had that happened? Maybe Ashe would share the story with her sometime, if she felt comfortable.

"Right?" Ashe grinned, reached over and placed her hand on Lydia's. "But after the shock wore off, I swear to you, I never knew such happiness existed. Being here, with Raphael and my baby, it's the best thing that has ever happened to me."

A soft smile touched Lydia's mouth. "It sounds wonderful. But you knew your mate, right? You wanted to be with him?"

Ashe nodded.

"That's not how this went down for me," Lydia said. "I didn't want a relationship. I'd done that and gotten hurt. Really hurt."

Ashe gave her a sympathetic look and squeezed her hand.

"I only wanted a child." Lydia touched her stomach with her free hand. "So being here in the Wildlands, it's not about romance and building a relationship with the father. I don't even know who it is. I'm nervous to find out, you know?"

"Of course. And no one is going to push you to have a paternity test. That'll be your choice. And when you're ready, *if* you're ready, all you have to do is let Doctor Julia know."

"I suppose the first thing is to find out if my baby is truly part Pantera." Lydia laughed softly. "The donor I used was supposed to be anonymous and…human."

"I understand," Ashe said. "I really do." She took a deep breath. "Listen, you're going to be around for a few days, right?"

Lydia nodded. She had agreed to that. She wanted that. Truly. She wanted to find out the truth about the baby's biological history. And if the child was half Pantera, she needed to learn as much as she could about them, so someday she could tell her child where they came from. It was amazing really, Lydia thought. Back in New Orleans, every human she'd come in contact with had wanted her to terminate her pregnancy ASAP. But here in the Wildlands it had been the complete opposite—they'd been almost reverent about the pregnancy, and her. She understood why Ashe felt so happy and content.

"You can, of course, stay here at Medical," Ashe began. "It's cozy." She shrugged. "In a clinical, Nurturers-gawking-at-you kind of way."

Lydia laughed. Nurturers seemed to be the medical staff here. The caretakers and scientists. Her eyes drifted to the door. She wondered if Roch was a Nurturer. She didn't think so. He didn't seem particularly nurturing. Protective, strong-willed, handsome, sexy, maybe. But not nurturing.

She swallowed hard and felt relieved when Ashe continued talking.

"I'd love it if you'd come stay with us."

Lydia turned to gape at the woman. "Us?"

"Me and my mate, Raphael. And our daughter, Soyala, of course." Ashe stood up. She looked very trendy. Human, come to think of it, in her black peasant top, skinny jeans and boots. "Now, I have to warn you, she's only a few weeks old, so you might be woken up at all hours of the night. But it's homey there and if you needed anything...well...to talk or whatever—"

The pull to say yes was a strong one. She liked this woman. A lot. And to remain in her soft, supportive light sounded so appealing. But the last thing she wanted was to impose on anyone. Especially a new family.

"I'll stay here," Lydia said quickly and gently.

Ashe looked instantly bummed. "It's the baby thing, right? I swear no one wants to hang out with us anymore. All the poopy diapers and breastfeeding."

Lydia laughed again. "No. God, no. Not at all. In fact, the baby thing is a huge plus for me. It's just—"

"What?"

"I don't want to impose."

Ashe made a shocked sound deep in her throat. "Okay, that's silly and crazy. You're staying with us. Period. End of story. I made lasagna for dinner tonight, and garlic bread. Who in their right mind can turn down garlic bread?"

It was virtually impossible to not like this woman. Lydia shrugged. "I do love me some garlic bread."

Ashe beamed, clasped her hands together. "Perfect. As soon as you're done here, I'll take you home. We're pretty much the same size and you can borrow anything you like." She glanced at her watch. "It shouldn't be more than a half hour, I think. Raphael, Baptiste and Roch are having a powwow out in the hall somewhere."

"They are?" Lydia felt her cheeks warm. She'd wondered where the man—the male, she'd have to get used to that—had gone off to. She wanted so much to get to know him. This man who had found her in *Break for Beignets,* saved her from whatever had been in her apartment, then brought her here. She wanted to know how he'd done that. And why?

"So, this Roch who found me," Lydia began, trying her damnedest to sound casual. "Who is he?"

"He works with my mate. They're what's called Diplomatic Faction. Or 'Suits.' They're like politicians or facilitators in our world."

Suit. Diplomat. Well, that certainly fit. And made him sound even more attractive than he already was. She cleared her throat. "Does he have a mate?"

"Roch?" Ashe started laughing. "Oh, no. He's a total loner. Really enjoys the single life, if you know what I mean."

Lydia did. Dammit.

"Totally unattached by choice," Ashe added. "But a good guy. Loyal, and deeply dedicated to his work. Even more so than Raphael, I think—which is saying something."

A loner, and a workaholic. Kind of like her. "So, no family dinners," she said with a forced smile.

"No. Not unless he's invited to one." Ashe paused, then her eyes narrowed playfully and studied Lydia. "Wait a sec. I could invite him?"

Lydia's heart seized inside her chest. "No, no, that's fine."

The woman smiled broadly. "I have more than enough lasagna."

"I was just curious," Lydia explained, hoping her cheeks weren't too pink. "He was the one who found me and brought me here. I wanted to thank him or…something." God, she sounded like a moron.

"It is pretty extraordinary how that all happened," Ashe remarked thoughtfully. "Actually, it's unheard of. Everyone's talking about it."

Lydia didn't understand. "What do you mean?"

"A male Pantera finding a pregnant human female." Her brows lifted. "Especially one he's never met. Or slept with." She nodded. "Extraordinary. And something I'm sure Raphael and the others are trying to figure out as we speak."

Chapter Five

ROCH paced the small patch of moonlit grass behind Medical. Due to his erratic and overassertive behavior when he'd brought Lydia in, Raphael, Dr. Julia and Jean-Baptiste had all thought it best that any discussion involving the human woman be done outside the building.

At first, Roch had blown them off, didn't believe that he was acting in any way but professionally when it came to her welfare and situation. But then he caught himself sniffing at her door, even growling at any Nurturers who tried to enter.

He'd gone willingly with them at that point.

"We have both Hunters and Suits dispatched to this Haymore Center," Raphael said, his tone just a decibel above a growl. "We'll find out exactly who they are and what happened. And how a mistake like this could occur. If indeed, impregnating a human woman with Pantera DNA was a mistake."

"It has to be a mistake," Doc Julia uttered, more to herself than to Raphael.

Jean-Baptiste inhaled deeply. "So, the blood samples show—"

"Yes," she said, her tone a strange combination of excitement and concern. "The baby is both human and Pantera." She lifted her gaze first to meet Raphael's, then Baptiste's. "Do you know what this means?"

Jean-Baptiste lifted his pierced eyebrow. "We need to find the father?"

Roch's lip curled with irritation, but he kept on pacing. Down the path aways he spotted Chayton, the man who had been taken over by Shakpi not long ago. He was working with a Nurturer and the Shaman-in-training, Sage, Lian's new mate, on some kind of trust exercise.

Poor bastard, he mused. Forget trust. It was going to be a miracle if the man actually managed to have some semblance of a normal life.

"Yes, we'll need to find the father," Julia put in. "When Lydia is ready to allow the testing. But it also means that with Shakpi gone, the curse has truly lifted. We could be seeing pregnancies throughout the Wildlands now."

Everyone was silent for a moment, letting that information seep in.

"My Genny," Jean-Baptiste uttered almost reverently. "She has wanted a cub so badly."

"This could be a new beginning," Raphael agreed. "But before we start the celebration, we must know how this human pregnancy occurred. Roch?"

Roch stopped pacing and turned to look at the three Pantera, who were all staring intently at him now. "What?"

"Are you certain you don't know her?"

"Am I certain?" He cursed. "Do you really think I'm the kind of male who wouldn't remember someone I bedded four weeks ago? That I'm that low, that vile?"

Raphael didn't answer. Just kept his gaze locked on the male. Whatever his personal opinion, he wanted an answer.

"Christ, no," Roch answered tersely. "All right? I've never seen her before in my life."

I would remember. Hell, I'd never be able to forget. Never be able to look at another female again after her.

"It seems improbable," Baptiste put in.

Roch whirled on the heavily tattooed Nurturer and flashed him a feral glare.

Baptiste chuckled and put his palms up in surrender. One had the name of his mate, Genevieve, inked onto it. "Easy, brother. My point is only that you went searching for her—"

"I went to New Orleans. There was no search."

"And you found her, brought her back here. And look at you now."

"What?" Roch ground out. "Look at what?"

"You're acting mated," Jean-Baptiste said calmly. "You're acting like me and Raphael and Parish when someone gets too close or threatens our females."

Raphael nodded in agreement. "I have to say it's true. I've never seen you like this, Roch."

"I've been ill, that's all," he tossed out.

"Don't think so."

Confusion, irritation and anger all rose up to claim him. "What the hell are you implying, Raphael?"

But it wasn't Raphael who answered.

"That this child could be yours," Doc Julia put in, her expression amazed.

A knot formed in Roch's chest. He ripped his gaze from them and stalked away. Just a few feet. Then he stopped and turned around. "Impossible," he hissed at them.

"Is it?" Raphael said.

"I've never seen her before." Roch looked up to the heavens. "I swear on Opela. And even if I had, I don't take risks like that. Even when we were cursed, I made sure the females beneath me were protected."

"Beneath him," Baptiste uttered under his breath.

"Beneath me, on top of me—"

"All right. Too much information, brother," Raphael said.

Roch snarled at them. "You can all go to hell."

"Hey," Julia put in, her eyes bright with amusement. "I didn't go there. I wanted to. But I didn't."

"Oh fuck," Baptiste said, his tone instantly grave.

"What?" Raphael said. "What's wrong?"

"Remember back when we found out about the curse? We all had samples taken from us for the purpose of testing. Blood, urine, semen…"

Something curled inside of Roch's belly.

"*Oh fuck*, is right," Raphael said, his mind working behind his green eyes. "That was over fifty years ago. I had forgotten."

"Would someone have given those samples to a human lab?" Julia asked, the moon above casting an eerie glow to her skin.

"It's possible, I suppose. We were trying in any way we could to keep our race going. But it would've been covert, against our laws. The experiments were only to be done in our laboratory."

Jean-Baptiste looked murderous. No doubt deducing that whoever had leaked samples was probably a Nurturer. "We need to find out who did this."

"Maybe Hiss will know?" Roch put in.

"I will take that bastard out with my bare hands if he's in any way responsible," Raphael threatened. Then he took a deep breath and cursed. "If this is true, we're in deep shit." His nostrils flared. "We can shut down The Haymore Center and recover the remaining samples, but who knows how many human women have been inseminated already."

"We could have males running off, going in search of their offspring," Baptiste put in. "All we can hope for is what Roch did. Find the mother of the cub and bring her back here."

"The child is not mine!" Roch roared.

All three of them went silent and turned to look at him.

"Most males would be pleased to know they had sired a Pantera cub," Jean-Baptiste said, his chin lifting a fraction.

"Not this way!" Roch returned, his chest tightening around his heart muscle. "Christ. Not this way." He cursed and uttered a battered, "Not in a lab."

"You have feelings for this woman," Julia said, her eyes going wide.

Roch didn't answer her. In fact, he didn't acknowledge any of them. He was done. Fractured by the possibility they'd just laid out before him. The impossible, amazing, horrifying possibility.

Turning away, he headed down the path, shifting into his puma state just before he was lost in the shadows of the garden.

———

Twenty-four hours ago Lydia had been in her apartment, standing at the kitchen counter, eating a supermarket salad and wondering what the following day would bring. Who knew it would bring so much: a firing, a possible Pantera baby, kindness, danger, beauty, confusion and—she glanced around the table at the small family gathered there—an altogether different existence.

Truly, she didn't know what was going to happen from this day onward, but here in the Wildlands she felt no fear about herself or her child's future. Maybe that was naive. Or maybe she had an example of what was possible right in front of her. Standing over the long, rustic wood table in her lovely two-story antebellum home, sliding a ginormous piece of lasagna onto Lydia's plate.

She started to laugh.

Ashe glanced up. "What? Does it look bad? Too runny?"

"It looks amazing," Lydia assured her.

"I swear I didn't go crazy with the sauce."

"*Ma chérie,*" Raphael put in, his gold-green eyes warm with love as he ran his hand over her hip. "I think she's just worried she can't eat it all."

"Oh," Ashe laughed, her cheeks flushing pink. "Well, no worries about that. Just do what you can." She gave Lydia a knowing smile. "But there is the growing baby to think of."

"Cub," Raphael corrected, then gave Lydia a gentle smile. "It's not too early to get used to that."

"Or how much the little fur ball likes to eat," Ashe said, glancing down at her beautiful blond baby, who was fast asleep in her raised bassinet beside the table. "Even when they're inside you."

"I'll remember that," Lydia said with a grin.

Ashe sighed as she sat down and picked up her fork. "We're so excited for you, Lydia. All the Pantera are. It's such a blessing, and we just want to make sure you have everything you need. We want you and the cub healthy."

"Yes, we do," came a male voice behind her.

A ripple of heat moved through Lydia's body as she turned and caught sight of Roch standing in the archway between the grand entryway and the dining room. Gone was the suit and tie. And in their place were black jogging pants and a black t-shirt. Both molded to his incredible body. He looked sporty and masculine and hot, and she tried not to drool as she stared at him.

"How did you get in here?" Raphael asked good-naturedly.

"Door was open."

"And you didn't think to knock?"

He walked over to the table and pulled out the chair beside Lydia. "I was invited to dinner."

"By whom?" Raphael demanded.

Ashe cleared her throat as both her mate and Lydia turned to look at her. She cut another sizable piece of lasagna and slid it onto an empty plate. "He hasn't been feeling very well, so I thought a little home cooking…"

"Poor little cub," Raphael said with heavy sarcasm, turning to his colleague and friend and giving him an amused grin.

Roch tossed the male a fierce glare.

"Are you going upstairs afterward and having Ashe tuck you into bed? Read you a story?" He paused, realizing what he'd just suggested. He rounded on his mate. "No, *ma chère.* Please don't do that."

"Not a chance," she answered. "Only one who's getting tucked in tonight is you."

He growled softly at her. "Mmm, I like that."

"Hey," Roch said, standing up. "I can go."

"No," Lydia said without thinking.

He turned to look at her, and the heat and hunger in his gaze was blinding. In fact, it made her heart race like a rabbit's. He liked her. She was sure of it.

"Sit down," Raphael called out to him. "I was just giving you a hard time. Let my mate serve you a piece of lasagna the size of your head. It would make her so happy."

"Hey!" Ashe said, then started laughing.

"Don't get upset, *ma chérie*. You know I live to make you happy."

"And you always do." She blushed, and he leaned in and kissed her deeply and hungrily until she sighed.

Roch turned to Lydia. "How are you?"

"Good. Fine." *Glad to see you. You look gorgeous. Then again, you always look—*

"Are you happy staying here?" he asked, his expression raw with concern. "You don't have to. I'm sure you won't get any sleep with the cub."

"We've already discussed that, Roch," Ashe remarked after coming up for air.

He turned to his plate and picked up his fork. "She needs more than food to keep her healthy and well. She needs sleep."

"Well, she wouldn't get that at Medical," Ashe replied, offering him some bread.

"There are other options."

"Like what? Your place?"

Lydia's heart sprang into her throat. She didn't want to hear his answer to that. Yes or no. Either option concerned her. "I'm happy here," she stated quickly, resolutely. "And I love being around that cutie-pie over there."

Roch glanced at the sleeping baby. "She's getting big."

Ashe nearly melted with motherly happiness. "She is."

"And she looks like you, Ashe. Which is lucky for her."

Raphael glanced up from his nearly consumed lasagna and gave his friend a good-natured growl.

Popping a piece of garlic bread in her mouth, Ashe turned to Lydia. "So, is your family from New Orleans?"

"They are. Were. They're gone now. My mom passed away a few months back."

Ashe's expression fell into a lovely mask of empathy. "I'm sorry."

"Thank you." She touched her belly, which now sported just the very beginnings of a rise. "I'm excited for new family to come into my life."

Ashe nodded. "Of course you are."

"What do you do for work, Lydia?" Raphael asked her.

"I'm a lawyer. Or was a lawyer."

Roch looked up from his plate. "What do you mean?"

"I was fired," she explained, feeling slightly embarrassed and still pretty pissed. "Lawyers don't have a lot of time to be mothers. Or so my bosses believe."

"Well, that's bullshit," Ashe exclaimed, then quickly turned to Soyala. "Sorry, honey. Mommy's a little upset about the issue of double standards."

"I'm actually thinking I'll go into solo practice," Lydia said after taking a sip of water. "Maybe a little office near where I live."

"In New Orleans," Roch said. It wasn't a question and his tone was anything but pleased. In fact it sounded pained.

"Of course, New Orleans," Ashe said, giving him an impatient look. "That's where she's from."

Roch's jaw tightened and he stabbed at a chunk of lasagna with his fork.

"Obviously there's a lot to consider," Lydia said, feeling the wave of tension in the air. It was the last thing she wanted to bring into Ashe and Raphael's home. "But if this baby is half Pantera, I would never cut the Wildlands or his species out of his life—"

"His?" Roch interrupted, his eyes cutting to her. They were a dark and stormy blue. "It's a male cub? How do you know?"

"I don't," she said, flustered by his quick passion. "I'm not sure why I said that."

"And there's no *if*, by the way," he added softly.

"What?" Her heart stalled and she looked around the room.

Roch glared at Raphael. "You didn't tell her?"

"Not officially," he uttered, uncomfortable.

"Oh, Raphael," Ashe scolded gently.

"I was easing my way into it."

Lydia was barely listening to them. Her heart was flickering hard in her chest, and her appetite was gone. "The tests are back? You know for certain…"

Raphael nodded. "Yes."

"Oh," she exclaimed. Her child was part Pantera. Her child would be a member of this tribe. It would be able to shift into a cat form like Roch. Her throat tightened. *A beautiful, powerful, remarkable cat, who might someday want to live here. Away from me.*

"Lydia, if I may," Raphael began gently. "How do you feel about the father having a relationship with the cub? If we can find him, of course. If you decide that you want the testing…"

"Do we need to talk about this now?" Roch put in darkly. He'd abandoned his food as well, and his eyes were pinned to Lydia's face.

"I don't know," she said, her voice reed-thin. "This is a lot to take in and I need to think about it." She put her napkin on her plate and eased her chair back. "I'm really tired."

"Of course you are," Ashe said with a quick and grim look at Raphael. "I'll walk you up, make sure you have everything you need."

"Thank you." She wasn't about to put up a fuss, or act like she could manage on her own. Granted, she probably could. But she kind of wanted Ashe with her. She looked at Raphael. "Good night."

"Sleep well, Lydia," he said gently, his eyes kind.

Then she glanced down at Roch. She wanted to say something, but she wasn't sure what. *Don't leave? I need you? To talk to you? Be around you?* But she couldn't form the words. Or she was afraid of them. Vulnerability was a terrifying gift to give another person. But, lord help her, she wanted to give it to him. Like it or not—understand it or not—she had this connection to him that couldn't be explained or denied. And when their eyes caught and held, she saw in those incredible blue depths the same connection she felt for him mirrored back.

He gave her a tight smile, but said nothing. And after a moment, Lydia left the table with Ashe and headed upstairs to her room.

CHAPTER SIX

THE sound of a female's cries woke him. He stirred against the soft rug on the cold hardwood floor, lifted his head and stared at the woman on the bed. In the glow of the moonlight through the window to her left, he could see that she was sitting up, blond curls perfectly disheveled, tears falling down her cheeks. She'd had a nightmare. He could tell it was still affecting her; she was trembling. The ache to crawl up on the mattress and sit beside her, comfort her, was shockingly strong. But he'd sworn to remain where he was.

She swiped at her eyes, her tears, sniffed hard and took a breath. She would lie down again and slip back into sleep. He too was about to settle himself when her gaze dropped to the floor and she noticed him.

For the first time.

On the rug.

She screamed, her eyes flaring with shock and terror. Then she quickly covered her mouth, realizing it was him. No, not him.

His puma.

Roch scrambled to his feet—all four of them—and shifted into his male form. He hated himself for causing her fear after an obvious nightmare. He only wanted to bring her happiness. Make her feel safe. He went to her, the mattress dipping with his weight, and pulled her into his arms.

"I'm sorry," he whispered against her hair. "Christ, I'm sorry."

"What are you doing in here?" she whispered back. Still trembling, she clung to him.

"I don't know." But that was a lie. He knew. The need to be close to her, protect her, had driven him to wait outside Raphael and Ashe's place until the lights had gone out. Then he'd climbed up the side of the house and into her window. He'd known exactly where she was staying because he'd scented her.

His eyes slammed shut and he cursed silently.

He'd scented her.

Just as he had in New Orleans.

"I can't seem to walk away from you, Lydia," he said, his voice gravelly from sleep and from the quick shift. "I have no claim on you, and yet..."

"Yet what?" she whispered.

He dug deep for control as he held her. He was wearing the same thing he'd come to dinner in, but she wasn't. Clad in only a dark green tank top and underwear, she looked soft and sexy as hell, and he wanted her desperately. Her breasts pressed against his chest, and her nipples were hard.

His mouth watered.

"I need to touch you," he uttered impetuously. Before she could answer, he eased back so he could see her. Half of her beautiful face was cast in moonlight. Her eyes were huge and her lips were slightly swollen. He reached out and swiped at one lone and lasting tear near her cheekbone. "Your belly," he clarified gently. "Can I place my hand there?"

She looked confused. "Why, Roch?"

Yeah. Why indeed? "I can't explain it," he said, his eyes pinned to hers. *Don't want to explain.* "I just need to. Please."

She stared at him for a moment longer, breathing in, breathing out. Then she moved away. At first, Roch thought she was rejecting him. A wordless refusal. And could he blame her? His request was strange at best. But then she laid down, her head on her pillow, her hair fanned around her face, and lifted the tank top to just under her breasts.

Heat slammed into Roch, and his cock filled with blood. For a moment, he just looked her over. Hungrily, covetously, sweetly. Her incredible body streaked with moonlight. From her sexy toes painted a fiery red, to her long, luscious legs, up to a pair of pretty, almost girlish underwear. White with tiny strawberries. And then there was her belly. Tan and taut with just a hint of a swell.

Need raged through him. Never had he wanted anything more. He lifted his gaze to meet hers. Clearly, she'd been watching him, and she gave him a gentle, encouraging smile. Christ, what he was doing—was this right?

"Come here, Roch," she said. "Lie down next to me. It's okay."

Her words and the warmth in her voice wrapped around him and squeezed. Shit. He'd never met anyone like her. It wasn't just that she was smart and strong and beautiful. That was amazing in and of itself. But she was also incredibly kind and warm. And he hadn't known—until that moment—that he truly craved those things. That he'd been missing those things in his life.

He stretched out beside her, inhaled her clean, floral scent, then laid his hand on her belly. He wasn't sure what he'd expected to happen in that moment. A sudden flash of insight, maybe? Or a blood-deep knowing that this woman and her cub belonged to him? But it wasn't either. Instead, a calming warmth suffused his skin. The kind of warmth that one liked to sit in for hours. A healing warmth. A happy, blissful warmth he'd never known existed. Or cared. Or had searched for.

She possessed that. In her heart and beneath her smooth skin.

Not wanting to hold her captive longer than she felt comfortable, or have her know how hard just being this close to her made him, Roch started to pull away. But Lydia covered his hand with hers. For a second he didn't move. His heart was slamming against his ribs, and every animal-like instinct he possessed wanted to pick her up and take her away. Maybe to his house. His bed. Claim her. Kill anything and everything that tried to get near.

But when she started slowly dragging his hand down toward her sex, his possessive instincts evaporated, and the desperate desire to mate took their place.

Lydia stopped when his fingers grazed the top of her strawberry underwear. The warmth from a moment ago—that delicate, gentle state of being—had already expanded into a ball of white-hot need within Roch and he needed to know if she felt it too. If she wanted his touch. Wanted his fingers inside of her? His mouth on her?

He lifted his gaze, and what he saw in those violet orbs was a depth of desire unlike anything he'd ever witnessed.

He growled softly at her, and her hand left his and went to his face. As her eyes melted into his, she brushed her fingers down one cheek and over his stubbled jaw. *Fuck them. Fuck them all.* He didn't care. At that moment, he didn't give a shit why he and Lydia were in Raphael and Ashe's house in the Wildlands—what challenges they faced outside in both their worlds. He just wanted to be with her, make her happy, and hot, and moan.

He followed the trail she'd set for him, slipping his fingers inside her panties. She lifted her chin and gasped when he cupped her.

"Oh, Lydia," he uttered, his skin going tight around his muscles. "You're bare. Soft." He ran his thumb over the top of her sex. "I can feel your heat, how wet you are."

She licked her lips. "It's you," she whispered. "It's all you."

Her words made his heart expand. Whatever this was, between them, he wanted it. That sounded insane given how long they'd known one another. And yet, he was Pantera, and she was here with him in the magical Wildlands.

He slid one finger through her folds. It was so slick with cream he couldn't stop himself from entering her pussy. A groan rumbled in his chest and he felt his cock turn steel-hard.

She pressed herself against him and moaned. "More."

Every inch of him rigid with tension and hunger, Roch eased another finger inside her.

She groaned. "Yes. God, yes."

Did he want inside her? Fuck, yes. More than he wanted to live, at that moment. But he wasn't going there. Not now. Tonight was about her pleasure. He needed to see that. See her body writhe under his care. Hear her cries of climax as he stroked her.

"Roch," she uttered, canting her hips, trying to take him deeper.

"I'm here, Lydia," he said fiercely, as he deepened his thrusts.

I'm always going to be here. If you want me to be.

He pressed the pad of his thumb against her clit and she gasped.

Want me to be, Lydia. Fuck. Please, want me to be.

Her eyes closed and she gave herself over to his touch. He didn't rush her. Hell no. He wanted to watch this incredible display for as long as possible. Watch her hips circle and grind, listen to her breathing change as she neared climax.

Her nipples were hard points beneath her tank top, scraping against the fabric as her breasts moved, as her breathing grew rapid.

"Oh, god, Roch," she cried out softly. "I can't hold on…"

"You don't have to," he cooed. "Come for me."

It was the sweetest hell, watching her, touching her. Wanting to be inside of her. A wave of heat and cream bathed his fingers as he thrust hard and deep inside her. And when she moaned and thrashed her head from side to side against the pillow, he quickened the pace.

"Come for me, Lydia," he urged, circling her clit with his thumb.

"Oh, god," she rasped, her walls tightening and pulsating against his fingers.

Roch couldn't help himself. Couldn't stop himself. He dropped his head to her breast and suckled her nipple through the thin cotton.

She cried out, her hips jerking. Come leaked from the tip of Roch's painfully hard cock, but he could only think of her. He wanted that climax. He owned that climax.

As his thumb flicked her swollen clit, and his tongue and teeth worked her nipple, he pressed hard against the sensitive spot inside her with the pads of his fingers.

"Oh, Roch," she cried out, writhing and moaning, coming apart under him. "Yes…"

His head swimming and his body roaring with unchecked desire, Roch lifted his head and watched her. Watched her ride each wave of orgasm as she rode his fingers. Watched her lips part and a cry emerge. She was so beautiful, so responsive. And he slowly thrust inside her until those glorious waves receded, until she couldn't move any more. Until she was so weary, she just stilled, and all he could hear was her rapid breathing.

Then he eased himself from her body. She looked spent, and for a moment he was worried. Was it all right to have touched her, made her come? Had he hurt her, or gods no—his heart seized—had he hurt the baby?

"Lydia." His voice was heavy with tension. "Are you okay? Did I hurt you?"

Her eyes opened and she blinked several times. Then she found his gaze and gave him the widest, most satisfied smile he'd ever seen. "Hurt me?" she laughed softly. "Roch?"

"Yes?"

That smile widened even further. "Hurt me some more?"

The apprehension left his body in a rush. Leaving only an intense hunger and a worrisome affection.

She reached for him, grabbed onto the waistband of his pants and tugged. Desire flooded his blood. But he put a hand over hers to stop her.

"No, Lydia." His voice was raw with tension. Fuck, he wanted her. Wanted to taste her. Bury himself within her.

She looked confused, pained. "Why? Don't you want me?" Her eyes dropped to his pants. "It looks like you want me."

"I want you more than I want to breathe or eat or see the sun set over the bayou for the rest of my life."

Her gaze returned to his. "Then…"

"I can't. Not yet." *Not until I know who you belong to.*

He hadn't said the words aloud, but she understood immediately, and her face fell.

"But I want to stay here with you," he said. "I need to. My cat and I are in agreement. But I'll return to the floor."

"That's silly," she said. "Don't go. I won't touch you."

"Christ, Lydia." She had no idea. She really didn't.

"I won't take advantage of you."

The teasing thread in her voice made him growl. He should say no. Should just leave the bed and park it on the rug. But he wasn't that strong. Not where she was concerned.

He lay back against the pillow and opened his arms to her. She went to him at once. And when he pulled her to him, she draped her thigh over his possessively.

"You slay me," he whispered against her hair, feeling well, healthy and strong in his male form for the first time in days.

"And you make me feel safe."

His chest constricted. No one had ever said something like that to him. What was he going to do? How was he going to deal with the truth when it came?

He heard and felt her yawn and he pulled her even closer. "Sleep now. I'm not going anywhere."

He closed his eyes too and tried to calm his breathing. After a few minutes, he thought she was asleep. But then she whispered, "Roch?"

"Mmm hmm?"

"Do you think it's true?"

Without even a hesitation, he knew what she meant. "That this cub is mine?"

"Yes."

"I don't know, Lydia." *But I want it to be. Goddess help me, I want it to be.*

When she didn't say anything in reply, he kissed her hair and stroked her back. And when her breathing evened out, and her limbs grew still, he let his mind go, too. And he followed her into sleep.

———

Lydia woke to the warmth of the early morning sun on her face and the feeling of a man's thickly muscled arms around her. As she opened her eyes and took stock of her surroundings, she blushed with pleasure. Most of the bedding was either on the floor or on its way there. She was completely wrapped around Roch's side and her underwear was still wet.

Her belly, and pretty much everything south of it, clenched. Last night had been extraordinary, to say the least. Her breath caught as she remembered his hands on her, *in* her. And her heart kicked as she recalled his reticence to make love to her.

Maybe that was a momentary hiccup. Maybe today will be different.

She lifted her head and let her eyes move over him. He was so beautiful, so...male. She reached up and dragged a thick lock of his blond hair away from his eyes. Tan skin, sharp angles, stubbled jaw, hard neck, powerful, wide shoulders.

Yes. Today will be different.

Without thinking, she leaned in and pressed her lips to his neck. One gentle kiss. Then she eased back an inch and swiped at his pulse point with her tongue. Oh, he tasted so good.

It was the only thought she could manage before she heard a growl and was swiftly rolled to her back.

She gasped and stared up at the male who had stolen her heart but had yet to take control of it. He looked fearsome and sexy, his eyes blue pools of sleepy hunger, as he easily held himself just inches above her.

"What was that, Ms. Page?" he said on a playful growl.

Her gaze moved from his eyes down to his lips. "I believe I was overcome with the need to taste you."

He groaned, then lowered his head and kissed her. A soft, deep, teasing kiss that went on for a good five minutes and inflamed every inch of her.

"How's that?" he asked confidently.

"How was what?" she said, deadpan.

His brows lowered. "I kissed you, woman."

"Oh, come on now. I'll need so much more than that to give my opinion." She grinned and pushed him off her—pushed him to his back.

Granted, Roch was pretty much built like a slab of iron. He could've easily remained where he was. But he let her direct him, let her do what was comfortable for her body. And lord, what was comfortable for her was being on top of him, straddling him, feeling his long, hard muscles—especially the one between his legs.

His gaze moved up her body, then settled on her face. A wicked gleam lit in his extraordinary blue eyes. "Take advantage of me, Lydia."

It was from their conversation the night before, she realized, grinning. She liked him this way. Playful and sexual, and not too serious. She leaned over and kissed him, her palms on either side of his head—her hair falling around them like a coiled curtain. Roch may have been a gentleman up until that point, trying to keep himself and his hunger under control. But once she started in on his mouth, kissing and licking his lips, nipping and suckling his tongue, he went wild. His hands came around to cup her backside possessively, squeezing the flesh as he groaned.

"I can't get enough of you," he uttered against her mouth. "Never enough."

They kissed hard and impassioned, ground their lower halves against one another, made out like teenagers with only stolen moments in the back of one of their parents' cars.

Her underwear soaked and her mouth desperate to taste the rest of him, Lydia sat up and pulled her tank over her head. After she tossed it to the floor, she found Roch's gaze once again. As he took her in, he looked like his puma. Or the male equivalent of it. Fierce, hungry, unable to quell its instincts. As in...if the puma wanted something, he took it.

And lord, she sure hoped he took it.

Her hands went to the front of his pants. She traced the outline of his cock, her mouth dropping open as she took in his extraordinary length. Her sex tingled in anticipation. Oh, she wanted him inside of her.

Roch reached for her then, palming her breasts. Massaging. Giving them a hard squeeze, before gently pinching each of her nipples.

"I want you," she told him on an impatient moan. "Inside of me. Please, Roch."

His eyes flashed fire. "I can't. Fuck, I can't take you, no matter how badly I want you."

"Why?" This was madness. What was he trying to prove?

In the soft light of morning, he looked doubly fierce. "You don't belong to me."

Was it possible for a heart to hurt and swell at the same time? she wondered. "I decide who I belong to, Roch." She slipped her hand inside his pants and wrapped her fingers around his shaft.

"Damn you," he growled, his hips jacking up.

"No. Damn you. Do you think I want to touch anyone else like this?"

That did it. Roch went crazy at her words. Growling, groaning, grabbing her hips and grinding her sex into the base of his cock. Over and over.

Until a knock sounded on the door.

Both of them froze.

"Lydia?" It was Ashe, in her lovely singsong voice. "You awake? I have breakfast downstairs if you're interested."

Lydia's eyes flew to Roch. He looked murderous. Like he might actually turn into his cat and attack.

"No hurry," Ashe continued. "But there are beignets. They make the best beignets here in the Wildlands."

With a nearly inaudible curse, Roch lifted her up and placed her down on the mattress. He was off the bed in seconds, running his hands through his hair. He looked wild and gorgeous.

"I'm awake," Lydia called out, worried Roch would do something foolish. Like snarl at the woman to get lost. "Sounds good. I'll be down in a few minutes."

"Okay, great!"

Lydia waited for the sound of the woman's footfall to disappear before she turned back to Roch.

"Don't go," she said to him. "Stay and have breakfast."

"That wouldn't be wise," he said, jaw tight. He wasn't looking at her. Anywhere but at her. Playful Roch was gone.

"Why not? You were here for dinner."

"I'm in no mood to be sociable. Besides, I've got to get home, shower and change before work." He turned to her then and stilled. For several long seconds, he took her in. Her eyes, her mouth, her naked torso. "You truly are the most beautiful woman, Lydia."

Her heart melted like a damn ice cream cone in the sun. She reached for him. "Stay."

"I can't." But he went to her anyway and kissed her. It wasn't a hungry, desire-filled kiss. It was more like a goodbye.

When he pulled away, Lydia couldn't help herself. She had to ask him. "Do you want to know, Roch? About the cub?"

Dread glistened in his blue eyes. "Of course I do, but—"

"You're scared?" she finished.

"Fuck, Lydia, of course I'm scared."

She scooted to the edge of the bed. "I'm scared too. Everything's changed for me. In the blink of an eye. My whole life. Where do I belong? What do I do?"

He sighed. "You will always belong here if that's what you want."

"What do you want?"

His jaw looked so tight Lydia was afraid it might crack. "You don't understand. The ways of a Pantera male are very different than that of a man. We have honor. A code we live by. But more important than that is the fact that our kind can finally, after fifty years, reproduce. We can continue." He took a deep breath. "This cub..."

"Is very important," she said.

"Yes." He was silent for a moment, then, "I have to go."

She didn't put up a fight this time. She understood the gravity of the situation. Love didn't or couldn't always trump practicality and allegiance. She may not have liked it. But she understood it.

"How are you planning to get out without anyone noticing?" she asked.

"Same way I came in." He gave her a small smile. "Have a beignet for me?"

288

She returned it. "Sure."

Then watched him go out the window with the supreme grace of the cat who dwelled inside of him.

CHAPTER SEVEN

"NOTHING?" Roch said incredulously. "No samples? No files?"

"How's that possible?" Damien asked in between bites of ham sandwich. "Did they search the entire facility?"

Raphael glanced up from his laptop. They were gathered in his private office inside Suit headquarters. "Not exactly. They were stopped before they could search the basement."

"Stopped?" Roch repeated, leaning back against the window. "By who?"

"The man who supposedly owns The Haymore Center. A Stanton Locke." He returned his gaze to the screen of his computer. "I put a few of the Geeks on it, and it seems Mr. Locke has friends in very high places. From politicians to celebrities to law enforcement. One of our Hunters was actually taken to a humans' jail."

"Holy shit," Damien exclaimed, putting down his sandwich and taking out his iPhone. "Which one?"

"Keira. She was protecting Reny."

"Sebastian's mate?"

Raphael nodded. "With her experience in the FBI we thought she'd be an asset in the field. She was. Until she saw this Locke bastard. She was convinced she knew the man. Wouldn't stop with the questions. When he got pissed and grabbed her arm, Keira stepped in. And you know Keira."

"Ballbuster," Roch said, crossing his arms over his chest. "Best Hunter I've ever known."

"Damn right. NOLA PD showed up pretty quick after that and Locke said Keira attacked him."

"What a pussy, and not the good kind," Damien said with a rare growl. "Is she still in jail?"

"No. Sebastian got her released. He headed to New Orleans the second he heard about Reny. They're all on their way back now."

Roch turned to face the window and the view of the meadow where the Pantera took meals together. "With nothing." In one sense he was relieved that there was no file on Lydia. If it got leaked to the human press that she was carrying a Pantera cub, she'd never be able to live easily outside of the Wildlands. Not that he wanted her to. Shit, he really didn't want her to. But with no records, no samples, no nothing, it was going to be near to impossible to track down any women who may have been given a Pantera sample.

"I say we question Hiss about this Stanton Locke, see what he knows," Damien suggested.

"You really think there's a connection?" Raphael asked.

Roch glanced over his shoulder, watched as the newbie Suit warred with himself on how to handle his leader's question. Finally Damien said, "I think it's worth a shot. If anything, I'll see how his eyes change, and his expression, when I ask him."

Raphael didn't contemplate this idea very long. "Do it. Head over to Medical."

"Now?" The male's eyes widened. "Alone?"

"You can handle it."

Damien tried like hell not to grin like a Pantera young, but it was impossible. He nodded at Raphael, and quickly left the room.

"That was nice," Roch said, pushing away from the window and walking over to Raphael's desk.

"Nothing nice about it," he replied. "He's going to be a formidable Suit. Just wanted him to find his balls and speak up."

Roch laughed. Then he dropped into the chair opposite his boss. "You think Hiss might know this guy?"

Raphael lifted his shoulders in a shrug. "My guess is no. I think Hiss is telling the truth when he says he was working with Shakpi's disciples. Don't think Locke has any connection there. But who the hell knows?"

"We need to find those samples," Roch said darkly.

"Damn right, we do. We can't have Pantera cubs being born outside the Wildlands. They're too important to the survival of our species."

The male's words raked through Roch. Lydia's cub. They needed to protect it. They needed to know who had sired it. He needed to know. Or Christ, did he? Would it truly make a difference? Now, or six months from now, or ten years from now? Would anybody remember, or care? And would she care?

"Just because they found no samples with the words Puma Shifter written on them doesn't mean they're not there," Roch put in.

"I know." Raphael lowered his voice even though they were the only two males in the room. Outside his door was a group of Diplomats, and some of the Geeks, working on a variety of issues. Including the very one they were discussing now.

"I didn't want to say this in front of the rookie," he began. "But we still have two Hunters inside. And when the lights go out and the alarm goes on, they'll continue their search."

Roch sat back, impressed. "You're damn good at keeping secrets, boss."

"Back at you, brother." Raphael too, leaned back in his chair.

"What does that mean?"

Raphael's brows lifted. "Loved that lasagna so much you came back for seconds?"

"You knew I was there."

The head of the Suits laughed, closed his laptop. "Are you really asking me if I knew someone was in my home with my mate and cub?"

Right. That was a pretty stupid question. Of course, Raphael and Ashe had been the last things on his mind last night. Or this morning. "And you allowed it?"

After a heavy exhale, the male said, "I am hoping..." He shrugged. "Ashe is hoping."

"For what?"

Green-gold eyes flashed with interest. "We want the woman to remain here. With her cub. You have a connection to her. A need to be around her constantly. It's like my connection to Ashe. And to Soyala. It's impossible to turn from. It's all-consuming."

Roch growled softly. "Yes."

"And you want her to stay."

"I want her, period," Roch ground out. "But what if the cub isn't mine?"

"Will it matter to you?"

"Of course not. I would claim it if she'd let me. But that's not the point. You know how we are, Raphael. Do you think a Pantera male would allow me to get close to the female carrying his young?"

That question weighed on the Suit leader. He scrubbed a hand over his chin. "It could cause a problem."

"Try a fight to the death." Because as much as he wouldn't want to rip any of his Pantera brothers apart, Roch was pretty sure he wouldn't be able to watch another male touch her.

Christ, just the thought of it made his cat feral.

"And fuck." He hadn't thought about what Lydia might want. "What if *she* wants this other male in her life?" *I lose my damn mind completely.*

"She wants you," Raphael said with a snort. "Shit, we all heard how much she wants you."

Roch snarled at him. "Don't make me make you fire my ass."

Raphael laughed. "What is the answer to this then, my friend?"

"The truth?"

"They say it sets you free," Raphael remarked.

At several points in his life, Roch would've appreciated that answer. Reveled in it even. But not today. Today there was nothing he wanted less than to be free. Of Lydia Page or the tiny life growing inside of her.

With a bluff of rugged hillside to her left and a curve of mysterious caves to her right, Lydia felt as though she was in a foreign land. Not that she'd been to all that many foreign lands. But she could imagine.

Thick, gloriously green vegetation hung from the rocks above her and rested languidly on the surface of the warm water of the bayou pool she was swimming in.

A bayou pool.

Never in a million years would she have thought she'd be doing this. *And* doing it buck-naked with three other women.

But seriously, that's what "recently fired, recently discovered by a puma shifter and brought to a magical spot in the bayous of Louisiana" people did, right?

"Are you sure Keira and Bayon aren't going to be around today?" Julia asked Genevieve with a quick glance at the beginnings of the couple's new home that was being built near the caves above them.

A Diplomat, Genevieve Burel was the Nurturer Jean-Baptiste's mate. She was a gorgeous blonde with pale blue eyes and a friendly smile. And she'd welcomed Lydia into the circle of friends like they'd known each other for years.

"Positive," Genevieve told her. "They're both on assignment."

"Top secret stuff?" Julia asked.

"If I told you I'd have to kill you."

Ashe and Lydia laughed while Julia splashed the female. Genevieve grinned and swam backwards toward a small alcove under a thick patch of greenery.

Growing up, Lydia had several close friends. But after high school, they'd grown apart. And well, she hadn't tried to make more. There just hadn't been time. Or maybe that had been an excuse not to get close to people. Fear of losing them again, or something. She had the same fear when it came to a certain Pantera male.

She looked at the women around her now, and wondered if there was truly a place for her here.

"Well this is very decadent." Ashe remarked before diving beneath the water and emerging five feet away with a wide grin.

"We all deserve a little decadence," Julia put in, making small circles on the surface of the pool with her index finger. "Especially the new mama."

"I can't tell you how excited I am for you," Genevieve said, swimming over. "It means there's hope for us here. To bring more Pantera cubs into the world."

It was shocking how different the reaction to her pregnancy was here in the Wildlands versus out in the wilds of New Orleans. Where the Pantera saw her half human, half shifter baby as a blessing, the assholes at Haymore had seen it as a terrible mistake. How would the rest of the world react, she wondered. And would she find out sooner rather than later? After all, she'd only agreed to stay here for a few days.

Her heart seized in her chest at the thought of leaving.

No. At the thought of leaving *him*.

"How long has it been since a Pantera cub was born?" Lydia asked.

"Not counting Soyala?" Ashe said. "Over fifty years."

"There was a curse put on our species," Genevieve explained. "Soyala changed all of that."

Curiosity pushed her to ask, "How?"

"Females," came a male voice at the shore. "Remain below the water, please."

Genevieve gasped and submerged herself to her neck, Ashe grabbed a piece of water plant and placed it in front of her, and Julia remained where she was, her eyes narrowing on the man—the male—standing on the bank.

"Roch, how the hell did you know where we were?" Ashe demanded. Then she glanced over at Lydia and sniffed. "Never mind."

Lydia stared at him. Standing there in a pair of faded jeans and a white t-shirt. She mentally sighed. The guy could sport casual or career and he would always be the sexiest male in the room.

Or the bayou.

His eyes, those summer sky blue eyes, captured hers. "I need to speak to you."

"Hey Roch, we're swimming here," Julia called out. "You know, girl time."

"Yeah, go back to the house, Roch, and wait for her there," Ashe said, though her tone was far from dictatorial.

"No." He said the word to them, but his eyes remained on Lydia.

As Lydia was held captive by his hot stare, Julia and Genevieve groaned simultaneously.

"If you hang out here and any of our mates see you they're going to kill you," Julia said, then turned to Lydia and explained. "Sounds uncivilized and barbaric, but there it is. It's what you sign up for if you get with any of our males, FYI."

Lydia nodded, but decided not to say that the idea of an uncivilized and barbaric Roch was intriguing as hell.

"She's not going for any of our males," Roch said tightly.

"Someone's acting a little possessive," Genevieve remarked. "Especially over a female who doesn't belong to him."

"Lydia," he called to her, ignoring the women's barbs. "Please."

"I'm not kidding about our mates, Roch," Julia called out.

He growled, and for the first time, he turned and glared at each woman in turn. "Let them come."

"Oh Jesus," Julia uttered.

The last thing Lydia wanted was for him to get into a fight. Get hurt. That gorgeous face did not need any bruises. "I'm coming," she called, then started swimming toward him. When she was ten feet from shore, she stopped and addressed him. "What's wrong?"

He looked tense. "I need to say something to you."

"We can talk back at Ashe's—"

"No. It can't wait."

She glanced behind her, then back at him. "Even for some privacy?"

"I'm not ashamed of what I have to say, Lydia." He came to the very edge of the water and dropped onto his haunches. His jeans hugged tight to his muscular thighs, and the white t-shirt strained against smooth, tanned, muscle. "Have the testing done."

Surprise caught and held her. "Roch…"

"We need to know the truth."

"We?" She held her breath.

"You, me, the Pantera."

A tight knot forming in her throat, she swam closer. "What if it's another male's—"

"Then the male should know." His nostrils flared, but he continued. "It's not about you and me anymore. It's about the Pantera. Pack first. The cub is what's important here. The cub and its safety is everything to our species."

Lydia stared at him, her heart pricked and bleeding inside her chest. Yes, she was grateful for what he was saying, how he felt about her child. But gone was his fight. For her. Or for the male who might try and claim her.

Pain lashed through her, but she pushed it away. It was important to know. Her value and importance was in her cub.

"That's what I came to say." He stood up, nodded to the females in the water. "I apologize, and will speak to each of your mates."

As he shifted into his puma and took off up the hillside, Ashe, Genevieve and Julia all surrounded her. They didn't say anything, but they didn't have to. It was something all females understood and sympathized with—Pantera or human. The pain of rejection.

CHAPTER EIGHT

HE despised himself.

He despised everyone around him, too.

It was a good thing that the one male Roch had told about his adventure to the bayou pool happened to be a Nurturer. Because as soon as Jean-Baptiste had given him the black eye he'd deserved, the male had quickly set about treating it.

Roch stalked through town in his puma state, a file folder between his teeth. According to Damien, Hiss had claimed to know nothing about the human male, Locke. But Roch had done some unconventional research on the man with Xavier, the head of the Geeks. Locke had been a foundling, taken in by a very rich man. A man who was rarely seen and rumored to be gravely ill. Seemed that Locke was devoted to him. Among his vast holdings, The Haymore Center was one of several research and/or medical facilities he owned. And though they offered a wide range of infertility options including egg donation, testing and surgery, it looked as though experimentation was their primary focus.

Cell and tissue rejuvenation, to be exact.

His jaw clamped a little tighter around the file as he leapt over a stretch of stream bordering Raphael and Ashe's property. He needed to talk to his boss.

"Afternoon, Suit."

Roch's puma whirled around and stalked forward, toward the voice. Which belonged to none other than Parish. The leader of the

Hunters wore a dark, irritated expression. So he'd gotten Roch's text. In seconds, Roch shifted into his male form.

The golden eyed male looked him over and sneered. "Only one black eye? I think you might need a set."

Right. Baptiste might have a genius at healing, but only time erased the bruising. Roch raised his arms in surrender. "Have at it, Parish."

The male sniffed, even kicked a rock with the tip of his boot. "Shit, brother, it's not as much fun when you welcome it."

"Look, I needed to speak with Lydia. It was the only way."

Parish was silent for a moment, then he lifted his shoulders and shrugged, the wind of battle now calm. "Well, I hope it was worth it."

Worth it? Seeing the look on her face when he'd made it pretty damn clear the cub was the most important thing to him, to the Pantera?

His jaw went tight. He truly despised himself today.

"Hey, if it wasn't," Parish put in, running a hand through his long, dark hair. "Or you didn't get what you needed, you can try again. She's over at Medical right now."

Roch's heart dropped like a stone into his gut. "What?"

"With my fully-clothed mate."

Shit. "Did you see what she was doing? Why she was there?"

The Hunter studied him, dark brows descending over those gold eyes. "Paternity test. She wanted to get it done today, as she's heading back to New Orleans in the morning."

The blood drained from Roch's body. He'd told her to get the testing. He just hadn't believed it would be right away.

"I know I shouldn't give a shit after the near-visuals in the bayou pool," Parish began reluctantly. "But are you all right?"

Hell no he wasn't all right. He'd made a huge mistake. If he lost the woman he—

With a growl, he shifted back into his puma. After a quick nod to Parish, he scooped up the file in his teeth and took off toward Raphael's place. Not just to give him the information he'd found, but to ask him—and his mate—for help.

Her heart beating wildly in her chest, Lydia stood on the porch of Roch's home. It was a lovely two-story Craftsman-style house, more modern than any of the dwellings she'd seen in the Wildlands. And it suited him perfectly. That warm, sexy, cerebral style.

As her hand rose to the door she wondered once again why Raphael had asked her to bring some paperwork over to Roch's place. Of course, she was happy to do it. Anything for the couple who were treating her like an honored guest. But in her gut, she knew it had to be an excuse to get her here. The only question was, who had the idea? And why?

After knocking, she stepped back and waited. It wasn't long before the door opened and the sunset behind her revealed the most gorgeous male in the universe. Her heart squeezed with love and trepidation.

His face split into a wide grin. He wasn't surprised to see her. In fact, he looked pleased.

She held out a large envelope. "I brought this from Raphael."

"Thanks." He took it from her, then stepped back. "Come on in."

"I should get back."

His eyes moved over her face. "Please, Lydia."

Resisting this male was like trying to resist air or light or water. He felt so strangely essential to her being.

The moment she stepped inside, she felt at home. Not that she was going to say that out loud. Instead, as she took in all the refinished wood, modern, yet comfortable furnishings and windows, windows, windows, she said, "I like your house."

"I like you in it," he said, taking her hand.

Lydia's breath caught in her throat. What was this? What was he saying?

"Come on," he continued with a soft smile, leading her out of the foyer. "I'll show you around."

Confused, yet happy in a way she could never explain, his hand holding hers, she followed him through several rooms. Kitchen, dining area, a back porch overlooking a small pond. It was all unfussy and gorgeous and clever. Like him. When he led her down another hallway and she spotted bedrooms, she wondered if she was going to get a look at where he slept. The idea made her blush and grin. But the bedroom he led her into wasn't his own.

"What's this?" she asked, suddenly breathless as she took in the lovely white crib, changing table, and pale green rocking chair.

"It's just a few things," he began, his voice low and deep and threaded with hope. "I thought maybe you'd want to choose colors and how everything is arranged. And if you don't like any of this, we can get something else. Maybe an animal theme..."

She turned to look at him. "I don't understand."

Ice blue eyes that were filled with only warmth and want stared back at her. "For the cub, Lydia."

"What you said today—"

He groaned. "I was an asshole. A male so deeply in love with a female he felt he didn't have the right to claim, he got scared."

Lydia's entire body erupted with heat, and her breath was locked inside her lungs. But she managed to push out a hopeful, "And now?"

He laughed, his eyes crinkling with affection. "Now he doesn't give a fuck. He wants her. He loves her. He's going to claim her, no matter what."

Lydia stood there, in the bedroom this male had declared was her child's. He'd told her he loved her, that he wanted her. And she could see it in his eyes. But she still had to know...

"I had the test performed today," she said.

Not a flash of concern crossed his handsome features. He only grinned at her. So happy. So confident. So sure.

"I don't care what it said, Lydia. I want you. I want this cub. I will be a strong, available father to it." He reached for her. "And if another male tries to claim you and the cub, we'll deal with it. No bluster. No fight." He lifted his chin and smiled. "We may be puma shifters, but we will be civilized and supportive."

It was all she needed to hear. It was everything. She went to him and wrapped her arms around his waist. Looked up into his beautifully fierce face. "I love your eyes."

301

He chuckled softly. "And I love you."

She squeezed him tighter. "I hope our baby gets them."

It was as if the air rushed out of the room. Those eyes she loved widened and Roch uttered hoarsely, "What did you say?"

The happiness that filled her in that moment was unlike anything she had ever experienced. She smiled up at him. "Just that I hope our cub has your—"

"Ours?" He didn't let her answer. His head dropped and his mouth covered hers.

Lydia wrapped her arms around his neck and kissed him back, so fiercely, so lovingly, both of them groaned with the pleasure of it.

She was in love. Deeply and desperately. With the father of her child. How in the world was such a miracle possible?

Roch eased her down to the carpet and started taking off her clothes. Her skin prickling with heat and excitement, Lydia helped him. Especially when it was time to undress him. She just wanted them naked and in each other's arms where they belonged. And when he stretched out over her, his hard muscle against her soft flesh, she sighed with ecstasy.

The magic of the Wildlands was here, with her and inside her. And she was never going to let it go.

As Roch took her mouth again, she wrapped her legs around his waist and lifted her hips in invitation. She wasn't going to play coy—she'd waited too long to know what he would feel like inside her. And when he entered her with one deep, hungry thrust, she cried out in both pleasure and intensity. He was long and thick and hot, and her walls instantly welcomed him, bathing him in cream.

Desperate for him to move, Lydia circled her hips. But Roch pressed her down into the soft carpet and held her there with unspoken authority and strength.

She looked up at him. "What's wrong?"

He gazed down at her with eyes so filled with hunger and love, her heart contracted. "This will sound insane."

"Tell me."

"We didn't get to make our cub this way..."

Pain, beautiful pain erupted within her. "Oh, Roch," she said on a sigh. "The next one. Our next one."

"Yes, but…" He eased out of her and thrust back in.

She gasped with pleasure. So filled. So desperate for more. Him. All of him.

"Can we pretend that we are?" he asked, lowering his head and nipping at her bottom lip. "Can we pretend that when I come inside you, when you cry out and take your release, and I follow you there, that we're making our—"

"Son," she said, tears pricking her eyes. She nodded. "Oh god, Roch. I love you. Yes."

He said nothing more. His mouth covered hers, and as he kissed her deeply, lovingly, he thrust inside her. Taking her to heaven. Building the heat and intensity within her.

Lydia wrapped her arms around him and held on tight. She wasn't going to last long. Roch was so big, so hard, the head of his cock rubbing deliciously against the spot inside her pussy that triggered her climax.

And when he ripped his mouth from hers and buried it in her neck, suckling, scraping his teeth against her pulse point, she exploded.

Crying out, she came. Her walls milking him until he too snarled and bucked and took his release.

It was moments—minutes, hours?—until he stopped thrusting inside her, until they cooled. But when they did, Roch eased to his back and pulled her in close. Satiated, Lydia snuggled against him. On the soft carpet. She smiled against his shoulder. On the floor of their cub's bedroom.

"Tell me you're not going back to New Orleans," he said with a possessive rasp to his tone. "Except to get your things."

Her heart stuttered. "You know about that?"

"Tell me, Lydia. Please. Before I lose my mind. I'm in love with you. I think I have been ever since you offered me your beignet."

She smiled and kissed his shoulder. This male made her deliriously happy.

"Tell me," he growled.

"I'll stay," she laughed. "Of course I'll stay."

He heaved an enormous sigh. "Christ, I'm glad. But you know, it's not enough."

She lifted her head, her heart jumping in her blood now. "What do you mean?"

He looked calm, satiated, tousled. Gorgeous. His eyes connected with hers and held. "You know about mating. Ashe and Julia and others too, I'm sure, have explained our ways."

She nodded, breath held. "It's like a human marriage."

He shook his head. "No, Lydia. It's deeper than that. Truer. It is a bond that lasts not just a lifetime, but beyond."

"Well, that's a good thing," she said with genuine feeling. "I love that."

His eyes moved over her face. "And I love you." He reached around her naked ass and yanked her to him.

She squealed.

"Will you be my mate, Lydia Page?" he asked in the most serious tone she'd ever heard from him. "Live with me, sleep with me, make love with me, laugh with me?" His eyes flashed with sudden humor. "Let me share in diaper duties for our son?"

It wasn't possible to be any happier than she was, but with that question—no, that proposal—she truly thought she'd died and gone to heaven. She was deeply and truly loved by the male who had given her a son.

"Is that a yes, Ms. Page?" he said with playful ferocity.

She smiled. "That, my gorgeous Pantera male—my mate—is an absolutely, definitely, love you, yes, yes, yes."

He kissed her, soft and gentle, then eased her onto her back.

"What are you doing?" she asked with a girlish giggle.

Up on his hands and knees and headed for the lower half of her body, looking as near to his puma as possible in his male form, Roch snarled sensually at her.

"I say we seal this with a kiss," he uttered, his breath near her belly now.

"My lips are up here, Roch," she said breathlessly, watching him, waiting.

His eyes went heavy lidded as he grasped her inner thighs and splayed them wide. "Not the lips I'm hungry for at the moment."

And as he proved that statement, all Lydia could do was sigh.

EPILOGUE

THREE days later

"Rosalie is home, but Mercier is dead," Raphael said to the small group of Hunters, Suits and Nurturers who were gathered in his office at Diplomatic headquarters. It was night, and they'd been at it for hours. "And our Hunters inside Haymore haven't reported back."

Sebastian cursed. "This new enemy is worse than the last."

"But what is it they want?" Genevieve asked, nonplussed.

"Our DNA," Roch said, glancing around the dimly lit room with its half empty plates and endless water bottles. "We don't know why yet. What they hope to use it for. But it has something to do with that Stanton Locke and the mysterious man he cares for. As you know, my mate is an attorney and she's calling all her contacts, trying to get a hold of Stanton's financial dealings. What, how much, with whom."

"Please stop saying that bastard's name," Keira ground out from her spot on the edge of Raphael's desk. "Do you know what he said when the cops hauled me away? 'Pantera are dangerous creatures.' He wants us all rounded up so human society can be safe."

"That piece of shit will come to know how unsafe we are," Xavier muttered. He turned to Raphael. "What do we do?"

The leader of the Suits looked at each one of them and sighed. "Maybe it's time to get on camera and speak. Tell the truth. Let the humans see us."

A slate grey puma burst into the room and snarled at the lot of them. In seconds, it shifted and revealed a very pissed-off Parish.

"What is it?" Raphael demanded.

"The elders are with Hiss, as he asked," the leader of the Hunters said with a sneer. "They are giving him the chance to confess what he knows."

"The three are visiting a prisoner?" Keira exclaimed, coming to her feet. "What the hell is happening?"

"Oh," Parish continued. "And we have photographers at our borders."

Calmly, every bit the formidable Diplomat he was, Raphael stood up and walked out from behind his desk. "Roch, I'll need to borrow your tie. Looks like our time on camera has come sooner than we thought."

BAYOU
HEAT

Book Eleven

HAKAN

New York Times and *USA Today* Bestselling Authors

ALEXANDRA IVY

Book Twelve

SÉVERIN
LAURA WRIGHT

HAKAN

By
Alexandra Ivy

PROLOGUE

HISS wasn't stupid.

He realized that most Pantera considered him crazy. Why wouldn't they? No one could possibly understand his obsessive refusal to believe that his family had been killed when he was just a babe.

But now they considered him more than just insane.

He was a danger.

A traitor.

The knowledge burned at him like acid on his soul.

This wasn't what he wanted. He'd never intended to betray his people, or to work with his enemies. But what choice had the elders left him?

Pacing the private room at the back of the medical clinic that kept him separated from the rest of the building, Hiss came to an abrupt halt as he caught a familiar scent.

Ah. Speak of the devil.

Or devils, as the case may be.

The elders.

A fierce smile curved his lips as he moved to stand directly in front of the door.

He'd waited for this moment for the past sixty years.

Ever since he'd been old enough to realize that the endless dreams he had of a pretty, dark-haired female clutching a child in her arms were more than just nightmares.

Even now he could remember the wild fear that had combusted through him as he'd rushed to the elders, convinced that he was having visions of his mother and sister. He'd been desperate to begin an immediate search for his family, but the elders had refused to send out the Hunters to track them down. Hell, they wouldn't even let him go in search of them.

Instead, they'd locked him in a small cell so he couldn't leave the Wildlands, claiming his parents and sister had died during a trip to New Orleans and his refusal to believe they were dead proved he was belatedly grieving their loss.

Bitches.

He'd been waiting for some sort of leverage to force the ancient females to tell him the truth of his missing family. And now, at last, he had it.

Outside the door he could hear the muted voices of the elders as they shared a private conversation. His hands clenched, his claws slicing out to draw blood as they carved through his palm. No doubt they were discussing how they were going to try to force information out of him without offering any in return.

Not. Going. To. Happen.

Even if he was going to be executed as a traitor, he intended to have the truth before he died.

Intent on trying to overhear the conversation from the outer hallway, Hiss didn't notice the sound of a window being opened behind him.

It wasn't until he caught the distinct scent of expensive cologne that he whirled around to discover a tall, human male standing a few feet behind him.

Hiss instinctively widened his stance, his fangs elongating as he prepared for an attack.

"Who the hell are you?" he growled.

The man smiled, his dark hair smoothed from his lean face and his blue eyes oddly compelling.

"A friend," he assured Hiss in a posh English accent.

Hiss curled his upper lip, flicking a disdainful glance over the slender form that was attired in a smoke gray suit that probably cost over a grand.

"I don't have human friends," he informed the intruder, his eyes narrowed.

"Fine." The smile widened to reveal perfect white teeth. "Then a potential partner."

Hiss spat on the ground, pretending that he wasn't being eaten alive by guilt. "If you're looking for your goddess, she returned to the mother-ship with her sister."

The man looked genuinely puzzled. "I beg your pardon?"

"Opela and Shakpi are reunited and have retreated from this world," he said in slow, deliberate tones. He wanted this idiot gone so he could concentrate on his meeting with the elders. "You're a day late and a dollar short, as usual."

"Ah." The stranger waved a slender hand. "You misunderstand my presence here. I have no interest in your deities, Hiss, or the strange allies you chose to use for your revenge."

Belatedly Hiss realized that the intruder didn't have the foul stench that clung to the disciples of Shakpi. Which meant that he wasn't one of the whackadoodles that Hiss had been forced to deal with for far too long.

So what the hell was he doing in the Wildlands?

Hiss stepped forward, the air sizzling with danger as he allowed the fool to catch a glimpse of the cat that prowled just below the surface.

"Give me your name," he commanded, his voice thick with warning.

The stranger gave a mocking bow of his head. "Stanton Locke."

Stanton Locke? Hadn't he heard that name whispered by the guards?

"Why are you here?"

"To give you what you most desire."

Hiss released a sharp, humorless laugh. "Thanks, but I don't swing that way."

"I have answers, Hiss," Stanton promised in soft tones. He had the voice of an angel. Pure temptation. "And the family that you've been seeking."

CHAPTER ONE

HAKAN returned to his small room in the Hunters' communal living quarters for a quick shower and a change of jeans and T-shirt before heading to the large plantation-style building that served as the nerve center for the Diplomats.

He was one of the most powerful Pantera ever born.

At six foot five he was heavily muscled, with skin the color of melted caramel and eyes a dark amber flecked with jade. But despite his epic stamina, he wanted nothing more than to crawl into his bed and sleep for the next twenty-four hours.

After three intense days of searching nonstop for Mercier and Rosalie his body ached and his mind was clouded with weariness. He was, quite frankly, running on empty.

Only the nagging knowledge he'd failed kept him moving.

Fury blasted through him. Mercier was dead. Shot in the head.

Someone was going to pay.

In blood.

Entering the large building filled with Geeks tapping on their computers or monitoring the surveillance equipment along the far wall, he moved toward the private offices at the back.

He'd just stepped through a double doorway when the hallway was blocked by a large Hunter with dark hair and an angular face that was scarred on the right side.

"Hakan." Parish arched a dark brow. "When did you get back?"

317

"An hour ago."

The leader of the Hunters folded his arms over his chest. "Then why aren't you resting?"

Hakan ignored the question. "Where's Raphael?"

Parish's face hardened. Any other day he would have commanded Hakan to get his ass to bed, but with yet another crisis looming, they were all on edge. Sleep was a commodity that would have to wait.

"He's busy with Sebastian, trying to play nice with the horde of reporters parked on our borders," the older male explained.

"Yeah, I noticed." Hakan curled his lips in disgust. He didn't have a problem with humans, but he'd been shocked by the dozens of vans that'd blocked the roads leading to the Wildlands, and the aggressive photographers who'd been lurking in the shadows to snap pictures of anything that moved. It'd been like a fucking feeding frenzy. "What are they doing there?"

"The humans have a bug up their ass about the beast-men infecting the bayous."

"Beast-men?"

Parish gave a short, humorless laugh at Hakan's outraged expression.

"Their words, not mine."

"Perfect. That's all we need right now…a bunch of humans treating the Wildlands like it's their personal zoo."

"No shit." Parish shook his head in frustration. "What do you need from Raphael?"

"I want to know how Mercier ended up dead."

Blunt. To the point. That was Hakan.

Only once in his life had he tried to hide his true emotions.

He was still paying the price for that piece of stupidity.

"They're both Hunters." Parish's voice was a low growl, the pain of his cat visible in his eyes. The grief for the fallen Hunter was still a raw wound for all of them. "They understood that Raphael would never negotiate for hostages, so they did what they were trained to do. Escape."

Hakan nodded. He didn't blame the leader of the Diplomats. Negotiating with blackmailers was unacceptable. Still, he needed to know how his childhood friend had ended up dead.

"And?"

Parish grimaced. "According to Rosalie they managed to break free of the malachite chains that were holding them, but they were both dangerously weak."

"Shit. They know we're vulnerable to malachite?"

"It seems we've been outed in more ways than one," Parish admitted. "Mercier sacrificed himself so Rosalie could escape past the guards who were patrolling the abandoned factory where they were being held."

Hakan pressed a hand to his aching heart. It was just like Mercier to play the hero.

"God. Damn."

Parish gave a grim nod. "That about sums it up."

"How is Rosalie?"

"Angel checked her out as soon as she returned. Physically she's fine. Mentally she's a wreck."

He could imagine. Knowing a close friend gave their life to save you…yeah, that would screw with anyone.

Hakan abruptly forced away his dark thoughts.

Eventually he would deal with the loss of his friend. For now, he had to make sure he didn't lose anyone else.

"Have you managed to figure out why the hell the kidnappers wanted to get their hands on Hiss?"

Parish shook his head. "Not yet. He's not talking."

Hakan bared his teeth, his cat straining to get free.

His mother had done her best to civilize him, but Hakan would always be a little feral.

"Give me ten minutes alone with him."

Parish twisted his lips. No doubt the Hunter had already tried to get his hands on their prisoner.

"The elders have demanded to speak with him before allowing us to interrogate him."

"Why?"

"If you want your balls handed to you, why don't you go ask them?" Parish drawled. "Personally I'd rather put my head in a wood chipper."

Hakan couldn't argue.

The three female leaders of the Pantera could be scary as shit when they actually bothered to take an interest in their people.

Usually it was Raphael making the day-to-day decisions.

"Damn." Frustration boiled through Hakan. He wanted to put his fist through something. Hard. "Shakpi's curse is finally gone and the land is healing. We should be celebrating the birth of Soyala, not worrying about another threat to the Pantera."

"Preaching to the choir, *mon ami*," Parish agreed. "And if that's not enough, the humans are becoming a genuine nuisance."

Hakan briefly considered the pleasure of shifting into his cat form and showing the gathered humans just how dangerous a Pantera could be.

Then he gave a wry shake of his head. "Thank the Goddess I'm not a Suit."

"Yeah, we're all happy about that," Parish said with a short laugh. "You have about as much diplomacy as a hungry gator."

"Which is twice as much as you."

The leader of the Hunters shrugged. "Painfully true." Their conversation was interrupted by a muffled chime. With a frown, Parish dug his phone out of the front pocket of his jeans and pressed it to his ear. "What?"

Hakan narrowed his eyes as his companion paced down the hall, clearly unhappy with the direction of the phone call. He hoped like hell it was Parish's mate complaining that the male forgot to take out the garbage, but there was a ball of dread in the pit of his stomach that warned it was something much worse.

At last Parish shoved the phone back into his pocket and prowled back to stand in front of Hakan.

"What's up?" Hakan demanded.

"I've been summoned by the elders."

Hakan grimaced. The poor bastard. No one wanted to be called before the three powerful females who shrouded themselves in mystery.

"I thought they were with Hiss?"

"He's gone," the leader said, his voice hard with anger.

"What did you say?"

"He's gone."

Hakan blinked. Then blinked again.

"What do you mean, gone?"

Parish's eyes glowed with the golden power of his cat. "Vanished. Departed. Vamoosed."

Hakan made a sound of annoyance. Now wasn't the time for his friend's twisted sense of humor.

"I understand the definition, but I thought he was being guarded. How did he escape?"

"A human who was armed with malachite darts managed to disable the guards long enough to unlock a back door to the clinic and sneak him away."

"How did a human get across the border—" Hakan bit off his words, remembering the large mass of people who were currently parked at the edge of the Wildlands. "Holy hell."

It could be a coincidence. The enemy might have noticed the flurry of fearful humans who were demanding answers from the Pantera.

Yeah, and he might sprout wings and a halo.

A low growl rumbled in his chest.

Parish studied him with a frown. "Hakan?"

"The humans were a deliberate distraction," he said, sharing his growing suspicion.

"Distraction?"

"What better way to slip past our defenses than to rile up the national press with stories of dangerous beast-men?"

Parish sucked in a sharp breath, swift to follow Hakan's logic. Then his golden eyes widened and he muttered a string of foul curses.

"It wasn't just the reporters who were used as a distraction," he at last said.

Hakan watched as his leader began to pace the hall from side to side. If he was in cat form his tail would be twitching.

"What else?" Hakan prompted.

"The kidnappers of Mercier and Rosalie," Parish snarled. "If they knew enough about Pantera to use malachite to capture them, then they would have known that we would never trade one of our people for another. Not even a traitor. Instead we did exactly as they expected and sent out our Hunters to search for them. Then, when we were concentrating on the search, they used the humans' growing fear of us to stir up yet more chaos so they could slip across the borders and get their hands on Hiss."

Hakan turned to smash his fist against the wall, his hand punching through the paneling.

Home repair was a daily occurrence in the Wildlands.

"We were played," he snarled.

"Like fucking violins," Parish agreed, his hands clenching and unclenching as if he was thinking about doing some remodeling of his own. "Could this week get any worse? First Mercier and Rosalie are kidnapped, then we discover The Haymore Center has been using Pantera DNA to try to create…" The older Pantera grimaced. "Hell, I don't even know what they're trying to do."

Talon had called Hakan when he was on his way back to the Wildlands to catch him up on the latest news. He was still wrapping his brain around the fact that a human female had been impregnated with a Pantera child without her knowledge.

"The Center has to have some connection to Hiss," Hakan pointed out, wishing he could get his hands on the traitor.

Long ago he'd loved Hiss like a brother, but that wouldn't stop him from beating the shit out of him to get the information they so desperately needed.

Parish gave a sharp nod of agreement. "We can hope the two missing Pantera aren't in the hands of our newest enemies."

Hakan went rigid. Talon hadn't said anything about missing Pantera. Of course, lately the disasters were happening at a fast and furious rate. It wasn't really surprising he had forgotten to pass along the information.

"Who's gone?"

"At first we thought it was Rage and Bayon, but it turned out that Bayon was at the police station dealing with a very pissed-off Keira." Parish's lips twisted into a wry smile. His older sister had a temper that could make grown men cower in fear. "Instead, Rage was with Payton."

Hakan's heart came to a sharp, agonizing halt as a savage terror scoured through him like hot lava.

No. This had to be a mistake.

He was suddenly overwhelmed by the image of a tiny female with a heart-shaped face that was dominated by a pair of pale green eyes and framed by a halo of copper curls.

"How the hell can Payton be missing?" he rasped. "She's a Geek. She's supposed to be sitting at a desk typing on her computer, not out in the field."

Parish arched a brow, clearly caught off-guard by the fury that vibrated in Hakan's voice.

"We hoped the doctors would allow her to look through the files to reveal who was behind inseminating Lydia," he explained. "They were a part of a larger group of Pantera who traveled to the Center..." His words trailed away as Hakan turned on his heel and charged toward the nearest door. "Hakan? Where are you going?" he called out.

"To get Payton," Hakan snarled, pausing long enough to glare over his shoulder. "Then I'm coming back to kick the ass of whoever sent her into danger."

———

The Haymore Center, just off the Pontchartrain Expressway, didn't look like a den of evil.

The three-story red brick building was framed by professionally trimmed hedges and a manicured lawn with large urns on either side of the glass doors. Even inside there was nothing to indicate it was anything but an upscale health clinic that offered in vitro fertilization.

It was only in the basement, which was accessible by a hidden elevator in the lab and was protected by two guards, that it became obvious there was something wrong beneath the carefully constructed façade.

What clinic had hidden rooms with prison cells, complete with iron bars? Or a line of steel walk-in freezers that were protected with biometric locks? Or a computer system that would make Homeland Security have a stroke?

Payton had immediately known that she had to discover the secrets The Haymore Center was so anxious to hide.

Ignoring Rage's vehement insistence that she return to the Wildlands, she'd entered the main computer room, not particularly concerned when the guards arrived and tossed her and Rage in the cells.

They were obviously rent-a-cops, not hardened warriors, and there hadn't been any malachite in the iron bars of the cells. If they truly felt in danger they would be able to escape.

Besides, the Hunters weren't the only ones who were willing to take risks to protect the Pantera. She might be a Geek, but she would do whatever necessary to discover who was behind the latest threat to her people.

And it had nothing to do with proving her worth.

Not one damned thing.

Leaning over the desk, Payton carefully monitored the numbers scrolling across the computer screen.

Over the past three days she'd been running the computer program that she'd personally developed to break through the firewalls that prevented her from downloading the files.

It should never have taken so long, but the complicated encryption system had meant there wasn't going to be an easy solution. Instead she had to peel away each layer of security, one at a time.

And of course, it didn't help that they had to pretend to be safely locked away whenever the guards stirred from their private break room to check on them.

It'd been a frustrating few days, but she was finally at the last firewall. She was close enough she could taste success.

Tapping an impatient finger on the edge of the desk, Payton pretended she didn't notice the large Hunter who stepped into the room packed with high-tech equipment.

As if any female could ignore the gorgeous male with short, dark hair that always looked as if it'd been tousled by an eager lover. He had skin tanned to a warm shade of bronze, a lean, perfectly sculpted face, and eyes that were a startling shade of violet, flecked with gold.

No big shocker that Rage had been breaking hearts since he'd left the nursery.

"It's almost halftime," the male warned. It was Sunday night and the Saints were playing football. Payton had hoped it would keep the guards glued to their TV until she was done. "You need to get back to your cell."

She absently chewed her thumbnail, psychically willing her program to work faster.

It didn't actually help, but it made her feel as if she was doing something.

"Just one more minute," she muttered.

"Dammit, you're going to give me a heart attack," Rage informed her. "Not to mention the fact that Parish is going to skin me alive for not checking in."

The guards had taken their cellphones when they'd first captured them, which meant they hadn't been able to contact the Wildlands and reveal what they were doing.

Payton didn't want to worry anyone, but this was too important not to stay and finish the job.

"I'm close to breaking through," she assured her companion.

Rage moved to stand at her shoulder, his impatience a tangible force in the air.

"I still don't know why we can't just take the computer and leave."

Payton swallowed her sigh. Hunters. They were always eager to charge in and take action. This waiting was driving the male insane.

"Because they'll know we have it and destroy the information we need," she explained for the tenth time, glaring at the numbers that scrolled across the screen. Rage wasn't the only one losing his patience. "Come on, come on," she urged softly.

"Does talking to it make it go faster?" Rage teased.

"Smartass."

"Hey now, is that any way to talk to the male protecting your very fine ass?"

She rolled her eyes, her lips twitching. Rage was a compulsive flirt, but she couldn't deny she enjoyed his companionship.

Every female enjoyed a male who made her feel beautiful.

Especially after she'd been cruelly rejected by the male she loved.

"You need to keep your attention focused on the guards, not my ass," she chided.

On cue, there was the sound of a door opening down the hall and Rage swore beneath his breath.

"Time's up, sweetheart."

Payton reluctantly straightened. "Crap."

"We'll try again after halftime."

"How long will that be?"

"Twenty minutes." Rage shrugged. "Thirty minutes tops."

Payton hesitated. If she shut down the program she'd have to start over on the last layer of security.

"Then I think I'll take the risk of leaving my program running," she abruptly decided. "Unless they try to use the computer they won't notice."

Rage snorted. "I doubt those goons know how to turn on a computer, let alone comprehend what you're doing."

Payton agreed. It'd become painfully obvious the human guards hadn't been hired for their brains.

Of course, whoever was running the clinic probably didn't think anyone would ever manage to stumble across this secret basement. And if they did, most people would have been easily run off by a guard pointing a gun in their direction.

"I'm not worried about the guards," she told him. "I'm afraid of triggering my presence once I break past the final firewall."

"Let's go."

Grabbing her upper arm, he gently tugged her out of the computer room and past the large lab that was locked up tight. Then, entering the storage area at the back, they pushed aside the shelves to reveal the double cells built in the hidden room.

"You have the gun I gave you?" Rage demanded as he opened one of the cells and urged her inside.

Payton glanced down to where the full cut of her slacks hid the weapon strapped to her ankle.

"Yep."

Rage shook his head as he closed the door and used a small piece of wire to tumble the lock. They both knew the weapon was more for show than actual protection. She couldn't hit the broad side of a barn.

Not that she was helpless.

She was far stronger and faster than a mere human.

"I don't like this," he breathed.

She rolled her eyes as the Hunter moved to step into the adjoining cell, closing and locking the door behind him.

"You've made your opinion clear," she assured him.

Rage moved to stretch his large body onto the cot, sending her a chiding glance.

"Not clear enough or we wouldn't still be here."

She headed to the back of the cell as she caught the smell of the approaching humans. It wasn't the same sour stench of the disciples of Shakpi. Nope, this odor was nothing more than a lack of soap and water.

None of them had been near a shower for three days.

Unfortunately.

"I'll be done tonight, I promise."

They fell silent as the two humans stepped through the hidden door. Unlike the other guards in the clinic, these two wore casual khakis and shirts instead of the official uniforms. They also carried high-powered guns that might have been terrifying if Rage hadn't disabled them while the men were asleep.

"Hello, pussy," the shorter of the two men drawled, moving to press his pudgy face against the iron bars. It was a tediously predictable taunt that he repeated every night. "Ready for a real man?"

The second guard made a sound of disgust, his gray hair and lined face revealing he was far older than his companion.

"Would you really do her?"

The man leered at Payton even as she gave a deliberate yawn.

"Hell, she has a cunt, doesn't she?"

"She's a fucking animal," the second guard muttered.

"I've had worse."

"Until she bites off your dick."

"I'm not scared of the mutants," Guard Number One assured his friend, only to ruin his manly boast when he gave a squeak of alarm and slammed against the shelves behind him as Rage shoved himself off his cot.

"Why don't you come in here and say that," Rage taunted.

"Let's get out of here." The older man backed out of the cramped room, his hand hovering above the gun holstered at his side. "I want to make a Hot Pocket before the game starts."

The two idiots stumbled out of the room with enough speed to make Payton chuckle, completely unaware that Rage was already out of his cell and shadowing them as they returned to their break room.

Once the Hunter was certain the two were once again engrossed in their game he would return to get Payton. Until then she would have to wait.

Too restless to sit down, Payton paced the small cell. Hopefully her program was on the edge of breaking through the firewall, without having actually penetrated the barrier. Anyone who had that level of protection would no doubt have installed a fail-safe to destroy the information if it was ever compromised.

Which meant she'd have only seconds to transfer as much data as possible.

Still pacing, Payton came to an abrupt halt.

What was that scent? It was Pantera. Not Rage, but it was familiar…

Oh hell.

Disbelief thundered through her as she watched the large male step through the doorway, his massive body consuming the cramped space.

Hakan.

She licked her dry lips, her gaze compulsively taking in his bluntly carved features and shaved head.

Unlike Rage, this Hunter would never be called gorgeous.

He was raw. Compelling. Potently male.

And dangerous to her on a primitive level.

Taking a hasty step backward, Payton was acutely aware that her linen pants and silk shirt were creased, and her hair a tangled mess.

Even worse, she knew that she smelled as bad as the humans.

Not how a female wanted to look when in the presence of the male she'd once begged to love her.

She winced, slamming the door on that particular memory.

Dammit. She'd devoted the past twenty years to scrubbing that humiliating night from her mind. When the hell was it finally going to disappear?

Angered at being caught off guard when she went to enormous lengths to avoid this particular male, she planted her hand on her hips and tilted her chin at a militant angle.

"What are you doing here?"

"Shh." He glided forward, his movements astonishingly graceful for such a large male as he easily broke the lock and stepped into the cell. "I'm here to rescue you."

"Why?"

He studied her flushed face, his expression impossible to read. She hated that. How could he so easily disguise his emotions while he always knew exactly what she was feeling?

"Why am I here to rescue you?"

She pursed her lips. Okay. It was a stupid question.

"Did Parish send you?"

The amber eyes narrowed. "Does it matter? You were missing and I came to find you."

"Well you can go back to where you came from," she informed him, her voice pitched low enough that it wouldn't carry. "I don't need your help."

He hesitated, glancing around the small cell. Was he trying to grasp why she wasn't falling to her knees in gratitude? Probably so. He had, after all, charged to her rescue like some knight in shining armor.

"This isn't the time to be stubborn, Payton," he at last growled, reaching out to lightly grab her upper arms.

Instant heat jolted through her, re-igniting the savage awareness that she'd tried so hard to deny. At the same time, her cat lunged toward the male who it'd chosen as her mate two decades ago.

The animal inside her didn't understand the meaning of betrayal. It only knew that this male was the most fascinating, gloriously sexy Pantera she'd ever met. And that the loss of his companionship had left a hole in her heart that refused to heal.

"You're right, it's not." She jerked away from his scalding touch, moving until the back of her legs were pressed against the cot. "So go away."

His jaw clenched, something perilously close to regret darkening his beautiful eyes.

"Not without you."

Payton watched his hands reach toward her again and she sent him a glance that she hoped shriveled his balls to tiny prunes.

"Try to force me and I'll punch you in the nose," she warned.

He stilled, then astonishingly his lips twitched, as if he was pleased by her fierce threat.

"Is that supposed to scare me?" he asked, stepping close enough that the heat of his body wrapped around her.

Payton shivered, the enticing scent of his musk clouding her mind.

Blessed Goddess. She'd wanted this male for so long.

Too long.

"Stop it, Hakan. You're going to ruin everything," she snapped, deliberately pausing. "Again."

He flinched. Had she actually managed to hit a nerve?

Amazing.

He stepped back, not bothering to disguise his wary confusion.

"Payton, what the hell is going on?"

"I came here to search the computer systems for any other females who might have been inseminated," she said.

A low growl rumbled in his chest. "Something I intend to discuss with Xavier. You're supposed to be in your office, not out risking your life on a mission."

"You most certainly will not speak with Xavier. This was my call," she informed him. When the hell had Hakan become so overprotective? Like her, he'd spent the past twenty years trying to make sure their paths rarely crossed.

"To put yourself deliberately in danger?"

"I didn't...." She made a sound of frustration. "Do you want to know why I'm still here or not?"

He folded his arms over his broad chest. The T-shirt stretched tight, emphasizing his bulging muscles.

"Go on."

Her mouth went dry, but she managed to resist the temptation to reach out and run her hands over those sculpted pecs.

"Reny got a little..." She hesitated, not entirely sure what had happened when Reny had caught sight of Mr. Stanton Locke. The one-time FBI agent had gone from cool and composed to *I'm-going-to-fucking-kill-you* in the blink of an eye. "...overheated when she recognized the director of The Haymore Center, and the cops were called. During the confrontation I slipped down here with Rage to have a look at their records."

His expression remained stoic, but the heat from his body warned he wasn't impressed with her resourcefulness.

"You mean to hack into their computer network," he said.

She shrugged. "Same thing."

"Only for a Geek."

She glared at him in frustration. "What's that supposed to mean?"

He ignored her question. "How were you captured?"

"We weren't."

Chapter Two

HAKAN scowled, his usual calm composure smashed by his smoldering frustration.

For years he'd been forced to keep a firm leash on himself or risk doing something he was certain he would later regret. A task that was almost impossible with Payton.

His emotions took on a life of their own when he was near this female. They became unpredictable. Treacherous.

Overwhelming.

He wanted to toss her on his bed and devour her. He wanted to wrap her in his arms and protect her from the world.

He wanted…

Her.

Period.

But even his cat understood that Payton was not only smaller, younger and far more vulnerable than he was, but she had yet to develop into the female she was intended to be.

He would never hurt her. He'd die before he'd let anyone, including himself, cause her to suffer. But he'd always feared in the past that his aggressive, dominant personality might very well stifle her ability to mature.

Now, however, the gloves were off.

He'd sworn to himself during his frantic trip to New Orleans that he was done keeping his distance. The stark terror of losing her had convinced him that the time had come to claim his female.

And the past few minutes had proven that she was more than capable of holding her own against him.

Hell, he was beginning to suspect that he was the one in danger of being bullied.

"You weren't captured?" he demanded, his brows arched in disbelief.

She waved a dismissive hand. "A couple of guards appeared and threw us in these cells that couldn't hold a flea. They're waiting for their boss to return and tell them what to do with us. We managed to pick the locks the second their backs were turned."

Fury at the knowledge she'd deliberately placed herself in danger continued to thunder through him. Dammit. She was supposed to be at her desk in the Wildlands. Not infiltrating into enemy territory.

"So why didn't you escape?" he demanded.

A stubborn expression that he'd never seen before settled on her pretty, heart-shaped face.

"I came here to get information and I'm not leaving without it."

"Fine. I'll get the computer and—"

"Absolutely not. Hunters." She rolled her eyes, as if exasperated beyond bearing by the entire faction of warriors. "We can't let anyone know that I have access to their system. Not until I've managed to break their encryption and download the records."

His fingers twitched. He would spare a minute to try to reason with her, but one way or another, she was leaving this cell.

Either walking. Or tossed over his shoulder.

"And if reinforcements show up and they decide to shoot you in the head?"

She sniffed at his perfectly rational argument. "I have Rage to protect me."

He snarled at the soft taunt. Now that his possessive urges had been unleashed, the mere thought of another Pantera offering his protection to this female made a red mist cloud his brain.

"Are you trying to piss me off?"

The pale green eyes that had once been soft with affection were now glowing with a dangerous light.

"What I'm trying to do is my job."

He leaned forward, meeting her glare for glare. "Your job isn't to put yourself in danger."

"That's not your call."

"It damn well is."

If he'd been in a rational mood, he'd have realized he was going about this all wrong. No female wanted to be told what to do. Especially not a Pantera female. His mood, however, was far from rational. From the second he'd heard that Payton was missing he'd been running on pure Hunter instinct. "And this mission just got cancelled." His hands grasped her upper arms, preparing to haul her over his shoulder, but even as he pulled her forward, she reached up to slam her fist against his nose.

More startled than hurt, he released her to stare in shock.

"Ow."

"I warned you." She bit her bottom lip, no doubt already feeling guilty at using violence against him.

Not that she backed down.

Pride flowed through him.

Payton had always been kind, and loyal, and terrifyingly brilliant. Oh, and sexy as hell.

Now she was confident.

It made his cat purr with pleasure.

There was a low chuckle as Rage stepped through the doorway, his gaze taking careful note of the way Hakan moved to stand protectively at Payton's side.

"As amusing as this little farce is becoming, the guards have returned to watching their football game," the younger Hunter informed them.

Hakan pointed a finger toward Rage. The male Pantera had allowed Payton to put her life at risk.

"We're going to have a discussion when we get back to the Wildlands."

With a sound of annoyance, Payton moved to exit the cell, her spine rigid.

"Go away, Hakan."

He prowled right behind her. "Not going to happen."

Rage gave a short laugh as he turned to lead them out of the hidden room.

"You might as well let him tag along," he told Payton. "He's not leaving without you."

Payton muttered something beneath her breath, but she gave up her futile attempt to get rid of him. Instead, she quickened her pace as they moved through the large lab and into a room that was packed tight with computer equipment.

Meeting Rage's questioning gaze, Hakan gave a nod of his head, sending the younger Hunter out of the room to keep watch. Hakan leaned against the frame of the door, watching as his soon-to-be mate slid into a chair at the desk in the center of the floor and did her thing.

He didn't understand all the numbers scrolling across the monitor, or what she was doing as she switched from screen to screen. Computers made his brain cramp. But he knew that Payton was a beautiful sight as she leaned forward, her expression intent as she absently nibbled on her thumbnail.

This was her world.

Well, not entirely.

Soon her world would also include being spread across his bed, her pretty face flushed and her copper curls tousled as he crawled between her spread legs and licked her sweet cream until she screamed his name as she climaxed.

He was instantly hard. Yeah, no big shocker. He had twenty years of pent-up desire blasting through him.

He was going to combust if he wasn't sinking deep into Payton's warm, willing body. Soon.

"That's it," she at last breathed, her fingers flying across the keyboard. "I'm in." Hakan moved to stand at her side, his entire body vibrating with impatience. Every passing minute increased their chance of getting caught. Then, Payton released a low growl. "Damn."

He placed a hand flat on the desk, watching the numbers as they rapidly disappeared from the screen.

"What is it?"

"The firewall has detected an intruder and is purging the data." She gave a sharp shake of her head. "I don't know how much I've managed to get."

Hakan glanced toward the door as the shrill sound of an alarm blasted through the air.

"It doesn't matter now," he said.

"I could try—"

"No."

Not about to waste time arguing, Hakan leaned down to scoop her out of her chair, holding her tight as he headed for the door.

"Hakan." She tilted back her head to glare at him. "Put me down."

"Forget it."

"How dare you." She squirmed in his arms as they reached the hall. "This is my mission."

"Sorry, sweetheart," Rage said as he fell into step beside Hakan. "We just ran out of luck."

"Don't call her sweetheart," Hakan snapped at the younger male.

Payton continued to squirm. "He can call me whatever he wants. It's none of your business."

Rage looked like he was trying not to laugh. "I'll scout ahead."

Hakan sent him a wry glance. "Wise choice."

Waiting for Rage to disappear down the hall, Hakan turned to carry Payton through a private office and into the attached storage area. The elevator would be the first place anyone would look for an intruder. Thankfully, he'd already located the utility duct that was large enough for him to fit through.

"You'd better check that caveman attitude, mister," she warned as he reached up to knock aside the ceiling panel and grabbed the first rung on the ladder that was built into the side of the duct.

Holding her furious glare, he dipped his head down to cover her lips in a kiss that spoke of his ultimate possession.

Pleasure detonated through his body. Oh hell. She tasted of fresh strawberries and innocence.

Pure female temptation.

"You haven't seen caveman yet," he warned against her mouth.

Her eyes widened, a vulnerable need darkening the pale green to jade before she was sharply turning her head away. As if she could close him out.

Hakan grimaced, urging her to wrap her arms around his neck so he could use both hands to pull them up the shaft and into the janitor closet above.

Payton could try to pretend that she hadn't responded, but he had felt her lips soften beneath his kiss, and her faint tremor of excitement.

She might not want to want him, but she was as eager as he was to finish what they started twenty years ago.

Once on the upper floor, Hakan exited the building out the side entrance that he'd left propped open. Then, crossing the nearly empty parking lot, he was jogging down the street when he caught sight of Rage.

He gave a low whistle, pressing himself against the side of a closed Chinese restaurant. Immediately the younger Hunter was joining him, his expression concerned.

"What?"

Hakan nodded toward the dark car that had appeared around the corner, trailing Rage at a distance. It hadn't come from the clinic, which meant that the alarm must have triggered reinforcements.

"You have a couple of shadows," he said.

Rage smiled with sudden anticipation. Like any cat, he loved to toy with his prey.

"I'll stay on foot and lead them into our special area in the swamps," he told Hakan, referring to a section of the bayou that was filled with lethal bogs. Humans foolish enough to go in rarely came out. "You go to the safe house." Rage turned his attention to Payton. "Can you use the computers there to find out whether or not you have the information you wanted?"

"Yeah. She nodded, her arms lightly looped around Hakan's neck as he cradled her against his chest. "I sent the data to an online account and Xavier had the safe house fitted with the latest equipment a few months ago. I should be able to check as soon as I get there."

Rage nodded, glancing toward Hakan. "Take care of her."

"That's exactly what I intend to do," he promised, his gaze locked on her pale face. "Even if I have to tie her to my bed."

Rage gave a short bark of laughter. "Good luck with that."

Hakan turned to head up the narrow alley, trusting Rage to lead away the humans.

"You're going to need more than luck if you keep saying things like that," Payton told him, a delectable flush staining her cheeks.

His lips twitched as he jogged through the empty streets, his instincts on full alert as they left behind the commercial area of town and headed toward the more graceful suburbs near the river.

"I promise you're going to enjoy being completely at my mercy," he murmured. "A soft bed, your arms and legs spread wide while I taste you from head to toe, making sure I take plenty of time to enjoy the places in between."

He caught the unmistakable scent of her arousal. So, his little Geek had a naughty side.

Nice to know.

Clearly embarrassed by her reaction, Payton pressed her hands to his chest.

"You don't have to carry me," she told him.

He turned onto a quiet, old-fashioned street that was lined with weeping willows and gracious homes.

"I know."

She muttered something beneath her breath that Hakan was fairly sure was a condemnation of the brainpower of the male sex and a derogatory reference to the size of his penis.

"Why are you being such a pain?" she demanded.

Halting beneath a large weeping willow, Hakan studied the street behind them.

"Because you deliberately put yourself in danger," he growled, using his acute senses to search for enemies.

So far he could detect nothing beyond a small cat that was hunting a mouse in a nearby flowerbed, and a human male who was seated on his porch a block away drinking from a bottle of whiskey.

"It wasn't deliberate," Payton denied. "Besides, you're always putting yourself in danger."

He shrugged. "I'm a Hunter."

"So what you're saying is that you think what you do is more important than being a Geek?"

Belatedly realizing his error, Hakan glanced down to study the pretty, heart-shaped face. He grimaced. She had the sort of expression a female got when thinking about slicing off a male's balls.

"I didn't say that," he hedged, surging back into motion to cross a manicured lawn and dart around the edge of a large mansion.

"Do you believe I should have walked away from our first opportunity to gain valuable intel on our enemies?" Payton pressed. "The Haymore Center is responsible for impregnating a human with a Pantera cub. We have to discover why and what else they were doing."

His lips twisted as he jogged through the back garden and then easily vaulted over the low fence.

He paused in the shadows, studying the white, plantation-style home that was set well away from the street. Then, certain there were no prying eyes, he headed directly for the back entrance.

"I don't have to be reasonable," he informed her, placing his hand on a scanner. The lock would only open to a Pantera.

The heavy metal door swung inward, and Hakan stepped into the cramped entry, sending a text message to the Hunters HQ in the Wildlands as the alarm automatically sounded.

With no guard on duty, the alarm would alert Parish there were intruders.

Seconds later the alarm went silent.

Hoping the distraction had brought an end to the uncomfortable conversation, Hakan swallowed a sigh when she narrowed her eyes.

"Is there a particular reason you don't have to be reasonable?" Payton demanded.

"Because you're my mate."

———

Mate, mate, mate...

Payton's heart clenched with a savage pain as Hakan carried her through the kitchen and into the main part of the house that had maintained the original moulded ceilings and sweeping staircases from the eighteen hundreds.

Once, she would have given everything she possessed to hear that word on his lips.

The large, barely civilized Hunter had fascinated her for as long as she could remember. And she certainly wasn't the only female who found a reason to hang around the training grounds when he was teaching the cubs how to fight. Or to jostle for a place to eat next to him during evening meals.

What female wasn't attracted to a tall, dark, and sexily dangerous male?

But she'd moved beyond her teenage crush when her cat had reached maturity.

Suddenly he wasn't just the male who made her heart pound and her knees weak.

He was the one.

The only one.

But while she'd rejoiced at the knowledge she'd found her mate, Hakan hadn't been nearly so excited.

In fact...

She stiffened in his arms, furious that Hakan would claim her as his mate after he'd nearly destroyed her.

"Nothing to say?" Hakan broke into her dark thoughts.

"I'm trying to decide if I want to punch you in the nose again," she snapped.

He arched a dark brow. "When did you become so violent?"

"When an arrogant ass decided he could push his way back into my life."

Turning to the right, Hakan carried her through a double doorway into what had once been the library filled with rare first editions and graceful antebellum furniture. Now the towering shelves held a high-tech computer system and military-grade surveillance equipment.

"You knew my retreat would only be temporary," he said with a calm composure that set her teeth on edge.

"Retreat?" Her own voice was closer to a screech. "Is that what you call sleeping with another female and then disappearing from the Wildlands?"

He came to a halt in the center of the floor, meeting her accusing gaze with a somber expression.

"I didn't sleep with Jessa."

She flinched, the memory slamming into her with brutal force.

Hakan had returned to the Wildlands after spending nearly a year away. Payton hadn't even known he was there until she'd been walking home from a night out with a group of friends and caught sight of him standing near her parents' home.

It was like being struck by lightning as she'd studied his big, beautiful body that looked as if it'd been chiseled by the hand of a master in the moonlight. And then she'd felt the pulse of his raw masculinity wrap around her, pulling forward until she'd stood directly in front of him.

She hadn't even hesitated as she'd lifted a hand to place it against his cheek, a sense of wonderment swelling in her heart.

"Mine," she'd whispered. "You're my mate."

The last thing she'd expected was for him to recoil from her touch, his expression hard as he'd simply turned and walked away from her.

She should have left it there.

He'd made it painfully clear he wasn't interested in pursuing their potential mating.

Instead, she'd foolishly followed him to the Hunters' communal quarters, watching in horror as a beautiful young Hunter with long, black hair and smoldering gold eyes had tossed herself into his waiting arms.

She'd heard all the rumors about Hakan and Jessa. But until that night it hadn't had the power to rip out her heart.

"No, I don't suppose there was much sleeping involved."

Regret darkened his eyes. "Dammit, Payton."

She abruptly turned her head to stare at the large window that overlooked the front yard, her body stiff in blatant rejection of his touch.

"Put me down," she commanded.

There was a second when she thought he might refuse to release her, then with a low curse he grudgingly loosened his hold and set her feet on the floor.

Without hesitation she was headed across the room to take a seat at the antique mahogany desk placed near the marble fireplace. Leaning toward the sleek computer that was set in the middle of the glossy wood surface, she flicked it on with one press of a button.

Hakan followed to stand at her side. His frustration filled the air with prickles of heat.

"What are you doing?"

She grimly concentrated on logging into her online account. "I'm going to start downloading the information I managed to get from The Haymore Center."

343

The heat of his body threatened to smother her as he planted his palm on the desk and leaned over her shoulder to study the computer screen.

"How long will it take?"

Her mouth went dry, her body shivering with an electric excitement as his chest pressed against her back, his breath brushing her cheek like a kiss.

"An hour," she managed to get past her stiff lips. "Maybe more."

"Good." He nipped the lobe of her ear. "Then we're going to talk."

Deep inside, her cat was roaring with need, anxious to feel the touch of its mate, but she wasn't ready.

Not when she was still pissed at him.

"I don't think so," she muttered.

"Maybe you're right." Without warning Hakan grasped the arms of Payton's chair and swiveled her to the side. Once she was facing him, he crouched between her legs, his eyes glowing with amber heat as he lifted his hand to cup her cheek. "Since we can't seem to communicate with our words anymore, let's try a more basic way to express our feelings."

"Hakan," she breathed, her heart pounding.

His features softened, revealing a vulnerability she'd once thought was only for her.

"I've missed you, little one."

She pressed herself back into the seat, desperately battling against the urge to rub her face against his hand.

"Don't say that."

"It's the truth."

She glared into the dark, fiercely male face that had haunted her dreams far more nights than she wanted to admit.

"You broke my heart."

He grimaced before he was rubbing his thumb over her lower lip.

"That was never my intention."

She knocked away his hand. She couldn't think when he was touching her.

"Of course it was," she hissed. "You walked away from me while I was trying to confess my love and had another female in your arms mere minutes later." She gripped the arms of the chair as pain lanced through her heart. Twenty years might have passed, but the wound had never healed. "And then, to top it off, you disappeared the next morning for over a year. No goodbye. No note. No calls. Only a male who deliberately wanted to hurt a female would do something like that."

With a stubborn insistence he returned his hand to her face, his fingers tracing the line of her jaw.

"Girl," he said, his voice thick.

"What?"

"You weren't a fully-grown female. You were a girl who was barely out of puberty," he insisted.

Her eyes narrowed. The…jackass.

If he was going to make up excuses for ripping out her heart and stomping on it, at least he could try to be creative.

"Screw you."

The rich scent of musk filled the air, the dangerous power of Hakan's cat shimmering in his eyes. Slowly he leaned forward, his lips lightly brushing over hers.

More a promise than a threat.

For now.

"Oh, there's going to be some screwing," he warned her softly. "But not until we get this mess straightened out."

Chapter Three

HAKAN watched with a sense of satisfaction as a flush stained her ivory cheeks.

Good.

He'd always known he was taking the risk of destroying her love for him. And if he'd been the sort of Pantera who had complete control over his animal side he would never have shoved her away. But he was who he was, and the only way to protect her had been to build impenetrable barriers.

Now he felt a soul-deep surge of relief as he caught sight of the pained longing that smoldered deep in her eyes.

She might be pissed as hell. And she might even think she hated him.

But at least she wasn't indifferent.

And that's all that mattered.

She frowned as his fingers lightly trailed down the length of her neck, trying to pretend she wasn't trembling with the same need that held him in thrall.

"Shouldn't you be out there keeping watch?" she demanded in husky tones.

"No one can enter the house without setting off the alarm," he assured her. "Not even another Pantera."

His fingers followed the neckline of her blouse before he grabbed it with both hands and ripped it in two.

"Hakan," she gasped, her eyes wide with disbelief as he tossed aside the destroyed fabric.

He'd always done his best to restrain his primitive side. Now he allowed the urges of his animal side to take the lead.

She might as well see the truth of the male she was about to mate.

And they were going to mate.

Period. End of story.

"Yes?" he murmured, grasping the lacy bra to dispose of it with equal ease.

He sucked in a deep, appreciative breath as her small, rounded breasts were exposed.

Holy hell. They were perfect. The precise size to fit in his palms, and tipped with nipples the shade of primroses.

"You're ruining my clothes," she choked out.

Shrugging, Hakan gently cupped her breasts in his hands, his thumbs teasing the tips of her nipples until they hardened into sweet nubs that begged to be tasted.

"They were headed for the trash," he muttered. His pretty little Geek was a true clothes fanatic. Which was why he'd added a walk-in closet to the house he was building in an isolated section of the Wildlands. She would never wear anything that had been soiled by three days locked in a basement. "Besides, you like it," he murmured.

"Bullshit," she rasped, her voice shaky.

He leaned forward, planting a lingering kiss between her breasts.

"Then why is your heart racing?"

"Because you're being an annoying ass."

He nuzzled a path of kisses over the upper curve of her breast, his fingers toying with her tender nipple.

"Do you know why I was standing outside your house that night you realized that I was your mate?" he demanded.

"I…" She clenched her jaw, blatantly trying to resist his ruthless seduction. "Does it matter?"

He pulled back, studying her pale face. "Look at me, Payton."

347

There was a long pause as she kept her gaze averted. Then, realizing that he was prepared to wait the rest of the night, she tilted back her head.

"Fine," she snapped. "Why were you standing out there?"

"Because I'd seen you out partying with those young males and I needed to know you made it home safely."

She stiffened at his soft words. "I already have a father. I don't need another one."

Hakan gave a sharp bark of laughter. The night he'd returned from his travels to see her surrounded by a group of adolescent males who were all sniffing around her was seared forever in his mind.

His cat had nearly gone insane with the need to mark her, to prove to everyone that she belonged to him, and that any touching from another male would lead to a slow, painful death.

"Believe me, my feelings weren't fatherly." His voice was harsh. "The minute I caught sight of you dressed in those short-shorts and tank top I knew I had to get away from you."

"That's why you crawled into bed with Jessa?"

He shook his head, holding her accusing glare. "No, Jessa and I have been friends for a very long time."

She studied him for a long moment, clearly finding it hard to believe he hadn't bedded the beautiful Hunter.

"Nothing else?"

His fingers skimmed down to span her narrow waist. He swallowed a low growl of pleasure. She fit so perfect in his hands.

"She's like a sister to me," he said, struggling to concentrate.

He logically understood the need to convince Payton that he'd merely been protecting her, but his body had waited far too long.

The need to possess her was a searing fire that threatened to consume him.

Payton pressed her lips together. "I saw her throw herself into your arms."

"She was trying to make her latest boyfriend jealous." He gave a lift of one shoulder. "It was unfortunate timing. Nothing else."

She hesitated, unable to miss the sincerity in his voice. Then slowly her brows drew together as she regarded him with an agonized disbelief.

"You knew what I believed," she accused, her voice shaking with a furious distress. "Why didn't you tell me the truth?"

He swallowed a sigh. Damn. He hadn't actually considered the fact that learning he hadn't been unfaithful would be as painful as her initial fear he'd taken another female to his bed.

"Because I no longer had the strength to resist my desire to possess you," he confessed.

Her jaw tightened. "I made it humiliatingly clear I wanted to be possessed."

"You were too young." His gaze swept over her heart-shaped face, lingering on the lush curve of her mouth. The thought of those lips on his body had tormented him for two decades. "And still so terrifyingly fragile."

"Just because I'm not a monstrous brute like you doesn't mean I'm weak," she informed him.

"I don't mean size." His gaze compulsively lowered to her bared breasts, his fingers lightly tracing the curve of her waist. "You were just starting your studies and finding your place with your friends. If I had taken you as my mate you would never have become the female you are today."

She grabbed his wrists, but she made no effort to pull away his hands.

Thank the Goddess.

It was going to take a long time for him to recover from his horror when he'd heard she was missing. He needed the physical contact to assure his cat she was alive and well.

"So it was for my own good?" she asked.

"For both of us," he insisted. "You might not have noticed, but I can be a little—"

"Arrogant? Pig-headed? Annoying as hell?" she interrupted with an overly sweet smile.

"Dominating," he corrected, his fingers skimming upward. "Even though I loved you, I would have demanded your complete surrender. And you were too eager to please me to stand against my overbearing nature."

Her pulse fluttered as he cupped her soft breasts, her nails digging into the flesh of his inner wrist.

"I'm not that eager girl anymore."

"Exactly." His cock hardened at the tiny pinpricks of pain. The intoxicating scent of her arousal was filling the air, making it almost impossible to focus. "You know who you are and what you want. Most importantly, you're more than capable of telling me exactly what's on your mind. You won't suppress your own needs in an effort to fulfill mine."

She shivered as his thumbs teased at her tender nipples, her eyes dark with desire.

"Stop that," she growled. "There's not going to be any fulfilling of needs."

"That's where you're wrong, my dear." Enough. Not giving her time to react, he slid his arms around her and scooped her out of the chair. Then, straightening, he crossed the library to the chaise longue that was tucked in a shadowed alcove. "I've waited an eternity for you." Laying her on the brocade cushions, Hakan stared down at her with a predatory hunger. "Tonight you become mine."

———

"You actually expect me to forgive you?" Payton demanded, her heart thundering as he slowly lowered his large form to kneel beside the chaise longue.

He looked big and dangerous and sexy as hell.

Shivering, she tried to ignore the sizzling anticipation that scorched through her as he tugged off her shoes and tossed them aside.

She wanted to be mad.

To remember all the reasons she shouldn't want this.

He'd hurt her, crushed her youthful dreams...allowed her to believe he'd been unfaithful.

So why was she trembling with a need that she couldn't control?

"Of course you'll forgive me," he murmured, leaning down to remove the gun holstered at her ankle before he was efficiently unzipping her slacks and sliding them off her body.

"Why should I?"

He smiled as he ripped off her tiny thong, leaving her completely naked.

"Because you know I was right," he assured her, allowing his hand to trail up her leg and over the curve of her hip.

"You always think you're right," she said, her voice husky with desire.

"True," he admitted, leaning down to replace his fingers with the destructive touch of his lips. "But you know you wouldn't be this bold, confident female you are today if I'd taken you twenty years ago."

She shuddered, her eyes squeezing shut as she savored the sensation of his mouth skimming over the soft swell of her stomach before heading slowly upward. He licked the bottom curve of her breast, then the acutely sensitive tip.

The pleasure exploded through her even as she grudgingly accepted that he might have a point.

Although she'd felt like a female when her cat had chosen Hakan as a mate, she could look back and see that she'd still been incredibly young. And it was true she would have done anything to please him.

Even if it meant denying her own wants and needs.

"You could have talked to me," she said. "You didn't have to be so cruel."

His fingers threaded through her coppery curls, arching her neck and at the same time holding her in place.

"Would you have listened?" he breathed, nibbling a path of kisses along the vulnerable curve of her throat. "Or would you have pressed me to complete the mating?"

351

"I...I don't know."

"You would have teased and tempted and I would have been far too weak to resist you." His fingers tightened in her curls, his free hand palming her breast as she arched toward him in silent invitation. Lightning bolts of bliss raced through her, a damp heat blooming between her legs. "I had to put a barrier between us."

A moan escaped her lips as his teeth nipped the sensitive spot where her neck met her shoulder, her cat responding with a snarl of urgency. She needed...more.

Bare skin.

Teeth. Claws.

Reaching up, she grabbed at his T-shirt and jerked it over his head, exposing the beauty of his hard, sculpted chest. Her breath tangled in her throat as she allowed her hand to glide over the heated silk of his skin.

She'd ached to touch him for so long.

"And now?" she asked.

He lifted his head to study her with eyes that glowed with an amber fire.

His expression was no longer aloof. It was possessive. And demanding. And stark with yearning.

"Now I'll fight to the death to earn back your trust."

Oh. The bastard. For a male who'd always claimed he was better with his hands than his words, he seemed to know exactly what to say to her.

"Sex isn't the same as trust," she muttered.

"I know, but it's a start to repairing the damage." He caught the tip of her nipple between his teeth, sending a shockwave of ecstasy through her. He gave a wicked chuckle at her gasp of pleasure. "Besides, if I'm not between your legs and buried deep inside you soon I'm going to explode."

Yeah, she totally got the whole about-to-explode thing.

Her entire body was clenched tight, aching to be filled by the male who was rising to his feet to strip away the rest of his clothing.

"Were there—"

She forgot how to speak as his jeans dropped to reveal the large thrust of his cock that was fully erect.

Oh. My.

She'd assumed he would be big. He was, after all, a massive Pantera Hunter. But she hadn't suspected he'd be so thick. Or hard.

Or that the mere sight of his erection would make her pussy clench with anticipation.

"Were there what?" he prompted, once again crouching beside the lounge chair.

She shook her head, abruptly realizing she didn't want the answer to her impetuous question.

"Nothing."

Of course he knew what was troubling her. He'd always known what she was thinking.

And feeling.

"My beautiful Payton." Hakan gently tucked a curl behind her ear, his male musk seeping into her skin and clouding her mind with a glorious sense of euphoria. "There's been no one else."

Relief seared through her. "No one?"

"Not since the night you accepted I was your mate."

He once again lowered his head, closing his lips around her nipple to suck her with an insistent need.

She groaned, her hands gripping his shoulders as the pleasure cascaded through her.

It felt like sensory overload.

The brush of velvet cushions against her back. The heat of male Pantera searing her skin. And the magical feel of his lips as they moved to press over the thundering beat of her heart.

"Oh," she breathed in wonder.

His hands gripped her legs, tugging them apart as his lips traced the curve of her breast.

"Does that surprise you?"

His fingers slid over her quivering belly, lowering between her spread legs. A groan was ripped from her throat as he found her sensitive clitoris.

She struggled to draw air into her lungs as he trailed a path of kisses from one breast to the other before heading back up her throat.

"I tortured myself with thoughts of you with other women," she admitted, her hands tracing the bulging muscles of his shoulders.

He gave a low growl, allowing his fingers to slide through her slick heat before slowly pressing into her body. Her back bowed in pleasure. Oh...blessed Goddess. He knew precisely how to touch her.

"My cat had already found its partner," he said, nibbling at the edge of her mouth. "I had no interest in any other female."

"And the male?"

He pulled back far enough for her to see the fierce sincerity that burned in his amber eyes.

"He was in complete agreement."

Oh...hell. She dug her nails into his shoulders, feeling the righteous anger she'd clung to for so long beginning to melt.

And her grudge wasn't the only thing melting, she acknowledged as his fingers pressed deeper into her body, his thumb rubbing against the sweet spot at the top of her clit.

Dammit. She'd wanted this male for what seemed like forever.

Was she going to allow her wounded pride to punish both of them?

Her hands smoothed down the sleek bronzed skin of his chest before lowering to the hard-as-steel six-pack.

Hakan was larger than most Pantera, with a power that made him one of the most lethal Hunters in the Wildlands, but he was careful to leash his strength as he claimed her lips in a kiss that demanded complete surrender.

Need seared through her, scorching away any hope of resistance.

Just a few hours ago she would have sworn that she would rather kiss a gator than crawl into bed with Hakan. Now she was desperate to feel his heavy body pressing her into the chaise longue, thrusting deep inside her as she reached her ultimate bliss.

Lowering her hand, she wrapped her fingers around the wide width of his cock, smiling at his violent shudder.

Ah. She'd never realized the rush of power that came from giving another pleasure.

"I need you, Hakan," she pleaded in rough tones.

He chuckled, blazing a path of kisses down her throat.

"Soon," he promised, continuing to press urgent kisses over her breasts and down the quivering plane of her stomach.

She made a sound of surprise when he tugged her until she was on the edge of the chaise longue so he could kneel between her spread legs. Then, holding her startled gaze, he leaned forward to trail his tongue along the tender skin of her inner thigh.

Payton gasped at the sensations that streaked through her.

She'd always known that Hakan was talented with his hands. She'd seen the homes he'd helped design and build for his fellow Hunters. But who the hell knew he'd be a magician with his lips?

She gripped the cushions, barely capable of holding still as his teeth lightly scraped her tender flesh. Oh, Goddess. It felt like she was being burned from the inside out.

"Not soon...now," she breathed.

CHAPTER FOUR

HAKAN sucked in a deep breath, his cat basking in the scent of vanilla and warm, willing female.

He wanted to ignore her breathless plea.

After all, he'd spent the past twenty years fantasizing about making love to this female.

He wanted to make it last for the entire night.

But as he spread her legs wider and headed toward that delectable pussy he knew he was fooling himself if he thought he could take this slow and easy.

His dreams of how this moment would be had been nothing compared to the brutal need that blasted through him. This wasn't the shallow attraction of his youth, or the playful games of his cat.

The need to possess this female was fierce, and powerful, and so raw he felt it to his very soul.

Deep inside, his animal roared in anticipation, spicing the air with a musk that would cling to her skin, warning other males this female was his.

Payton bit her bottom lip, a sweet little moan wrenched from her lips as he finally moved to stroke his tongue through her slick pussy.

Hakan tightened his hands on her legs, licking and sucking at the thick cream. Christ. He'd never tasted anything so good.

A heady excitement charged through him, stiffening his cock until it throbbed with a painful need.

He was desperate to impale himself in her female heat, but he grimly squashed the urge to lean her back and shove himself into paradise.

This had to be perfect for Payton.

He'd spoiled her tentative declaration of love. And spent the last twenty years keeping her at a distance.

Now he had to make this night so special that it would help to erase the past.

Attuning himself to her every sigh and moan, Hakan held her in place as she squirmed against the ruthless swipe of his tongue.

Over and over he teased her tender nub, his cat delighting in the sexual play even as the male was barely holding on by a thread.

"I love the taste of you," he growled, his voice thick with the power of his animal. "Vanilla and honey. My favorite."

She studied him from beneath half-lowered lashes, her cheeks flushed.

"I want to taste you," she breathed, her tone shy.

His cock twitched, silently pleading to give her what she wanted.

Only the knowledge that he was going to come at the first touch made him give a rueful shake of his head.

"Next time," he promised. "Tonight is all about you."

"But..."

Her words broke off in a soft gasp as his tongue plunged into her body, thrusting in and out in a promise of what was to come.

Muttering something beneath her breath she lifted her hips, instinctively moving in rhythm with the ruthless stroke of his tongue.

His cock throbbed with a hot, aching need as the taste of her slid down his throat. She was like a drug. Intoxicating him with a heady pleasure he knew would be addictive.

The intensity of his sexual drive would have been terrifying if it wasn't for the knowledge this female was his.

His mate.

The female meant to stand by his side for all of eternity.

The fact that she was driving him out of his mind with lust was only more proof that she was his destiny.

Intent on giving her more pleasure than she'd ever experienced before, he continued to explore her sweet cunt, sending her to the very edge of her climax.

"No, Hakan," she rasped in thick tones. "I want you to be inside me when I come."

Leaning back on his heels, Hakan took a minute to appreciate the sight of her in the throes of passion.

The halo of coppery curls. The heart-shaped face that was flushed a pretty pink. The green eyes that glowed gold as her cat studied him with a hungry gaze.

She was so fucking beautiful.

Feeling a sense of awe that fate would have given him this exquisite female, he surged up to claim her lips in a kiss that spoke of possession and need and utter surrender.

He slid an arm around her waist, turning her on the chaise so he could push her back against the cushions. Then, continuing to kiss her with a fierce desperation, he settled on top of her slender body, groaning in pleasure as she wrapped her legs around his hips.

Balancing on his elbows to keep from squashing her, he tilted his hips forward. They both hissed in anticipation as the broad head of his cock slowly breached her body.

Oh…Christ.

She was tight. So blessedly tight.

Sweat beaded his brow as he pressed into her damp channel, penetrating her with his thick length.

Threading his fingers in her damp curls, Hakan nipped the sexy fullness of her bottom lip before he was planting a trail of kisses down her throat.

"There's no going back," he breathed, heading lower to suck the tip of her breast between his lips. "You're mine."

Tormenting her nipple with his tongue and teeth, he gave one last push, battling to maintain control. She needed time to adjust to his invasion.

Of course, Payton couldn't remain passive.

Once, his shy, eager Geek would have simply waited for him to take the lead. Now she grasped his shoulders and arched her back, angling herself until he was pressed so deep his balls were fitted against her ass.

"Shit, Payton," he groaned, hoping like hell he didn't embarrass himself. "I'm trying to make this good for you."

"It's good," she rasped, her breath hissing between clenched teeth as he pulled out until just the tip of his cock was inside her and then surged back in with a powerful thrust. "Oh hell, it's perfect."

It was.

Hakan pressed frantic kisses over her breast before he was burying his face in the curve of her neck.

She was clenched around him like a hot fist, intensifying the electric pleasure of every stroke. He groaned, the tip of his cock tingling and his balls drawing up tight.

Around them the scent of male musk and sweet vanilla arousal saturated the air, the whisper of their soft moans the only sound.

"Come for me, Payton," he commanded softly, driving into her with a quickening pace.

His orgasm was thundering through him, threatening to explode. Sliding a hand beneath her hips, he angled her to take him even deeper, his teeth sinking into the soft flesh of her throat.

"Hakan," she rasped.

"I've got you, little one," he murmured. "Give me what I want."

She released a cry of pleasure, her heels digging into his lower back as she met him thrust for thrust.

Over and over he plunged into her welcoming body, his cock torturously sensitive as her silken heat wrapped tightly around him.

Then, feeling her stiffen in stunned pleasure, he moved to press his lips to her mouth, capturing her shout of frenzied fulfillment.

His cat roared in wild pleasure as he unleashed his hunger and drove into her at a ferocious pace, his fingers digging into her hips as he held her in place.

White-hot bliss arrowed down his spine before it was tightening his balls and then shooting through his cock in a violent climax.

He lifted his head to cry out in sharp ecstasy, his muscles clenched so tight he felt as if he was going to shatter into a million blissful pieces.

Minutes—or perhaps an eternity—later, he heaved a heartfelt groan and pressed his lips to Payton's damp forehead.

Her soft convulsions squeezed his cock, milking the last of his bliss.

Yep. Perfect pretty much summed it up.

———

Two hours later, Payton stumbled across the bedroom, and flopped onto the mattress as she struggled to catch her breath.

Wow.

She'd thought that nothing could match the pleasure Hakan had given her in the library. That had been...stunning. But when he'd joined her in the shower, he'd verified that you really could improve on perfection.

Now she sprawled across the bed and allowed Hakan to dry her off with a fluffy towel. She felt boneless as sated pleasure flowed through her with liquid heat.

Of course, that didn't halt her appreciation of the sight of the naked Hunter as he gently bent over her.

The moonlight streamed through the large upper-story window, gliding over his carved muscles and adding a rich sheen to his dark caramel skin.

Dear Goddess. He was so deliciously male.

Purring beneath his touch, Payton sighed with regret when Hakan at last finished and tossed aside the towel.

Standing at the edge of the bed, he stared down at her, his expression uncharacteristically tender.

"Are you okay?" he asked, his voice low. "I wasn't too rough?"

Her lips twitched as she pushed herself onto her elbows. "Are you fishing for compliments?"

"Do you have some to share?"

"I think your head is big enough," she said, her attention lowering to his cock that instantly hardened beneath her gaze. "Along with other parts of your body."

"I just want to know that I pleased you," he said gruffly.

He had to ask? Payton would have assumed that her screams of pleasure might have given him a clue.

Oddly, his need for reassurance made her feel all warm and gooey inside.

"You pleased me very, very much," she murmured softly.

"Good." A slow smile of satisfaction curved his lips as his musk filled the room with an intoxicating fragrance. "This wouldn't have been my first choice as a setting for our mating, but—"

"Wait."

The euphoria that'd been clouding her mind with a sexual contentment abruptly shattered as Payton hastily shoved herself off the bed.

Hakan watched her awkward movements with a frown. "What's wrong?"

A sudden, acute awareness of their mutual lack of clothing made Payton blush. Pantera possessed the ability to absorb whatever they were wearing when they shifted, so it wasn't as if she was used to waltzing around naked. Still, she forced herself to stand her ground.

Dammit. She'd been so caught up in the sizzling passion that she hadn't really considered what was going to happen when the momentary madness ended.

Now she felt an unpleasant knot of tension settle in the pit of her stomach.

"Who said anything about a mating?" she demanded.

The amber eyes abruptly narrowed. "Don't play games, Payton. Not with this."

She wrapped her arms around her waist, refusing to be intimidated by the force of his glare.

"I've never been the one who plays games, if you'll recall."

"We've discussed this," he growled in frustration. "You know why I had to walk away."

"I do." She wasn't lying. She could look back and see that she'd been unbearably young when her cat had decided on Hakan as a mate. But that didn't mean the past twenty years had been erased. "I even understand you were probably right."

"And?" he pressed.

"And while I can logically accept our past, my heart isn't ready."

He abruptly stepped forward, framing her face in his hands. "Then what the hell were we doing in that shower?"

Heat flushed her cheeks as she recalled in precise, Technicolor detail what they'd been doing in the shower.

It'd involved hot water, shower gel, and Hakan on his knees...

Payton slammed the door on the memories.

It was distracting enough to feel the press of his thick arousal against her lower stomach.

"I told you that sex wasn't the same as trust," she reminded him.

His thumbs brushed her cheeks, his touch so tender it brought tears to her eyes.

"That wasn't sex," he said in husky tones. "We made love."

She gave a slow nod. She wasn't going to lie about her emotions. Even if she wasn't ready to make the leap he was demanding.

"Yes. I do love you." She tilted back her head, allowing him to see the sincerity in her eyes. "I have always loved you."

His jaw clenched, his features looking like they'd been carved from granite.

"But you won't mate with me."

She winced at his flat tone. The less emotion Hakan revealed the more intense his feelings.

Which meant that she'd just deeply wounded him.

"I..." She licked her lips, a part of her yearning to simply accept what he was offering. She had belonged, heart and soul, to this male for the past two decades. But another part rebelled at the mere thought of giving in so easily. It wasn't pride. It was...hell, she didn't know. But she wasn't ready. She firmly pulled from his grasp and headed for the walk-in to pull on a pair of jeans and a sweatshirt from the spares that were always kept in safe houses. "Not now."

Hakan was standing in her path when she stepped out of the closet, his arms folded over his chest.

"Then when?" he rasped.

Turning, she reached to grab a pair of jeans off a shelf and tossed them toward him.

Dammit. That huge, naked body was making her want to do things with her tongue that weren't going to convince him that she was serious about putting their mating on hold.

Things that involved licking that thick cock until he was pleading for mercy.

"I don't know."

Snatching the jeans before they hit his chest, he pulled them on with jerky motions.

"So this is my punishment," he snarled.

"This has nothing to do with punishment," she protested, even as a small doubt gnawed deep inside her.

A doubt she easily squashed.

Blistering heat filled the room as he straightened to glare at her with a barely leashed frustration.

"I understand. I hurt you," he said, not sounding like he understood. At all. "Now you need to hurt me."

"That's not fair."

"You know we belong together." He leaned down until they were nose to nose. "Even now I can sense your cat's hunger for us to complete the bond."

It was true, but she refused to back down.

The needs of her cat didn't control her. Not since she'd left the nursery.

"Just a few hours ago I hated you," she pointed out, trying to be reasonable despite his annoyance. "I can't just turn my feelings off and on."

"Payton..." The infuriated male stiffened in alarm at the shrill beeps that echoed through the hallway. "What the hell?"

Taking advantage of his distraction, Payton stepped around his large form and headed for the door of the bedroom.

"The download is finished," she muttered.

She managed to reach the sweeping staircase before Hakan was standing directly in front of her, his expression grim.

"We're not done with this conversation, Payton."

She shoved a weary hand through her still-damp curls. When was the last time she had a decent night's sleep?

It seemed like an eternity.

"Hakan—"

"You're my mate," he stubbornly interrupted. "Nothing is ever going to change that."

He turned to jog down the steps before she could answer. A good thing, considering she didn't know what the hell she wanted to say.

They *were* mates.

No doubt about it.

It was just...

Giving a resigned shake of her head, Payton followed Hakan down the staircase and into the library. Then, trying to pretend she wasn't vibrantly aware of his large form standing next to the desk, she crossed the room to peer at the computer screen.

Tapping in her private password, she studied her account, unconsciously chewing her thumbnail as she scanned through the long list of files.

"I think I managed to get something," she at last said.

Hakan moved to stand behind her as she slid into the chair and used the mouse to click on the first of three files that she'd managed to retrieve that weren't fragmented.

"What are they?" he demanded.

Payton skimmed through the various documents, swiftly realizing she didn't have the skill to decipher the medical forms.

"This first one is some sort of lab work," she said. "Blood. DNA."

"Is it Lydia's file?"

"It's impossible to say, but it looks like there's more than one patient. I'll need the Nurturers to look at it to make sure."

Hakan stiffened. "How many?"

"At least ten."

"Damn," he breathed. "It's one thing to suspect that they're screwing around with Pantera DNA, but to think they're impregnating women with our semen…it's intolerable."

"I don't think that these files are dealing with creating cubs," she said, clicking open the next icon.

His breath brushed her cheek as he leaned over her shoulder. "Then what?"

She grimly concentrated on sorting through the documents. "I'm not sure. This is the only complete file I can open."

"Patient Z," he read out loud. "Why wouldn't it have a name?"

She shrugged. "I don't know much about medicine, but I suppose if you were doing some clinical trial…" She sucked in a shocked breath as she located a folder of pictures and clicked them open. "Hakan."

She felt him grip the back of her chair as they studied the grainy photograph of a female strapped to a gurney in the center of a lab.

There was no mistaking the dark-haired Pantera.

"Reny," he growled.

Payton made a sound of distress as she zoomed in. She could detect wounds on the unconscious Reny that suggested that the chains that bound her to the gurney were laced with malachite.

Not only must the pain have been unbearable, but the separation from her cat would have been a constant torture.

It was no wonder she'd blocked out the memories even after Sebastian had brought her to the Wildlands.

"This is why she went ballistic when she entered The Haymore Center and caught a glimpse of Stanton Locke," she said. "She might not consciously remember what happened to her, but her cat no doubt sensed it'd been held captive there."

Hakan leaned over her shoulder to study the picture, the heat from his body blazing around her. She didn't doubt that it was taking every ounce of his willpower not to charge back to the Center and destroy everyone associated with it.

"Why would she be in a human medical facility?" he snapped.

Payton searched through the remaining photographs, hoping to discover some clue to those responsible for her captivity. Instead what she saw was pictures of Reny going back more than fifty years.

"Dear Goddess," she breathed, her voice tight and tears flooding her eyes. "She'd been there since she was just a newborn baby."

The back of her chair cracked beneath the force of Hakan's grip.

"Is there any mention of her mother?"

Payton pointed a finger toward the last picture of a pretty, dark-haired female with jade green eyes.

"Not directly, but this looks like it might be a photo of her."

Chapter Five

HAKAN abruptly straightened and paced from one end of the shadowed library to the other.

Inside, his cat roared, demanding vengeance for the helpless female Pantera who'd obviously been abused since she was a mere cub. Unfortunately, until they knew exactly who was behind the secret lab in The Haymore Center, he had no true enemy to battle.

"Hiss was right," he at last said between clenched teeth.

"What do you mean?" Payton studied him with a wary expression and just for a crazed minute he was nearly overwhelmed by the urge to haul her back up the stairs and keep her in the bed until she agreed to complete the mating.

Okay. It might be arrogant to assume that after twenty years of denying the attraction between them, she would be eager to bind herself to him just because he'd decided it was time.

And maybe he deserved to do some squirming.

But dammit, she wasn't the only one who'd suffered. Couldn't she at least give him a lifeline? A smidgeon of hope that she wasn't going to make him wait forever?

Then, with a muttered curse, he forced himself to focus on what they'd just discovered.

The mess he'd made of his personal life was going to have to wait until they'd identified and destroyed the people responsible for holding Reny captive.

Dammit.

"Hiss always swore that his family was still alive, but the elders insisted they'd been killed in a fire," he explained, belatedly wishing he hadn't dismissed his one-time friend's insistence that the elders were lying to him as the grief of an orphan.

Payton frowned. "Could he have been involved with the Center?"

"No." Hakan paced back toward the desk. "The bastard might have helped the disciples of Shakpi, but he was genuinely shocked by the blood tests that revealed Reny is his sister."

"The kidnappers did try to negotiate to get their hands on Hiss," she reminded him.

His hands clenched at his side. "And now they have him."

She studied him in confusion. "How? I thought he was being guarded?"

"Yeah, that was the general assumption," he said. "But right before I left to follow you, Parish learned that someone had taken him out of the Wildlands."

She stiffened. "A Pantera?"

Hakan didn't blame her for her painful assumption. Once he would have sworn that no Pantera would ever betray them. Now they'd discovered that no one was above suspicion.

"No, they believe it was a human."

She studied him with an anxious expression. "And you still don't think Hiss is involved?" she asked.

Hakan shrugged. He'd been shocked and deeply wounded when he'd discovered that Hiss had been working with Shakpi's disciples, but he'd accepted the truth without hesitation.

He'd known his friend had suffered throughout his childhood. It made sense he would try to punish those he held responsible for his pain.

But this…

He shook his head. "It doesn't feel right."

She blinked, studying him as if she thought she might have misheard him.

"Feel right?"

"Geeks depend on facts and logic. A Hunter uses his gut instincts."

"Hmm." Clearly unimpressed with the idea of depending on intuition, she returned her attention to the computer. "I'll stick with facts and logic."

Hakan moved to stand behind her chair, watching as she scanned through the medical documents that were in the file.

"Is there anything that reveals what the humans were doing to Reny while she was here?" he asked.

"It looks like they were taking several vials of blood from her every week."

"Were they testing it?"

She continued to scroll through the information that all looked like Greek to Hakan.

"They wouldn't need that much blood just for testing," she said, her tone troubled. "They had to be using it for something else."

Hakan agreed. There was something in her blood they needed. But what?

The realization struck without warning.

Oh, not the answer to the puzzle of why they'd taken Reny and held her captive. But why they'd risked everything to sneak into the Wildlands.

"And now they have Hiss," he said.

Payton glanced over her shoulder, instantly following the direction of his unwelcomed thoughts.

"His blood would match Reny's," she said.

A sense of urgent unease pulsed through his body. He might not know what they wanted with Hiss's blood, but he knew it couldn't be good.

They had to get him back.

He watched the data flicker over the computer screen. "Are there any other files?"

"Yes, but they're corrupted." Payton gave a frustrated shake of her head. "I'll have to send them to Xavier. He has a program that can salvage fragmented bits of data and piece them back together."

369

Hakan turned his head to glance toward the row of monitors set on the bookshelves. The live feeds from the outside cameras revealed nothing moving in the surrounding yard and no cars hidden in the alley.

"We need to get back to the Wildlands," he said, knowing they had to take a calculated risk.

The sooner he could get Payton home safely, the sooner she could help to decipher the files. And the sooner he could be on the hunt.

She instantly rose to her feet. "I'm ready."

His gaze slid down her slender body, resting on her ridiculously bare toes. Suddenly the biting need to be on their way was tempered by the tidal wave of tenderness that rushed through him.

"Don't forget that we have unfinished business," he warned.

She shrugged, turning to hide her expression as she shut down the computer.

"Later."

Hakan swallowed a curse. He'd wanted Payton to develop a will of her own, but...Christ.

Clenching his hands, he moved across the room to pull on his T-shirt before heading to the ugly-ass velvet Elvis painting that was hung over the fireplace. A joke from Lian, no doubt, who'd been stationed at this safe house until he'd recently mated.

Pushing the painting aside, he pressed his hand against the fingerprint reader and waited for the door of the built-in strongbox to spring open.

He reached in to grab a set of car keys, turning to toss them toward the startled Payton.

"You drive."

Her eyes widened in disbelief. Hakan could be a little...anal when it came to being in charge.

"Really?"

He reached into the safe to pull out two loaded handguns. "I need my hands free."

"Oh." She stepped toward the door, only to abruptly turn back toward the desk. "Wait."

Hakan watched in confusion as she pulled open a drawer and extracted one of the extra phones that was always kept handy.

"What are you doing?" he asked.

She kept her gaze locked on the small screen as she tapped in her personal codes.

"Lian said the enemy has a sophisticated GPS system, so I developed a signal that any Pantera can download to jam tracking devices," she murmured, seemingly unaware that she was a fucking miracle to her people. Hakan, however, was well aware of her worth. And he couldn't be more proud. "I doubt the guards were competent enough to hide a bug on me, but I want to make sure we can't be followed." At last she lifted her head, looking puzzled as she met Hakan's awed gaze. "What?"

He slowly shook his head.

He'd always admired her razor-sharp intelligence. It was one of the reasons he'd been so determined that she would finish her training before they mated.

But he'd never seen her in action until the past few hours.

"You dazzle me," he said softly.

She blushed, a pulse fluttering at the base of her throat as she hastily headed toward the door.

"Let's go."

———

Stanton Locke stood in the basement of The Haymore Center, looking distinctly out of place in his thousand dollar Armani suit and his black hair smoothed to a short tail at his nape.

Currently his brilliant blue eyes were narrowed as he glared at the two stooges who'd managed to create a minor disaster.

Perhaps he should take a portion of the blame.

When the guards had called to say they'd locked two intruders in the cells, he'd told them to keep a watch on the captives, even knowing they were idiots barely capable of tying their own shoes.

But he'd been in the middle of his delicate mission to capture Hiss. There was no way in hell he was going to risk his one opportunity to get his hands on the well-guarded Pantera. So he'd waited until he had his prisoner secure in the warehouse before at last coming to the Center to deal with the interlopers.

Now he realized he'd made a tactical error that might very well cost him his life.

Planting his hands on his hips, he ignored the icy chill that inched down his spine.

Bloody hell. He hated this place.

The stench of antiseptic. The squeak of shoes on the waxed floor. The knowledge that before he'd torn down the previous building and constructed this modern clinic, it'd been a private sanatorium where they'd experimented on the Pantera females.

It was, after all, one thing to hold a full-grown male hostage. It was quite another to be responsible for a fragile child stretched on the gurney as she screamed in agony.

Grimly he slammed the door on his dark thoughts.

He'd known since his master had taken him off the streets of London that there was a cost to his new life. It was too late to fear that the price had been higher than he'd ever dreamed possible.

"So who wants to explain how this little clusterfuck happened?" he demanded.

Both men flinched at his low tone, capable of detecting the lethal edge beneath his polished English accent.

"It wasn't our fault," the older guard said, denying any blame.

Stanton arched a brow. "No?"

"We had the prisoners locked up just as you ordered," the guard insisted.

Stanton allowed his gaze to move from one upturned face to another. One was lean and wrinkled. The other was plump with heavy jowls. Both, however, were drenched in sweat and pale with a fear that tainted the air.

"You're certain?" Stanton demanded.

The younger guard pumped his head up and down. "Of course. They were locked up tight."

Stanton's lips thinned. "Then how do you suppose someone managed to use my own computer to steal highly sensitive information?"

The two exchanged baffled glances before the older one tried to scramble for an excuse.

"After they broke out of their cells they must have stopped by here and hacked into the system."

Stanton gave a shake of his head. It was difficult to believe they could truly be that stupid. His master would tell him to kill them. Such incompetence had to be nipped in the bud.

Tonight, however, it all seemed like a colossal waste of energy.

"Impossible," he instead snapped.

The older guard licked his lips. Smack, smack, smack.

"I don't understand."

"Clearly." Stanton reached beneath his jacket to pull out a thin dagger, deliberately running his finger along the razor-sharp edge. He wasn't going to kill them, but he was willing to scare the shit out of them. "Even the most sophisticated program would have taken days to break through my layers of security."

"Someone must have snuck in and—" The older guard's words ended on a shrill scream as Stanton leaned down to place the point of the dagger beneath his chin.

"Do you know what I think?" he asked.

The man's breath sawed in and out of his lungs. "What?"

"I think that the supposed prisoners could have waltzed past you two morons any time they wanted," he said. "And that the only reason they stayed was to steal my private information."

"No, we would have known if..." The guard pissed his pants as the dagger dug into his flesh hard enough to draw a bead of blood. "Please, don't kill us."

He curled his lips in disgust. "Give me one reason why I shouldn't."

"We..." The younger one cleared his throat. "I...I...have kids."

"They have my condolences." Stanton stiffened as his phone gave a distinctive ring. "Bollocks," he breathed, straightening to pull out the phone and press it to his ear. "Sir, I'm afraid there's a problem," he said, pacing away from the guards as he listened to his master's icy reprimand. "No, we have the male Pantera, but there's been a breach in our security. I have my men trying to track them down." He grimaced at the mere thought of his security chasing after the escaped Pantera. There was no way in hell the guards were going to catch the animals before they reached the Wildlands. "I fear it's too dangerous for you to travel to New Orleans until we can be certain that we haven't been compromised." He winced, capable of feeling the fury humming through the phone. "Yes, I know we're running out of time, but we can't risk having you exposed. I will call as soon as it's safe." Pushing the button to end the long-distance connection, he turned to stalk back toward the guards who cowered on the floor. "You made me disappoint the man I consider my father," he said, holding the dagger so the silver blade shimmered in the overhead lights.

"We're sorry," the pudgy guard sobbed, his face pale with terror.

"Not yet." Stanton crouched down, a deadly smile curving his lips. "But you will be."

Payton stood at the window of her office in the Wildlands, watching the tall, dark Hunter stride away from the Diplomats' official headquarters. Even from a distance she could detect the rigid line of his spine and the stiff set of his shoulders.

With a grimace she hoped that there weren't any humans remaining on the borders. She knew that Hakan had been working with Parish to clear away any reporters who were foolish enough to linger despite Raphael's warning that there would be no more interviews. In his current mood he might create a diplomatic disaster.

It was the sixth time he'd tried to see her since they'd returned to the Wildlands ten hours ago and she'd retreated to this place that'd always been her haven.

She told herself that her refusal to speak with Hakan was necessary. After all, she might not be a warrior, but she did have the skills that could help them learn more about their enemies. For now, she needed to concentrate on deciphering the files.

But deep in her heart, she knew that the true reason she was avoiding the Hunter was because she couldn't hide her intense physical arousal whenever he was near.

It'd been bad enough before she knew what she was missing. Now the memory of being wrapped in those strong male arms as he buried himself deep into her body made her ache with the need to ignore everything but the physical pleasure he could offer her.

Giving a sharp shake of her head, Payton stepped through the door that led to the communal room where a dozen computers had been arranged on a long table. Each of them was running the fragmented files through the filtering programs in an attempt to piece them back together.

At her entrance a tall, dark male with blue eyes and buzzed haircut rose to his feet.

Xavier was leader of the Geeks and one of her dearest friends.

"Anything?" she asked.

He arched a dark brow, planting his hands on his hips. "The program's still running," he said. "Just as it was fifteen minutes ago."

It'd only been fifteen minutes? Shit, it'd felt like an eternity.

She wrinkled her nose. "I don't mean to pester you. I'm…"

"Trying to avoid the large Hunter who keeps stalking through our offices causing panic?" Xavier finished as her words trailed away.

"Yeah." No use trying to lie. This male knew her too well. "I'm not ready to speak to him."

His gaze never wavered. "It's none of my business, but I suspect that you've been doing more than speaking with Hakan."

She bit her bottom lip. There was no way to hide Hakan's musk that continued to cling to her skin.

And if she was being honest, she didn't want to.

She liked being surrounded in his comforting scent.

"You're right, it's none of your business," she said before she realized how bitchy she sounded. This male wasn't being nosy. He truly cared about her. "Oh, hell. I'm sorry, Xavier," she muttered, shoving her fingers through her tangled copper curls.

He moved forward to place a finger beneath her chin, tilting back her head so he could study the shadows beneath her eyes.

"Don't be. You're like a sister to me, Payton," he said. "Which means that I've been tempted to kick Hakan's ass more than once for hurting you." He held her gaze. "If you need me to take care of him, I will."

She shook her head. The last thing she wanted was violence between the two men.

"He claims he was protecting me," she told her companion.

She didn't know what she'd been expecting, but it wasn't for Xavier to give a nod of his head.

"He was."

"You agree with him?" She frowned, feeling a tiny jolt of betrayal. Whether she was right or wrong, Xavier was supposed to be on her side. "You just said you wanted to kick his ass."

Xavier gave her chin a squeeze. "For hurting you, but I would have sliced off his balls if he'd tried to mate you before you were mature."

She rolled her eyes. "Males."

Dropping his hand, Xavier took a step back. "I'm assuming he's decided it's time to pursue you?"

"Not pursue," she corrected, recalling Hakan's arrogant assumption that he could decide they were mates whenever it was convenient for him. "Capture."

He hesitated, studying her with a searching gaze. "I understand there must be some distinction between the two, but my poor male brain can't figure it out."

She gave a lift of her hands, trying to explain the tangled emotions that were knotted in the pit of her stomach.

"Hakan spent twenty years pushing me away," she said. "Now he wants to snap his fingers and have me come running back to him."

"Ah." Xavier gave a nod. "You want to make him suffer."

"No…" She hesitated, realizing she wasn't being entirely honest. She couldn't deny a small desire to see Hakan squirm. "Well, maybe a little." She shrugged. "But mostly I just need time to adjust to the change in our relationship."

"You want him to woo you."

Payton's lips twitched at the old-fashioned word. "Woo?"

"He's seduced your body, now he has to seduce your heart."

As usual, Xavier managed to hit the nail directly on the head.

All those years ago Hakan had walked away from the invitation her cat had offered. He hadn't been interested in the playful games that marked the beginning of the mating process.

Now he wanted to leap directly into a committed relationship without the flirtatious fun.

"Yes," she agreed.

A slow, wicked smile curved his lips. "Don't make it too easy on him."

"Trust me, I won't."

Chapter Six

HAKAN heaved a sigh of relief when he received the text from Payton.

'I need to see you.'

He wasn't stupid enough to think that she had a sudden change of heart. It'd been less than a half hour since she'd refused to see him. No. This had to be about the information she'd stolen from The Haymore Center.

Still, it had to mean something that she would chose to contact him instead of simply calling Parish or Raphael.

Right?

Perfectly happy to clutch at straws, Hakan jogged through the communal eating area where a number of Pantera had gathered for breakfast. His stomach growled at the smell of food, but his pace never slowed as he entered the large, plantation-style building and moved past the Geeks who were monitoring a long line of computers arranged on a table.

He stepped into a small reception area that set apart the private offices to discover Xavier standing in the center of the hand-woven carpet.

The large Pantera Geek had his arms folded over his chest and an expression that said he was itching for a fight.

Hakan smiled and stepped directly into the male's grill.

Xavier wasn't the only one with a need to release some aggression.

"Hakan," the Geek greeted him in cold tones.

"Xavier." Hakan glanced over the male's shoulder at the empty room decorated in shades of pale lemon and ivory. Payton's favorite colors. "Where's Payton?"

"Going through the data we managed to salvage," Xavier said.

Hakan narrowed his gaze as the male remained parked between him and the door to Payton's office.

"You have something on your mind?"

"Yep." Xavier poked a finger into the center of Hakan's chest. "Hurt her again and I'll rip off your balls and shove them down your throat."

A growl rumbled deep in Hakan's chest, his cat roaring with fury that another male would dare to try to offer Payton protection.

That was his right.

His alone.

Only the knowledge that Xavier was happily mated kept him from punching the bastard in the face.

"I realize that you consider Payton a part of your family so I'm going to let that slide, but try to get between us and I'll go through you," he snarled. "Got it?"

Nose to nose, the males were indulging in a good old-fashioned glaring match when the sound of the door opening had them both spinning toward the female who was studying them with a stern expression.

"You two can measure your dicks later. I have something you need to see."

She whirled on her heel, stomping back into her office.

Hakan exchanged a startled glance with Xavier.

"I don't think she needs your protection," he told the Geek, pride and exasperation laced through his voice.

Xavier gave a short laugh. "Maybe I should be more worried about you."

Hakan nodded. Payton was not only dangerously clever and sexy as hell, but she'd developed a spirited independence that was going to make life with her extremely...interesting.

"No shit."

"Are you coming or not?" Payton called through the open door.

Hakan and Xavier obediently headed into the inner office that was as neat and organized as Payton, with two delicate oak desks that were covered by a number of computers and precisely stacked papers.

"What have you got?" Hakan asked, resisting the urge to reach out and brush his finger down her too-pale cheek.

She looked as weary as he felt, with bruises beneath her beautiful green eyes and her coppery curls tangled. But with an effort, he bit back the urge to tell her she needed to rest.

Not only were their people depending on her skill to discover the truth of their latest threat, but he currently didn't have a place in her life to scoop her into his arms and carry her to the nearest bed.

Leashing his primitive instincts, he moved to stand at her side as she flipped open a file and pulled out the top sheet of paper.

"I printed out the files we managed to repair," she said, handing it to him. "The first is a newspaper clipping."

"*Unidentified woman discovered bound and gagged in back of delivery truck*," he read out loud.

"According to the records, Reny..." Payton wrinkled her nose. "Or rather, Patient Z, as they called her," she corrected herself, "was being moved to New York when the truck was hit from behind. The driver was killed and the human authorities arrived before she could be retrieved."

Hakan nodded. "That's how she managed to escape. Does it say anything about why she was being taken to New York?"

"Nothing."

"I'll see if I can do a background check on the dead driver. It might lead us to who hired him." Xavier leaned against the edge of the desk. "Anything else?"

She pulled out more paperwork and handed them to the leader of the Geeks.

"These are reports from various private investigators who've been looking for Reny after she was found," she explained. "It looks like the cops did a decent job of hiding her identity to protect her."

Xavier studied the reports before he tossed them on the desk.

"I hate to admit it, but the human authorities probably saved her life."

"Yes," Payton agreed. "They kept her identity hidden in case the people holding her captive tried to find her." She grimaced. "Which, of course, they were trying to do. Thankfully, they didn't have any info on her until she arrived in New Orleans and was caught by a photographer during the spree of supposed puma attacks."

Hakan grimaced. The disciples of Shakpi had been responsible for that fiasco, although their newest enemy appeared eager to use the humans' growing fear of the Pantera to their advantage.

"Shit," he muttered, glancing at the paper that Payton handed to him. The picture was blurry, but there was no mistaking Reny walking out of the FBI headquarters with Sebastian at her side. "She made the front page."

Xavier gave a puzzled shake of his head. "So if our enemies know where Reny is, why didn't they make any effort to retrieve her instead of Hiss?"

Payton grimaced. "They didn't know about Hiss until they managed to plant a bug in The Cougar's Den."

"What?" Xavier roared, heat blasting through the air as he snatched the file from Payton.

"That's where they overheard someone discussing the blood tests that revealed Reny and Hiss are siblings," she said, unfazed at the large male's fury.

Hakan was beginning to suspect that Payton had developed the ability to stand up to anyone and anything.

"Goddammit." Xavier glared out the window that offered a view of the communal eating area. "I've had the damned place swept for electronic devices a dozen times."

"Lian claimed our enemies have access to military-grade equipment," Hakan pointed out.

Xavier jerked his head around to glare at Hakan. Clearly he took the electronic breach as a personal insult.

Hakan got it.

The knowledge that someone had slipped past the guards into the Wildlands and disappeared with Hiss continued to piss him off.

"I don't care if they have fucking X-Men technology," the Geek snapped. "I would have found it."

Hakan rolled his eyes. Any other time he might have enjoyed provoking Xavier. The Geeks and Hunters enjoyed baiting each other, attempting to prove which faction was superior. But this was too important. They were Pantera. Which meant that they worked together.

"Not if it wasn't actually in the bar," he said.

Xavier scowled. "What the hell are you talking about?"

"They seem to have an enormous amount of money and political connections. It would be easy to bribe or blackmail a local to wear a listening device and hang around the bar."

Xavier gave a lift of his brows, as if surprised that Hakan actually had the ability to do more than punch or bite things.

"Shit, you're right," he breathed, pulling out his phone. "It could be a customer carrying the listening device in and out of The Cougar's Den. We need to put the place off-limits until we've managed to find out who our latest enemy is and what they want."

"Wait." Hakan halted the Geek from making his call. "We don't want them to suspect that we've discovered how they're getting intel on us," he said. He might not be a Geek or a Suit, but Hunters understood how to stalk their prey. "Besides, we can send in trusted Pantera to give out false information. It might give them a sense of security if they think we're chasing after shadows."

Xavier gave a nod. "I'll speak to Raphael."

There was the sound of footsteps before a pretty female with blonde curls and violet eyes poked her head into the office. Lydia, Roch's new mate, had been using her legal contacts to try to discover information on Stanton Locke.

"I think I found something you'll be interested in on Mr. Locke."

"What is it?" Hakan demanded.

"I know that you've had Hunters watching his home in the Garden District, but I've found another address that I've traced to him through a dummy corporation."

"Where?"

"An old warehouse near the docks." She held out a sheet of paper that had the coordinates printed on it. "Here you go."

"Thanks."

He shoved the paper in his pocket, preparing to follow Lydia as she left.

"Hakan."

The soft voice immediately had him spinning around to meet Payton's worried expression.

"Yes?"

"Be careful," she said in soft tones.

A fierce satisfaction surged through him at her obvious concern.

"Don't worry." He moved to gather her in his arms, pressing a tender kiss to her forehead. "I have every intention of returning." Lifting his head, he held her gaze, letting her see his unspoken pledge that he wouldn't take any unnecessary risks. Not when he was so close to getting everything he desired. "We have unfinished business."

With a last kiss on her lips, Hakan pulled his phone from his pocket and headed out of the office.

"Parish, meet me at the garage," he said as his leader answered. "We have a lead on Hiss."

Less than two hours later, he was seated beside Parish as they took the narrow backstreets to New Orleans East.

"Do we have any research on the property?" Parish at last broke the silence, his expression tense.

He'd commanded a dozen Hunters to surround the area. It was never easy to put his people in danger.

Hakan glanced at his phone, skimming through the series of messages that Payton had sent him since leaving the Wildlands.

"It's listed as a cold-storage warehouse although it's not currently in operation," he read out loud, scrolling to the next message. "Payton checked and the electricity is still running."

"Which means someone is using it," Parish said.

Hakan tossed aside his phone and pulled out his gun, his body tense as he prepared to engage the enemy.

"A perfect place to hide Hiss," he growled.

Parish nodded. Keeping a Pantera locked in a freezer wouldn't kill him, but it would weaken him to the point he would be far easier to control.

"These shitheads are starting to piss me off," Parish muttered, turning onto the road leading toward the nearest canal. "I thought the disciples were a pain in the ass, but they weren't nearly so well-funded, well-armed, or well-organized."

"True," Hakan agreed. "But they're not Pantera. Which means they'll eventually make a mistake that we—"

His words were cut short as Parish stomped on the brakes and yanked the vehicle to the side of the road. At the same time he shoved open his door to take a deep sniff.

"Do you smell that?"

"Smoke," Hakan growled.

Together they were leaping out of the car and jogging down the street. Rounding the corner they came to a halt at the sight of the long building that was swiftly being consumed by flames.

"We'll only have a few minutes before the human authorities arrive," Parish said, his voice tight. "You circle right. We'll meet back here."

Dread clutched Hakan's heart as he headed directly toward the burning building. Hiss might be a traitor, but Hakan wouldn't wish his worst enemy to be trapped in that inferno.

Ignoring the fierce heat that seared his skin and the smoke that threatened to choke him, Hakan did a thorough sweep, his senses on full alert.

At last he was forced to back away as the first fire truck was pulling next to the nearly destroyed building.

Avoiding the throng of humans that were gawking at the disaster with fascination, he joined Parish at the edge of the empty parking lot.

"Anything?" the leader demanded, his voice harsh as he carefully scanned the crowd for any hint of danger.

"Hiss was here," Hakan said.

Even with the thick smoke and nearby humans, he'd managed to catch his friend's distinctive scent.

"Shit." Parish clenched his hands. "Did he get out?"

Hakan nodded his head toward the parking lot. "His scent was near the road as if he was carried to a car, so we have to hope he survived."

Parish scowled as his phone rang, and hastily yanked it from his pocket.

"It's Raphael," he muttered as he pressed it to his ear and stepped away from the sirens that threatened to pierce Hakan's sensitive ears. "Yeah, we're here, but we're too late," Parish told the head of the Suits. "The place has been torched." He listened for a second before his eyes abruptly glowed with the power of his cat. "Shit."

Hakan moved to join him as Parish ended the call.

"I'm afraid to ask," he muttered.

Parish turned to head back toward the Jeep. "The Haymore Center just burned to the ground."

Hakan swore even as he had to admit from a tactical standpoint it made sense.

If you feared your secrets had been compromised, then simply get rid of them.

"They're brutal, but efficient," he said.

"A dangerous enemy." Parish said, his expression tight with concern. "And I have a nasty suspicion that we'd better find out what the hell they want from us before it's too late."

———

Payton was so weary she could barely keep her eyes open, but it was only Xavier's threat of having her hogtied and carried home that finally forced her to leave her office and return to her parents' house.

Not that she planned to go to bed.

How could she sleep before she was certain that Hakan had returned safely to the Wildlands?

Instead, she sought the peace of the small garden that she'd devoted years to creating. This was her sanctuary. The place she went when she needed to think.

Pacing through the camellias that were loaded with soft, pink flowers, she chewed her thumbnail, her concern growing with every passing hour.

Where was Hakan?

He should have returned long ago.

Unless something had happened to delay him…

Shadows had shrouded the garden in darkness when Payton at last caught the familiar scent of earthy male musk.

Without hesitation, she was flying across the garden to throw herself in his open arms.

"Hakan." She snuggled against the broad chest that was covered only by a muscle shirt that was tucked into his black jeans, savoring the heat of his skin that was still damp from a recent shower. "I heard about the fire." She pulled back to study his dark features, her heart squeezing with a love that was impossible to deny. Dear Goddess, if anything had happened to him…"Are you okay?"

"I'm fine." His big hands skimmed up her back, his touch gentle, as if she were some fragile treasure he was afraid of hurting. "Unfortunately our one lead is gone."

She struggled to concentrate on his words as he pressed her tight against him. Being held in his arms was sending all sorts of delicious sensations zooming through her body.

Not to mention X-rated thoughts of tumbling him back into the lotus flowers and giving in to her cat's urge to rub against that huge, beautiful male form until she was saturated in his musk.

"Now what?" she forced herself to ask.

He shrugged, looking as distracted as she felt. "We start fresh tomorrow."

She nodded, shivering beneath the force of his amber gaze. There was an intense focus about him that made her feel as if he was on the verge of pouncing.

The question was…would she let him catch her?

There was no doubt that the hours she'd waited for his return had shaken her.

What if she'd lost him without having told him just how much she still loved him?

"Have you eaten?" she abruptly demanded, caught between the urge to simply give in to her fierce desire to complete the mating and the need to make him work for her trust.

"Not yet," he said, lowering his arms and stepping back. "I have something I want to show you."

Payton frowned, instantly missing the heat of his body. "What is it?"

"A surprise." He held out his hand. "Will you come with me?"

She didn't hesitate in laying her fingers on his palm. She didn't know if she was prepared for a mating, but she desperately needed to be near him.

"Yes."

Assuming they would be going to the communal area for dinner, Payton was surprised when they instead turned to head into one of the numerous untamed areas of the Wildlands.

"I'm running a background search on Stanton Locke to see if he has any connection to the Pantera," she said, oddly needing to fill the silence as they walked along the narrow trail. "And I think Lydia is continuing to look for additional properties he might own."

"Tomorrow," he murmured, leaning down to steal a fleeting kiss. "Tonight is for us."

Excitement jolted through her, making her heart race and her palms sweat. Deep inside, her cat purred with anticipation.

They'd walked in silence for nearly a half hour when he tugged her off the pathway and into the thick underbrush.

She frowned in confusion. It'd been years since she'd been in this area, but she didn't recall anything being around that was worth seeing.

"Is there a reason we're in the middle of..." Her words were forgotten as he steered her around a patch of cypress trees to reveal a pretty cottage that was nearly hidden among the thick foliage. "Oh, how pretty. Did you build this?"

"I did," he admitted.

She gave a slow shake of her head.

"Why?" she demanded. "You've always lived with the other Hunters."

"Because I wanted a home that was ours," he said with a stark simplicity that made her heart miss a painful beat.

"Ours?" she breathed.

"Of course." In the darkness his eyes glowed with a green sheen, his brows lifted as if wondering why she would be surprised he'd built them a home. "I've been working on it for the past twenty years." He studied her wary expression for a long moment. "Do you want to see?"

Payton unconsciously chewed her thumbnail. "I'm not sure."

He stepped forward, brushing his finger down her cheek. "What are you afraid of?"

She sucked in a deep breath, a thousand butterflies fluttering in her stomach. Blessed Goddess. She felt as nervous and uncertain as an adolescent on her first date.

"I'm not sure I'm ready for this," she admitted in a breathless voice.

"Give me a chance, Payton." His fingers cupped her chin, tilting back her head so he could lean down and kiss her with a piercing yearning. "Please."

She hastily stepped back. It was that or melt into a puddle of need at his feet.

"Okay."

A rare, heart-stopping smile curved his lips. "Thank you."

Once again reaching for her hand, Hakan walked up the flagstone path and stepped onto the porch that wrapped around the two-story home that was painted white with green shutters. Then, pulling open the screen door, he led her across the small foyer and into the main living room.

"What do you think?" he asked in soft tones.

Payton blinked, a hand pressed to her racing heart.

It was...perfect. The large stone fireplace where the logs were burning with a cheery fire. The pale lemon walls and ivory, overstuffed furniture. The hand-woven carpet and open-beamed ceiling.

It was warm, and cozy, and everything she'd ever wanted in a home.

"Did you talk to my mother?" she demanded.

He stood at her side, his thumb lazily brushing the inside of her wrist.

"Why?"

"These are my favorite colors."

He chuckled at the edge of disbelief in her voice. "Do you think anyone knows you better than I do, little one?" he asked. "Let me prove it."

Payton pressed her lips together, trying to hide her flare of amusement.

There was such eager pride in his voice.

Like a little boy who was trying to impress her with his shiny new toy.

Stepping through the connecting door, Payton's amusement was replaced by a sense of awe as Hakan flipped on the lights.

Her feet automatically carried forward before she halted in the center of the polished wooden floor and turned in a full circle.

The breath was wrenched from her lungs as she caught sight of the beautiful library Hakan had created.

"This is..." Her feet carried her across the polished wood floor toward the walls that were hidden behind heavy shelves that towered to the ceiling, each of them loaded with leather-bound books.

Lightly her fingers trailed over her childhood favorites: *The Secret Garden, Oliver Twist, Pippi Longstocking...*

"I know that while you enjoy all your techie toys, you still love to have a real book in your hands," Hakan murmured.

She pulled out a copy of *Treasure Island*, carefully opening it.

"First editions?" she breathed in shock, unable to comprehend how much money and time had been devoted to creating this room.

"My mate deserves the best," he said without hesitation.

Barely resisting the urge to plop herself on the floor and surround herself with the books, she instead moved to the back of the room where a hand-carved mahogany desk was situated with the latest computer system already up and running.

She sent Hakan a startled glance. "You did this?"

"With some wise council from Xavier," he said with a lift of one shoulder. "He helped me set it up before I came to get you."

She licked her lips, feeling overwhelmed. "I don't know what to say."

"There's more," he assured her, taking the book from her hand and setting it aside before he was pulling her through the house and out the back door.

Lanterns were already burning to reveal the perfect replica of her beloved garden. The only difference was the wicker table and chairs set in the center, loaded with candles, a bottle of wine, and silver-covered plates.

"Hakan." She gave a disbelieving shake of her head. "This is amazing."

With the grace of a predator, he moved to lift the covers from the plates.

"Lasagna, garlic bread and your favorite wine."

Her lips parted as she met his smoldering amber gaze, the truth suddenly hitting her.

"You're wooing me," she breathed, pleasure racing through her.

He prowled toward her, wrapping his arms around her waist as he studied her upturned face with a brooding gaze.

"I've been wooing you for the past twenty years. You just didn't know it."

Wonderment melted the last of her bitterness as she gazed into the harsh male face. No male could spend so much time and effort to please a female unless he truly was devoted to her.

"No more barriers?" she demanded.

Regret darkened the amber eyes. "Never again."

"And no more assuming you know what's best for me?"

His lips twitched, the scent of his musk teasing her senses like the finest aphrodisiac.

"I would be too terrified," he assured her, his voice thickening with the power of his cat. "You've grown into a formidable female."

Her own cat brushed against her inner skin, eager to get out and play with her mate.

Going onto her tiptoes, she caught his bottom lip between her teeth, giving it a punishing nip.

"Don't forget it."

"Will you be mine, Payton?" he rasped. "I want to have you wrapped in my arms when we go to sleep, and standing at my side when we walk through the Wildlands." He grabbed her hips, pressing her tight against his thickening cock. "I want you to grow round with my young and be angry when I get home late. I want to spoil you, and aggravate you, and love you until I take my last breath."

Tears flooded her eyes at the words she'd ached to hear for so very, very long.

"Damn you," she sighed.

He stiffened with genuine concern. "What have I done now?"

"I intended to make you suffer."

A low growl rumbled in his chest. "Believe me, spending two decades trying to keep my hands off you has been sheer torture."

"Hmm."

He suddenly lowered his head, nipping a path of kisses down the curve of her neck.

"Say yes."

"Hakan." Her hands landed on his broad chest, lightning bolts of pleasure streaking through her. "I can't think when you're doing that."

"Doing what?" His teeth sank into the flesh where her neck met her shoulder, hard enough to leave a mark. "This?"

She clutched at his T-shirt, sheer bliss flowing through her like molten lava.

"Unfair," she moaned.

He used his tongue to ease the tiny wound. "Then say yes," he commanded.

"Yes."

There was a tension-charged pause, as if Hakan couldn't quite believe he was hearing her right. Then, with an explosion of movement, Payton found herself swept off her feet and carried back into the house.

"Thank the Goddess," he muttered as he headed toward a staircase that led to the upper floor.

"What about dinner?" Payton teased even as she wrapped her arms around his neck and snuggled against his chest.

Her hunger had nothing to do with lasagna.

He lifted her up to brand her lips with a kiss that made her toes curl and her core clench with raw, joyous anticipation.

He spoke against her lips. "You can consider me the appetizer."

"I do want to lick you from top to bottom," she repeated his words back to him, her claws already extended as she sliced her mating mark down the length of his back. "With several long stops in between."

He stumbled on the stairs, nearly falling on his face.

"Holy shit, Payton."

She offered him a wicked smile, fiercely pleased by the stunned expression on her mate's face.

"I think there might be more than one way to make you suffer."

Epilogue

HISS opened his eyes, not surprised to discover he was strapped to a gurney.

Fuck.

He'd known when he escaped with the well-dressed Englishman that it was a trap. Still, he'd been willing to take the chance that he could discover the truth of his family before he died.

But minutes after sneaking out of the Wildlands the bastard had injected him with pure malachite, knocking him unconscious.

He had a few weird-ass memories of being icy cold, followed by the unmistakable stench of smoke, but he'd been floating in and out of a black, clinging fog so he couldn't be sure if it had been real or a figment of his imagination.

Now at last his body had burned through the malachite and he could take in his surroundings with a clear brain.

It was dark. And musty. Like a basement or cellar.

No, wait.

His eyes adjusted enough that he could see the long cabinets with stainless steel counters, along with the sort of equipment that went with a medical lab.

Not a hospital...the place looked like it hadn't been cleaned in the past decade.

Maybe an old government facility.

Straining against the chains that bound him to the gurney, Hiss abruptly stilled as he caught the sound of a door opening.

"Who's there?" he snarled, his gaze searching the darkness. "Dammit, you promised me answers, you cowardly bastard."

The soft sound of a woman's voice came from one of the tall, metal cabinets.

"Shh."

Hiss scowled, trying to lift his head off the gurney. Was this another trick?

"Show yourself," he commanded.

"No, do not look in this direction," the mystery woman commanded, cracking the door of the cabinet just far enough to reveal a slender female form.

"Why not?"

"You're on camera."

Hiss's gaze flicked toward the ceiling, easily locating the blinking red light in the far corner.

"Yeah, that's no big newsflash," he said.

"I don't want them to realize I've found you," she whispered.

On the point of telling her to go to hell, Hiss caught an unmistakable scent.

The female was Pantera.

God. Damn.

"Are you another prisoner?" he rasped, jerking his head so his gaze was fixed on the ceiling.

There was no way in hell he was going to endanger her by allowing his guards to realize anyone had entered the lab.

"Yes."

The voice was textured with an unbearable sadness that made Hiss's gut twist in response.

Christ. He'd never heard such grief.

"You're Pantera," he said, his voice softening.

There was a long pause before he heard her give a soft sob. "Oh, I'm so much more than that, Hiss."

Hiss stiffened, his instincts on full alert. "You know me?"

"Only in my heart."

An icy chill of premonition inched down Hiss's spine. "Who the hell are you?"

"Your mother."

SÉVERIN

BY
LAURA WRIGHT

CHAPTER ONE

THE cool night air pulsed in and out of Taylor's lungs. Her muscles threatened to seize. Rain pelted her skin like tiny bullets. The ground beneath her feet was thick with mud and brush.

And yet she ran.

She ran faster than she'd ever run before—faster than she believed herself capable of. Maybe it was the drive to keep breathing another day—to keep at bay that one person who wanted to extinguish her breath. Or maybe it was to finally know the feeling of being safe again.

The bayou terrain was exactly what she'd expected: thick foliage, stands of cypress, wildlife around every corner—their eyes a glowing pulse with every blink. But it was far more difficult to maneuver. She'd dressed appropriately, in boots, jeans, tank and an all-weather light jacket. But the rain was growing heavier by the second, the sky darker, and her compass had stopped working five minutes ago. All she could do was keep going, hope she was crossing the border—pray that Edgar and his 'friends' hadn't followed when she'd snuck out the back of the quaint La Pierre bed and breakfast she'd been staying at.

The bed and breakfast her ex had tracked her to.

"Shit!" she cried as her foot sank into a large bog of brown sludge that smelled faintly of rotting eggs.

Please let me be close, she begged, easing her foot out gingerly so she didn't lose her boot or twist her ankle.

Then, heart beating so fast it was painful, she took off again. Running, pushing herself, faster and faster, deeper and deeper into the lush, green wildness until she came to the shoreline of the bayou. She stopped, put her hands on her thighs to catch her breath and glanced back. Just a couple of seconds, just a couple blinks. She couldn't afford any more than that. But there was nothing. No lights. No sounds but the rain and brackish water to her right.

Keep going. Just keep going.

They had a town. She'd read about it. They had leaders, one who was purported to be kind and fair. God, it was a long shot. But that's the chance you had to take when you were pretty much out of chances.

She was about to continue on when the breath was suddenly ripped from her body and she felt herself falling to the ground. Her butt hit wet earth with a loud thud, and she reached out for something to grab on to. But there was nothing. *What...?* Gritting her teeth against the pain, she glanced up, and the breath left her body in a rush.

Holy shit! An animal!

A puma?

No, a Pantera!

Is this really what they look like? No drawing could do them justice. It was huge! And no more than three feet away, hackles raised, paws the size of dinner plates. She stared, both panicked and awestruck. Even with the rain falling, she could see its thick, golden fur.

"I'm sorry," she began stupidly, as if she'd just bumped into a pedestrian on the streets of New Orleans. "I'm...I..."

Nothing else stumbled from her tongue because deadly silver eyes were pinned on her—a cat ready to spring.

Ready to attack.

She had to say something. Speak up. Not lie here ready to be dinner. God...But what? What did she tell it? That her ex-boyfriend was stalking her? That he was determined to either have her again or make sure no one else did? That she was terrified and desperate? That she had no one. That she thought—maybe foolishly, but here she was—this magical place called the Wildlands could protect her?

The cat started toward her, a slow, calculated progression, head bent, nostrils flared. Her heart kicked and her fingers dug into the wet ground. She hardly felt the rain pounding on her head and shoulders. Had she been prepared for this? Meeting up with a wild cat who could kill her as easily as Edgar had threatened to do? Was that her choice? Claws and teeth...they came in so many different packages.

She gasped, drew back as it approached. It was massive, its eyes so beautiful, yet so feral. She could feel its hot breath on her face. Her muscles flinched, ready to propel herself backward. Ready to run. But her mind refused those calls. Fear had ruled her for so long now. Every move she made. The state was a constant in her life. She'd made it here, to her destination. Now she had to do everything she could to stay.

It loomed over her, its nostrils flaring slightly as it took in her scent. She wondered what it smelled. A poor little frightened human, not worth its time or its taste buds? Taylor knew what she scented: wet fur, wet earth and something else...Something she'd never taken into her lungs before—but she swore was almost floral.

It leaned in a few inches.

Bracing herself to feel the sharp sting of claws or teeth, Taylor held its gaze. *Whatever you think you see or smell, I'm not afraid.* She gritted her teeth. *I know what true fear feels like and this isn't it. Anticipation, anxiety...yes. But not fear.*

Its head dropped then, to her legs, and it slowly started to sniff her. First her thighs, then between her legs—Christ!—then her belly, up her chest to her neck. Finally, it lifted its head again and those silver eyes pinned her where she sat.

She nodded. "Yes, I'm human," she rasped. "But I'm not here to hurt anyone."

It cocked its head to the side, studying her.

"The opposite, actually," she continued, rain pelting her face and mouth as she spoke. "I'm trying to get away from someone. He's a really bad...man. Dangerous. I..." Her throat closed up for a moment and she cleared it. "I need help."

Taylor had no idea what the cat understood or didn't. But when it leaned in, stopping only inches from her face, panting, its warm breath a heartbeat against her skin, she knew if she was going to die she'd rather have it be here, beneath the feral hunger of an animal instead of under the thumb of a calculated, insecure sociopath.

But the gold puma didn't kill her.

Instead, it ran its pink tongue from her chin to her forehead. Then over her right ear. Then across her neck.

As she sat there, ass-deep in muck, the strangest feelings rushed over and through her. Panic was still there, yes. In the back of her mind, warning her to jump up and run. But there was something else too...below the surface of that panic...something that hummed with knowing or awareness. And when she glanced up once again to meet those silver eyes, she swore the cat felt it too.

"Please. Can you take me to your town?" she asked, her voice unrecognizable to her. Breathy, strained. "To someone called Raphael?"

The moment she said the name she knew it was a mistake. The cat jerked backward, pawed the ground, then bared its impressive set of teeth. *Oh shit.* What was the problem? Was Raphael a bad guy? Was she going from one bad guy to another?

She pushed to her feet and tried to get her bearings. She was soaking wet, and, as night descended fully, getting colder. The cat remained where it was, watching her, eyes fierce.

"My name is Taylor, I..." Oh, god. *Yeah, tell it your name. Like that's going to do something.*

A growl unlike anything she'd ever heard before erupted in the rain-scented air, and the cat leapt at her and landed a foot away in a puddle of dirty water. Taylor cried out from the splash and the attack and jumped back. But it didn't stay where it was. It leapt again. Then pounced. *What the hell?* Taylor dropped back. Again it bounded at her. Again, she stumbled back. But when it did it a fourth time, she suddenly realized it wasn't trying to attack her at all. It was pushing her back toward the border. It was trying to get her to run away. Get out of the Wildlands.

No. She couldn't.

When it pounced a fifth time, she didn't move. Refused her instincts. Breath stalled, teeth gritted, she held her ground. Pissed, the cat snarled. Snapped its teeth at her. *Move, foolish human,* it seemed to be saying. But it didn't touch her.

Tears pricked Taylor's eyes, but she willed them away. She shook her head, feeling like her heart was going to explode. "No."

Nostrils pulsing with each breath, it glared at her.

"I can't go back there." She glanced behind her.

"My life is over if I go back there."

When she turned to face it again, the cat's head was swaying from side to side as if to say, '*What do you think awaits you here, human?*'

"I was hoping for protection," she said, her voice cracking. She was done. Done running. Done planning every move she made. "I was hoping to stay here. Live here. Contribute in any way I could. I was hoping to hide." She laughed suddenly. "Do you know what that's like? Being so afraid you just want to crawl into a hole and stay there?" She shrugged. "Indefinitely." Her eyes came up and locked with those silver orbs. "Do what you gotta do, puma. I know I'm in your world, on your land. Kill me if you must. Because if I go back there, I'm dead anyway."

For long seconds, the only sound in the bayou was the rain and the rushing water. The massive cat stared at her, regarded her, then started to move. But it didn't come at her. Instead, it paced from side to side, every once in a while glancing her way, as if it were pondering an idea...or a question. Then suddenly it stopped.

Taylor held her breath. *Please don't make me leave.* This time, when it padded toward her, it didn't leap or pounce or back her up against the border. Instead, it sort of corralled her down the shore of the bayou like a sheepdog. Light wasn't in abundance so she had to trust that it wasn't leading her into a sinkhole or swamp—hope it was taking her into town.

"I'm sure you get people coming across your border for the wrong reasons," she said as she trudged through the overgrown wetlands. "Or trying to. Curious tourists and irritating reporters. I'm not curious or a reporter." Her voice dropped. "I'm not anything."

The cat didn't make a sound, but she felt its head, solid with muscle, warm breath at her back. It nudged her onward.

"I just want to be safe," she continued, swiping rain from her eyes. "I just want to know what that feels like again."

She knew she was rambling. But she wanted the cat to see her as more than a pesky, unwanted human. She wanted it to see her as a being it could help.

After a few minutes of walking, they came to a stand of cypress. Taylor started to veer left, but the cat darted out in front of her, cutting her off. Taylor stopped sharply, looked from the trees to the cat.

"What?"

Once again, the cat came forward and nudged her toward the tallest, broadest tree. The power in just that small movement was staggering. Confused, Taylor looked all around. What was it trying to tell her? The panic rose again in her throat and she swallowed hard. Was this the border? Just in another area of the Wildlands? Then she saw it. In the trunk of that one massive cypress. Or what should be a trunk.

She squinted against the rain and her pulse kicked in her blood. There was a doorway in the trunk, as tall or taller than she was. How was that possible? To her left, the cat growled, then knocked its head in the direction of the hollowed-out tree.

Oh, god. Her heart sank into her soaking wet shoes. It wasn't taking her to town. Wasn't forcing her across the border. "You want me to go in there? Why?"

The cat looked up at the sky, then back at her and snarled.

She shook her head. "I don't understand. Please. I need to find Raph—"

Her words were cut off by a strike of lightning and the rain that had been falling lightly just seconds ago upgraded into a virtual torrent. Within seconds, Taylor felt as though she was underwater. And without another thought, she bolted for the door in the cypress.

———

Want.

Not food.

Female.

Not puma.

He rolled his neck, dug his claws into the wet ground.

Human.

Raphael? She wanted Raphael. He knew the name. Had come across the Hunter when he'd found his way to the Wildlands so many years ago. When he'd finally escaped.

Bite. Claw. Tear flesh of humans. Release...

A low, satisfied growl rumbled in his chest as he padded into his nest. He gave a good shake, then sank to his belly and watched the woman. Human woman. It was a stench he normally despised. Anything human, really. But she also carried the scent of warmth inside her, and desire and vulnerability. That was new. That he didn't understand.

She was looking around his dwelling like she was surprised to find it clean.

Should it be filled with shit and bones, human?

No. He lived as puma only, true, but he liked his dwelling kept with fresh moss, clean blankets. He hunted and consumed and relieved himself outside the den.

She turned to look at him then, sodden and hopeful, her dark green eyes desperate to understand—know her fate. As if he carried that power within him. He would admit to her beauty. The fur on her head was long and thick and lighter than the sun. Her body was perfect for mounting. Her breasts were large and could feed young. Her face...it made him momentarily forget what human women were capable of. What they had done to him, both in and out of his cage. That they had wanted his suffering, then demanded he give them pleasure. His mind ventured back. His senses too. He could catch their stench on the air before they even unlocked the door to the clinic's hallway. Disgust, desire, anticipation.

His eyes narrowed on the woman before him, and he opened his nostrils further. This human did not scent of anything like that. It was strange, yet intriguing. She carried some fear and panic in her pores. But there was something else. Something he hardly recognized. Something from long ago. Something he'd shared with the Pantera female he'd been caged with. A hope for comfort?

He growled low and blackly.

"Please." She sat down, her back against the wall. "Please, don't."

What did she expect of him? To rush? Attack? To lick? Bite? Feast on her delectable human flesh?

Heat rumbled through him. His caustic thoughts and suggestions had been only sarcasm. And yet, they'd entered his mind and instead of remaining, had snaked through his body like liquid fire. He tucked his head into his chest and closed his eyes. He should force her to leave. Rain was just water. It hurt nothing. Especially a human. They were, after all, made of slick, impenetrable grease. She would find her way to town, perhaps. Find the male she sought. Raphael.

His lip curled. Now he remembered. This Raphael was a leader in the Pantera. A Suit, they called it. He was the go-between with humans and Pantera. Yes, he sometimes heard the Hunters speaking of it as they passed by on patrol.

He lifted his head. Now she was sitting with her knees to her chest. She looked exhausted. Her eyes wilting like a Dyesse lily after that fete the Pantera loved so much. He should ignore her until the skies dried up. But instead, he got up and padded over to her. Eyes wide, biting her lip, she pressed as far back against the wood as she could. He had liked licking her. At first, he'd wanted to taste her emotions, her fear, to know her mindset. But he'd gotten carried away. Her neck intrigued him. The beat of pulse under his tongue.

Her eyes moved over him. "I don't know what you're thinking," she said in an almost-whisper. "Or if you're thinking. Maybe this is an instinct thing to bring me in here. Maybe it's protecting your borders. Maybe it's the crazy rain, and you're actually protecting me. But all I'm asking for is safety for a short time. Until I can figure out what I'm going to do."

Safety. He had asked for that once. Not for himself. But for the Pantera female. His friend. Instead they stuck another needle in her arm.

His nostrils flickered, catching a scent. He inhaled deeply.

Blood.

Human.

It was faint.

Hunger roared through him. He dipped his head to the woman's hand and nudged his nose up the seam of her wrist until...A low growl vibrated in his throat. She'd had something put around her forearms. Something that had dug into her skin. Caused her to spill blood.

His gaze flipped up.

She was staring at him. "It was the day I told him I was leaving," she said, her eyes tired but strong. "That I never wanted to see him again. He didn't accept that."

A sudden tornado of fury exploded within him, and he let loose a series of cries, a wild cat's way to curse and howl and rant. She had been caged too.

She grabbed her arm and held it to her chest protectively. "But I got out. When I could I got out and ran. That was three weeks ago. He won't stop looking for me."

Fuck! Was he truly sitting here, feeling empathy for a human? After all they had done to him? All they had inflicted on him?

"I'm not a wimp, I swear," she said quickly. "I tried the police. Tried friends, hiding out. Changing my address, phone number. But nothing worked. He's got too many connections." She inhaled deeply. "I saw an article in the newspaper about the Wildlands. How there are some humans here. Mates, they called them." Her eyes pricked with sudden tears. "I was hoping…" she added softly. Then she swiped at the tears with one of her paws and sagged against the wall. "It smells so good here. The minute I crossed the border, the air changed. Wet and fresh and cool."

He glanced over his shoulder at the open door. Outside, the rain had receded to a fine mist, and a sliver of moonlight was trying its best to break from a cloud and spread some light across the bayou.

He turned back. She was leaning on a mound of blankets, her eyes heavy-lidded. "I'm so tired. I've been running for two days."

What was left of the male inside him reacted to her words, pushing the cat forward until it placed a paw on her shoulder and pressed her gently until she lay down on the strip of clean rug. As she stared up at him, unsure, he scratched at her, very softly on her shoulder and arm until her muscles relaxed and her eyes closed.

Go to the doorway, curl up in a ball and rest.

But the puma remained where it was, watching the woman sleep. He didn't know what he was going to do with her. But he worried that she might be cold. Or hungry.

CHAPTER TWO

TAYLOR woke to the gray-green light of dawn and a man's naked body curled up next to her. For a second or two she lay there frozen, trembling, believing she'd failed—believing she was back in New Orleans, Edgar beside her. But as the dust of sleep faded from her eyes, she realized the man pressed to her side was the antithesis of Edgar.

Her ex was of medium height, thin and wiry, with short black hair. The man beside her now was tall, had a mane of thick hair the color of caramel, and every inch of him was hard, smooth muscle.

She let her eyes move over him. He reminded her of a sculpture from the Renaissance, perfectly carved and chiseled muscle from calves to buttocks to torso and even to his face. His face...was it possible for something so fiercely beautiful to exist outside of a museum? Such strong features, like granite, yet his heavy mouth was soft and his eyelashes were long and thick.

Without thinking, she reached out and ran the pad of her thumb across his cheek. Soft. She smiled.

A low, tense growl vibrated from his throat, and in seconds the man was up on all fours, eyes blazing down on her, teeth bared.

"I'm sorry," she said quickly, pressing back against the wall of the cypress. *Oh my god.* What had she done? "I didn't mean anything by it. I—"

Her words were cut off by the look on his face. A moment ago he had been all predatory antagonism. Now, alarm, panic and shock registered in his features. He glanced down at his body. So did Taylor. *Oh*...She swallowed thickly. He was erect. And very, very large. She'd never seen...anything...

It's true. God...it's all true. The pumas are human. Or can change into humans. Amazing. Incredible.

Her eyes lifted. He was staring at her intently, those silver eyes now flecked with pale blue trying to comprehend what was happening.

"I'm so sorry for touching you," she whispered, her heart kicking against her ribs. "It's just I've never seen anyone like you before. You're...magnificent."

His eyes narrowed, and once again, he looked down. At his hard sex, and his thighs, belly, forearms. When he lifted his head again, his eyes held stark, icy panic.

"How..." His voice sounded raspy, unused.

"What?" What was wrong with him?

"This." He reached up and clutched his throat. "How am I... male?"

She didn't understand. "What do you mean?" Wasn't this how it worked for the Pantera? Shifting from one state of being to the other? She shook her head. "When I went to sleep you were a cat. And when I woke up..." *You were lying next to me, warm and nude and glorious.* "You were like this."

The color drained from his handsome face. "No...I...am puma," he managed. "Always. No."

His anxiety was palpable and Taylor wasn't sure what to say or do. Was this not how the Pantera shifted? Were they not males or females at all, but always in cat form? Again, on instinct, she leaned in and touched him, offering him some level of comfort. Her hand on his shoulder. His skin was hot to the touch. Not the kind that burned, but the kind that melted. She felt her insides liquefy, felt her belly tighten.

"You," he growled softly, his eyes probing her.

"Taylor," she whispered.

They were close. So close she could feel his warm breath on her cheeks. His gaze swept over her face, hesitating when he came to her lips. Taylor swiped at the bottom one with her tongue.

"Human," he uttered.

She nodded. "Yes."

He leaned closer, but didn't touch her. A sense of urgency erupted within Taylor, and she wanted nothing more than to feel this male's lips on hers. Crushing against her, stealing her breath—

The thought was seized from her mind as a feral snarl burst from the male's throat. He jerked back, and his nude body stiffened. In seconds, hair began to sprout from his skin. Taylor watched in shock and fascination as the man with the chiseled muscles and beautiful mouth became a glorious golden beast.

Her back to the wall of the tree, heart beating a violent rhythm in her chest, Taylor stared at the animal, mouth open. It stared back. For one moment, she believed she saw him—the male—behind the puma's silver eyes; his anxiety, his curiosity, his desire. But that look was gone in an instant, and something else had taken its place. Something vicious. Ears flat, teeth bared, he cocked his head to one side.

"We're supposed to be patrolling," came a man's voice outside the tree.

Taylor tried to sit up, but the puma remained where it was.

"I scent human female, Rage." This time it was a woman's voice.

"Are you sure?" Rage returned.

"Yes, Lena," another man put in. "Be sure. You know how he gets when we try to engage him in anything."

"I know what I smell, Parish," she said with a snort.

Taylor stared up at the puma. It stared right back at her. *What do we do? What do I do?* she silently asked him.

The man called Parish cursed loudly, then bellowed, "Séverin, do you have a human in your treehouse?"

Séverin. The name coated her skin like honey. "Is that your name?" she asked him.

He didn't answer. He wasn't looking at her anymore. His ears were pinned back. His entire being was aggressive animal ready to spring.

"I can't believe you called his place a treehouse," Lena said dryly. "Bad form, boss."

"Séverin?" Parish yelled again. "Come out here and talk to us before we have to come in."

"Talk to us?" Rage put in with a sniff. "He hasn't uttered a word since he came here, and you expect—"

"No expectation, brother," Parish cut in. "Just hope. Always hope." He growled softly. "Dammit. Séverin! Last time I'm saying it—"

Without warning, Séverin turned and barreled through the opening in the cypress. *Shit!* He was going to get into trouble because of her. Maybe even hurt. Taylor was on her feet in an instant, following him. Cool morning air rushed her skin as she hit the doorway and remained. *Holy hell.* Séverin was directly in front of her, just a foot or two away. He was in full fighting stance, ears pinned back, teeth bared—his growl a warning for the three people standing in a semicircle beside the shore of the bayou. No, she corrected herself. Not people. Pantera. They were staring at Séverin, no doubt worried about his sudden show of ferocity. They only looked up when Taylor spoke.

"It's okay," she said quickly. "I'm okay."

Three sets of incredible colored eyes took her in. Taylor glanced at each one in turn, acknowledging them with an encouraging nod. Both the males were tall and dark-haired, and like Séverin, heavily muscled. The woman was about Taylor's height with straight, shoulder-length red hair and a wicked expression. She spoke first.

"Who are you?" she asked.

Séverin growled and lunged at her.

Lena held her ground, but crouched slightly as if ready for whatever was about to come her way. She glanced at Parish. "What the hell?"

The male with the long dark hair didn't reply. He was staring intently at Séverin.

"My name's Taylor," she called out quickly. Last thing she wanted was a fight. And one she had brought on because of her presence.

"Are you okay?" the male she believed to be Rage asked. "Has he hurt you?"

"No," she said with feeling.

Parish, who seemed to be the leader of the group, narrowed his fierce gold gaze on Séverin. "This is not part of your agreement with Raphael."

Raphael? Taylor's heart kicked. *So he knows the male I sought?*

Séverin bared his teeth at the male in the sort of universal symbol for *fuck off and die.*

The male shook his head with irritation, then turned his attention to Taylor. "My name is Parish. I'm the leader of the Hunters in the Wildlands. What are you doing here? We do not allow humans on our land without invitation. Are you lost? Are you a reporter? Or were you lured here?" His eyes once again flickered toward Séverin who was crouched and ready to spring.

"No, no," she said rapidly. "I'm not here for a story…and I came here by myself." Oh, how did she start this? She turned to the female. Lena. "I need help. A place to stay. Protection."

"Protection?" the female repeated. "Someone outside wishes to harm you?"

Taylor nodded.

"We don't protect humans," Rage said, his tone rigid. "You are the ones trying to destroy us."

Taylor knew some of what was happening between her world and this newly-found Wildlands. There was fear, ignorance, even a desire to capitalize on the shifters' existence. But she wasn't after any of that.

The leader stepped forward, then stopped when Séverin sprang at him, landing just a few feet away. "Taylor," he began. "I appreciate your quest, sympathize with it even, but we don't offer protection here. We have humans who live among us, yes, but they are mates only."

The words weren't something she wasn't expecting. Why would they want her here? Why would they want to open it up to anyone who wasn't their kind or their mates? But she had to try.

She swallowed hard, nodded. "I understand. I really do. Perhaps if I could speak to Rapahel..."

Rage interrupted. "How do you know Raphael?" he demanded, then looked to Parish. "Goddess! She could be the enemy. Wrapped up in a poor little beautiful human in trouble package. That would be clever. She could be sent in to infiltrate. Find out our secrets."

"I'm not," Taylor insisted. "I swear. I don't want to hurt anyone. I only want to stop someone from hurting me."

Lena stepped forward. "Is it a male?"

Taylor nodded. "An ex."

"Who doesn't want to be an ex?"

"Yes. And I don't want anything to do with him."

"We're not a fucking halfway house!" Rage erupted. His violet eyes settled on Séverin. "Send her back where she came from."

Séverin snarled.

"Fine," the male said tightly. "I'll do it myself."

Rage only managed to take a few steps before Séverin was on him, canines sinking into flesh.

———

Séverin's eyes bolted open. Wet, green earth below. Sun overhead. Inside, his organs were still asleep. But he shouldn't be sleeping. He should be hunting. But for what? What? Who...He blinked.

Woman.

Human woman.

My woman.

A low growl rumbled at the back of his throat. *Remember.* They had drugged him. His cat. Parish. Lena. Rage. Rage wanted to take the woman from him. Out of the Wildlands. Hadn't he wanted that, too? No...not today. She had touched him today. Her fingers on his skin were soothing. He had felt...that was all—he had felt.

He rolled to his belly and pushed to his feet. The sun was too bright. He liked the rain, the clouds. They brought the woman.

Woman.

Eyes up, he looked around. Where was she? He padded into the nest. Scent lingering, but starting to fade.

She is gone.

A deep, feral snarl erupted from his throat and he turned slowly around. They took her from him. His prize. She was his. He found her. She belonged to him. Her scent, her touch, made him feel good, comforted. She made him—

A male.

A sharp pain went through him as he padded out into the lush, wild lands once again. How had it happened? He hadn't been male for many years. He didn't want to be male. When he was male, bad things happened.

Yet he needed the woman.

Lifting his head, he inhaled deeply. Once he had her scent in his lungs, he took off toward town.

Chapter Three

THE baby cried and fussed as she waited for her mother to sit and unhook her nursing bra. Ashe Pascal was obviously well practiced because she had the slip of cotton down and the baby latching on before her backside even hit the leather.

"Boy, was she hungry," the woman said, relaxing back in the chair and giving Taylor a soft smile.

"She's beautiful," Taylor said.

"Thank you. I think so too. But I suppose that's a mother's lens I'm seeing her through." She lowered her chin conspiratorially, a few of her black curls falling about her face. "Some of these Pantera think she's a crying poop machine."

Taylor laughed, but the sound was slightly hollow. Granted, she was grateful to be in town, in the lovely Colonial-style house that served as the headquarters for the Pantera's diplomats. She was going to meet with Raphael—this woman's mate. It was exactly as she'd wanted it. And yet, all she could think about was Séverin. Whatever the other Hunters had believed, he had been trying to protect her. Seeing him go down that way, a needle in his neck…she'd been so angry at that dark-haired Hunter. Rage. A perfect name. They'd given her the choice of going with them to town or being escorted to the border.

Hadn't been much of a choice. But all the way into town, she'd vowed to talk to Raphael about Séverin, make sure he was okay. Ask if she could see him again. She owed him.

"So, I hear you're looking for a place to escape?"

Taylor looked up, realizing she had been deep in thought. "Excuse me?"

"A place to escape?" Ashe's cheeks flushed pink. "I'm sorry. Maybe it's not my business."

Taylor shook her head. "No, it's fine. I hadn't meant to keep it a secret. I'm looking for asylum. I'm looking for a place that can keep me safe."

"Lena mentioned a man…" Ashe pressed gently.

"My ex," Taylor explained. Maybe she should've been shy or embarrassed about the truth. But she wasn't. It was her truth. She'd fallen for a slick, intelligent, seemingly worldly man who she'd allowed to control her, and ultimately hurt her. But that was over. The shame would be if she let that man break her now—force her to come home. Force her to live in fear.

"I lost my family when I was sixteen," she started, fidgeting against the brown leather couch she'd been instructed to take a seat on when Parish had led her inside Raphael's office about fifteen minutes ago. "My brother and my parents, in a car accident."

Ashe's brown eyes warmed with sympathy. "Oh my god, I'm so sorry."

"It's okay," Taylor assured her. "I did really well, actually. One of my teachers helped me out, let me stay with her and her husband. They were so wonderful, so supportive. I graduated with honors and went to college. I wanted to be a teacher too." She smiled to herself at the memory. "English lit. I found an incredible middle school, and worked there for three years. Then one night, going home, a car sideswiped me. I was physically fine, but it did something to me mentally. I tried to go back to teaching, but my anxiety was overwhelming. It wasn't fair to the kids." Taylor's eyes came up and connected with the woman before her. "The man who hit me was Edgar, my ex."

Ashe nodded. "Was it on purpose?"

"No. I don't think so. But he definitely saw me fall apart and he took advantage of it. He liked me weak." Taylor cringed, every inch of her feeling not the pain of his hand, but the sickness of humiliation. "I hated me weak."

"You weren't weak," Ashe said with quiet passion. "You know that, right? You had PTSD or something. From the accident. Then you probably felt like he was taking care of you…"

"I started to understand that after about a month. I was getting stronger, and Edgar was growing more insecure. Had to know where I was every second of the day. If I didn't answer the phone because I was in the bathroom…" She shook her head, disgusted. God, how could she have allowed herself to put up with that for so long? "He's a finance guy, and worked for this clinic in New Orleans. He would make me hang out there, just so he could keep an eye on me."

"What a freaking nightmare."

"It was. When I felt ready to go back to work, he didn't want me to." She sat up a little straighter. "But I did it anyway. Started a tutoring business. It was okay at first, but one day I was working with an eighteen-year-old boy on his senior paper. Edgar picked me up afterward and was convinced I'd slept with the boy." Sickness moved through her. "He told me I wasn't going anywhere without him ever again. I told him he was wrong about that. It was the first time he put his hands on me."

"Oh, Taylor…"

Dammit, she didn't want pity. She really didn't. She was good now, strong, capable. She just needed to live in a world without Edgar.

"Here's the problem," she concluded. "He refuses to believe we're over. He said I'm his forever, until the day we die. I made a statement of harassment to the police, but that's all I could do. Not that a restraining order would matter. He has friends everywhere. And I realized I didn't have friends anywhere."

Before Ashe could say anything, the door opened and a man entered. He was tall and gorgeous, had long, golden hair, and Taylor instantly recognized him. From the newspaper. This was Raphael. He went straight to Ashe and gave her a kiss.

"*Ma chère*, I didn't know you were here today." He leaned down and gave the baby a kiss, too. "Are you taking your repast, my little one?"

Surprisingly, unexpectedly, the words and the action brought tears to Taylor's eyes. That…Oh, that was how a real man treated his partner. With gentleness, affection, vulnerability. Ashe was a very lucky woman.

After giving his baby one more kiss on the head, Raphael went and sat on the edge of the desk. He acknowledged Taylor, then turned his gaze back to his mate as if he'd forgotten something. "*Ma chère*, didn't you say Soyala had a check-up at ten?"

"I cancelled it." Ashe gave him a very pointed look. "Rescheduled it."

He returned the look with one of his own. "Perhaps Miss Taylor would like to speak to me alone."

Ashe smiled. It was a coy, almost wicked smile. "I don't think so. And I want to hear what you're going to say to her."

"Ashe—" he began.

She cut him off. "Not happening, Raph. Taylor here needs a friend, and I'm it."

Taylor turned to her. *Are you sure? Are you sure you want to take this on? Take me on?* she asked her silently. Ashe gave her a brilliant smile.

"Friend?" Raphael repeated, his brows lifting.

"That's right," Ashe said. "Now, go ahead. Get all Diplomatic Faction on me. You know I love it."

Raphael stared at her, his lips turning up at the corners, his eyes filled with an obvious love. Finally, he sighed, beat—happy. "You are so beautiful like that, *ma chère*. Our cub at your breast."

She grinned back at him. "Our first cub."

A low growl vibrated in his throat and his eyes flashed gold fire. Then, seeming to remember where he was and with whom, he turned back to Taylor. "I apologize, Miss Taylor."

Taylor smiled too, shook her head. "It's fine." Actually it was more than fine. It was a reminder that strong, confident men loved strong, confident women.

"I have to ask," Raphael began, his expression wary. "Did Séverin hurt you?"

"No. No, not at all." The passion in her voice was obvious. Not just to herself, but to both Ashe and Raphael. "What I mean is that he protected me. It was raining heavily and I was…lost." The leader of the diplomats didn't need all the details.

"Oh, thank the Goddess," he muttered. "That would've been a nightmare. Human hurt or killed in the Wildlands. I can see the headlines now. See the angry humans at our borders. It's just the press we need."

"Raph," Ashe scolded.

"What?"

"Insensitive much?"

He grimaced, turned back to Taylor. "Once again, my apologies, Miss Taylor—"

"It's okay, and please, call me Taylor." She smiled softly. "Listen, I know I'm putting you in an awkward position. This isn't something you normally deal with. I get that. I really do. I'm just asking that you make an exception this once."

"It's not that simple, Taylor," Raphael told her. "I wish it were. I gather you're in trouble. But we'd need more than my okay on something like that. And as a species, we're in the middle of dealing with—"

"Raph," Ashe broke in, taking her now-sleeping baby off her breast and covering herself. "There is a man outside our border who wants to hurt her. Will stop at nothing to hurt her." Dark eyebrows lifted over sharp brown eyes. "You would send her back to that?"

The Pantera leader sighed. "I would not want that, *ma chère*. Of course. Any male who puts his hands on a female in anger deserves nothing less than death. But we are already accused of being barbarians. Beast Men. What if this human male tells the press we took his mate?"

"I am not his mate!" Taylor exclaimed, then pulled herself back. "I belong to no one but myself." She crumpled a little. "I'm so sorry I'm bringing my problems here. Edgar could very well do that. Make a huge stink. He's powerful, and with the clinic where he works having just burned down, he's become even less rational than—"

"What did you say?" Raphael moved closer to her.

Taylor stilled. "That he's becoming irrational—"

"No. About the clinic burning down."

A sudden commotion erupted outside Raphael's office. Loud voices intermixed with the sounds of desks crashing to the floor and lamps breaking. Taylor knew those sounds. Knew what came after those sounds—in her world, anyway. She fought down her body's reaction to it as the door burst open and Séverin, the massive gold puma cat, stalked in.

———

Woman.

My woman.

Fear in her blood.

At me? No. She would not fear me. I am the one who cares for her. Must be the Suit.

He narrowed his gaze on the puma before him, silver eyes to gold, and growled. Raphael had shifted into his cat quickly, and was poised in front of his mate, snarling a graphic warning.

"Okay, that's enough," Ashe hissed in a fiery whisper. "If either one of you wake this baby, you're going to have to deal with me."

Baby?

Cub.

Oh, yes, he had heard of the little one being born. A miracle, she was called by the Pantera. And perhaps she was. Séverin knew nothing of that. Cared nothing for that. The goal of creating new life, a new species, had been his daily nightmare before escaping and coming to the Wildlands. Needles and blood, endless samples of his piss and semen…

But though he didn't care for creating the kind of life that lay in the female's arms, he cared even less for frightening it. He drew back, sheathed his claws and sat.

For several long moments, Raphael paced in front of his female. No doubt deciding if he trusted Séverin. But with one look from the woman he shifted back into human form, into his fancy clothes and faced Séverin.

"What the hell are you doing, bursting in here?" Raphael demanded. "The woman—Taylor—is already living in fear! Goddess only knows what more damage you did, keeping her caged in your fucking treehouse—"

"Raph," Ashe uttered in warning as Séverin's lip curled.

He looked at her and nodded. "Of course. I'm sorry, *ma chère*. I won't curse in front of our cub."

"It's not the cursing," she said. "Soyala doesn't have a clue about that yet, and frankly with this pack she might have to get used to it. It's the yelling."

"I wasn't afraid," Taylor burst out. "And I wasn't caged."

Séverin turned his gaze on her. She was looking at him too, her green eyes as soft as a caress.

"In fact," she added. "I haven't felt that safe in a long time." She smiled shyly at him. "Even waking up next to all the naked male flesh."

A rumble of pleasure moved through Séverin's chest. No, she didn't fear him.

"What did you say?" Raphael asked her. "You saw him naked?"

Taylor's cheeks flushed. It was beautiful, the rush of blood to her skin, Séverin thought. It made her eyes bright, like emeralds in the sun.

"Nothing happened," she stumbled on, turning her attention back to the Suit. "It's just how he was when I woke up. Not in his cat form anymore. I'm sure that's normal." She looked at Ashe for clarification. "Right?"

"No," the woman said. "That's impossible, Taylor."

"What do you mean?"

"Séverin hasn't been out of his puma form since he came to the Wildlands a decade ago," Raphael said. His gaze flickered Séverin's way. "None of us know where he came from or what happened to him before he got here. None of us know what he looks like, what he sounds like. In fact, we don't even know his real name. Or if he had one. The elders gave him—"

"Séverin," she uttered, turning to look at him.

Confusion.

But softness.

She wants to know more.

She wants to know everything.

But can I give her that?

Trust her with that?

A human.

His fur bristled at the idea as Raphael explained, "Because it sounds like 'save.' To the elders, he was saved."

Taylor stared at him for long seconds, her eyes running over his cat's face. Then she spoke softly, but clearly. "He has silver eyes, like the puma—but with flecks of pale blue. Like the sky just before dawn. And long hair. Not as long as yours, Raphael, but thick like yours and the color of caramel. He's tall, with the body of a marble statue. And when he allows himself to smile, it's like the whole world lights up."

The room grew very quiet at her description, and Séverin felt strange inside his muscles and blood.

Her words.

How she saw me as a male.

My eyes? My smile?

Had I smiled?

I barely know what a smile is. And yet I smiled at her?

"Séverin," Raphael began, breaking into his thoughts. "If you showed yourself to her, would you do the same with us? Let us know you?"

The question was like a punch to the gut. So many years in his nest, wishing, wondering if he could shed his fur and allow the male inside him a little freedom. The fear of being that vulnerable made Séverin turn and give the Suit a hard look. Whatever had happened this morning, it was an anomaly. Waking up beside Taylor in his male

423

form—feeling the hungers of a male, the desires. It wasn't a change he had made consciously. He shook his massive head.

No.

Raphael sighed. "It's a prison you choose to live in, brother. In your mind and heart. We pose no threat to you. We only want you to be part of the community, know your family, your kind. Come to the clinic, let the Nurturers help you. Let them draw you out of your cat."

Séverin gave the male a snarl of defiance.

Never.

Never go back to the clinic.

I am free.

"Stubborn." Raphael gave him a pointed look. "We can't have you hijacking humans. No matter if they believe themselves safe in your company."

Séverin had had enough. He was growing more and more uneasy here, in town, under many watchful, curious eyes. He needed the air, the space, his nest.

And her.

He padded over to Taylor and began to rub his head and muzzle against her side. Then he opened his jaws and closed them gently around her hand. She pulled in a breath, but didn't resist him.

"Shit," Raphael uttered behind them. "He marked her."

"You're going to have a hard time forcing her to leave now, *mon chèr*," Ashe remarked dryly.

"Taylor?" Raphael asked.

She glanced up at him.

"That clinic you said burned down? Was it called The Haymore Center?"

Her mouth dropped open. "How did you know that?"

Sighing, Raphael turned to his mate, a look passing between them. "She's not going anywhere."

CHAPTER FOUR

THE trip back into the bayou was very different than the trip Taylor had taken into town several hours earlier. The latter had been on foot, and she'd been scared and worried and guilty about leaving the male who'd helped her. Now, with the sun bright and warm overhead, relief and excitement coursed through her. And her manner of transport? The strong, muscular, fur-lined back of a very beautiful, very fast puma.

Her pulse jumped as he raced through the thick, wet undergrowth, dodging bushes and cypress. She leaned in further, tightening her grip around his neck. He made a sound, something hungry, yet contented in his throat, and quickened his pace. Thoughts and questions zinged through Taylor's mind. Was this real? Was she passed out somewhere? Dreaming this? Not only had she made it to the Wildlands—but she was being hosted, for lack of a better word, by the one being her heart seemed to trust. Maybe because he was like her. Running…hiding, from a past etched with pain.

"Thank you." She whispered the words in his ear. Two words that encompassed so much.

He growled back at her and sped up.

Granted, she didn't know what was going to happen from here. Raphael had allowed her to stay because he believed she might have some information about The Haymore Center. Which was baffling. Why would the Pantera be interested in a random fertility Regardless,

425

Taylor was pretty sure she was going to disappoint him. And when she did...he might make her leave. But for now, she and Séverin were going back to the treehouse. And for the first time in so long—in her heart and her guts—she felt safe. With him, she was safe.

Séverin slowed his pace, coming into the familiar stand of cypress. He stopped before the door in his tree and allowed her to get off. When she did, he turned to face her.

"Home sweet home?" she asked with a little laugh.

He nodded, his gaze intense.

"You're sure you're okay with this?" she asked. Though she was grateful to be there, she still felt slightly like a burden.

For a brief moment, Séverin just stared at her. Things happened within Taylor under the intense study of those silver eyes. Warm belly, warm heart, and a strange awareness south of her navel that was quite new and worrisome. He was a puma, and yet he was a male too. It was strange to reconcile this within herself.

He moved toward her then, and very much like the housecats she'd known in her life, started rubbing himself against her. Against her left side, then her right. His shoulder to his hip.

Was this his way of answering her? Yes, he wanted her there. A smile broke on her lips and she laughed. He stopped and looked at her—and Taylor would've sworn the puma smiled as well.

Over the next couple of hours, Séverin showed her where the fresh water stream was located and where dry firewood could be collected. She was starving by the time they returned to the treehouse.

"I used to go camping with my teacher and her family, so I know how to build a fire." Her brows descended. "I'm guessing you eat your food raw, though..."

Séverin didn't answer. In fact, he wasn't looking at her at all. He was scenting the air. He'd caught a whiff of something. But instead of growling or assuming a predatory or defensive stance, he released a heavy breath.

Something was coming through the brush. Taylor looked passed him and saw that it was Ashe. Hiking very capably through the wetlands. She looked like she knew her way around. Even had a large pack on her back. What was she doing here?

She waved when she saw them. "Thought I'd get my cardio in and bring you a few things at the same time," she announced.

As she sidled up to them, Séverin acknowledged her with a nod, his eyes slightly narrowed with suspicion. Then he turned and took off into the trees.

"Going hunting?" Ashe asked her.

"I hope so," Taylor replied with a grin.

The woman dropped the pack on the ground, then stood with her hands on her hips and surveyed the landscape for a good thirty seconds before declaring, "Okay, you can't do this."

Taylor laughed. "Of course I can."

"Come, on. Look at this place." Ashe pointed to the cypress. "It's a hole in a tree. You're not a rabbit."

"I love it."

Ashe grimaced. "Why?"

"It's got everything I need, I assure you."

She sighed. "Fine. I know better than to argue with a woman smitten with a Pantera."

"I'm not smitten," Taylor returned quickly. Though something in her gut was telling her otherwise.

"Mmmhmm." Ashe picked up the backpack and headed for the door in the tree. "Well, everything you need plus a few essentials."

"You didn't have to do this," Taylor said, following.

"Yes I did," she returned, gazing around the small interior. "Good Goddess, it's smaller than a studio apartment. Where are you going to shower or go to the bathroom?"

"It's not forever. It's for now. It feels good here, with him." *Is this smitten?* "Look, I know this all seems crazy. First the running away from the ex, then running into Séverin and wanting to stay here with him." Her gaze lifted and locked with her new friend. "It's just, for so long I was going against my gut, you know? It feels good to follow it this time. Feels right."

Ashe nodded, smiled. "I understand." Her smile widened. "Better than you can know, actually." Impulsively, she reached out and hugged Taylor. "I'm glad you're staying. I love what we're building here. Us human girls." She laughed. "I didn't come to all of this with many friends either."

"Well, I owe this respite to you," Taylor said. "Your mate obviously can't say no to you."

"It's how the Pantera males are. Rough and predatory and stubborn. But to their mates, they're kittens. Ready to lick and play and please." She wiggled her eyebrows.

"Maybe I'll find that out."

Ashe snorted. "No maybe about it..."

That strange heat, that awareness was back. Running laps inside Taylor's belly.

"Okay, okay, settle in. I'm going. I need to feed the cub in an hour." She headed out of the treehouse den and into the light of the early afternoon. "But remember, we're expecting you for dinner tonight. Some great people for you to meet. My sister's going to be there, too."

"How fun. I'll be there. And Ashe?"

"Yeah?"

"Thank you. For the quick, uncomplicated friendship, and whatever's in that pack."

Ashe grinned as Séverin appeared in the trees. "You're welcome."

The puma trotted up to Taylor, something furry and dead in his teeth. She stared as he promptly dropped it at her feet. For a few seconds, she let the grossness of the act wash over her, then she laughed.

"So charming," Ashe remarked. She turned to Séverin. "Make sure you escort your guest to my house at seven."

He snorted at her halfheartedly.

"I'll take that as a '*yes, ma'am.*'" She gave Taylor a wave, then headed off toward town.

With a deep breath, Taylor turned around and faced her puma. No...not *her* puma. *The* puma. Ashe's observation had really done a number on her brain. "I could cook some of what you brought for us," she said, bracing herself for a quick lesson in skinning a bayou critter. "Just give me a few minutes to start a fire."

But she only got a couple of feet before Séverin did that mouth around her hand thing. He was so gentle, she barely felt his teeth. When she turned, he motioned for her to climb on his back—just like he had when they'd left town.

"We're going somewhere?" she asked.

He nodded, his eyes warm, liquid silver.

Her heart leapt into her throat as she climbed onto his back and wrapped her arms around his soft, strong neck. With a howl to the air, he took off down the shoreline of the bayou. Water kicked up, splashing her and she laughed. Was this how she would live? For a short time, anyway? Racing through the beautiful Wildlands? Campfires at night. The puma curled up against her side as she slept. God...knowing she could sleep in peace and not with one eye open?

Séverin slowed and padded up a small incline. The other side looked to be a very remote spot along the bayou. There on a large patch of clean, dry moss was a picnic set-up. Taylor sat up and slid off his back. She stared. A red blanket was spread out on the green, a picnic basket in the center, a plate on either side.

Séverin came up alongside her and she turned to look at him. "Did you do this?" Then amended, "With some help?"

He nodded.

Her smile was so wide it made her face ache. "It's beautiful. Thank you."

He rubbed himself against her side, then went over to the blanket and sat down. The golden cat on the red fabric, a male's silver eyes...

"When I was a child," she said, joining him on the blanket. "I used to love coming to the bayous. My mom and dad would surprise me sometimes. Pick me up from school and away we'd go." She opened the basket and started taking things out: bread, chicken, fruit, water..."Being here makes me miss them. But in the best way, you know?"

He stared at her, but there was understanding, empathy behind those silver eyes.

"Do you have family, Séverin?" she asked, popping a grape in her mouth.

He nodded.

"Do they know you're here? Do you see them?"

He shook his head, and his nostrils flared slightly.

"Do you want to?" she pressed gently.

He didn't answer right away. His expression changed. From relaxed to pained. After a moment, he nodded.

"We're a lot alike, you and I." She tore off two pieces of bread. One she placed between his paws, and the other she kept for herself. "Both hiding. Both wanting to protect ourselves against something painful. Both wanting to be free."

His eyes were piercing as they looked into hers.

"Both accepting each other for who and what we are at this moment," she added.

Séverin leaned toward her and nuzzled her foot. So warm, a little wet. Her belly clenched. God. To anyone on the outside looking in, what she was doing and allowing and basking in, it was crazy. But she didn't care. The outside world had offered her a different crazy—one that had nearly destroyed her.

She sighed and ate her bread and a few slices of salty cheese. "It's beautiful out here. I see why you're drawn to it. The colors and the air and sounds. Although, it is a little hot today," she added with a laugh.

Séverin pulled up and gave her a wry look.

"What?" she said, grinning.

He turned and padded down to the water's edge. Taylor wiped her mouth and hands with a napkin and stood up. He glanced over his shoulder and growled softly at her.

"What are you thinking?" she said.

In answer, he dove into the bayou with a heady splash. Taylor gasped. Not from fear, but from the suddenness of it all. She scanned the surface, and when he came up she laughed.

"But cats don't swim!" she called out.

He dropped his head back and roared as if to say *This one does!*

She couldn't believe him. He looked totally at ease as he waited there, expectantly. Waited…Oh, no…

"You can't be serious," she called.

The puma cocked his head to the side and splashed the water with one enormous paw.

"I didn't bring a bathing suit," she said.

A low sound made its way across the water at her. He didn't give a shit. He wanted her to come in, join him—swim with the kitty cat.

He dove down once again and surfaced with an impatient snarl, his silver eyes sparkling against the sunlight off the water.

"Can't believe this," she muttered as she unbuttoned her jeans and slipped them off. Her tank, too. She kept her bra and panties on, of course.

When she walked toward the edge of the bayou, she felt his eyes on her. She wondered what he thought, what he saw. As the puma, and as the male. Then she was gasping. The water was shockingly cold. Without thinking, she followed suit and dove beneath the surface. When she came up, she cursed, then laughed.

"This is crazy! We are crazy!" She turned around to face him. "And I've never felt so happy. How is that possible?"

The cat locked eyes with her, and something solemn yet contented passed between them. He drew nearer until they were face to face treading water, then Taylor reached out, wrapped her arms around his neck and pulled herself close.

Later, she would think about this impulsive action, and how she wasn't a forward person. Didn't normally make the first move. But right then all she could register was warm, wet fur one moment and solid, smooth, male flesh the next. And hands…big, impatient hands, pulling her even closer. She felt hard abdominals. And an even harder sex against her belly.

He eyes went up and connected with silver and blue. Her breath was somewhere lodged in her lungs. But she managed a shy smile and a breathy, "Séverin."

But the male had no smile. Only an expression heavy with hunger, desire and fear. Instinctively, Taylor tightened her grip on him. But the male had ten times her strength, and he wanted to get away.

In a clash of splashes and groans, he disentangled himself and started swimming for shore. Treading water, Taylor watched powerful arms rising out of the water and cutting back in. But the very second he hit shore, he was a puma again.

Her heart confused and slightly bruised, she stared at him. She didn't understand. Why he pushed away. She accepted him in his cat form. Anytime. For as long as he wanted. Forever, if that was what he wanted. But he had been a male. When she'd touched him, he'd become his male counterpart. And that male had wanted to hold her.

Her eyes implored him. "Why?" she asked.

But the cat gave her nothing except its wet back as it turned around and lay down.

———

Hunger.

But not for the nutria.

The large rodent lies uneaten outside the nest.

Inside the nest, the woman reads.

Or pretends to read.

Angry.

At me.

Doesn't understand me.

I don't understand me.

"Let me know if I'm in your way," she stated from behind the book Ashe had brought her.

Ashe had brought her many things. Canned and bagged food, clothing, female's things to bathe with, a small pillow and blankets. Séverin's lip curled at the last two. Taylor didn't need soft and warm blankets for sleep. She had his body to lie against. To lie beneath—

432

He growled. At himself. The errant thoughts of a male who kept emerging without permission. He was puma. An animal. His fur, thick. His heart strong for catching prey. His mind clear.

And yet, when he caught sight of her long, bare legs peeking out from the pale pink robe she'd put on after they'd returned to the nest, he felt the male inside of him pound against his ribcage. He wanted her. Wanted more of her smile, her laugh, her stories, her hopefulness…

"Séverin?"

He glanced up.

She put her book aside and gave him a solemn look. "You know I want to stay here. But I don't want to screw things up for you. Make it uncomfortable for you. With what's going on inside of you. The battle that seems to be taking place. If there's one thing I under-stand it's desperately needing peace." She inhaled sharply. "Ashe has offered to let me stay with them—"

He didn't allow her to finish. He was on her, straddling her, licking her mouth with his long, pink tongue. Forcing her to stop talking.

Mine.

Every inch.

Mine.

She wants to stay here.

I want…

"Séverin," she cried out.

He froze. Stared down. Taylor's robe was open. She was wet. Everywhere. Her face, neck, chest, belly, bra and panties…

My cat.

Me.

What is happening?

Her eyes were pinned to his. "It's okay." Her breathing was labored. "It's more than okay. It's you. Don't go away again. Kiss me. And don't go away again."

Male.

I am male.

He'd felt the shift. A second ago. A second in time. His gaze raked over her. His blood rushed hot through his veins. He wanted. So much. So much of her.

His head came down and his mouth crushed against hers. Hunger unlike anything he had ever known slammed into his body. His male body.

"Fuck!" he ground out as he ripped his mouth away.

Her arms went around his neck. "No! Please."

"Taylor," he growled, then took her lips again, suckling the bottom, nipping the top, then kissing her, hard and demanding.

Séverin had felt the urge to consume many times. Prey. Fresh water. But it had been a long time since he'd felt that way about a female. And with this one, his Taylor, he wanted more than to just take her. He wished to devour her. Feed off her breasts, drink from her sex.

He dipped his head and nuzzled her breast until it sprang free from the soft piece of fabric. A low, feral sound erupted in the back of his throat as he gazed upon the dark pink nipple, which rose even higher as he envisioned drawing it into his mouth.

Taylor arched her back. An invitation...as if he needed one. The moan escaping her parted lips and the erotic scent of her wet pussy was more than enough. He lapped at her, for the first time in so long, using his tongue to give pleasure instead of to glean sustenance for his body.

She moaned and slipped her hand between their bodies. Séverin took her into his mouth and suckled. Pain and pleasure collided inside of him, two whitecaps fighting for dominion. She tasted so sweet, so hot. He wanted inside of her body. Wanted to thrust himself so deep he was lost.

He was hidden.

Pictures started flickering through his mind. His once-clear puma's mind. Needles, impatient hands, pain...

But she isn't pain.

My woman.

She is pleasure.

She is happiness.

And comfort.

She can be my hiding place.

Then her hand wrapped around his cock and the light turned instantly to darkness.

He was puma.

CHAPTER FIVE

THE long redwood table inside Ashe and Raphael's dining room was one of the most beautiful things Taylor had ever seen. Votive candles and small silver vases filled with white flowers dotted the spaces not laden with food. And overhead, a chandelier made up of crystals and long tubes of green glass sparkled warmly, gently. What a life this human woman had created for herself. A home, a mate, friends and family.

Some of whom were seated around the table with Taylor. To her right were Ashe's sister, Isi, and her mate, Talon. And across the votives and flowers and food was a male called Roch, a diplomat like Raphael, and his human mate Lydia, who was pregnant. Both couples were fun and engaging and welcoming. And Taylor wished more than anything that she could join them in their high spirits.

Outside, the puma howled.

Again.

And again, Ashe glanced over at her from her spot at the head of the table. "I'm sorry, Taylor."

"Don't be," she assured the woman.

"Sounds hungry," Roch remarked, tossing Talon a grin.

"Starved," the male said, chuckling, his pale gold eyes dancing in the light of the candles.

"He's been invited inside," Taylor informed everyone for the third time. "But not his puma."

Isi shook her head, showing off the tattoo that ran from her ear to her bare shoulder. "Hard-ass."

Pouring herself another glass of sparkling water, Ashe said very calmly, "Is it too much to ask to have a nice dinner without cat hair all over the food?"

"That's cold, *ma chérie*," Raphael said in between bites of alligator fritter. "And don't forget our daughter will have fur as well."

"You know very well how much I love fur," she said, her eyes lifting to meet his. "Yours in particular. Very soft." She grinned wide as she brought the glass to her lips. "Just not at my dinner table."

Raphael growled lovingly at her, and at the same time, the front door burst open. Taylor's head came up to see Séverin stalk in. Not Séverin the puma. Séverin the male. Her heart twisted and heat spread through her limbs like wildfire. There he was, all six foot three, naked and ferocious, silver eyes running accusingly over each face at the table. Until he got to Taylor's stunned face, that is. Then, his mega-feral expression softened.

"Holy shit," someone muttered. "So that's what he looks like?"

Taylor thought it was Talon, but she wasn't sure. Kind of didn't care, actually. She was too busy looking at Séverin, admiring Séverin, worrying about Séverin. Though he was massive, nearly taking up the whole doorway into the dining room, he seemed a little lost. A little confused. She wondered if he'd shifted on his own, or had done so involuntarily, as had seemed to be the case lately.

"There's a seat next to me," she called to him, pulling out the chair and patting the cream fabric.

His eyes instantly warmed and a smile touched his beautiful mouth. Her heart kicked as he started toward her.

"Raph," Ashe said quickly. "Grab those sweatpants you left in the kitchen earlier."

The leader of the diplomats didn't move. He, like everyone else, was staring. Taylor could hardly blame them. It was the first time any of them had seen Séverin as a male. And he was rather impressive.

Ashe hurried from the room and was back just as Séverin was about to sit down. "Please." She held the gray sweats out to him. "I won't make you put on a shirt. But pants are a must."

He made an impatient sound from the back of his throat.

"Why does he get to go topless?" Roch complained with a fake pout and a laugh.

Talon and Raphael turned to stare at him.

He shrugged. "What? Oh...Yeah. Didn't really hear myself say it until just now."

Taylor was giving Séverin an encouraging smile. He'd come so far. She knew this wasn't easy for him. Finally, with a grumble, he took the sweatpants and, because he obviously hadn't worn clothes in a long time, awkwardly slipped them on.

"Alrighty." Ashe gave everyone a tight-lipped smile as she headed back to her seat. "Please continue. I don't want your food to get cold."

But even though some of the parties at the table picked up their forks, their eyes and their attention were entirely devoted to the shirtless god now seated beside Taylor.

"Want some chicken?" she asked him.

He didn't answer. His gaze was moving over her face, taking in every inch.

"It's delicious," she said.

"I think he thinks you're delicious, Taylor," Isi said on a laugh.

"Isi," Ashe said, shaking her head at her sister.

"Come on. Look at the guy. He's practically drooling, and it isn't over your potatoes."

Ignoring them, Taylor put a chicken leg on his plate, along with some mashed potatoes, spinach salad and a roll. "Please. Eat."

His eyes flashed with fire, and he leaned in and brushed his nose across her cheek.

"Oh dear," Ashe muttered.

"The food, Séverin," Taylor chided, knowing that cheek and the other one were red with embarrassment.

His gaze lifted and in it she saw his want, his need, his care for her. None of it laced with force or intimidation, or threats. He hadn't changed from puma to male because the food at Ashe's table called to him. He'd changed because he wanted to be with her.

She reached out and placed her hand over his. The simple act made his face light up with pure, unabashed pleasure, as if she'd given him a car on Christmas morning. On a growl, he took her mouth, kissed her hungrily until she moaned and melted into him. Lord, she wanted to care about the others at the table, but she didn't. Her heart was beating and threatening to burst. Her breath was stolen. And below her navel, wet heat reigned.

When he eased back and sat up in his chair, a megawatt grin on his face, Taylor could barely breathe. She watched as he grabbed the chicken leg with one hand, a scoop of mashed potatoes with the other and went to town. Oh, Séverin. Table manners…highly overrated.

To her right, Lydia sighed.

"What's wrong, sweetheart?" Roch asked her, instantly concerned.

"Oh, nothing," she said, a few of her tight blond curls escaping the bun on top of her head. "I just remember when you kissed me like that."

There were a few chuckles around the now lively table, as everyone had resumed eating. Roch, however, was both dejected and defensive. "I don't wish to harm the cub."

Beautiful violet eyes gazed at the male with sympathy and longing. "How many times do I have to tell you it won't?"

"It?" Talon put in, brows raised mockingly.

"Shut up," Roch snarled. He turned to Raphael. "Tell me truthfully, will it hurt the cub if I…take my mate…"

"No," the male answered, his eyes bright with amusement.

"Now this is dinner conversation I can get behind," Isi remarked in between bites of salad.

"But," Roch continued seriously. "As Pantera, we are not the most gentle…"

Ashe glanced Taylor's way and winked. "Our poor, terrified predators."

Taylor laughed. So did Lydia and Isi.

Raphael drained his beer before answering. "These human women are very sturdy, brother."

"Indeed," Talon agreed, giving his mate a broad smile.

Roch stood up quickly, knocking his chair down. He didn't appear to notice. "Have you filled your belly sufficiently, my love?" he asked Lydia, his voice low and eager.

Her eyes lifted to meet his, and they flickered with heat and amusement. "I couldn't eat another bite."

He reached for her hand. "Come, then. We are going home."

Soft laughter moved around the table. And as the couple said their goodbyes and thank yous and quickly bolted from the house, Taylor found herself studying Séverin. He had finished his chicken, the meat sucked clean off the bone, and the potatoes as well. Now, he was holding up a piece of spinach, sniffing it.

"Like this," she told him, picking up her fork and stabbing it into a few of the green leaves on her plate.

He watched as she brought the fork to her mouth and slipped it inside. His nostrils flared, lips twitched, his eyes utterly focused on her mouth. Taylor stabbed at another pile of spinach, but this time instead of eating it herself, she brought the fork to his mouth.

"You'll love it," she said, hearing the provocative tone in her voice. "I promise."

Silver eyes went liquid and as he flashed his teeth and bit at the salad, he made a growling sound deep in his throat. Taylor inhaled sharply as that sound traveled all the way down to her sex.

"Every dinner party," Ashe said. "I swear."

"Don't worry, sis," Isi told her. "We're not going anywhere until after dessert. Talon's already had me three times today. He's beat."

Ashe dropped her head in her hands and moaned. "Who wants coffee? I need coffee."

"Beat?" Talon repeated, his face darkening. "Are you suggesting I am too tired to mount you, my love?" Without waiting for an answer, he reached out, scooped her up and placed her down on his lap. "Answer the question now, mate."

Isi curled into him immediately and sucked air through her teeth. "Nope. My mistake. Not tired. Not tired at all."

Laughing softly at the very open way these Pantera shared affection, Taylor pushed her chair back and stood. "Excuse me."

Séverin turned to her, grabbed her hand.

"Just going to the restroom," she assured him.

"I'll show you where it is, Taylor," Raphael offered, rising from his chair.

She followed him down the long stretch of hallway and into an office space. A masculine-looking office space, so she guessed it probably belonged to him.

"Right through there," he said, pointing toward a door at the far end of the room.

"Thank you."

She didn't expect to see him waiting for her when she emerged a few minutes later. But there he was, seated behind a metal desk.

"Are we having coffee at the table or...?" she asked, not sure if she should wait for him or just go on back to the dining room herself.

"I actually wanted to speak with you about The Haymore Center," he said. He gestured to the chair opposite him. "If you could spare a moment."

She glanced at the open doorway, wondered if Séverin would come looking for her if she was gone too long. Then realized she owed the leader of the Pantera a few minutes of her time. After all, he'd not only allowed her to remain in the Wildlands, but let her stay with the one being who made her feel safe and cared for.

She slipped into the leather seat. "I want to help. Any way I can."

He smiled evenly. "Do you know what went on in there?"

"I always assumed it was what it was purported to be. A fertility clinic." She'd never heard Edgar refer to it in any other way. "But I'm gathering you believe otherwise."

"We believe human women were being impregnated with Pantera DNA."

441

All warmth bled from Taylor's body. "Oh, my god."

"The woman you met tonight, Lydia, she's one of those women."

Shaking her head, Taylor uttered a confused, "How? Why?"

"We don't know."

"I do," came a male voice behind them.

Both Raphael and Taylor turned to find Séverin at the door. His gaze was gunmetal. His expression, bleak.

"They want Pantera blood."

———

The urge to shift back into his cat was almost unbearable. He felt on edge, ready to spring, both inside his body and out. The only thing that kept him from doing it was Taylor. The way she was looking at him. Confused, sickened, worried. She cared for him. As he cared for her.

"Why do they want the blood?" Raphael asked, pulling his attention.

Séverin remained where he was, in the doorway. "There is a human male. His name is Christopher. I saw him only four times in the many years I was caged there."

Taylor gasped. "No…Oh, god, no…"

He couldn't look at her. Didn't want to see pity or disgust or any of the vile things he already felt about himself mirrored in her eyes.

"The first time I saw him," he told Raphael, "he looked to be a ninety-year-old human. The second time, a male in his sixties. Every time after that, even younger." Cold dread scratched like fingernails up his spine as he recalled his time in that prison. "I was, of course, strapped down. The human male lay on a bed a few feet away. For hours, they took my blood and put it in his body. Afterward, I was weak as a newborn cub. He appeared in perfect health. Even thanked me." A snarl rippled through the room. "I wanted to rip his skin from his body."

"That piece of shit," Taylor whispered, vitriol lacing her tone. She didn't pity him at all. She was pissed.

Raphael's expression was measured, but his eyes flared with the heat of revenge. "So, they believe our blood is the fucking fountain of youth, do they?"

"Why the pregnancies?" Taylor blurted out. "Why do they want to create Pantera children?"

"I don't know," Séverin answered, his gaze moving to the window to his right. "They never told me." He felt his jaw go painfully tight. "Just forced the semen from my body and left."

The room went silent. And for several moments, only the sound of breathing could be heard. Then Raphael leaned back in his chair and cursed.

"I imagine," he began acidly. "Like any great, profitable discovery, more must be created. More blood, longer lives to sell to the highest bidders. Black market Pantera blood." Raphael looked at Séverin. "You escaped."

He nodded, but inside he wasn't sure that was really true. It was all still there. Attached to his male's mind.

"Did you ever see anyone else while you were there?" Raphael asked him. "Any other Pantera?"

Pain licked at his insides. "A female. She was taken from me. To another clinic, or maybe she was killed. I will never know."

"What was her name?"

"We didn't have names," he ground out. "Male subject. Female subject."

Raphael sat forward. "Do you remember what she looked like?"

He would always remember. "She was beautiful. Dark hair, green eyes, kind, strong." His gaze went to Taylor, who looked utterly bereft.

"She was your mate?" Raphael asked gently.

"She was my friend. They wanted us to…But no. We were friends. We kept each other sane." An unnatural heat started to expand within him. "I need to shift. I can't…"

"Go," Taylor said. "It's okay. Raphael can bring me—"

"No. I will be outside. Waiting. When you are ready."

Pain lancing through his body and mind, he left the room, stalked down the hall and was a puma the second he passed over the threshold of the front door.

CHAPTER SIX

THE ride home was a quiet one. As her hair whipped about her face and she wrapped her arms more tightly around Séverin's neck, Taylor thought how normal this could seem in the world outside the Wildlands. Just switch out the cat for a car. Driving home from a dinner party where…shit happened. Both parties deep in thought, and not ready to talk. Not just yet. Not until they got home and could breathe the familiar air again.

The night was comfortably cool, a full, bright moon following them as they raced through the brush and trees. Taylor's stomach ached slightly, not from the food, but from what she'd heard in Raphael's office. What Séverin had revealed. She'd come here looking for a place to hide, and been taken in, cared for, protected, by someone who had only known suffering at the hands of humans.

Séverin was the very antithesis of Edgar. He could be the most brutal creature imaginable, and yet he chose not to be. With her—to her—he was gentle and kind and generous. He'd shared things about himself and his past. He'd been vulnerable.

Could she say the same?

She slipped off his back in front of the treehouse and went inside. She was tired. Both mentally and physically. And the idea of curling up with the warm, solid puma, falling into a deep sleep, sounded wonderful. But Séverin hadn't followed her into the tree. She could see him outside, pacing back and forth.

She went to the doorway. "Are you okay?"

He looked at her as he moved, those silver eyes shockingly bright in the full moon's light. A strange sound exited his throat. It was like a strangled cry. Taylor wasn't at all sure what was wrong. The dinner? The others seeing his male form? The conversation with Raphael? It wasn't until she saw the stress in his expression that she realized he was trying to shift. Trying and failing. Or trying and not really wanting to let go of that protective outer layer.

"Don't," she said, leaving the doorway. "You don't have to."

Still pacing, he snarled. Not at her, but at himself.

"Séverin?"

He kept his eyes to the ground.

Fine. I'll meet you there.

Taylor moved directly in his path and sat down. The hard earth was cold and unforgiving. Not unlike the puma's spirit. "I want to talk to you. Ask you something. Please."

A few feet away, he slowed, his shoulders falling.

"Did it feel good today?" she asked him softly. "To touch me? Kiss me?"

For one moment, he stared unblinking at her. Then, like a freshly painted canvas in the rain, the stress bled from his features. He padded over to her and put his muzzle in her hands.

Tears pricked Taylor's eyes. "To me, too," she whispered. "But it was also terrifying."

His head lifted and his tired eyes locked with hers.

"I let someone take my body before and they abused it," she explained. "I gave that same person my heart, and he crushed it. And trust?" She laughed without humor. "He shattered it."

The puma made a sad, mewling sound.

"I was scared when you were kissing me because I felt my body and my heart, and maybe the soul I thought was dead and buried, reaching out to you. This stranger. And yet, not so much a stranger really." She reached up and stroked his soft head. "I think that might be why the male part of you is growing stronger. Braver. Because it's reaching out for me too."

To watch the shift from beast to male so closely took Taylor's breath away. Or maybe that was just Séverin. He was so startling, so beautiful. Even more so when he stood up, displaying a body that was a true work of art.

He offered her his hand, and when she placed hers in his, he lifted her up and carried her inside the treehouse. It was no five-star hotel, and there was no king-sized bed with Egyptian cotton sheets. But the den was scented with fresh cypress and soft, sun-warmed blankets. And the view...oh, the view. Moonlight on dewy green.

With the gentlest hands, Séverin removed her clothes. And as he did, his gaze took in every inch of skin that was revealed to him.

"You are so beautiful, Taylor," he said. "And yet..."

Her heart stuttered. "What?"

His eyes locked with hers. "I can't have you look at me. When you touch me. I...every time they took a sample—"

"Hey." She took his face in her hands. "It's okay."

His nostrils flared. "I want you like I've wanted nothing else. But my mind won't...I may shift back if..."

She kissed him. To shut him up. To allay his fears. And to show him how much she wanted him too.

His hands drove up her naked back and into her hair. He fisted the thick tresses and kissed her with utter abandon and barely restrained hunger. Taylor felt dizzy as she pulled away.

"Taylor...my beautiful, wonderful Taylor."

"Séverin. I want you, too." She turned away from him then and went over to her blankets, got down on all fours. Then she looked back at him. "Can't you see how much? Take me. I'm yours."

For one brief second, she saw the puma flash behind his eyes. But it was gone in a flash, a flicker, a blink. And before she could take another breath, he was behind her. *Oh*, she groaned. Just the feel of his skin, all that hard muscle, pressed against her. And that cock. That thick and very impressive muscle she wanted inside her. So deep inside her.

447

His head was near her shoulder. His mouth at her ear. "The need to bite you, hold you still, hold you in place while I fuck you," he growled. "Is so strong."

Shards of heat battered her insides, making her sex clench. "Do it," she urged.

He laughed softly, his breath tickling her face. "Not yet. But I will be gentle if I do. I won't break the skin. I promise."

Taylor wanted to scream at him that she didn't care—that she wanted his teeth inside her just as she wanted his cock inside her. But Séverin was doing things to her, raking his fingers down her back as he kissed the length of her spine. She moaned and arched her back. Why couldn't he just take her? Fill her? Why did he have to tease and torment—

Her words were cut off, or maybe her mind just shut down, because when he reached her backside, he started nipping at the flesh. First one cheek, then the next.

Hot curls of awareness moved through her, and she felt moisture leak from her sex. It seemed Séverin knew it too as he inhaled deeply and groaned.

"Cream," he growled. "Mine."

It was all he said before he spread her wide and licked her from clit to pussy. She inhaled sharply and her fingers dug into the blankets. He was masterful, a hungry cat, and she couldn't stop the image of his puma entering her mind. He lapped at the entrance to her sex, even drove his tongue up inside her with a snarl of possession.

Yes, I belong to you.

To Séverin and to the puma.

Taylor arched her back and groaned as found her clit and licked it furiously. Hot, hard swipes. Back and forth until she was about to explode. And then he covered her with his mouth, and started to suckle. Heat and unquenchable desire roared through her. *It's not enough. It's perfect. More. Harder. Inside. Come in me.*

Come.

On a cry, she broke apart. And as Séverin continued to suckle her pulsing clit, Taylor bucked her hips. Back and forth. Riding it out as long as she could. It had been so long…so long since she'd felt the thrill of climax run though her body, but those moments in time were nothing to this. This was Séverin.

Could he be hers?

Before her body had a chance to cool or calm, his arm slipped around her waist, and his hand cupped her breast. Sucking air through his teeth, he squeezed the tender flesh and rolled her nipple between his thumb and forefinger. Taylor groaned with desire.

"Mine," he uttered, his teeth grazing the skin of her shoulder as his cock found her entrance—hard, thick, pushing, pushing until he thrust inside.

Taylor stilled, gasping for air as her body grew accustomed to him. So deep. So big. Wet heat surrounded his cock and she started to rotate her hips. She wanted to feel him everywhere. Wanted him to grab her hips and fuck her hard. Fuck her until—

Suddenly he was no longer there. She was empty. Cold.

"Séverin?" she panted. Oh, god, had he shifted? Was he a puma?

Would she ask him to stop if he was?

The stray, insane thought dashed through her mind and was out in a flash when Séverin flipped her onto her back and opened her legs as wide as they would allow.

She stared up at him, breathless.

"I need to see you," he said, his expression a mask of desire and longing.

"But I thought…"

"No. Not with you." He shook his head. "This is right," he growled. "You and me. Male and female. Eyes locked, mouths playing, nipples brushing my chest. This is how we are meant to be, Taylor."

Such overwhelming feelings ran through her. "Yes," she cried out. *God, yes.*

Pushing her knees back to her chest, Séverin drove up inside of her, so deep it took her breath away and left a body that desired no other—and a heart that belonged to the one who had only to claim it.

———

Hot.

Wet.

Tight.

Squeezing his cock.

I am male.

I want to be male for you. With you. Inside you.

As his eyes locked with hers, Séverin moved inside Taylor's body in a rhythm so perfect he wanted to weep. The humans he'd known in his long life had taken so much from him. And yet this one— this beautiful human with her open and understanding heart—had given it all back times a thousand. He couldn't let her go. Wouldn't.

No, he thought darkly, rolling his hips, giving her what she was crying out for. He wouldn't take from her, demand anything from her. That was what she'd come from. He would offer…

Oh, but fuck. What did he have to offer? A hole in a tree—

"Séverin." Her legs were around his waist and her hands were on either side of his face. Her eyes implored him. "Kiss me. Make love to me. Fuck me. Come with me, and stop thinking."

How had this creature wandered into his life? His sorry life?

Stop. Thinking.

Take.

Give.

Fuck.

Come.

His mouth closed over hers, and he drove his tongue deep. Taylor groaned with approval and sucked on the welcome invader as her sex squeezed around him. Come leaked from the head of Séverin's cock, and he knew it wouldn't be long. He slipped his hands beneath her glorious ass and lifted her. As he kissed her, taking every moan, every sigh, he thrust deep. Over and over. Grinding his hips, trying to hold on as she came, bathing his cock with the cream he still tasted on his tongue.

Her hands plunged into his hair, and as they kissed, biting and sucking and showing their hunger, she pulled the too-long strands. It was the quick and hot pain that sent him over the edge. He rode her hard and deep, then drove up inside her and bathed her womb in his seed.

"Taylor," he groaned, burying his head in her neck. "You don't know…you can't know…"

"Tell me," she said, her voice so soothing it made his throat tight with emotion.

"It was the first time." *Fuck. Just say it. Tell her.* "I've given my seed freely."

For a moment, everything got quiet. Even Taylor. Then she released a weighty breath and wrapped her body around him so tightly, he could hardly move.

"Mine," she said. "All mine."

Séverin didn't know if she was talking about his seed or him, but it didn't matter. He rolled them to his back, then when she loosened her hold, he pulled her close again, grinned when she draped a leg over his thigh and still-hard cock. And as she snuggled into him and drifted off to sleep, he allowed himself the same pleasure.

Not as a puma. But as a male.

Taylor's male.

CHAPTER SEVEN

THE dream Taylor was having was so delicious, so perfect, she never wanted it to end. She was in Séverin's arms and he was carrying her into a house...or was it a tree? A tree inside a house. But they lived there together beside the spot at the shore of the bayou where they'd had their picnic. Taylor hadn't seen the house before. She believed it was a surprise by the look on Séverin's face. So proud, so happy. Content for the first time in his life.

It was only when that smile faded, when he shifted abruptly into a snarling, pissed-off puma, that she realized her dream was over. No. It had never existed. Happy endings weren't in her future. Because the Wildlands wasn't far enough or magical enough to keep fate away.

She woke to the barrel of a gun pressed to her temple. A Glock 19, to be exact. She knew because she'd felt it before. Several times before. Not on her temple—that was new. But other parts of her body.

"Wake up, you stupid bitch," Edgar whispered in her ear.

Taylor's eyes opened, and at first she felt no panic. Edgar's threats. His ugly, demeaning language. It was almost a normal state of being for her. Or had been before she'd come here and met—

Oh shit. She sat up, saw Frankie, one of the assholes who worked with Edgar, holding a gun to Séverin's head. He was in his male form and naked. He sat with his back against the wall, calm as death and looking straight ahead.

"Séverin," she breathed.

"Shut up!" Edgar spat. He was wearing his customary black jeans and gray sweater. Upscale prick, she'd called it. Not to his face. Never to his face.

"One more word from you, whore of mine," he said. "And I'll have Frankie take the kitty cat out."

"You sure you wanna do that, boss?" Frankie asked. "Mr. Locke would want him alive, wouldn't he?"

Edgar glared at the man. "Did I tell you to speak?"

The man gulped and shook his head.

"But you have a point…" He cocked his head and regarded Séverin. "He'll fetch a very nice price. Take him outside. I'll be right behind you. We want to cross the border before dawn."

"Get up," Frankie commanded, poking Séverin in the ribs with the barrel of his gun.

Séverin! she screamed silently. Why wasn't he looking at her? Did he blame her? He should. She'd brought Edgar here.

"Don't take your eyes off him," Edgar added as Frankie led Séverin outside the treehouse. "And if he shifts, shoot him. We have the other Pantera male now. It'd be nice to have a spare. But not necessary."

What other Pantera? Utter terror rippled through Taylor. She had to get to Séverin. Find a way…

"Just take me," Taylor begged as her piece-of-shit ex forced her to stand. "Please, Edgar. You know that's what you came for."

He grabbed the pink robe Ashe had given her off the floor and threw it in her face. She nearly ripped through a sleeve in her rush to put it on.

"Yes, I did, my sweet, foolish Taylor. I came to rescue you. From a group of disgusting creatures who had obviously abducted you." He reached out and ran his thumb down her cheek. She felt bile rise in her throat. "But look what I found. You fucked an animal."

He'd meant to bruise her with that comment. Unfortunately for him, it only made her smile.

Edgar's eyes filled with hate. "You like him. You wanted to be fucked by him." He grabbed her by the wrist and hauled her outside, pushed her to the ground.

She looked up, and this time her gaze met Séverin's. She didn't know what was going to happen to them. Torture or death—with Edgar it could go either way. But she knew she loved the male before her. And days, hours even, with him were worth a hundred lifetimes in Edgar's hellish company.

"Did you know him before, Taylor?" Edgar taunted. "Is that why you never wanted to fuck me? Because the animal had already claimed your worthless cunt?"

The word was barely out of his mouth before a vicious snarl erupted in the pre-dawn air. Taylor screamed as Séverin shifted. *No. Please no!* The puma was on Frankie, teeth buried in the man's throat.

Stumbling to her feet, Taylor turned to Edgar. He had his gun aimed at the puma, his finger curling around the trigger. Without thinking, she rushed him, smashing her body into his. The gun went off, the bullet hitting the treehouse. Séverin roared and tossed a limp Frankie to the ground.

Pain rippling through her body, Taylor saw shapes coming out of the mist. Three Pantera pumas. Running—teeth bared, snarling and hissing. They were focused on Edgar, who was diving for his gun. It had flown out of his hands when Taylor had hit him.

But he never reached it.

Like a hawk with a rabbit in sight, Séverin leapt through the air and slammed down on Edgar—paws striking gut and chest. As the man hit the earth with a thud and a crack, Taylor rolled to the side and grabbed the gun. She was on her feet with the thing pointing at his face just as the three pumas shifted. But it wasn't needed.

"Is he dead?" Raphael called, shifting into male form and rushing forward.

"I think he broke his neck," Taylor said, panting.

One of the Pantera, a woman, kneeled down and touched his throat. "No pulse."

No pulse. Taylor stared at Edgar. Eyes closed, face still, body crumpled. This man who had once made her feel special, then decided to ruin her. Or try to. She wasn't ruined. Lost, maybe. But she'd been found.

She glanced up, needing to see Séverin. Know that he was okay. He'd shifted back into his male form. But his gaze wasn't searching out hers. It was trained on the female Pantera who had attempted to find Edgar's pulse.

"It's not possible," he uttered. "Can't be…"

Still shaking from Edgar's death, Taylor looked from one to the other. The female was staring at him too, her face going pale.

"Reny," Raphael said gently. "Do you know him?"

Know him? Why would she…She remembered Séverin's words. *The female. Dark hair, green eyes. Beautiful.*

"Reny?" Séverin repeated. "Is that your name?"

"Male subject," she whispered.

He nodded. "Yes, it's me."

Horror-struck, Taylor watched as the female cried out, then ran into Séverin's waiting arms.

———

He couldn't believe what he was seeing. In the flesh. She hadn't died. She was here. Safe. He pulled her back so he could look at her. "What happened to you? Where did you go? I tried to find you."

"You escaped," she uttered, her smile just as he remembered it. "Oh, I'm so glad."

Too many thoughts, too many questions were running through his head. "How long have you been here?"

"Not long." Her gaze ran over him. "What about you?"

"Ten years."

Her eyes grew wide. "Ten years. Why didn't you tell anyone what happened? Why—"

"I couldn't leave my puma state," he explained. "Didn't want to. Didn't want anything but freedom. After all that happened…"

"I understand." She gripped his arms. "After I lost my memory—"

"You lost your memory?" Séverin cut in.

She nodded. "But later, I found my freedom working for the FBI." She glanced back. "Then with Sebastian."

Séverin took in the blond male who stepped forward. Who gathered Reny in his arms the moment she came to him. His friend knew love. Just as he did.

"We have truly escaped our bonds," he told her.

She smiled, her eyes filling with tears.

"You with your Sebastian, and me with my Taylor."

"Where is she?" Reny asked. "I want to meet her."

Séverin glanced around. She'd been right there. At his side, fighting with him. For him. And ending the life that had held hers captive.

She must be in the treehouse, he thought, heading inside his nest. "Taylor?" But she wasn't.

What the hell? He stalked back to the other Pantera, his gut tightening with every step. "Raphael?"

"I don't know," the male said. "I didn't see her after you and Reny…" His voice trailed off.

"Fuck," Séverin ground out. "I need to find her." He eyed Reny. "We will speak—"

She nodded. "Of course. Go. Find her. Your mate?"

"I hope so," he said, his heart heavy.

"Do you want us to go with you?" Raphael asked. "Help you find her?"

"No. Stay here. Deal with this." He took off and was halfway to the bayou's shoreline when he turned and called back, "That dead bastard said a man named Mr. Locke held another Pantera male. Didn't give a location, though."

"Fuck!" Raphael returned hotly. "Did he give a name?"

"No."

Séverin said nothing more. He was already shifting into his puma and sniffing the air. Following the scent of his woman.

His mate.

Chapter Eight

THE water was sun-dappled this morning, Taylor mused as she swam from one shore to the other. But cold. Cold as her nerves, as her heart. Edgar was dead. And the male she wanted more than life itself had just been reunited with the female who'd saved him from madness.

His best friend.

The beautiful dark-haired Pantera female who'd rushed him like a linebacker—like a woman who'd found the love of her life once again.

Tears pricked her eyes and she dove beneath the surface. Was this really her fate? To lose the one person on earth who truly understood her heart? Her lungs started to ache and she kicked up toward the early morning sunlight. But what greeted her when she surfaced was a golden puma standing stock-still on the shore. Its silver eyes were wide with fear, but when it saw her, relief took over. It growled at her.

"What do you want, Séverin?" she called, moving into shallower water until her feet made contact with the bottom of the bayou. "Everything's fine here. You can go back to your reunion."

She sounded like a jealous, insecure bitch. Probably because she was one.

A gasp escaped her throat as the puma quickly shifted into its male counterpart. For five seconds she stared. She couldn't help herself. He was breath-stealing, heart-wrenching, pulse-jumping.

And...furious?

Was that the look on his handsome face? Was he angry with her? Oh, god. Of course he was. She'd brought Edgar here. Into the Wildlands. Into his refuge. Séverin had almost lost his life because of her. No doubt he was looking for her now to bring her straight to the border. Out of his life. Clearing the way for him and Reny.

He dove in, swam directly for her and surfaced with a curse. Taylor was ready. Ready for his anger. But the anger that spilled from his lips had nothing to do with her ex.

"You ran from me," he uttered blackly, his eyes wild. "Does this mean you fear me?"

Confusion gripped her. What was he talking about? "Fear you? What—"

"You came to the Wildlands—ran to the Wildlands—out of fear. You ran from that walking, talking maggot. And now you run from me." As his gaze traced her face, his eyes softened. "You don't want to be with me?"

Oh my god. "What? No. I left because..." *Reny was in your arms. The female who saved you.* "It's over, Séverin."

His face turned ashen.

"Edgar's dead. There's no reason for me not to go back where I came from."

"You want to go back?"

"No." She shook her head, tears pricking her eyes. He didn't understand. "You found Reny. That's amazing."

"It is," he agreed, watching her intently, his gaze bewildered.

"I'm happy for you." And truly she was. Maybe not for herself. But she cared about Séverin. She wanted him to be happy.

"Reny is wonderful, Taylor," he said. "The only friend I ever had. Before you came along, that is." His eyes demanded that she look at him, hold his gaze. "She deserves all the happiness in the world."

God, this was hell. Tears streamed down Taylor's face as she stood in the cold bayou and waited for the inevitable. She was going to leave this place. The one place that felt like home. And the male she...loved.

"I deserve happiness too, Taylor."

Her eyes never left his as she nodded. "Yes, you do. I want that for you. More than anything."

"Do you mean that?" he asked.

Her heart bled. "Yes."

He reached out and took her in his arms. "Here in the Wildlands, males enjoy claiming their females. As Sebastian claimed my friend, Reny."

Breath stalled in Taylor's lungs. Sebastian. And Reny. *She has a mate. She has a mate!*

"But I would not do that to you, Taylor."

"What? Claim me?" *Why not? Oh, god, I want you to. I want you more than anything.*

He pulled her closer. "I too was used without my consent. Without choice. It won't be that way with us. No claiming."

This time, Taylor calmed and listened to him. What he was saying. What he wished for.

"I would ask that you stay with me," he said, his eyes bright and hungry. "I would ask if you would love me. I would ask that you allow me to care for you and any cubs we may have." He grinned at that. "I ask, Taylor."

As understanding dawned, happiness unlike anything Taylor had ever known spread through her. She wrapped her arms around his neck and held on tight.

"Oh, Séverin," she said, leaning in and kissing him. "It was a blessed day when you knocked me on my ass."

He laughed. "Do you accept, my sweetest love?"

"Oh, I accept," she said, her eyes shining with love. "With everything I am, I accept."

Then he kissed her. Softly, sweetly, hungrily. Her male, her mate. Séverin. And she was home.

HAKAN

Hakan never apologizes for being a lethal, barely civilized Hunter, but he understands that he has to be careful when it comes to his future mate, Payton. The pretty young Geek captured his heart long ago, but he was forced to keep her at a distance until she was mature enough to handle his feral nature. When he discovers she's been captured, however, he's done waiting. It's time to claim his female. Unfortunately, he didn't anticipate that Payton might refuse the mating.

Payton understands that there's nothing more important than discovering why their newest enemies are targeting the Pantera. And if that means putting herself in danger, then that's exactly what she's going to do, no matter what the arrogant Hakan might say. Of course, that's easier said than done. Especially when Hakan is clearly determined to seduce her. Does she listen to her pride, or give in to the urgings of her fragile heart?

SÉVERIN

Humans have always been the enemy.

Séverin has lived the last ten years of his life in his puma form. He is feral, predatory and angry at the human world. Born in captivity, the male is haunted by years of torture and abuse. And when he comes upon a human female running scared through his Wildlands domain, he wants nothing more than to get her back to the border. But as she finds shelter with him in his rustic treehouse, the male inside him starts to emerge, threatening his still-caged heart.

Until he meets her.

Running from her abusive ex, Taylor is desperate for a place to hide. She believes her only chance at life is the magical Wildlands. But with a war brewing, the Pantera species aren't too keen on letting a stranger into their fold. Luckily, there is one Pantera who might want the beautiful teacher to stay. A male who, like Taylor, is running scared. Can they both listen to their hearts and allow the first real love of their lives in?

About the Author
Alexandra Ivy

Alexandra Ivy is a *New York Times* and *USA Today* bestselling author of the Guardians of Eternity series, as well as the Sentinels and Bayou Heat that she writes with Laura Wright. After majoring in theatre she decided she prefers to bring her characters to life on paper rather than stage. She lives in Missouri with her family. Visit her website at alexandraivy.com.

Book list:

Guardians of Eternity
Hunt the Darkness
May 28, 2014
978-1420125153

Darkness Avenged
June 4, 2013, Zebra
ISBN 978-1420111385

Levet
March 26, 2013

Fear the Darkness
September 1,2012, Zebra
ISBN 978-1420111378

Bound by Darkness
December 6,2011, Zebra
ISBN 978-1420111361

Devoured by Darkness
November 2010, Zebra Paranormal
ISBN 978-1420111354

Beyond the Darkness
April 2010, Zebra Paranormal
ISBN 978-1420102987

Darkness Unleashed
November 2009, Zebra Paranormal
ISBN 978-1420102970

Darkness Everlasting
May 2008, Zebra Paranormal
ISBN 978-0-8217-7939-2

Embrace the Darkness
November 2007, Zebra Paranormal
ISBN-10: 0821779370
ISBN-13: 978-0821779378

When Darkness Comes
January 2007, Zebra Paranormal
ISBN 0-8217-7935-4

SENTINELS:

Born in Blood

Book #1 Sentinel series

December 31, 2013

ISBN 978-1420125146

Blood Assassin

Book #2 Sentinel series

January 6, 2015

ISBN 978-1-4201-2516-0

About the Author Laura Wright

New York Times and USA Today Bestselling Author, Laura Wright is passionate about romantic fiction. Though she has spent most of her life immersed in acting, singing and competitive ballroom dancing, when she found the world of writing and books and endless cups of coffee she knew she was home. Laura is the author of the bestselling Mark of the Vampire series and the USA Today bestselling series, Bayou Heat, which she co-authors with Alexandra Ivy.

Laura lives in Los Angeles with her husband, two young children and three loveable dogs.

Book List

Mark of the Vampire
Book 1: Eternal Hunger
978-0451231499

Book 2: Eternal Kiss
978-0451233844

Book 2.5: Eternal Blood (Especial)

Book 3: Eternal Captive
978-0451235879

Book 4: Eternal Beast
978-0451237729

Book 4.5: Eternal Beauty (Especial)

Book 5: Eternal Demon
978-0451239754

Book 6: Eternal Sin (November 5, 2013)
978-0451240163

Bayou Heat Series
Bayou Heat Raphael & Parish
Book #1 and #2 in the Bayou Heat Series
January 7, 2013
ISBN 978-0-9886245-0-4

Bayou Heat Bayon & Jean-Baptiste
Book #3 and #4 in the Bayou Heat Series
April 15, 2013

Bayou Heat Talon & Xavier
Book #5 and #6 in the Bayou Heat Series
July 9, 2013

Bayou Heat Sebastian & Aristide
Book #7 and #8 in the Bayou Heat Series
November, 2013

Bayou Heat Lian & Roch
Book #9 and #10 in the Bayou Heat Series
April 19, 2014

WICKED INK CHRONICLES (New Adult Series- 17+)

FIRST INK

SHATTERED INK

CAVANAUGH BROTHERS

BRANDED
(Out now)

BROKEN
October 7, 2014